THE
MAGE'S
OATH

Book Five of The Dark Angel series

COURTNEY LILLARD

ISBN: 979-8-9914485-0-5

Cover Design by Etheric Tales & Edits | MC Damon

ACKNOWLEDGEMENTS

This book is dedicated to everyone who contributed some fraction of their time to help shape the person I am today, including my parents, siblings, friends, teachers, and colleagues from across the country. I also must thank my husband, Darren, who not only gave me the push I needed to begin writing seriously and reads the drafts but who also listens to my ideas with honest, eager ears.

A NOTE FROM THE AUTHOR

The Dark Angel series has gone through several editions. This final version combines what used to be the first two books, The Shadow's Grasp and The Guardian's Deception, into Part One and Part Two of the former. The Demon's Curse also used to be the first book in The Yeluthian Duology, a sequel story meant to be two books. This book has been altered to continue The Dark Angel series as its fourth book. This decision was not made lightly considering the amount of effort it takes to rebrand a series, as well as my readers who were familiar with the original book order, but each part of the story has been kept the same. Chapter titles have also been added, and the rest of the series will follow a new order, so to speak.

This note serves as a notice for those of you who may see The Guardian's Deception, whether online or a physical copy. That book will now be considered the second half of The Shadow's Grasp, and the rest of the series will be numbered appropriately. The Yeluthian Duology is no longer its own entity since The Demon's Curse is now Book Four.

Other changes will be mentioned in future notes.

Contents

Nim-Vala
Parnic
Verona
Sindaly
Fester
Western Woods
Umbridge
Twindela
The Vall
Dala
Medina
Marinich
Umbrich

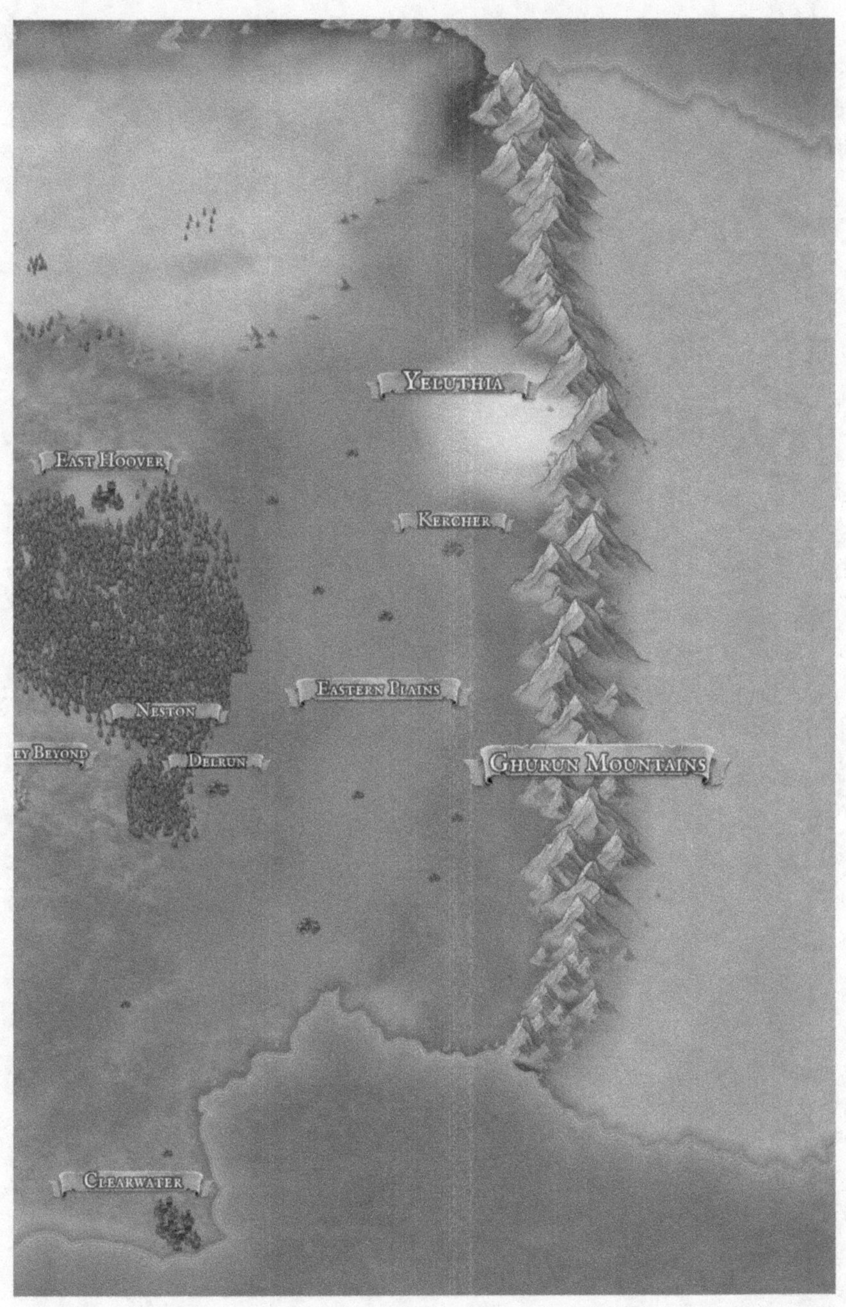

Yeluthia
East Hoover
Kercher
Eastern Plains
Neston
Ghurun Mountains
ey Beyond
Delrun
Clearwater

Part One

Shared Weakness

For the first time since he entered the medical station, Byron sat alone without someone standing an arm's length away attempting to converse. Sunlight peeked above the tree line from the southern field, through the open window, and into his face, signaling the arrival of dawn. He closed his eyes as he leaned forward and bent his head over his clasped hands in an effort to stop the throbbing behind his temples. There seemed to be no point in courting sleep; even though the healers appeared to have settled the chaos, the level of noise remained loud enough to wake the entire palace.

Hours ago, he and Clearshot decided to call it a night after visiting a mutually beloved tavern where they enjoyed the company of wandering soldiers and lively music. Neither noticed the unusual amount of activity despite it being nearly midnight, and both assumed Emilea and Cintra would already be in their quarters. It wasn't until somebody recognized Byron in the grand hall that he learned what took place that night.

His first thought when his comrade shared vague details of an attack within the private dining space had to do with whether or not Cintra fled to Katrina's; however, her haunting vision lingered in the back of his mind, leading him to search for her. With every step, an added weight continued bearing down on his shoulders. Clearshot stayed on his heels as he hurried to where a line of guards patrolled outside the room. A building frustration grew as soon as he recognized the lack of urgency among the soldiers, and that overshadowed his sense of dread.

After demanding answers and hearing a summary of the event, including where the victims had been taken, he and Clearshot dismissed the dining hall in favor of locating their partners. Light mages and medical personnel met them at the station. Men and women glided from one bandaged patient to the next while ignoring them before they wordlessly split apart to scan the weary, pained, and grief-stricken faces of the ladies.

Cintra lied in a bed surrounded by four mages maintaining a light spell while she stared upward without really seeing what was going on. Her blonde hair no longer possessed its glossy sheen as it covered the pillow, and beneath the smeared makeup, her face grew pale. While Byron watched without considering anything else, somebody commented on her legs, even though blood soaked her midsection. Despite the numbness overwhelming his senses, a slight flicker of sanity urged him to find Clearshot while the mages worked. He scanned the station for Emilea's body to no avail and gave up on locating the pair a minute later.

The final healer doting over Cintra by that point seemed to recognize him and turned as she cleared her throat. Whether or not she cared about their relationship, or knew they were romantically involved, she didn't say.

"This woman is alive and in a stable condition now, so you can take it easy," she started, though she averted her eyes. "I've been monitoring the damage to her back, specifically her spine. Those who caused this mess directly stabbed the lower part. We did what we could, but there's no way to determine the effect that injury had on the nerves. The worst-case scenario, and what I can deduce, is she won't be able to move her legs."

Byron's jaw dropped in response, and his mind went blank. The healer attempted to reassure him her theory wouldn't be confirmed or rejected until Cintra stirred, but he barely heard the words through a fog clouding his mind.

She tried warning me… I assumed her foresight hinted at her death, but this may be much worse. It's my fault. I didn't listen…

That was how he remained until morning, and how he would have remained until somebody gently shook his shoulder, rousing him from his slump. He figured Clearshot, Emilea, Coura, Marcus, or anyone else who knew him intended to check on him, but he glanced behind to find a palace servant instead.

The boy in his late teens offered a brief bow before fidgeting uncomfortably, as if he didn't expect the results of the massacre in the medical station. "Master Byron, General Tont sent me to fetch you. King Aaron has called for a council meeting and requests you join as soon as possible."

Byron understood he wasn't thinking clearly and knew the servant just obeyed the general's order, but he still scoffed in response. Without a word, he faced Cintra again while praying the world would leave him alone.

After a minute passed, the young man cleared his throat and began repeating his words only for Byron to raise a hand, prompting silence between them. The noise grated against his fragile nerves, so when the servant continued a few seconds later, his temper snapped so suddenly he couldn't restrain himself from cutting off the boy's next sentence.

"I've been awake all night in the midst of this!" he exclaimed while sweeping his arm in a gesture to the entirety of the space, startling the servant into backing away. His shout also drew the attention of the healers, patients, and other visitors, so he lowered the volume of his voice. "There are more important matters I'm dealing with now. Tell the general they can manage without me for once."

The young man's wide eyes and stiff posture reflected his alarm, though he appeared to notice Cintra lying asleep in the nearest bed. His glance transferred between her and Byron twice, then he dipped his head before hurrying out of the room.

This left Byron to process the consequences of his outburst as those in the area returned to their business. *I shouldn't have said that. It's been a long night, but I must uphold my responsibilities. Cintra, you were right when you accused me of choosing this role over a life with you. I truly am a fool.*

The exhausted figure didn't react to his internal comment nor his touch when he took her hand in his. Seeing her so weak and imagining the pain she experienced, as well as her imminent realization of the future in store for her, tugged at his heartstrings. With her vulnerability in mind, Byron crafted a vow, kissed her hand, and took his leave of the medical station to head toward the council's meeting chamber.

I promise, from the moment you stir, I'll be by your side. I refused to listen to your concerns and dismissed our attempts at a compromise. It's my fault you ended up here and why you might never be able to walk again. We'll prepare for a future together. Whatever you want, whatever you need, I will be there.

***

The day following the incident in the dining hall felt like an odd limbo for Grace, who remained in her quarters after being released from the healers that morning. What transpired seemed like a dream, or rather a nightmare, which lingered to occupy her thoughts. Her mind grew fuzzy, though her caretaker mentioned such a reaction was a normal aftereffect of the shock. In response, the woman gave her a set of potions to calm her when it came time to rest. Once she returned to her room, Grace sat on her bed, stared out the window facing Verona, and observed the bustling city below.

That was how the first day passed.

The following morning, she ventured to the mess hall and found a solemn atmosphere. Soldiers and mages spoke in hushed voices to one another without giving her any attention. Out of consideration for the cooks' efforts, she ate about half the food on her plate before returning upstairs to lie on her bed again.

This time, she faced the banner embroidered with a pair of bronze wings draped along the opposite wall. A sigh escaped her then as a surge of emotion inexplicably rose.

I could not stop them… Grace clutched her chest, embracing the tightness resulting from the first coherent thought she had all day. *Emilea and the other ladies are dead because I did not act sooner. I dismissed the doors being sealed and what servants roamed about, like everybody else. How could I be so careless?*

Tears slid down her cheeks, and a repressed sob threatened to strangle her upon recalling the bodies and faces of those she'd grown familiar with over the years. Twice she allowed herself to gasp for air, fearing the flood would never end if the dam broke. Then, she remembered the potions. In a swift motion, she grabbed a bottle on her nightstand, twisted off the wax seal, and drank the bitter liquid in a single gulp. She figured whatever she drank would ease the trauma eventually, and that notion calmed her enough for her to lie back; however, her mind remained restless despite her desire to sleep.

The sky swiftly shaded darker until evening fell upon the capital city, and Grace moved to stand beside her window and study the many lamps lit across the area below. For some reason, the scene settled her rising nerves enough for her to consider the future without panicking.

Father was right about my life being in jeopardy if I stay in Asteom, she admitted. *This incident will no doubt encourage them to remove me from my position and push me into one where I can live in Yeluthia, probably surrounded by guards. Perhaps that would be best. I did not prove my abilities in the dining hall, and Emilea, Lady Katrina, and others died because I lack the strength to fight. The enemy easily overpowered me; that could become dangerous in the future if I ever seem useful enough for them to capture. I cannot imagine being anything less than an object for political gain. After all, why else would they not harm me and mention my kingdom?*

The truth stung, but her tears seemed to have run out, leaving her exhausted enough to drop onto her bed and fall asleep.

The following morning, Grace prepared to depart for the mess hall but found a guard posted outside her door. She didn't recognize the woman, though the soldier offered a polite smile and salute.

"Lady ambassador, I am here under High Highness' orders to escort and protect you," came the explanation. "My comrades and I will rotate throughout the day, so please don't hesitate to request anything from us."

Grace nodded, mentioned her desire to eat, and trailed behind as her guard led the way. Having an escort both comforted her and drew additional attention, yet Aaron took the time to consider her safety, so she refused to act ungrateful.

The soldier enjoyed conversing without appearing nervous or intimidated in a Yeluthian's presence. When Grace questioned this by asking about the woman's familiarity with her people, her guard seemed confused.

"Forgive my bluntness, but I've been training with the angels ever since they arrived. General Tont also issues patrol shifts around the palace and in Verona, so you're not the first foreigner I've conversed with. However, you are the most important figure."

Grace could only stare at her escort before resigning to finishing her meal and returning to her room. When the guard remained at attention on the opposite side of her door, she closed it, went to sit on her bed, and rested her head in her hands. The soldier's reveal of the interactions with her people sounded completely normal, yet the idea lingered.

I suppose I never put in the effort to imagine what life would be like when Yeluthians and humans interact with each other every day. The nobility always treat me special to earn my favor, and I never visit the training grounds. Have I closed myself off from the world these past few years in order to help plan the future? As she continued wondering if others built relationships through daily activities like her guard did, a new thought sprang into her head. *I know I focused on establishing Yeluthia's presence in Asteom, but could this be part of the result? Has my position contributed that much toward the alliance?*

Grace longed to answer that question with a definitive confirmation, yet she refused to overemphasize her role, even if doing so made her feel better.

With nothing else to do and no impulse to leave her quarters until the next meal, she selected a book from one of her shelves, opened it to a random chapter, and dove into the words halfheartedly. The information pertained to her people's development of a trading system with the Mintelians, who shared their work with the citizens in Clearwater, which had always fascinated her. She allowed herself to become so enraptured with the fantasy of acting as a merchant in a new land that a sudden yet gentle knock on her door caused her to jump.

"C-Come in," she stuttered while promptly closing her book. She hadn't planned for visitors, not that she expected any, so she wondered who would wish to see her, especially with the chaos still surrounding the palace.

To her relief, it was Marcus who stepped inside and lingered by the door. The shadows under his eyes showcased a lack of rest, though he held a smile after she greeted him.

"You look much calmer than our last encounter," he commented in a softer tone to project his sympathy. "How are you feeling?"

Grace forced herself to maintain a pleasant expression despite the memories returning to her. "I appreciate your concern and am much better."

When she didn't continue, a pause stretched between them broken only when the assistant general released a tired sigh.

"I hate to say this, but that's the best news I've heard lately," he revealed. "Not many of the survivors are as optimistic, and those of us assigned to the investigation keep facing dead ends."

A part of Grace knew she should refrain from inquiring about the situation due to her mental state which could shift upon hearing negative updates; the other part selfishly wanted to remain involved, if only to keep her position relevant. The latter side won out after a few seconds to contemplate her point of view.

"What is happening with the search?" she asked when he didn't elaborate.

He raised an eyebrow while losing his smile. "Honestly, nothing too exciting. The culprits our troops captured refuse to talk, my father and his soldiers took care of the private dining hall and are planning a funeral pyre for tomorrow or the day after, and King Arval offered his commanders to aid in locating those who fled."

"How is Aaron?"

"He'll leap into his grave if he attempts to handle every concern at once," her friend grumbled, as if commenting more to himself than to her. "I don't blame him though. The fights with the Nim-Valans and demonic creatures seemed to be taking place in a different world for the citizens of Verona. This incident just proves we're not invulnerable."

Grace could hear the strife in Marcus' words. "What about you?"

His resulting, startled glance showed he hadn't intended to display such emotion, but to her relief, he didn't attempt to hide the negatives plaguing him personally. "I'm worried about a lot. You,

Aaron, my comrades, Dala… Everyone is in distress and needs help. I can't do what needs to be done and be in every place at the same time."

This is not so much about his problems but the problems of others, she noted when his eyes lowered until he stared at the ground. *His conflicts revolve around being unable to assist those he cares about, and I would wager he somehow blames himself for the attack in the private dining hall. That is just the kind of person he is.*

"Please, do not berate yourself for what is out of your control," she began in an effort to ease the burden on her friend's shoulders. "You possess weapons training and strategic skills that most people lack, making you a valuable asset anywhere in Asteom. I believe your guilt stems from your inability to do more; however, you will benefit others no matter where you are stationed."

By focusing on him, she hoped her own concerns would lessen, at least until he departed. Marcus sensed her lies in the past, so she spoke with enough confidence to assure him what she claimed was true.

Her friend raised his eyes while she waited for his response, and the sincere smile returned to his lips. "Thank you, Grace. What you said is correct, though I often forget the significance of just being there for others."

A warmth filled her center. *The significance of being there for others…*

Marcus' laughter cut through the silence. "I came here to see you after all! If General Tio or Calin heard our conversation, they'd call me a fool for forgetting that and dismissing it."

Grace chuckled too. "They sound like proper role models for you."

"That's putting it nicely," he mumbled, yet his grin meant he was only teasing. "Now, enough about me. Is there anything I can do to help you? I was surprised when the healers released you from the medical station so soon."

"I appreciate the sentiment, but I am feeling better," she replied while ignoring her rising anxiousness at the reminder of the past three days. "I was not harmed during the attack, remember? They were dealing with more pressing patients."

"The light mages can aid a physical recovery, but mental damage is arguably a greater challenge to combat." The volume of his voice lowered, and he moved to sit beside her on her mattress. "I know you've seen a battlefield, but it's different when you're around family and friends in a mess like that. Don't risk your sanity by bottling your emotions up. Even if you don't talk now, you can always find me later."

Grace could only stare at the assistant general with a bit of shock. *I only spoke with Aaron about my concerns regarding my position because he had been the only person available, then I resigned to devoting my time to an arranged marriage. That may still be my only path toward freedom, but perhaps I would not feel so poorly about myself if I had Marcus' validation.*

"I am…embarrassed," she prefaced while looking away. "What troubles me is more selfish than losing friends and witnessing the massacre; however, it does not dismiss the fact that I am weak. I *was* weak during the attack, and Emilea and others died because of my carelessness."

For some time, Grace shared what she had been reflecting on, including her parents' letters, the potential uselessness of her role as ambassador, and her inability to defend the noblewomen in the private dining hall. What she hadn't planned to reveal was the idea of an arranged marriage, yet the suggestion slipped out when she started rambling. Still, Marcus didn't interrupt or appear to be judging her for any of her thoughts. She finished by explaining her worry regarding her safety in Asteom. By that point, tears slid down both cheeks as she gave up on controlling her shame.

"I trust you, the generals, and the soldiers, but not all humans are as diligent," she admitted while covering her mouth with her hands.

"You're right," her friend responded after a minute when she composed herself. "I wish I could tell you you wouldn't be in danger if you stay in the palace. I wish I could say all humans are kind and don't use others for their own gain, but I'd be lying. That's just a risk you would have to take."

Grace nodded.

"With that being said, you shouldn't let fear dictate your choices," he continued and averted his gaze. "You don't have an obligation to stay in Asteom or go back to Yeluthia. It's your decision. Just know Aaron and I, and plenty of other people, will support what you do."

"I appreciate that."

Although she expected to end the conversation there, he surprised her by adding more in that same, thoughtful manner.

"Also, I recommend not looking back at the negative moments too often. There are lessons we can learn from the experience, but we'll get nowhere if we linger on the lives lost. It's not your fault Emilea and the noblewomen died. We can speculate on alternative actions until we go insane. That's all it will do."

"Marcus…"

Hearing his name had her friend glancing at her with a sad smile. "As long as you understand you're not to blame and stop viewing yourself as a pawn, you'll be fine."

Grace let the words sink in before returning the gesture and leaning over to let her head rest against his shoulder. "I promise to try."

He responded by wrapping an arm around her shoulder in a partial embrace. Then, the assistant general departed.

***

The meeting chamber housing the king's council grew stuffy due to the dozen or so people wandering in throughout the day. Marcus had volunteered to act as one of Aaron's guards for these sessions, opting to remain by his friend's side from the moment the two reunited the morning following the incident in the dining hall. They would both be forced to address a lot personally, but Aaron's business affected thousands within the palace and Verona alone. All Marcus had been ordered to do was prepare to return to Dala once the council arranged what paperwork General Tio needed. Until then, he stayed with the king, which happened to be in the meeting chamber for hours on end.

Father said I should be leaving tomorrow at the soonest, he recalled as the next topic of discussion regarding the scouting parties' observations continued. *I'm somewhat surprised he won't keep me around here considering recent events. Then again, if the demon creating the creatures to the south takes advantage of the chaos stemming farther north, the capital will remain caught in the middle of multiple conflicts.*

"Is there anything more to report?" Aaron asked once the soldier finished speaking.

Nothing new came of the middle-aged man's briefing as far as Marcus could tell. From what he gathered during the initial meeting three days ago, Aaron and the generals delegated assignments in order to complete the most tasks without their subordinates bumping into each other. The soldiers and mages who had not been invited to join the search or recovery process resumed their regular schedules.

When the scout shook his head, General Tont dismissed him with a grunt. Marcus took the opportunity to make note of who remained in the space during the resulting pause.

His father and General Garvish sat together since they were in charge of organizing and supervising the search for the enemies who infiltrated the palace, as well as the ones who decided what soldiers entered to present observations to the council. High Priest Jurek sat closest to Aaron with his hands folded in his lap to assume a calming manner, and King Arval and his commanders wished to be in any council meetings going forward for the time being due to their troops' involvement.

General Terrell and Byron were also present, though neither seemed too inclined to contribute much toward the conversations. The former appeared to be actively listening but never attempted to speak, which made Marcus wonder if the man ever dealt with an issue of this scale or simply left matters in more capable hands. The master mage only shared his thoughts when Aaron asked for his input; that uncharacteristic, closed-off behavior bothered Marcus.

The damage done to those involved with the massacre in the private dining hall must be weighing heavily on his mind. I don't blame him for being concerned, especially after what the victims mentioned.

After escorting the Yeluthian ambassador to the medical station, he decided to rejoin his father and assist with the aftermath of the incident; however, the general ordered him to focus on Grace instead. The request sounded sincere, and when Marcus questioned this, the answer startled him.

"Based on her account and what mumbles I've heard from the survivors, she was most likely being targeted," the general had shared at a lower volume. "The attackers mentioned Yeluthia before leaving her alive and didn't strike when they had the chance. It also seems like disposing of the master light mage had been a priority."

Hearing those words struck like a blow to Marcus' gut. He learned of Emilea's death then, and his shocked reaction led to his father dismissing him from the area a second later. Instead of returning to the medical station though, he found himself wandering through the halls, as if he had been ordered to patrol the palace and not guard the ambassador. Concerns and grief-spurred thoughts plagued him until he needed fresh air, leading him toward the bridge at the front of the structure where a mixture of soldiers and citizens meandered around the guards without hiding their curiosity and worry.

Why Emilea? he wondered once he could process the news. *They must have known Grace would be present, so it stands to reason they would've been informed about Emilea as well...*

A chill had swept through his body at the notion.

Before the event, she mentioned Aaron received an invitation. Could that have been their ultimate goal? Killing the only light mage besides Grace ensured what injuries they inflicted would not be healed.

He pushed the memory of that night away in order to focus on the present meeting, which continued with another scout. In time, he planned on mentioning his conclusion to his closest friend, if Aaron didn't understand already, but the wound would remain fresh for a few more days, at the very least.

The master mage's death bothered others outside the chamber, Clearshot most of all. The soldier locked himself away without accepting food or drink and rejected anybody who tried seeing him, including Marcus. When he took advantage of his authority as an assistant general to schedule guards for Grace while he stayed with Aaron, he also arranged for others who knew Clearshot to adjust their routes in order to patrol his friend's quarters.

One of Emilea's subordinates assumed her duties and represented the light mages on the king's council. The woman named Jenna had to be around the former's age based on her appearance, which looked similar in just about every way except for their faces. Unfortunately, she lacked any sort of personality or strategic sense, for she acted awestruck from the moment she arrived in the chamber. Nobody addressed her, not even Byron, so she kept quiet for the most part or provided brief answers.

After a while, they reached the point in the meeting where Marcus focused on the discussion again since Aaron summarized the events of the day before opening the floor for new or pending matters.

"Based on General Tont and General Garvish's information, the rest of the group who committed the crime in the private dining hall isn't in the area anymore," his friend concluded. "The scouting parties will continue patrolling their regular routes, and we will place additional guards around the palace to specifically assess those who enter. This includes the servants, who will be monitored by their superiors through written reports containing inconsistencies from this point forward. General Garvish, I would like you to continue overseeing this transition."

The man nodded before Aaron continued.

"I received news from the guards in the prison who dealt with an additional attack, though nobody was hurt; however, it seems the former high priest managed to escape during the chaos."

Many mutters cursing the traitor followed, though no one interrupted the report.

"General Tont, can you remain where you are at in the investigation and find Hendal's whereabouts?"

"Your Highness, it would be an honor," his father replied in a serious manner.

Marcus had some inkling the general's pride had been damaged because multiple killers snuck into the palace under his nose. What he most likely didn't realize yet was how everybody else in the room felt the same.

"Until we hear from General Casner about the border, I suggest we divide our attention," Aaron shared. "We know the creatures to the south are being controlled by a demon and are plotting their attacks to avoid detection by Yeluthian soldiers. Stopping them is our first priority while Nim-Vala isn't moving. There are enough troops on the border to intimidate the northern country into remaining stagnant, and I trust General Casner will manage for the time being. The palace is heavily guarded, but as I mentioned, we will take no chances here."

"Besides, it would be foolish to strike the same place twice," General Garvish threw in with his usual confidence.

Aaron nodded. "This leaves us with an opportunity to aid General Tio and the Dalan base, as well as the Sie-Kie in the Western Woods. Before that, I invite King Arval and his commanders to add their thoughts."

The Yeluthian ruler expressed his gratitude for the opportunity to speak, then his deep, melodic voice filled the space. "Decreasing the number of demonic creatures is a task both our soldiers and yours can handle. What we need is a way to locate and eliminate the source in order to prevent more from spawning. For this, I believe two methods must be acknowledged and achieved, if possible."

"You intend to seek out the ancestral weapons again, don't you?" Aaron asked into the resulting silence.

"I do."

"We'd be wasting our time," General Tont grumbled after a pause. "The only one we know of that had been kept with the royal family for generations is no longer accessible. The others have been missing for decades."

"What we need is a means to kill a demon, not just seal its power," Byron startled them all by suggesting. Then, he turned to raise an eyebrow at King Arval. "I assume you were about to bring that up as well?"

"You and a few others witnessed the prism sealing spell and goddess fire, which burned away demonic energy. Commander Detrix can train the light mages, both human and Yeluthian, and use that combination to weaken the creature's power."

"If I may interject, the spells were used on a human," Marcus added, drawing everybody's attention to him. "They didn't ultimately kill the former high priest. Even if we drain all the demon's energy, someone else will need to be present to deal the final blow. After facing the first being in combat, I'm not entirely sure how much effort that will take."

"You are correct," Commander Detrix replied with an expression reflecting his understanding, as if he considered that as well. "To my knowledge, goddess fire burns demonic energy into nothing, but the creature would most likely survive the ordeal."

Silence filled the chamber while everybody seemed to be waiting for someone to add more. When nobody did, Aaron cleared his throat before addressing his council again.

"If that is our best option, we will begin training the light mages as King Arval suggested. We can brainstorm ways to search for the ancestral weapons at a later time."

"We should hope nothing interrupts our planning this time," the high priest commented after, prompting nods around the room.

*

The council completed additional, less pressing matters before breaking apart for the evening. Marcus and four guards waiting outside the space escorted their king to his quarters where he ate meals now that the private dining hall needed to be cleaned, not to mention how it became tainted with horrific memories.

Every day since the incident, Marcus shared dinner with his friend when they could stomach the food. The past few days had been rough, both from the added responsibilities and the stress they endured, but they managed to clean their plates while silently reflecting on the day.

Just as they set their dishes aside, a knock on the door interrupted the almost relaxed atmosphere, spurring a quiet yet irritated groan from Aaron. Marcus ignored the pity he felt for the consistently busy leader and rose to open the door. He expected one of the soldiers patrolling the hallway or standing guard to be on the other side; however, a glimmer of bronze caught his eye before he recognized the man in front of him and straightened.

"Commander Evern, what can we do for you?" he asked loudly enough to give Aaron a warning in case his friend didn't already spot their guest.

The Yeluthian's sapphire eyes shifted from Marcus to the king and back again without hinting at any sign of danger or worry. "Forgive my intrusion, Your Highness," he began as he offered a polite bow. "I bring an update regarding the intruders at the prison."

Marcus stepped aside to allow the commander to enter the room and closed the door after. Once the three were alone, Aaron cleared his throat.

"You may share your report."

The bronze-clad soldier prefaced his news with a frown, something Marcus found interesting since the Yeluthian never appeared to show much emotion.

"I am not certain what information has been shared with you regarding the prison, but my king granted me permission to reveal the entire situation, which needed to wait until your people and immediate problems were handled and delegated. I apologize for the secrecy."

How Commander Evern began intrigued Marcus, though Aaron's unexpected reply left him wide-eyed.

"This has to do with Coura, doesn't it?"

Coura? Marcus wondered when her father nodded. *Why bring her up? Now that I think about it, I haven't seen her at all since before the massacre.*

"She visited me the night of the attack, or rather, after she had been attacked."

Aaron tilted his head a bit. "What do you mean?"

"My wife and daughter met in the queen's garden during the event in the private dining room. There, a pair of men presumably apart of the group we are searching for, led Coura away and injured her when she mistook them for servants, for they wore the plain uniforms. She managed to shield herself and her mother until the invaders fled. Then, the two came to me outside my king's quarters. This took place after the incident involving the noblewomen, so they entered a chaotic scene. Still, I informed my king before bringing them to their rooms. I ordered Coura to remain there for the time being just to be safe, but she argued for another route."

When the Yeluthian paused to contemplate his next words, Marcus glanced at Aaron and found his friend wearing a perplexed expression.

"My daughter's connection to demonic energy is what continues making her a target for their kind," the commander explained slowly, as if he needed to consider how to simplify the issue for the humans lacking magic. "She claims the same might be true of any person who becomes involved with such malicious power."

"That must be why she went after Hendal," Aaron muttered while pinching the bridge of his nose.

"She did what?" Marcus snapped in response only to be hushed by his friend.

"I'll tell you later. Commander, please continue."

The Yeluthian nodded. "You are correct, Your Highness. If the former high priest attracts demons and their creatures, he could lead them to the capital city from the comfort of his cell. I can sense the dark presence within my daughter and believe her suspicion, so I proposed a solution. The Mintelian people in the mountains have a process to cleanse bodies damaged by magic. She agreed to seek them out with the former high priest in order to prevent additional trouble in Verona and the palace."

The room fell silent while Coura's father let the news sink in. Marcus felt confused, betrayed, and fearful all at once and expected the same from his closest friend, who stared at the floor for a while before responding.

"Commander, why did you wait to bring this up? Why not include it in the council session?"

Aaron didn't sound like he accused the Yeluthian of doing anything wrong, and Marcus planned to ask him why when they could discuss the situation.

"As I mentioned, your kingdom took precedence in its time of need," came the reply. "General Tont agreed to manage the investigation at the prison, and I imagine he sent troops to search for the former high priest. The reason behind that attack and the confrontation in the queen's garden are one in the same, do you not agree?"

"I do," Aaron offered, then he released a sigh. "I would like to learn why the enemy attacked the private dining hall too, but I doubt you or King Arval have a clear answer.

"No, Your Highness."

"In any case, I appreciate you taking the time to share your information," Asteom's ruler added while moving to stand. "If more news arises, I would like to know as soon as possible from now on. Please share this with King Arval."

Commander Evern bowed again. "You have my word."

With that, the Yeluthian took his leave. Marcus remained on his feet even when Aaron dropped back into the chair.

What does this mean?

"Just when I thought this mess couldn't get any more complicated," the king mumbled and ran a hand through his blond hair.

Marcus faced his friend and met the weary gaze with a glare. "How did you already hear about Coura and Hendal?"

"It's late," Aaron replied before covering a yawn. "Are you sure you want to keep talking about this?"

Instead of answering, Marcus waited until his friend went on.

"The prison alarm sounded the evening of the massacre, and they sent a messenger with a report to explain the noise. In the document, the supervising guard mentioned an attempted break-in, Assistant General Benedict's visit to manage the situation under General Tont's orders, and how Coura arrived before fleeing with Hendal on her heels. The soldiers stationed there recognized her when she entered, though she created a shield to prevent anybody from pursuing her immediately."

"So, you knew about this for over a day and never brought it up until now?"

"It's as Commander Evern said. The prison is back in order, and we have troops searching for Coura and Hendal. The real question is, what are our enemy's motives if they struck three separate locations at once?"

Marcus shook his head to reflect his annoyance. "I understand that much. I want to know why you hid the details of Hendal's escape? Why did you never mention Coura's involvement?"

"Because I trust her," came the immediate response.

No sign of doubt, embarrassment, or concern crossed Aaron's face while Marcus stared at him in disbelief. He scoffed yet couldn't piece together a serious rebuttal.

His friend took advantage of that pause to elaborate. "Coura's father gave us enough reason to believe her actions are to solve an issue we don't, and can never, comprehend. She didn't hurt anybody in the prison, so her only crime is assisting with Hendal's escape. We have an idea of where she's headed too."

"I suppose you're right," Marcus grumbled.

"Besides, King Arval wouldn't permit Commander Evern to share this with us unless he believed no further action is necessary at the moment."

"You shouldn't have kept this hidden from your council, at least the part about Coura. They deserve the entire picture in order to assist you."

"I'm sorry." This time, Aaron fidgeted and wore a guilty expression. "I just couldn't reveal her involvement until…"

"Until you could justify her decision to free Hendal," Marcus finished for his friend. Seeing the royal figure react in an appropriate manner to the secrecy, at least appropriate to him, eased the building tension between the two.

"I'll tell the council everything tomorrow."

When Aaron rose to shuffle toward his bed, Marcus realized the hour and remembered how draining a busy day felt. *He has plenty to worry about already. I shouldn't give him another burden before I leave for Dala.*

He place a hand on his friend's shoulder and met the deep blue eyes when they fell on him. "I trust Coura too, but I trust you more. I'll support what you choose to do, but don't overwork yourself."

"I appreciate that," Aaron replied with a genuine smile.

Just to ensure they would separate on positive terms, Marcus shrugged and offered a final comment. "All the problems here make me grateful I'll be heading south again. Their answer to a problem is to either strike the source into submission or chase it away."

Hearing the king's laughter removed a weight from his shoulders he didn't realize he had been carrying.

*

The next morning, Marcus prepared for the upcoming journey since his father dismissed him from the king's side for the day; however, a new issue replaced his concern over the news he learned regarding Coura and the former high priest. Whispers reached his ears containing a rumor spreading throughout the palace like fire on dry hay. When he attempted to snuff out the lie, the soldiers informed him of the truth: A messenger from General Casner's company returned to inform Aaron and his council of Nim-Vala's attempts to cross the border at multiple locations.

He hurried to confirm what he heard with his father or closest friend when the opportunity arose, and he found the former first. The general didn't appear pleased with being stopped as soon as he departed from the council's chamber, but he gestured for Marcus to join him on his way toward the mess hall.

The northern country had indeed planned to invade Asteom without hiding their presence, as they supposedly did with the group who struck during the event in the private dining hall. Some of the troops managed to reach the town of Parnic, which housed General Casner's troops before when Marcus had been directly under the man's authority, and announced their king had declared war. Of course, with no proof to back up such a bold claim, their words could not be seen as entirely accurate.

When the pair reached their destination, Marcus' father ordered him not to become involved with the discussion since he would be departing the next morning. He swore to inform General Tio of the news before the two parted ways and struggled to suppress his desire to remain in Verona and assist with the ongoing dilemmas.

That feeling remained with him during his ride to Dala and for days after. Calin had been the first to welcome him back, then they met with General Tio in the meeting room.

Nothing changed from his previous assignment. The additional troops from the capital, including the Yeluthian soldiers patrolling their unique routes, continued dealing with sporadic attacks from the demonic creatures. Marcus made sure to share what the council decided regarding the light mages' spells and the ancestral weapons, leading the general to begin a tirade on how incompetent the leaders in the palace have been when considering the appropriate precautions against demons. Then, the man vowed to locate all the golden items before his fellow generals, a declaration Marcus found amusing despite the circumstances.

Looking to Heal

Although three days passed since they fled the capital, Coura and Hendal didn't stop moving until they were just outside Fester for fear of the soldiers they envisioned pursuing their trail. The former high priest remained quiet during most of the journey, which she became immensely grateful for, and he proved to be able to sleep in the saddle. At least, that was what she figured since they only paused for a brief nap when she began stumbling over herself and he appeared well-rested.

The pair and their horse kept to the main road until it split east where they found a path leading through the woods toward Clearshot and Emilea's home. Then, they merged with another, worn trail, taking them closer to the nearby towns. The looming threat of demonic creatures lurking in the forest still remained, and Coura hoped the pair stayed too far north for such an encounter to be a possibility.

At dawn on the morning of the third day, she decided to have them halt in order to prepare camp so she could venture into the city and purchase food and other supplies, such as waterskins, fire-starting stones, and a metal pot for boiling water.

That was when they ran into a dilemma.

Hendal dismounted after Coura instructed him to assist by locating a water source and collecting firewood, but he revealed he had never set up a campsite. This led him to ask several questions about the basic tasks that she attempted to answer without judging him too harshly. She departed for Fester after. The city seemed as lively as she remembered from her visit years ago, and despite her heartbeat picking up while her eyes darted around for the guards, nobody bothered her. Once she collected what she needed, she returned to Hendal and the mare only to find the former high priest standing beside a pile of twigs he assumed would suffice. Instead of berating him, she asked about a water source.

"I circled the area, but there doesn't seem to be a stream nearby," he admitted in a defeated manner. "You should have searched before going to Fester."

Coura bit her tongue to prevent herself from snapping a retort. *This is my fault for overestimating his survival instincts.*

After pausing to pent up her frustrations, she ordered Hendal to rest, seized the horse's reins, and led it away to look for water on her own. A source evaded her for a while, which she figured based on her companion's experience, but she eventually heard a promising sound that drew her toward a brook. The mare drank enough to satisfy its thirst while Coura filled the waterskins with a mental note to boil the contents before they departed from the area. She rinsed her face last in an attempt to ward off her weariness.

When she returned, she tied the animal's reins to a sturdy branch, scoped out the perimeter for decent logs, and collected enough to maintain a proper fire until evening. The flames flickered to life, so she let them grow until she could use them to heat what water she gathered. Hendal continued snoring softly when she finished. With the tasks complete, she wrapped her cloak around her body tighter, propped herself against a sturdy trunk with the sword across her lap, and drifted off.

*

The shuffling of feet had Coura jolting awake what felt like seconds later. She reached for her weapon and grasped the hilt before realizing it was Hendal who moved nearby. He strolled with the animal's reins in hand before letting his mount graze. Though the animal ignored Coura's startled reaction, Hendal responded with a stare that reflected concern.

"What are you doing?" she asked while setting the sword down to rub her tired eyes.

"I thought she should be able to roam a bit for fresh grass."

Coura pushed herself to her feet before moving toward the dwindling fire. "She would have been able to reach whatever she needed."

Hendal didn't offer a rebuttal. Instead, he watched as she dug through her pack for the dried jerky she picked up in Fester and an apple. Once she selected her share, she extended the bag over to him.

"Take what you want, but we'll need to ration what's inside for a few days until we reach Kercher."

"Why go that far east?" he protested, obviously appalled by either the limited food supply or the idea of continuing until they traveled a safe distance away from the capital. "Surely there are other towns to hide in."

"We don't have time to make extra stops, especially when word will spread of your escape. The guards, and probably the Yeluthians posted around the country, are going to start looking for you. Our best option is to get to our goal as soon as possible."

"You still haven't told me what happened in Verona or how I'm involved in all this," he added.

Coura finished her lackluster meal and set about banking the fire without answering his unspoken question since she hadn't planned how to go about explaining the situation and danger regarding Terran, Soirée's lingering connection, and the massacre in the palace.

With the camp properly taken care of, she raised a hand to shade her eyes as she observed the sky to gauge the time, as well as what direction they should set off in. *I wish I woke up sooner. It looks to be around mid-afternoon, so we can push through the night again and rest when the opportunity arises. I'll find a decent spot after I see how far we get.*

She spent another minute assessing their remaining supplies before feeling prepared to begin the trek again. Meanwhile, Hendal stood scratching the mare's snout while wearing a slight smile as the horse leaned into his body.

"Let's go," she ordered and turned to lead the way until his casual response caught her mid-step.

"No."

"No? Did you forget we need to hurry?"

"I was promised an explanation," he replied in a cool manner reminiscent of his previous persona in the palace. "I won't be riding around Asteom blindly."

Her hesitation made her next words sound less forceful. "We don't have time. Besides, would you rather risk getting caught?"

"That depends on why we're fleeing to Kercher. Considering you were the one to free me and the guards didn't act like they received a warning, I would venture to guess this has to do with the demon and her manipulation over us. If that's true, I could be walking into a trap. If not, I would still be captured and locked up again if anybody recognizes me. The guards might decide to kill me on the spot, so we would both be wasting our time and energy by rushing."

Coura sensed no fear or anxiousness behind his words, only acceptance of his fate. This bothered her as she hoped to use his lack of knowledge to pull him along until she could reveal her concerns.

To buy additional time, she tried urging him on once more. "Right now, it doesn't matter why we're going there. If you don't follow, I can go on my own and leave you behind."

"I doubt you would do that. Why go through the trouble of liberating me just to stop short by abandoning me?"

He frowned when she didn't respond, yet his narrowed eyes dared her to challenge the decision. At last, she released a sigh in defeat.

I'll face this one way or the other...

"Fine, but I can explain on the way," she agreed and pointed toward the trail.

Hendal contemplated this before nodding. She helped him mount the horse after, then the two continued at a brisk walk.

The best place to begin the discussion proved to be her initial encounter with Terran, prompting her to share what drove her to visit Verona's prison in the first place. This included what the Sie-Kie witch shared regarding her soul space as a result of acting as a host for Soirée's power. Finally, Coura told Hendal about the attack in the palace. By that point, evening had approached, though enough light lingered to allow her to catch glimpses of stress-induced lines across the man's forehead.

"Before I got you, I spoke with a Yeluthian commander about this," she shared without informing him of her connection to Evern. "We agreed I should see the Mintelians who specialize in soul cleansings in order to heal my body and stop me from being a target."

"And you brought me along for the same reason," her companion concluded. "You also assume someone in Kercher is familiar enough with the mountain people to direct us to their villages."

"The commander believed so."

"What if they were wrong?"

"No matter what does or doesn't happen, we're keeping any demonic threats away from the capital."

"Forgive me for being skeptical, but Kercher was once my home. I loathe the idea of hiding there when we increase the likelihood of another massacre, especially in a place without soldiers and mages for protection."

"We can figure out our next steps when we get there," she cut in to end the discussion.

Hendal attempted to make idle conversation about his time around the country twice after that, which seemed odd given his normally hostile character. Still, she had no interest in befriending the man.

Later in the evening, Coura didn't sense anybody following them and decided it would be in their best interest to rest during the night and begin traveling again in the early morning. They stopped, she set up camp while her companion took care of the horse, and once she got a fire going, they ate their portions. Despite the season, the air grew chilly within the hour, leading them to huddle close to the flames' radiating warmth.

She hugged herself as she stared into the orange glow, letting it lull her into a comfortable, near-sleep trance. If Hendal hadn't spoken then, she would have drifted off shortly after. His voice sounded neutral and hung above the air between them while he lied on his back with his eyes gazing up at the bright stars.

"Now that I understand the situation, I suppose I should thank you for freeing me from Verona's prison. Before you mention it, I know you didn't do that for me. You act on behalf of your friends in the palace and the rest of the people in the capital city. Regardless, I appreciate the effort you spent for my escape."

Coura had no response for what she just heard; however, the man started snoring almost immediately after. Part of her shrugged off the thanks as words anybody in his position would say in order to ease some of the tension and cause less trouble. The other part, the one that had felt enough pity for the high priest behind the demon's influence to visit him on multiple occasions during his imprisonment, took his humility to heart.

*

After four more days of traveling along woodland trails, Coura believed they were close to reaching the edge of the trees that would reveal the eastern section of Asteom, which consisted of even plains and farmland. She tried pressing their urgency every time they set out, yet Hendal kept his horse to a strict, steady walk. His lack of effort made her irritable, and soon they were forced to stop for the night in order to prepare a camp before the sunlight faded completely.

"You wouldn't recognize the area around Kercher, would you?" she threw out when they settled by the fire and finished the evening meal.

Hendal shifted to the side and shot her a less-than-amused look. "It's been over a decade since I went this far east."

Coura sighed, lied on her back, and covered her eyes with one arm. She expected his answer, but for some reason she hoped he would surprise her with a useful hint. *We should have enough food to last through tomorrow. After that, we'll need to find a road and follow it to the nearest town. I'm not sure how much I can get with a few coins either. We may have to cut our rations again.*

The fire's crackling usually relaxed her enough to bring about sleep, so she listened to its lulling sound and focused on resting.

"Did you give more thought to what we will do in Kercher?" Hendal asked to interrupt the peaceful atmosphere, drawing her awake in the process.

27

"I already told you. We're going to find the Mintelian village and request their soul cleansing."

"What if nobody knows where their people are located? Or worse, what if they recognize us and turn hostile?"

Coura's temper began simmering, though she understood her body's weariness contributed to her pessimistic attitude. She prepared to offer a retort about how they would figure it out once they arrived; however, the man's dry chuckle filled the silence to stay her tongue.

"I can't imagine what they'll think when they see me," he admitted with a wry sense of humor. "I'm a disgrace to their people, a blemish on the timeline of honored priests."

Coura had no response to his sudden, personal comment. It wasn't until he went on that she understood he spoke to her and not just himself.

"It's been a few months, but you should remember my history with the town. I abandoned them for my own, selfish reasons. There's no forgiving what I've done, so I suppose I intended to warn you. They will most likely turn us away instead of offer aid."

She opened her mouth, though no word came to mind, nor did she decide whether to be hopeful or realistic in response. During the pause, she realized how quiet the woods around them had grown. This caused her to rise in a deliberately slow manner, scan the illuminated area, and listen.

The insects and night animals aren't making a sound.

"Get up," she ordered at a hushed volume and as calmly as she could manage without removing her eyes from the darkness beyond the firelight.

Hendal started questioning her but stopped when she extended a hand for him to quit talking.

"Move to the horse. I'll help you up."

As if on cue, the mare began fidgeting in place with stressful whinnies. That had Hendal scrambling to his feet and hurrying over. Meanwhile, Coura grabbed her sword without worrying about the other, replaceable items and secured it to her waist.

They managed to get him in place just before a set of growls hummed in the air. Coura put her back to Hendal and the horse and searched for the source with a hand on her weapon's hilt. When nothing became visible, she turned her head to the side in order to tell him to go east without sacrificing her position; however, as she finished, three, shadowy figures emerged at once from across the fire bearing vicious snarls.

The memory of her first fight with the wolf-like demonic creatures came to mind, reminding her of when she rescued Mace and Lexie. The beasts appeared the same, showcasing violet eyes, which glowed against the flames, and slick, black fur that shined like oil. Their lengthy claws dug into the dirt, as if in anticipation for an attack, though instead of standing nearly as tall as Coura, they proved to be no bigger than a large dog. That observation seemed to be the only positive she could come up with since she was outnumbered. To avoid baiting the creatures into action, she drew her sword painstakingly slow, though the three growled louder at the sight of the blade.

We need to run. There's no way I can handle multiple opponents and keep track of Hendal, especially if they possess venom in their claws. There's also the issue regarding their energy. If I kill one, would its power go straight to me, Hendal, or both? Would Terran become aware of its death?

More questions came to mind until the creatures began fanning out around the fire, causing the horse to buck in fear. For all he was worth, Hendal somehow hung on by clinging to the animal's neck.

"What are we going to do?" he begged. His voice trembled to reflect his terror.

"Go!" Coura yelled while glancing over her shoulder and sheathing the sword. "I'll catch up!"

Before he could argue or distract her further, she slapped his horse on the rear, causing it to jump with a cry before bounding ahead into a gallop. Hendal continued to remain in the saddle before the animal led him into the woods. Coura spun around and chased after them.

The demonic creatures snapped at her heels a minute later as she wove around trees and leapt over what obstacles she could spot in the dark forest. Her lungs started burning, yet she knew any pause or decrease in speed would cost her her life. Soon, she completely lost track of the horse's noise and what direction she moved in.

I need to find a tighter area where they can't follow me, she thought instinctively as she twisted to her right and slid between a pair of thick trees.

The breath of the nearest creature reached her then. In a desperate act to buy additional time, Coura noted the next, wide trunk ahead and dove behind it to hide. Her pursuer sprinted by before noticing her disappearance and backtracking; however, Coura already adjusted to sprint in the opposite direction from the continuous snarling.

Her objective became finding a new spot to remain out of sight or hold them off, but the trees started spacing out farther instead of compacting. The realization spurred a sense of panic until a push from behind accompanied by a surge of pain struck her left shoulder. It didn't prove to be enough for her to lose her balance, though she stumbled a bit, and she dismissed the stinging sensation in favor of pressing her pace. The bushes and branches thinned as she focused only on running straight before she burst away from the forest and out into an open, grassy field.

Despite the environment, Coura kept going. A crescent moon hung overhead to illuminate the area a bit, yet nothing met her away from the woods. She also noticed the growls growing fainter and halted while drawing her sword again. Instead of following her into the field, the creatures remained under the shelter of the trees. What started as three beasts appeared to have multiplied, as shown by the several pairs of glowing eyes watching her.

They're not pursuing? she wondered and lowered her blade. *Are they afraid of being out in the open? No, that's not it. I've never seen a demonic creature fearful of anything.*

One by one, the shadows and eyes disappeared into the forest, leaving Coura alone and confused. Her panting steadied into deep breaths, and the pain from her shoulder returned. Although the wound stung, she touched the spot to judge its severity before removing her hand and observing the blood-soaked palm.

I would have felt the effects of venom already. That's some positive news.

She returned her hand to her shoulder, closed her eyes, and focused on the Yeluthian power resting within her center. The energy sprang into action at her call, so she directed it to the scratch until she sensed no indication of an open injury.

My healing ability is weak, so I should be gentle with this shoulder until it finishes healing on its own, she told herself while dismissing the light spell.

With that issue taken care of, Coura looked around and began shouting Hendal's name. There was no telling where they each ended up, so she questioned choosing a direction to explore in until a male voice answered hers. From the south, she soon made out the mare, though it limped, with its rider guiding it toward her.

She released a sigh of relief before jogging over to meet them. "What happened?"

"After you sent us flying off, I didn't see where we were going," Hendal explained without hiding his displeasure with their unexpected escape. "When she steadied enough for me to try calming her down, she shied away and wound up catching her front leg on a broken branch. She didn't fall, but her leg isn't in the best shape."

"The creatures didn't chase you then?"

Hendal shook his head. "Not after we started moving. We found our way out of the forest and waited until we heard your call."

"At least we managed to find each other," Coura said as she crossed her arms and considered their current situation. "A few others joined the original three and chased me to the edge of the trees, but none went any farther. For some reason, they won't go beyond the woods. It should be safe enough to rest, at least until morning."

"You mean to say the creatures didn't come after you once you reached the field?" he asked and raised an eyebrow.

"I figure it's because they prefer the cover of the forest."

"I'm not so sure. It sounds uncharacteristic based on what I learned about them."

This time it was Coura's turn to shoot him a dubious glance. "What do you know about demonic creatures?"

"Well, the one aspect I remember is they often assume the qualities of the animals they possess," he began while shifting to study the trees. "Those appeared like wolves, even going so far as to hunt in a pack. Usually similar types of predators hunt in a certain area."

"You think they were being territorial?" she asked in disbelief.

Hendal shrugged and returned his eyes to her. "I don't see why it's not possible. If that's the case though, there might be others nearby. At any rate, I would rather not stick around past morning to find out."

Coura voiced her agreement while turning around to survey the land to the north. No buildings revealed themselves during their conversation, meaning another day of straight traveling was ahead of them. She also recognized the additional burden of losing Hendal's mount, as well as walking the mare without causing it too much strain.

"What happened to your back?" she heard her companion inquire, prompting her to face him again. When he pointed at her shoulder, she understood he referred to her torn, bloody shirt.

"One of the creatures managed to scratch me. Thankfully, it didn't carry venom in its claws, so I closed the wound."

Hendal's resulting expression reflected a mixture of concern and fear.

"What?" she snapped when his lack of a response made her feel uncomfortable.

"None of the demonic creatures pursued me. Those three, and whatever ones came after, were all targeting you."

"I mean, you were on a horse," she retorted. "I was the obvious, easy prey."

"You know that's not what I'm implying."

Coura averted her gaze without admitting anything, so Hendal continued at a lower volume.

"You might recall I mentioned this before during your visits to the prison. My connection with Soirée never became as personal as hers was with you. She may have granted me use of her power, but what you two shared was…different."

I hate agreeing with him, she admitted. Despite the passing years, the memory of the demon recounting her manipulation and experimentation remained fresh in Coura's mind. *Whatever damage Soirée did to him is nothing compared to how she destroyed my soul space and morphed my center into absorbing demonic energy. This encounter just proved these creatures are after me for that reason, and probably not Hendal. At least, not entirely.*

She forced the issue aside as a yawn approached. "Whatever's going on, it can wait until later. We should try to sleep while we can and figure out where we are tomorrow."

*

In the morning, the mare's limp significantly weakened, though they didn't want to push their luck by trying to ride it. Hendal continued leading the animal as they wandered northeast. Coura figured Kercher would be noticeable even at a distance given the flat land, which seemed to be true when the pair spotted buildings grow from tiny dots on the horizon into decently sized homes as they drew near. It would be another few hours until they'd enter, so she chose to spend the evening in the grassy area and reach their goal the following day.

She felt a sense of relief when the pair crossed into farmland filled with corn stalks and what appeared to be grain. The eagerness of accomplishing part of the journey pushed her onward until she realized her companion stopped farther behind to stare at the town with a worried expression.

"Hurry up," Coura urged, letting her impatience show and waving a hand toward the path ahead.

He wiped his forehead with his free hand twice before taking another step and halting again. "I don't think this is a smart idea."

"If you're that paranoid about being recognized, keep your hood over your face," she suggested.

33

Hendal jumped, as if he never considered the idea, and threw the upper fabric of his cloak over his head. The cover provided him with enough courage to move, and soon they strolled along the town's main road.

Based on how the former high priest once described Kercher, Coura figured it would be devoid of people or they would only pass those who were out on business. Instead, they merged into a welcoming, energetic atmosphere full of noise and life. Children played games near the edge of several buildings while the adults spoke with one another in a casual manner. Although no merchant booths lined the street like in Verona, shop doors remained open to let their sights and sounds wander through the area. Those who noticed the newcomers offered waves and nods as the two went deeper into town.

"I remember you saying nobody had fun around here," Coura commented as she returned the smile of an older woman carrying an armful of wrapped packages.

Hendal kept his head down to stare at his feet the entire time. "It never used to be like this. At least, it wasn't for many years when I was young."

"Well, who do you recommend we ask about the Mintelians?"

Before he could answer, someone bumped into Coura while her head had been turned in the opposite direction. Several, thin books floated to the ground, and their owner, a woman around Coura's age, gasped in alarm.

"I'm sorry!" the stranger exclaimed before dropping to her knees to collect the items.

Coura knelt, picked up those at her feet, and rose to hand them over. "It's fine."

Upon first glance, the woman looked skinny, so much so that her arms were practically all bone and no muscle underneath pale skin. She stood about a head taller than Coura and possessed light brown hair, which had been cropped to her shoulders, and unique, gray eyes. Despite her off-putting appearance, her voice sounded as cheerful as the rest of the town acted.

"You must be new around here, or else I would have recognized you. My name is Lyla."

"It's nice to meet you," Coura began without offering her name. "And you're right. We traveled from Fester to find somebody to guide us to the Mintelian villages. We have business with their mages."

Thankfully, Lyla didn't pursue additional details. She tilted her head and raised her eyes in thought. "I'm afraid I don't know much about them, though my uncle might. If you have a free evening, would you care to join us for dinner? It's nothing special…"

"We'd love to," Coura replied while allowing herself a chance to hope for answers.

"Excellent! Follow me."

As soon as the woman put her back to them, Hendal shot out a hand to seize Coura's arm. "What are you doing?" he hissed without attempting to hide his anger.

"How else are we supposed to find our way?" she countered at a lower volume.

"Not like this!"

"Are you two coming?" Lyla asked from farther ahead when she noticed them lingering.

Coura yanked her arm free, glared at her cloaked companion, and started forward. Part of her expected Hendal to abandon their mission altogether; however, when she glanced over her shoulder a minute later, the man trudged behind a few steps back.

Once they reached their destination, she understood his hesitance.

They approached a clean, white building and passed through a similarly painted gate attached to a wooden fence, leading them into a backyard full of wilting flowers and ripening vegetables. Their escort allowed them to tie the horse's reins to the fence before she stopped after the trio spotted a man standing near the entrance. His woolen, gray robe was the only indication of his status as a holy man, and his peppered hair had been neatly combed into a short braid, revealing a chiseled, shaved face.

He faced Lyla with a kind smile that broadened when his eyes fell on Coura and Hendal. "Who do we have here?" he asked in a manner as gentle as his expression.

"These travelers wandered into town and inquired about the Mintelians. I figured you would know more than me, so I invited them to dinner." Despite how confident she acted when she first suggested the idea, Lyla dipped her head as she repeated the request.

The priest's lips stretched farther. "That's thoughtful of you; however, it's polite to ask for their names so they aren't introduced so informally."

His resulting laugh assured them the comment wasn't meant to offend his assistant, and she even raised her head with her own, weak smile.

"Forgive me," she said next before apologizing to Coura while her cheeks heated into a blush, which became stark against her pale complexion.

In response, Coura waved her hand to dismiss the concern. "Our names aren't important. We do appreciate your hospitality though."

"Nonsense," the priest added as his smile faltered slightly. "We greet everyone with the respect they deserve."

"Everyone?"

Coura started at Hendal's deep voice, especially compared to the lightheartedness of those in the yard. She planned to lie about his name, at the very least, and avoid becoming involved with his past and potential confrontations.

The priest's smile disappeared when he focused his attention on the cloaked figure. "In this place, all are worthy of being treated as equals. Our god Summa and goddess Izina believe caring for another as your own brother or sister leads to salvation and benefits the entire community."

Hendal began a mumbled response before abruptly quieting. Then, he lifted his hands to remove his hood with obvious reluctance as he spoke again. "They would be pleased with you for showing such compassion to a miscreant."

Coura pressed her lips together to express her displeasure with the direction of their conversation, but she didn't dare interrupt. Lyla remained silent too, and Hendal stared at the ground with a grim expression. Meanwhile, the priest's eyes widened to show he recognized the man in front of him. Despite that, he made no attempt to confront Hendal.

They all stood still and waited for somebody else to respond first. Finally, when Coura's stomach rumbled, Hendal spun around to head toward the gate.

"I shouldn't have come here," he started before the other man verbally stopped him.

"Please, wait!" the priest exclaimed while reaching out a hand. His fingers twitched, his mouth worked for a response, and what was once a calm expression shifted into a mixture of pain and sympathy. "Is it really you, Uncle?"

"It is."

A sneeze from Lyla cut through the tension hanging in the air, distracting them for the moment. The priest's eyes fell on her before darting to Coura and back again.

"Lyla, would you bring this young woman inside and prepare dinner?"

She nodded eagerly, as if waiting for such an excuse, and gestured for Coura to join her in the building beyond.

The first room they entered proved to be a chapel with a dozen wooden benches lined up before an altar. Windows stretched to the ceiling, but no decorations adorned the space except for a pair of vases holding colorful flowers. While Coura inspected the dull yet peaceful space, Lyla hurried into another area through a hallway to the right.

Of course Hendal had to ruin this opportunity for us to make progress, she couldn't help but note bitterly. After a moment, she took a seat in front of the rear window where she could observe the men outside for any sign that the priest would betray them or leave to find a guard.

The two faced each other where Hendal stopped, though his eyes remained downcast. For a while, she caught their mouths moving in a conversation she couldn't hear. Suddenly, the priest outstretched his arms to hug Hendal with enough force to reflect a surge of emotion behind his action. Hendal looked completely bewildered as he stared down at his nephew until he spoke again. When nothing changed, his face scrunched as tears slid down his cheeks before he returned the embrace just as passionately. Coura decided she had enough eavesdropping then, prompting her to rise and go into the next room.

She recognized it as a kitchen immediately, though it appeared as ordinary as any except for the lack of personality, such as pictures or artwork. Lyla noticed her arrival, beamed as if they didn't just leave an awkward encounter, and pointed at a cabinet.

"The dishes are in there if you wouldn't mind setting the table for four."

Coura obeyed, mainly so her assistance would bring them closer to eating. Not long after, the glasses for water, a matching set of plates, and dull silverware were in place.

Lyla placed a loaf of warmed bread at the center before wiping her forehead with the back of her hand. "Thank you..."

"Coura," she supplied during the intended pause.

With a giggle, the young woman spun around to finish adding the rest of the food to the table. "How lovely! It's been weeks since we hosted guests; that is, outside the holidays. Where are you from?"

"Neston."

"I've heard of that town. What's it like?"

"About the same as Kercher."

"I see."

Coura slid into one of the chairs while eyeing their meal in the process. "Should we wait for them?" she asked politely despite the urge to do the opposite.

Lyla chose the seat to Coura's right and pushed herself closer. "They might be a few minutes. Priest Wesley tends to ramble when he's excited about something."

"You consider that as him being excited?"

The priest's assistant didn't respond until they loaded their plates with boiled potatoes, roasted chicken, and buttered bread. "Priest Wesley has always been such a friendly person, but rarely does somebody push him enough for him to grow uneasy. If your appearance brought trouble, he would have dismissed you and your friend or sent for the soldiers to remove you from church grounds."

Coura grunted in approval, then she shoveled a spoonful of the flavorful food into her mouth and chewed slowly enough to savor the taste. The dried rations served their purpose, but nothing could compare to a real meal.

Lyla noticed her cherishing each bite and grinned. "Does Neston not have potatoes?"

Coura didn't understand the comment had been meant as a joke until the other woman laughed at it herself. "That's funny," she added before noticing Lyla's untouched plate. "Are you not hungry?"

The priest's assistant jumped in alarm, as if someone poked her in the back. "N-No," she stuttered while dropping her eyes to her plate. "I mean, I am. I just…"

She cut herself off by shoving the diced pieces of vegetable into her mouth, sparing Coura from continuing the conversation. Soon, Hendal and his nephew, Wesley, moved into the kitchen. Neither attempted to hide their flushed cheeks and pink eyes, though they wore matching, genuine smiles.

"Come," the priest began as they took their seats. "Let us offer a prayer that we are all together this evening."

*

The church's attic acted as a spare room with two mattresses consisting of hay bales, which the priest offered to his guests. Despite how uncomfortable the bed felt and how Coura despised being closed up with Hendal, she slept soundly and awoke only when her companion rose to leave first. The silence of the space allowed her to recall their host's response the previous night when she asked about a guide to the nearest Mintelian village.

"Although their peoples' connection to Kercher is limited, I believe the messengers are aware of their locations," Priest Wesley explained after their meal. "I will visit my sister tomorrow and see what she can do. If anything, I can request a guard who should be able to contact a Yeluthian scout to assist you."

Coura and Hendal had shared a look but accepted the offer.

Once she felt prepared for the day, Coura met the others at breakfast before retreating to the garden while Hendal and Lyla remained in the kitchen to catch up. She occupied an outdoor bench, propped her elbows on her knees, then leaned forward to rest her chin in her hands. The atmosphere proved to be as relaxing as the church's chapel, and she stared at the insects crawling and buzzing around the nearby plants without thinking. In an attempt to meditate, she closed her eyes while focusing on her soul space.

As usual, the Yeluthian energy responded to her prodding and awaited instruction, though she merely studied the flow of power, like watching fish swirl around in a pond. It was then she noticed a faint presence lingering underneath that reminded her of a shadow. She longed to explore by calling it forth, yet the subtle fear of the potential results kept her from doing so, and she opened her eyes just as Lyla called her name.

The priest's assistant approached with a basket in one hand and a cheerful smile across her face. "I'll be in town for some visits and to pick up ingredients for dinner. Would you like to join me?"

The offer sounded tempting, mostly because Coura didn't want to hurt the young woman's feelings by refusing. For some reason, Lyla clung to her, as if they developed a close friendship, and she wondered if it had to do with the sheltered life of a priest's assistant.

"I'm sorry, but I would prefer to stay and meditate."

To her relief, Lyla didn't appear bothered. "That's fine. Priest Wesley should be returning soon if you need anything."

Coura watched as she moved to the gate; however, Priest Wesley appeared on the other side at the same time, causing the two to laugh before he let her pass. He then greeted Coura with a wave, entered the yard, and came over to converse.

"I have good news for you. My sister and I found somebody to escort you to the nearest Mintelian village."

She perked up. "Really?"

"He is familiar with one to the south and claims it is a three-day journey on foot before the climb."

"That's perfect!"

The priest chuckled at her enthusiasm. "I'll pass the message along to Hendal as well. Your guide will plan on departing tomorrow morning when you arrive at his home."

Finally, we're getting somewhere.

Coura kept the comment to herself but thanked her host. Despite what certainty she showed during the past few days, she secretly worried what she would do if the guards caught the pair or she needed to request assistance from a Yeluthian scout.

*

The rest of her day remained as ordinary as the previous had been, except Coura retired earlier in the evening than the rest. When she crawled out from the fog of a dream, she found Hendal wasn't in the attic. She spent a few minutes physically and mentally preparing for the day ahead of them before emerging to find Priest Wesley and Hendal conversing in the chapel. When the former noticed her, he stopped talking mid-sentence to stand and greet her.

"I figured you would aim to depart as soon as possible, though I hoped Lyla would've been awake by now to see you off."

Coura brushed her guilt aside in order to concentrate on the importance of her task and looked at Hendal. "Are you prepared for the hike?"

He stared up at his nephew without answering.

"I'll give you two a moment," the priest started before addressing her directly. "Join me outside when you are ready, and I will escort you to your guide's home."

With that, he left the building. Coura looked after him as silence fell upon the space once more. Despite her curiosity at his sudden desire to leave them alone, she didn't press the subject.

Instead, she glanced at Hendal, who kept his eyes on his folded hands. "What was that about?"

He inhaled deeply through his nostrils, released a sigh, and met her gaze. "I've decided I won't be accompanying you to the Mintelian village."

"What? Why?"

Hendal didn't answer.

"That's been the plan this entire time," she snapped while avoiding the urge to raise her voice. "Did you forget who you are and why I brought you here? If you don't come along, you could be in danger. You'll be luring the-"

"No, I won't," he interrupted in a firm enough tone to startle Coura.

"What do you mean?"

He studied her for a moment while wearing a patient expression before shaking his head. "Surely you've realized it by now. I'm not impacting the demon or its creatures, at least not the way you are."

"We don't know that."

"I do." The volume of his voice lowered as he went on. "While Soirée manipulated me through my pride, she only allowed me to act as a conduit for her power. The demonic energy never belonged to me. Besides, any part that might have remained afterward was burned away by the Yeluthian and Lady Emilea. They were both present before my sentence to ensure no power remained."

Coura hadn't heard that detail from Emilea, Byron, or Aaron, but she didn't doubt their thoroughness given the severity of the issue. Still, she shook her head. "Even if that's true, you can't stay here. You're not a free man and will be labeled as worse once the guards capture you."

"I understand the consequences."

His confession shocked her enough to let him continue.

"If they question me, I could honestly admit I intended to visit the mountain sages for a soul cleansing in response to the demon's attack on the palace. I would rather spend what precious time I have been given outside that prison cell with my family. There's no forgiving what I did, especially to you and the others who risked their lives to protect Asteom, but allow me this bit of mercy."

Coura crossed her arms and turned away when his hopeful yet understanding expression became too much to bear. The person who sat before her was just that: a vulnerable man searching for whatever leniency she would give him.

Why does he bother asking me? she wondered amid her frustration. *It's not like I control his life. I guarantee I'll be in trouble too once I return to Verona.*

Perhaps it was the church's atmosphere, but her mind and heart leaned in a sympathetic direction. She also grew fond of Priest Wesley and Lyla and believed they would be a better cure for Hendal's isolated mentality than any mountain sage.

"If you want to stay, I'm not going to stop you," she responded after contemplating the potential results. "I trust the people of Kercher and their judgement, as well as the Yeluthians, and the guards posted here will drag you back to Verona if you cause trouble again."

"I believe so as well. In a way, I'm counting on that." He rose to his feet before offering a slight bow. "Thank you, Coura."

She watched him for a moment without acknowledging his gratitude. Part of her debated whether or not she made the right decision while another recoiled the idea of informing those at the palace. Without reaching a clear conclusion about either thought, she moved to pass him and exit the chapel.

Priest Wesley didn't question their exchange nor why she would be departing alone, leading her to realize he probably discussed the matter with his uncle before Hendal brought it up with her. Instead of lingering on the past, she walked beside him as he went into town, moved east, and knocked on the door to a shed-like building near the perimeter.

Coura felt conspicuous as everybody seemed to recognize the holy figure and waved with smiles or words of greeting. He responded to each in his own, respectful manner until a stranger emerged from the building carrying a pair of packs. The two men shook hands, then the newcomer inspected her with beady eyes. She did the same, allowing her to spot the family resemblance as their square faces looked nearly identical.

"This the one?" the stranger asked in a gruff yet not unkind manner.

"Borus, this is Coura."

Her new guide grunted, presumably to greet her, looked her over for a final time, and nodded. "She's sturdy enough."

"In that case, I'll let you two be on your way." Priest Wesley faced Coura with his signature, gentle smile. "We will be praying for a safe journey."

She thanked him while Borus dipped his head, then the pair started down the road.

"It'll be about three days before we reach the base of the mountain, if we don't stop too frequently," the man shared, which matched what Priest Wesley explained the day prior. "The trail south is the easy part since it cuts straight through the fields and grassland. Climbing the mountain can get rough, so don't be shy. If you need a break or aren't comfortable with the trek, tell me, and we can find another route."

His sudden, hospitable offer sounded out of character based on his tough exterior, but Coura agreed to communicate any issues. With a final glance behind, they left the safety of the structured town for the open world beyond.

44

Royal Requests

Despite the lack of additional conflicts in the palace after the initial week, Grace remained hesitant to leave her room except for meals. The people around her seemed to be recovering from the chaos that took place mere days ago as they fought for justice, yet she struggled to overcome the haunting images of the terrified, injured, and dying women she knew. The potions dulled her senses enough for her to sleep, though she hated drinking them during the day when she preferred to be thinking without their effects.

She continued reading in her free time and visited the library once for a new set of books. The female solider who guarded her daily agreed to purchase painting supplies, yarn for knitting, and various, common materials when Grace requested them since she found art projects soothing throughout her time in Asteom. Those, in addition to Marcus' check-ins before his venture to Dala, kept her from growing too bored or lonely.

After breakfast one morning, she contemplated an examination by a healer at the medical station in order to acquire more potions. She contemplated whether or not the medicine was still necessary; however, noise from outside her door, including multiple voices and shuffling feet, distracted her until a knock sounded.

"Come in," she called while rising from her seat near the window where she gazed out over Verona.

Her curiosity piqued when King Arval stepped inside with Commander Isan lingering behind to remain in the hallway. Grace promptly offered a curtsy before he addressed her.

"May I trouble you for a few minutes?" her uncle asked.

When she nodded, he closed the door, smiled, then closed the space between them.

"You have made this space your own, Grace. It puts my quarters to shame."

"Thank you, Uncle," she replied without hiding her pride. "It is a collection I amassed throughout the years. Perhaps you will build a similar assortment of decorations in time too."

The king's resulting chuckle sounded rich and genuine. "Perhaps. Your aunt prefers I deliver what I discover to Yeluthia so she does not need to trouble herself with traveling. She is a homebody through and through, yet her fascination with the human world grows with each new gift I return with."

Grace rarely heard about the queen even before being appointed as ambassador. Most updates came from her mother since the two worked closely together in the kingdom's political landscape.

"To what do I owe the pleasure of your visit?" she inquired and offered the king a seat. After he accepted, she stole the stool from her vanity in order to be near him. Her uncle never came to her room or sought her out personally, so she figured he had a valid reason.

"I will not assume you are ignorant of the troubles Asteom faces to the south," he began while letting his smile fade. "King Aaron wishes to resolve that matter as soon as possible with the threat of a war to the north. I desire to assist him without offering more of my troops since monitoring each Yeluthian soldier is becoming taxing on myself and my commanders."

Grace nodded and decided to respond when he paused, as if waiting for her to comment. "I can understand the choice you face. We are Asteom's allies, but that does not mean we should donate our resources in order to aid them. Yeluthia would end up suffering from the lack of attention."

Her uncle's lips curved upward to show her words pleased him. "After all the time you spent among the humans, you still put our kingdom first. Nullan and Elenor nearly had me convinced you all but abandoned your responsibilities."

Grace's face fell before she composed herself a moment later and cleared her throat. "I apologize for concerning you."

When King Arval didn't respond, she averted her gaze. *Father and Mother would actually lie to remove me as ambassador? Unless they honestly believe I am not striving to support Yeluthia. Have I given that impression? That might be why Uncle is here, then.*

"In any case, I would like to request your assistance with a search King Aaron has agreed to," he went on. "It requires the use of your goddess gift."

"My goddess gift?"

Her uncle nodded before revealing the details. "I suggested the council locate the ancestral weapons to wield against the demonic creatures and the being controlling the beasts; however, I fear time is of the essence. That is why I would like for you to use your goddess gift to peer into the minds of those living in the palace, city, and towns nearby. You should be able to hear mention of the items, or a golden blade or enchanted bow, and we will utilize that information to track them down."

The idea spurred mixed emotions. "What if nobody knows about the weapons?"

"If that proves to be true, we will eliminate this area and explore elsewhere. You may even assist further by traveling south, but we would assess the risks first."

King Arval's intelligent eyes studied Grace until she dropped hers to stare at her hands. Hearing about her parents and how they doubted her dedication to Yeluthia stung, yet she wished for nothing more than an excuse to prove her loyalty. Still, what her uncle asked went against what morals she developed during her time in Asteom.

Every human deserves to be treated with respect, just like my own people. It would be selfish of me to turn by back on that fact after developing such meaningful relationships. I do not believe Aaron, nor any member of his council, would be pleased with me either.

Grace inhaled a deep breath through her nose to calm her nerves before raising her eyes to her uncle again. "I am afraid I cannot use my ability in such a way."

"Is your energy that limited?" he inquired, though he appeared to be genuinely curious and not testing her.

"I did this before," she shared and shook her head. "When the former high priest controlled the palace and I assisted those fighting to end his reign, my goddess gift helped locate an ally hiding in Verona, as well as General Casner and his troops, and I informed them of the situation. Although it was useful, I only did so because of how dire the situation became."

"Do you not believe the threat of a demon is enough?"

She paused to reflect on his question before countering with her own. "Has Aaron exhausted every other option?"

"Not yet."

"Until my ability is your last resort, I refuse to invade the citizens' privacy by observing their thoughts without their knowledge. It would be disgraceful to turn by back on the people I built trust with over the years."

Grace's body grew tense when her uncle didn't push her again. *If respecting our allies makes me a traitor to Yeluthia, then I suppose I am fine with losing my position. This is an odd course for him to try anyway.*

"You developed into a mature young woman," came King Arval's next comment.

His words startled her into bumbling her thanks, and he released a relieved sigh before smiling at her without a hint of malice.

"I never expected you to agree to participate in the search," he admitted. "Your goddess gift gives you plenty of opportunities to spy on others, human or Yeluthian, yet you choose to hold yourself accountable. Most people would not hesitate to further their own ambitions through such means either."

Grace felt her cheeks heating into a blush. "That is kind of you to say, Uncle."

"It is nothing more than the truth, and I will gladly share this with Nullan if he pesters me again with his lack of faith."

"Really?" she practically squeaked to show her surprise.

As he rose, King Arval shot her a knowing look. "My brother nor his wife visit enough to learn what type of effort you contribute. They do not converse with the humans; they only hear what news others bring them. I discuss such matters with King Aaron, as well as the generals and master mages, and they speak highly of you. I prefer to keep an experienced ambassador who is familiar with the people than assign a new one as well."

"You should not be troubled by my disagreements," she mumbled. The idea of her parents bothering the ruler of Yeluthia for a personal squabble embarrassed her when she considered what he dealt with in Asteom.

"I believe so too; however, family and friends sometimes disregard being considerate when they grow desperate. I suppose that includes my previous request, so I apologize."

Grace rose to curtsy. "Thank you, and if there is anything else I can do to assist with the search for the ancestral weapons, please do not hesitate to summon me."

After mentioning he would hold her to her offer, King Arval took his leave.

***

Of all the appointments Will volunteered to attend for the Nim-Valans, he was looking forward to that afternoon's the least. The patient experienced similar symptoms of the illness rampaging the capital city for weeks, which he became well-equipped to treat. Unfortunately, the positives ended there.

The afflicted boy was the fourth of six children born to a busy father and an overbearing mother who already belittled Will during his first visit for being unable to hear, an act he continued to uphold. Two of her children recovered from the sickness during his original appointment, then another fell ill almost immediately after. Their mother grew furious, blaming Will's incompetence for creating a third case. When Finn defended his skills, she wept and assumed the role of a victim in matters she knew nothing about. It gave Will a headache, especially since he could only ground his teeth to keep from making a sound that would ruin his disguise. He expected her to act similarly, if not worse, with this child.

The days spent in the northern country's inner circle began blurring together. He couldn't leave Yukin's father's estate except for the appointments, but the young lord remained sympathetic and allowed Finn to collect anything he requested from the city, ranging from medicinal ingredients and tools to local foods and finer clothing. Although he didn't care too much about possessions, Will accepted whatever the spy brought him with indifference, knowing if he acted enthusiastic Finn would catch on that something bothered him.

What that was, he couldn't identify.

He spent the morning lying in bed to mentally prepare for the day before dragging himself to the bathing chamber to wash and change into proper clothes. Fortunately, everybody left him alone as he moved throughout the rooms to grab breakfast after and return to his quarters where he stared out the window. The stray thoughts that swam around his head eventually led him to remember Clara, the other light mages in Muld, Geneva, then his friends in Asteom. Each memory widened the hole in his chest, though it felt too familiar to pester him much.

"Are you ready?" a male voice asked from behind.

Will jumped at the sound, hitting his elbow against the windowsill in the process, and shifted to see Finn waiting in front of the closed door. The Nim-Valan's ability to sneak into an area without producing a sound was a skill Will would never grow accustomed to.

"You could at least knock," he grumbled with a glare while rubbing his throbbing arm.

Finn just shrugged indifferently. "It would seem suspicious if I did."

Will rolled his eyes. "In the weeks I've stayed here, no one has come near me or my room."

"Better to be safe than sorry. Now, are you ready?"

"For what?"

Finn narrowed his eyes. "You haven't forgotten today's appointment, have you?"

"No, but it's only…" Will glanced outside again and found the sun high overhead, indicating how much time passed. "It's already afternoon?"

He hurried to gather what few items were not already packed, such as a spare, clean shirt and rags, before throwing on his boots. Finn continued to linger by the door yet gave him an odd look.

"What?" he finally asked and got to his feet.

As he reached for his cloak hanging in the closet, the Nim-Valan slid in between. "Something's upsetting you."

Will recoiled his outstretched hand and took a step backward. "I don't…"

"Is it the noblewoman? She shouldn't be so obnoxious this time. I made it clear when her servant came with the request that she wasn't to interfere."

"That's not it," Will added. His glum tone appeared to startle the usually serious spy, as Finn's eyes widened a bit.

"Then, what is?"

"It's not important right now."

"When will it be, if not now?"

He reached around the Nim-Valan for his cloak and threw it on, hoping to cover his unhappiness for the time being. "Come on. We have a job to do."

*

The ill child wasn't nearly as sick as her siblings had been, and what Finn mentioned about not allowing the mother to be anywhere near Will held true. In fact, everybody he saw looked relieved by the peace as he worked while his assistant went through the regular routine of instructing the caretakers on the girl's care and medicine doses. The only hint of an argument sparked when they prepared to leave. One of the servants handed over a pouch possessing their payment to Finn, who weighed it gingerly in his hand before scowling.

"This is less than normal," he commented while lowering his voice to be more menacing.

It worked, for the older woman dipped her chin when her cheeks and neck reddened. "My lady told me to give you this and no more. She claims there are other medicine men now who charge less for the same treatment, and she already paid you for visiting her other children."

Will worried that Finn's resulting glare would somehow set the poor servant on fire because of how furiously it bore into the top of her bowed head. She remained unmoving even as the pair departed. Will had no interest in the money they made, not that he ever saw any of it, and Yukin never seemed to care either. For some reason, Finn kept his temper after they returned to the estate and entered the young lord's private office for the usual debriefing.

Yukin stood from where he lounged at his desk as soon as the door opened and only spoke once Will closed it. "What's wrong?" he asked after without hiding his concern.

Finn tossed him the pouch before taking one of two empty chairs along the back wall. Under his breath, he muttered several, nasty curses without meeting the young lord's gaze.

In response, Yukin blanched before turning to Will. "Could you leave us alone? I'll send him for you if we need to talk."

Will couldn't exit fast enough. Finn's behavior made him uncomfortable, mainly because he didn't understand why the man grew so aggravated. Once he left the Nim-Valans, he swung his head around out of instinct to confirm the hallway beyond was clear and took a couple steps before halting. The pair of voices proved to be loud enough that he could hear them clearly through the door if he tried.

Why not? What's the worst they could do to me for eavesdropping? he figured before sitting against the wall next to the door and pulling his knees up to his chest.

"I can't help you if you don't talk to me." That was Yukin.

"She shorted us! Not by a little, either. You should have been able to tell too."

"I did, but that's not the point. Why does it infuriate you? It's not like we don't get enough payments."

A pause followed the young lord's comment. Will had to strain his ears then because Finn's voice returned to its normal, controlled volume and professional tone as he responded.

"I'm sorry. I overreacted."

"Why? What has you so worked up, especially in front of Will?"

"I should be at the border searching for the advisor, not playing escort to a medicine man for ungrateful wenches."

"Finn…" Will could hear Yukin's frown as he said his partner's name. "Your responsibility is here with me, not in Asteom."

"What if they request I return before the fighting breaks out? Who do I obey when both sides are at war?"

Light footsteps sounded, followed by the gentle scraping of the desk chair along the floorboards.

"I won't pretend to hold any control over where your loyalties should lie. When I promised Elena I would house you here, she made it clear that you belong to her, not me."

"I know."

"Whoever you serve across the border gave you free reign as long as you report in every once in a while, correct?"

Finn grunted in confirmation.

"Of course, I want you to stay, but I also understand your responsibilities elsewhere."

"Does that mean-"

"I'll cover for you with Elena as best as I can while you're away. You better be sure Lupin's at the border, or else we're both going to be in trouble."

"Yukin…"

Will heard more footsteps before the room fell silent, leading Will to wonder if he should return to his quarters.

"What about Will?"

At the mention of his name, Will froze, as though he had been caught.

"I'll take care of him here."

"Why not send him back to Muld?"

"Don't worry; I'll talk with him tonight. You need to hurry if you're going to get anywhere before it's dark outside."

While Finn thanked Yukin, Will scrambled to his feet as quietly as possible, ducked behind the nearest wall, and held his breath. As soon as he got into his hiding place, the office's door opened and closed, and the lighter footsteps hurried down the hallway before disappearing. Only then did he breathe against the ache in his lungs and crawl out from his hiding spot.

Many new thoughts gave him much to contemplate, so he prepared to return to his room until Yukin's voice reached him.

"You can come in now."

He spun around, uncertain if the young lord addressed him. Evidently, the Nim-Valan did.

"Hurry up, Will."

With heavy feet, he poked his head in first to observe the man writing on a piece of paper at his desk.

"Please, close the door," Yukin instructed without looking up.

Will obeyed, then he moved to stand in the center of the room with both arms at his sides and his head bowed in a sheepish manner. "I'm sorry. I didn't mean to listen in on your conversation."

To his relief, Yukin laughed and raised his deep brown eyes, which looked full of life and humor. "Of course you did! Why else would you wait outside the door?"

Will felt his face grow hot, even though the rest of his body started to relax. "Fine, so it was on purpose. I was worried about Finn."

Yukin's smile faded, and he nodded. "I know. Actually, I hoped you would do that."

"You did?"

"Now I don't need to repeat the previous conversation."

*

Their meeting would be the last time Will saw Finn at the estate for a while, according to the young lord. Yukin reiterated that the spy had been given permission to search for their target on the border while doing his best to prevent an immediate conflict. As far as any of them knew, nothing changed recently to push for a war.

Will prayed that would stay the same, especially after what he heard next.

"What Finn mentioned about needing to serve both sides is…" Yukin paused to search for the word while circling his hands over one another. "It's complicated, to say the least. He'll probably berate me for telling you, but years ago he got caught snooping around Nim-Vala's inner circle."

"You mean, he's…"

"That's right. He's originally a spy from Asteom."

Will's mouth hung open in disbelief. "How? I thought-"

54

"Let me explain this all at once," the young lord interrupted while raising a hand. "He never revealed his past in the southern country other than he was recruited as a child and trained by a mentor. He had been sent to infiltrate the king's estate twelve years ago, but Elena's soldiers found him sneaking around her quarters. Lying is something she's adept at spotting. I'm not sure how, but she can and did during their first interaction; however, when he was prepared to die with his secrets, she offered him the opportunity to work for her too."

"Too?"

He paused to lick his lips in a nervous manner. "Elena is tricky, to put it kindly. She manipulated a lot of people to keep herself in the king's presence, then she seduced him in order to become his wife. Still, all she's ever been is true to her morals, at least as far as Finn and I can tell."

"And what are those?"

Yukin didn't answer for a moment, opting to stare at the pen he had been twiddling between his fingers. "Nobody in Nim-Vala desires a war with Asteom. Sure, the outer ring has longed for justice for decades, but that's a grudge with the inner circle. Elena desires to maintain her position, as do most here. Potential conflicts along the border jeopardize that because if these issues continue, Asteom *will* invade to seize land and hold it. What prevents them from conquering the rest of the country while the lords and ladies idly sit back and let it happen?"

Will pushed his glasses farther up his nose to hide the fact that his head began spinning. "The people within the inner circle don't want a power shift since it would risk the lavish lifestyles they live."

"Exactly. That's Elena's goal, and that's why she kept Finn near the border all these years. He makes routine visits to share reports for Asteom, then he returns to the palace to do the same for her."

"How did you get mixed up with them?" Will asked next.

Yukin visibly relaxed as his lips curled upward into a smile. "My father brought me to her when I was younger, and we always got along. I find her blunt behavior refreshing considering I mostly deal with nobility who search for methods to scheme their way to power.

When Finn began serving her estate, she noticed we're around the same age and introduced us. The three of us grew close over the years, but one day I went over just to visit him. Elena laughed at me for hiding this from her. She said if I enjoyed his company so much, I could have him so long as he remained loyal to her."

"Does your family know?"

Will regretted not clarifying that he referred to Finn's relationship with Elena, not Yukin, for the young lord's cheeks flushed a deep crimson.

"No," he replied quietly and glanced away. "They don't ask or care about that."

An uncomfortable silence stretched between them until Yukin could face Will again.

"So, that's it. Our current goal is to monitor the king's estate while Finn is away."

"*Our* goal?"

"Without Finn, you won't be going around as a medicine man anymore, and I can't spare the upper servants to escort you to Muld. You'll be my new assistant for the time being. Speaking of which, Elena wishes to meet you; I was just answering her summons actually. We'll leave before dinner."

Will felt as though he should be arguing for his freedom, yet something prevented him from making an outburst. *I agreed to stay and help where I could. Besides, I'd need Finn in order to cross the border again. Remaining here is the only opportunity to hold him to that, but I didn't expect to become this involved in Nim-Vala's politics.*

*

Somehow, the king's estate appeared more serine against the gray backdrop of the overcast sky, which threatened a heavy rain for the season. Even as Will stepped out of the carriage behind Yukin, plump raindrops descended, and their drumming soon echoed on the roof while the pair were led down the corridor. They passed in silence, then the guards guided them into an unfamiliar room.

"Queen Elena will be with you momentarily," one said before exiting to stand in front of the opening.

Yukin didn't offer a response, so Will stayed quiet.

A few minutes later, the sound of footsteps slapping against the stone flooring reached them, and the king's wife barged in with a displeased expression. The young lord leapt to his feet, leaving Will to do the same a second after.

"Elena, what's wrong?"

"I wish you hadn't sent Finnley away," she practically growled with a glare, though it was not directed at either of them. "We have the perfect opportunity to…"

Her words faded when she noticed Will.

"What's going on?" Yukin pressed at a lower volume as the woman approached Will, who could only watch in bewilderment.

"My Lord, I need to borrow this boy."

Yukin stepped forward without hesitation to place himself between the two. "Tell me what this is about."

"We don't have time to waste!"

To Will's relief, the young lord held his ground, and Elena backed off a moment later. She glanced over her shoulder at the entrance, or rather the men standing guard just outside, then leaned closer.

"Advisor Lupin has returned."

Yukin gasped at the news, nodded, and matched her whisper. "You wish to spy on him?"

"Not me," she replied before her rich, brown eyes shifted to Will.

He purposefully kept silent since he hadn't been sure if she became aware of his feigned lack of hearing; however, that look confirmed her knowledge of their lie. *Yukin was right about her.*

"He's meeting with my husband shortly. I would like to arrive before then and leave this one until I return. In the meantime, he can listen and repeat what they discuss."

"Is it safe?" Will hoped to ask.

To his dismay, she grabbed his arm before he could vocalize the question. With a wave at Yukin and a promise to return, Elena dragged him behind her until they left the room. Then, she strolled ahead, leaving him to follow on his own.

*

Will couldn't figure out who he should be more afraid to meet: the king or this mysterious advisor. He got the impression Elena wasn't the type to be inclined to help someone in his position, so he devoted himself to playing the part of her servant as they reached their goal.

Instead of a throne room, the space appeared to be a lounge area possessing oversized pillows scattered around cushioned chairs and couches. King Syrus draped over a seat in the back. Gems and metal adorned every part of the hefty man, from piercings and jewelry on or around his face to the colorful tunic he wore. Black hair trailed over his shoulders in an unkempt manner, like a spilled vial of ink, while his short, trimmed beard gave the opposite impression. As soon as Elena entered, his wide eyes became glued to her.

"My beautiful flower!" he exclaimed while outstretching his hands with a grin. "To what do I owe this visit?"

"Your Highness," she purred before accepting his embrace and dropping to sit at his feet. "It's been days since you made time for me."

Will remained standing awkwardly as the two shared a lustful gaze. A minute later, Elena turned her head to meet his eyes and pointed at a chair, which he promptly occupied. The movement caught King Syrus' attention, and he raised an eyebrow before scanning Will up and down.

"Who is this boy?" he asked with nothing more than innocent curiosity.

"He's my newest servant," the woman explained. "I took him in out of pity because he lacks the ability to hear, though he is smart enough to know where he should and shouldn't be looking. I thought to bring him along so your guards would recognize him in case he wanders off."

Will let his eyes steadily coast around the space in a casual manner while he listened. His main focus was on ignoring the audible directions and cues in favor of responding to only physical touch and visual gestures.

Still, when a guard at the entrance announced the arrival of Lupin Olim a minute later, he couldn't stop himself from growing tense.

"Lupin, my friend!" The king laughed in the resulting silence and rose to his feet.

Will forced his attention to stay on the man and Elena again. She stood and clung to her husband in an attempt to remain relevant; however, King Syrus indirectly brushed her aside when he opened his arms wide to welcome his advisor.

"You've returned at last. What riches do you bring?"

As the newcomer crossed the space, Will took a moment to observe what he could without staring for long enough to draw attention to himself.

Lupin wore a formal robe similar to every other lord's, except his proved to be an emerald color adorned with patches of decorated designs in silver thread. No nobleman he had encountered used that particular shade or such intricate patterns either. The advisor held his hands in front of him, allowing the elongated sleeves to cover them until the king rose. Then, he extended both with the palms facing upward and revealed several rings and other pieces of jewelry that caused his superior to giggle like a child.

Will noted how he couldn't identify Lupin's size or build because of the heavy-looking, loose garments; however, the advisor's choice of headgear interested him the most. A maroon scarf had been wrapped around his head in a bundle that acted like a layered hood, preventing anybody from assessing his face. What skin he showed looked starkly pale, especially against the darker clothing. It wasn't completely new to Will, though he had never seen the accessory used to hide a person's facial features.

For the most part, Will didn't feel threatened by the advisor, yet his suspicion rose once Lupin addressed the king.

"My Liege," he began while bowing. "I possess finer gifts than any before; however, I was under the impression our meeting would be private."

Will noticed Elena's frown, which deepened when King Syrus nodded, turned to his beloved, and kissed her cheek.

"Leave us," he ordered gently.

"Shall I wait nearby?" The woman's playful tone suggested she intended to continue her seduction.

"If you wish."

That satisfied Elena, so she returned the kiss and sauntered to the exit. Meanwhile, Will got to his feet and stared after her, like an abandoned child.

"Now then, what about these gifts you mentioned?" the king asked as soon as she disappeared. He rubbed his hands together in a gleeful manner, and his voice displayed a possessive nature.

Will listened for a response, yet none came. He glanced at the king again but found the advisor facing him. The stranger's lip curled, as if in disgust, and despite not being able to meet Lupin's eyes, Will felt his glare, prompting a shiver.

"You should be more attentive to your master," Lupin growled with none of the pleasantry he used before.

Will hoped his expression projected his genuine mixture of confusion and fear.

After a pause, King Syrus groaned. "This one can't hear. Leave it alone."

The advisor didn't reply, yet he didn't move either.

If Will wasn't purposefully trying to eavesdrop, he would have bolted after Elena, if only to ease the growing tension. *If he won't continue their discussion, the king might turn on me. Without Yukin or Elena's support, I'm in serious trouble.*

With that in mind, he acted dumb. He swung his head between the opening and the king twice then backed away, as if realizing he should be following his master. When he chose to spin around and scuttle toward the exit, he heard Lupin begin the conversation again at a lower volume. Instead of leaving the space, Will dropped into a cushioned chair at the rear before hunching over and wringing his hands to emphasize his feigned nerves and uncertainty.

The king and his advisor didn't seem to notice, or at least they ignored Will; however, the set of guards posted nearby spoke to each other in mutters. He chanced a brief, hopeful glance their way and found them avoiding his gaze.

"Poor boy," one said loudly enough for Will to hear. "The least Queen Elena could do is train him to stay by her side. He's clueless."

"Don't worry," the other replied. "She'll be back as soon as they're done. Just keep an eye on him in case he decides to do anything funny."

Will attempted to listen to the farthest voices after that, but the guards' continuous chatter drowned out what happened with Lupin, aside from a laugh from King Syrus. The tension in the space also remained, giving it a stuffy sensation.

The meeting went on long enough that he began to wonder if Elena would burst in and demand affection from her husband, but nothing exciting came to pass. Will placed his elbows on his knees, rested his chin in his hands, and dipped his head to relax his neck and shoulders. For a while, he focused all his attention on discerning the advisor's words.

Then, the atmosphere around him changed. The air in the enclosed space became heavy enough that the guards commented on the humidity so late in the year; however, unlike natural weather patterns, it didn't seem stagnant. Will thought about a lightning storm and how the clouds would crackle to signal the presence of energy. The image he crafted in his mind had him sitting upright with a start.

That was magic! Did they just…

King Syrus let out a maniacal, uncharacteristic laugh unbefitting the man's upbeat personality, startling Will. It took all his self-control not to look at the opposite side of the room.

Clara nor any of the other light mages ever produced this haunting sensation. That must mean one of them is using dark energy instead. What would a mage be doing in Nim-Vala anyway?

Before he could even consider possible answers to that question, he caught Lupin bowing a second time, turning away from the king, and crossing the space to exit. The advisor kept his head dipped and hid his hands in his sleeves, like he did when he arrived. Will considered keeping his eyes glued to the floor to avoid incurring a tongue lashing should he be scolded for lingering but decided to risk his position in favor of memorizing what he could about the man.

A second later, Will learned the figure was not what he seemed.

From the moment the advisor passed him, he scanned the clothes, headwrap, and what he could see of the pale face. His previous, standing position caused the scarf to hide the upper half of Lupin's face; this time, the lower angle allowed him to spot a pair of violet eyes, which remained fixated on the exit. They shone with a sense of satisfaction in the brief glimpse he caught, and the implication of their color dawned on him as the figure went to the curtained opening, slid through, and vanished.

No, it couldn't have been… A demon? Does this mean the advisor did use magic? Is that creature even the real advisor? He wrestled with his disbelief and shock before jumping to his feet and hurrying to find Elena.

As soon as the guards stepped aside and let him out of the space, the woman stood in his way, leading him to nearly stumble into her. One glance at his expression must have been all she needed to understand something was wrong. Without giving the guards or her husband an explanation for her departure, she seized his wrist and dragged him away.

*

"Are you absolutely sure that's what you saw?" Yukin asked without attempting to hide his skepticism.

Will continued pacing while Elena remained near the entrance after she dismissed her guards. The Nim-Valan pair had listened to his observations of Lupin, including his claim that the advisor wasn't human, at least not entirely, and considered the shocking news for a while in silence.

"I made sure to remember every detail," he replied after avoiding the urge to snap at the young lord.

"Forgive my doubt, but it's unlikely a creature as distinguishable as a demon could pretend to be somebody so well known in the inner circle."

"Is it though?" Elena countered in a hesitant manner. "Think about it, Yukin. No one has been able to confirm how Lupin reappeared, and he controls the Olim estate's new servants with an iron fist. Nobody can meet with him or interrogate those in his household. He earned favor with my husband by sharing exotic

62

presents, hides his body and face as much as possible, and departs from the inner circle to supposedly contribute to the issues on the border."

At the reminder of Asteom, Will stiffened before meeting the other man's eyes. "When my friends and I were attacked in our camp and fled to Nim-Vala, someone used magic against the light mages in order to have them killed. That figure was also cloaked and held power over the soldiers, or what I thought were soldiers. Finn told me he tracked their leader before rescuing us too. Even if I mistook Lupin's eyes, I felt the use of dark magic in that room."

"You understand what he did, right?"

Will shook his head, so Yukin turned toward Elena.

"What we've feared is coming to pass through his manipulation. If the advisor is indeed using spells and greed to sway King Syrus into gifting him authority in Nim-Vala, nothing will hinder Lupin from continuing to strike along the border."

"That explains why the capital is becoming closed off from the rest of the country," Elena added. "My husband isn't the brightest man under normal circumstances, but he would never place this level of trust in anybody without reason. A spell to influence his decisions is the most logical explanation for such reckless behavior."

Although Will wondered what the leader of Nim-Vala was like without Lupin's interference, he kept such irrelevant questions to himself. "What should we do now?" he asked instead.

A minute of silence passed after his question.

"I'm worried about Finn," Elena admitted to spark the discussion once more. "He needs to hear what we learned before Lupin returns to the border."

Yukin bit his bottom lip, displaying his own worry. "You're right. Besides, he's able to cross over as well. Asteom might be more reluctant to become involved in a war when dark magic is involved."

"I wouldn't count on it," Will threw in without hesitation. "Because of their history with the creatures, I'd wager they will be less reluctant to eliminate any threat related to demons." He stopped himself before he dove into the previous conflicts he experienced firsthand.

"What do you suggest then?" Elena practically demanded.

He glanced at Yukin and addressed the young lord. "Send me after Finn. Someone needs to warn Asteom about Lupin before it's too late. This way, he won't stretch himself thin in order to obey both sides. I'll just require a map of Nim-Vala and provisions to last a few days."

"Going alone is too risky."

Will paused to consider this until he realized what opportunity the situation presented. "I won't be alone. I'll return to Muld first for my friends. Their light magic can shield and heal, and the extra sets of eyes will allow us to rotate shifts to sleep and scout. We'll meet up there, leave for the border together, and search for Finn-"

"How much extra time will that take?" Elena interrupted. Given her defensive tone and unamused expression, it became obvious how much she despised keeping Finn in danger.

Thankfully, Yukin favored Will's argument. "He prefers to stay near Muld between his snooping in order to buy supplies. I trust Will won't dally and that his friends will understand the gravity of the issue."

The woman pursed her lips but didn't question the idea again. The young lord appeared satisfied with this and returned his attention to Will.

"Let's return to my estate. Once you're sufficiently prepared, you are free to head south."

Soul Cleansing

The journey to the Mintelian village would have been grueling for anyone inexperienced with traveling for days on end. Fortunately, Coura's guide continued to be respectful by offering breaks at regular intervals so they didn't wear themselves out. It wasn't the worst trek she'd ever been on, though it became far from the best.

The fields outside Kercher stretched south for an easy hike over two days. Borus explained how he needed to search for a trail leading into the mountains, which had been purposefully disguised to appear as natural as possible. As odd as it sounded, this proved to be the case when he abruptly turned east toward the Ghurun Mountain Range. The man noticed her hurrying to catch up, chuckled, and pointed to a fist-sized stone on the ground. It looked as ordinary as every other object they passed, if not more so considering the longer grass covered part of it; however, Coura inspected it closer and found a hole where violet amethyst glimmering within.

"These people are rather clever," Borus shared once they began moving again. "They leave hints like this so people with the right sense can find their way. If nobody pays attention, they don't care. I'm one of two people in my family who understand their meaning with these signs."

Coura's eyebrows rose as he went on to explain various examples he encountered in the past. Besides the gem-filled rocks used to signal a change of direction, they would place claw markings on the boulders near the mountain's base and plant a certain type of grass where the ascending trail began. For the first time during the trip, she became grateful that somebody else led and reconsidered her previous idea regarding flying above instead.

When the pair reached the base, they began following a steep, upward path requiring their full consideration and precise footing.

Coura slipped at one point and stumbled, nearly resulting in her tumbling down the way they came. From then on, she kept her Yeluthian energy at the ready in order to manifest her wings should she fall off completely.

When her guide announced the next landmark, she released a sigh of relief.

"We're almost there," he added with a reassuring smile after.

They camped out for another night alongside a vertical wall, and around noon the following day, they could make out the shadows of huts nearby. Coura's stomach growled as they approached and entered the village to the welcoming scent of smoke from a bonfire.

The layout of the buildings suggested each person or family maintained their own property possessing individual gardens, pens for sheep and goats, or chicken coops. The foundation for each home appeared to consist of stones with logs used as the roofs and straw laid on top. Everything looked similar, except for a worn trail in the grass to act as a road. An eerie sensation loomed over Coura and her guide while they walked through the seemingly abandoned place.

"They are extremely wary of strangers," the man from Kercher said, lowering the volume of his voice as he did so. "Years ago, I learned the children are taught to hide at the first sign of another living creature. Their people don't hunt, and they like their privacy. Don't take it personally."

She longed to ask how she would ever locate their sages if everybody stayed away, but he stopped in front of the farthest home and waited in silence. Like the Yeluthians and Sie-Kie, each doorway possessed a single opening shielded by a piece of cloth instead of metal or wood on hinges.

After a minute, he cleared his throat. "I am Borus of Kercher. My partner seeks a meeting with your people for your soul cleansing ceremony."

They heard the shuffling of feet inside before a man shoved the curtain aside to stand in the opening. He looked strikingly similar to the Mintelian Steiner: Both were bald, had deep brown skin, and showcased a muscular chest and arms. His matching, silver eyes bore into Coura first, then they shifted to her unphased guide.

"You wish to see the village sage?" he inquired. Despite his formidable appearance, his voice sounded husky and grim.

"We do."

The man extended his right arm to point left. "Sage Vidar and his company live on the outskirts."

Borus nodded and began moving in that direction without thanking the Mintelian.

Meanwhile, Coura gazed after him. When she faced forward again, the home's owner dropped the curtain in a gesture similar to slamming a door in her face. She rolled her eyes before catching up to her guide.

"This is going well," he muttered while raising his eyes to assess the sky.

"Are they not normally this friendly?"

He didn't respond or comment on her sarcasm, so she resigned herself to focusing on the task at hand.

Soon, they reached another, duplicate home with several, less-developed shacks beyond. Her guide introduced himself at the entrance again before the cloth opening waved and pulled back slightly to keep the person behind it hidden.

"You wish to speak with Sage Vidar?" asked a feminine voice just softly enough to blend in with the noises of the animals in the surrounding pens.

Borus tilted his head. "I am from Kercher and was assigned to escort this woman for the soul cleansing ceremony."

A pause stretched until the voice responded. "I will fetch my master."

Footsteps faded from inside and returned sooner than Coura would have expected. This time, the curtain fully parted to reveal a middle-aged woman standing a head taller than Borus. Her lighter chestnut-colored hair had been tied into a bun, though several strands found their way loose. She slipped one behind her ear as she stared down at Coura with striking, silver eyes.

"You may follow me."

Coura glanced at her guide instead. "What will you do?"

He threw up the hood of his cloak and turned away from the hut. "Now that my duty is fulfilled, I'll return to Kercher. The people here can send for me when you need to return. The times of these cleansings differ in my experience, so I don't want to be a burden on their people."

She nodded and thanked him for the assistance even as he left her standing alone in front of the Mintelian woman.

"Let's get this over with," she mumbled after and stepped inside the space.

Ever since she entered the village, a numbing sensation dulled her mind slightly yet noticeably enough. She figured the climb would affect her due to the elevation, similar to her flights, and that change was the explanation; however, as the woman led her through an opening at the rear and into the field beyond, Coura felt her thoughts slipping away until she merely reacted to the new world around her through her physical senses.

"What is this place?" she asked aloud since she remained unable to contain the question in her head.

The Mintelian didn't answer.

They passed a herd of sheep and goats fenced in the grassier areas, then they neared the mouth of a cave built into the side of the mountain.

"Master Vidar is through here," the woman explained without stopping.

Once inside, Coura's distrust of this new guide grew. She realized there was no plausible way the woman could have reached the sage to announce her arrival at the previous building in such a brief amount of time, even at a sprint. Despite that fact, she decided to save her questions for later.

The cave exited into another field enclosed by rock walls, reminding Coura of the Valley Beyond between Dala, Clearwater, and Fester. A shudder slid through her body at the idea of being lured away for an ambush. Thankfully, nothing of the sort awaited her.

Sitting cross-legged in the center of the area was an older, Mintelian man. His darker skin appeared to be the lone similarity to the previous citizens, for he sported white hair, which trailed down his back, a round face complimented by a gray moustache, and a slim figure. He wore a robe dyed bright green to match the grass, and he didn't move when the woman brought Coura over.

"M-Master?" the Mintelian started. Her stutter betrayed a nervousness not hinted at earlier. "We have a guest. She wishes to speak with you about the soul cleansing ceremony."

Coura stepped closer to stand at the woman's side. She noticed how the man kept his eyes closed and rested his hands on his knees in a serene manner. When he remained silent, she decided to try speaking on her own behalf.

"Sage Vidar, my name is Coura Galdwin. A man from Kercher escorted me-"

"Did I ask for your name?"

Her mouth hung open at his interruption, though his words were void of any inflection. After a moment, she cleared her throat to answer. "No, but I was-"

"Did I invite you here to disturb my meditation?"

Coura put her hands on her hips, glanced at the woman, who stared at the ground, then returned her gaze forward again. "I wouldn't say I was uninvited considering your servant led me here. The people of Kercher also-"

"So, you enter onto my property without my permission and insist I sacrifice my time for you?"

"I didn't insist anything," she snapped before gesturing to the woman at her side. "I came here to request a soul cleansing. She brought me here after agreeing we could meet."

At that, the Mintelian man opened his eyes to stare at her, revealing their bright, amber color. He spent no more than three seconds looking Coura over before narrowing them at his servant. "Harriette, is what this stranger said true?"

The woman dug her chin into her chest, hunched her shoulders forward, and muttered a confirmation.

"Speak up," he ordered impatiently.

"Yes, Master Vidar. I sensed the energy within her. She must see you."

"Any fool with an ounce of magical capabilities knows that. Approving who should visit me is not your decision to make. Is that understood?" Without waiting for a response, he turned his glare on Coura. "Get out of this place. I don't welcome people like you into my home."

She repressed a retort, let out a frustrated breath through her nose, and shook her head. "I need your help. My soul space was damaged, and-"

"That much is obvious," he interrupted once more. "What I sense from you is repulsive. Only somebody who purposefully accepted demonic power so recklessly harbors such results."

Coura's cheeks grew warm, and her hands clenched into fists as she resigned to fight for his assistance. "I messed up and I understand the consequences, but Asteom is in danger because I can't prevent my center from attracting demonic energy. I didn't come here because I need approval from others. The Yeluthians sent me because they believe you're the only person who can help. If I can't fix this, people I care about are going to get hurt."

She felt satisfied the sage hadn't interrupted this time and waited while his piercing stare seemed to be peering into her mind. Steadily, his expression softened until his eyes closed again, reverting him to his original appearance.

"The process of cleansing one's soul space comes from the individual. My responsibility is to act as a guide throughout the process. There is no spell to erase the past. The experience is not merciful to those without the devotion to their goal of recovery."

He paused, as if waiting for Coura to respond. When she kept silent, he continued.

"Those I worked with in the past had been victims of demonic activity. Those who meddle with such power on purpose are not worthy of redemption, but I pity those forced to endure such pain for the sake of somebody else. So, which are you?"

She swallowed around a lump in her throat before replying quietly. "I don't know."

Despite the urge to elaborate, no words came to mind that would do her situation justice. Her eyes rose to the cloud-covered sky, and she reached into her center for the Yeluthian energy that usually supported her; however, it didn't respond due to the numbing sensation. Coura felt absolutely alone in the isolated space.

The sage produced a long hum that drew her attention. He had opened his eyes, though his expression remained neutral.

"Harriette, leave us."

His servant spun around before hurrying back toward the entrance, leaving Coura to look after the woman.

"Your indecisiveness intrigues me," he went on. "Please, sit."

She obeyed and matched his pose after removing her pack.

"I would like to hear how you damaged your center of power and how it was able to mend itself into what it is now."

Although she got the urge to cross her arms in an attempt to comfort herself, Coura forced herself to keep still. *I haven't reflected on my past since I shared it with my parents. Even then, I didn't reveal the entire experience. If I'm going to get anywhere with the Mintelian sage, I need to be vulnerable and honest about how I came to possess demonic power.*

"This might take the rest of the day," she added with a half-hearted smile to lighten the mood.

The words and gesture were ignored, so she started at the beginning with her first, nightmare-like interaction in the woods outside Neston. She covered Soirée's personality, the demon's manipulation of her through her parents, their venture to live in Yeluthia, and how her life moved to Verona. Then, she shifted to meeting Terran on two occasions, her visit to the Sie-Kie's witch and the woman's words, and finally the attack on the palace that forced her to flee east. When she neared the end, her voice wore away, leaving her coughing and pausing multiple times in order to finish.

Sage Vidar remained patient during the entire recounting. He never interrupted, let her clear her throat until she could continue, and kept his eyes closed, which avoided putting extra pressure on her. By the time she fell silent, insects chirped in the night, and darkness completely enveloped them to the point where Coura couldn't see her hand when she put it in front of her face. She continued to feel utterly exposed and alone since her Yeluthian energy never stirred.

"Come."

A shuffling sound followed the Mintelian's order to signal him rising to his feet. She grabbed her bag, trailed behind him based on the noise he made across the grass, and exited the secluded area. Once they reached the field beyond, oil lamps hanging on the fences provided some light. The sage said nothing as they moved to the most developed building and called for Harriette.

Like a spirit, the woman appeared in front of them.

"Take her to the guest space," he instructed before entering the hut without providing a clear dismissal for Coura.

His servant began walking in the opposite direction, so Coura trudged behind until they reached the designated shack.

"Someone will wake you for the morning meal," Harriette commented, then the woman left.

Coura brushed the cloth along the opening aside and found a room similar to those used by the Sie-Kie. No furniture adorned the space, a woolen, square rug covered a majority of the floor, and a blanket woven from the same material had been laid out. Since she had nothing else to do, she stripped off her cloak, pack, and weapon before curling up onto the makeshift bed.

*

A shuffling of feet dragged Coura out of her slumber, and as soon as she realized she didn't recognize her surroundings, she grabbed for her weapon. A second later, she slid the sheath off while adjusting into a half-crouch, then the tip of her sword pointed at the intruder, who proved to be a young woman. Either the girl had experienced this type of reaction in the past or she was made of tougher stuff, for she stared at Coura, frowned, and set the bundle in her arms on the ground.

"New clothes," the apparent servant explained. "The morning meal is served at sunrise."

With that, Coura found herself alone once more. She took a moment to compose herself from the experience before changing into the loose, gray-colored shirt and black pants and departing from the hut.

Two dozen or so men and women of varying ages moved toward a shack reminiscent of the stables in Verona's training grounds. Its extended length provided extra space for a table able to seat everybody comfortably, as well as a kitchen at the rear where a handful of children brought out pots and pans containing various breakfast items.

Coura sat by herself, accepted a bowl of bland-looking oatmeal from one of the young servants handing them out, and began eating. There were several other options, such as fried eggs, toasted bread slices, butter and jam for the former, and what appeared to be pieces of fruit similar to a pear, but she decided to stick with a light diet for her first day. After, she fell into the established system of returning the empty dishes to a basin filled with clear water. Nobody paid her any attention as she stood around wondering what she should be doing until people started departing from the building.

Should I find the sage, or maybe Harriette?

A tiny psst from behind had Coura glancing around. She caught the head of a child peeking out from the doorway acting as an entrance to the meal area.

"Over there," they whispered and shifted their eyes from her to the mountain.

Coura believed that path to be the one she followed to see Sage Vidar the previous afternoon, and her curiosity grew. When she faced the opening again to thank the child, they were gone.

*

Every adult from breakfast sat just as she found their sage the previous afternoon in the same, enclosed area surrounded by rock walls. She planned to join their meditation session until an older woman approached. The hunched figure possessed colorless hair, which had been pinned to the top of her head, and a pointed nose. She gestured for Coura to follow her to the opposite side with a thin, wrinkled hand.

"We start here," she croaked when they were completely separated from the group, showcasing a voice steadily worn down over the years. "Or else you will distract the others."

In a single, fluid motion, the older woman dropped into the cross-legged position with her palms resting on her knees. Coura did the same, though much less gracefully, and released a breath as she mirrored the hand placement.

"Today we learn how well you can focus on your center," the Mintelian shared before closing her eyes and visibly relaxing her entire body.

Meditating had never been an exercise Coura was successful with for a number of reasons. There were surface distractions, such as noise and physical discomfort, stray thoughts, and a general sense of boredom after a while. The first of these began mere minutes after she closed her eyes when a blade of grass brushed against her leg, tickling the spot. She instinctively scratched the itch until something struck the back of her hand. With a startled gasp, her eyes flung open, and she coddled her skin where a pink line began to swell slightly. Across from her, the old woman held a branch thin and long enough to be mistaken for a miniature whip.

"What was that for?" she demanded out of surprise rather than anger.

"Your mind should be disconnected from your body enough so minor distractions do not remove you from the experience," came the impatient reply. "As soon as you break that tie, your focus and progress are lost."

Coura stared down at her hand and avoided the urge to bite her lip when she understood how bothersome of a morning it would be.

*

She found no inner connection that first day, instead earning herself three more strikes to her right hand, one on her left, two on her right bicep, and a couple on each knee. By the time her overseer dismissed her for lunch, she felt disheartened.

Fortunately, the afternoon brought a familiar session. Harriette came to fetch her as soon as she dropped off her empty plate and utensils, and the two hiked farther in the opposite direction of the village. They came upon Sage Vidar, four men, and three women standing in front of a dusty, dirt patch in the shape of a wide circle.

"We are going to assess your fighting prowess," the sage explained, then he gestured to the woman on his right.

As the Mintelian stepped forward, Coura noticed two, wooden blades in her hands.

"Consider this a sparring match," he went on when she accepted the extra weapon and took a few seconds to gauge its weight with mock swings. "Being a soldier, you're obviously comfortable with combat. The goal is to get your opponent to surrender, nothing more."

She dipped her chin to acknowledge the rules before taking a regular stance. The woman who handed her the practice blade did the same, and for a brief moment, Coura wondered if these people secretly trained as fighters equal to those she faced across Asteom; however, the idea soon proved to be farfetched.

The first opponent lost her sword after blocking Coura's second swing and muttered her surrender afterward with a mixture of fear and shame. Sage Vidar motioned for another woman to take her place. This one appeared to be a decade or so older and lasted a minute longer before Coura made her stumble onto her backside with a feigned stab at her exposed stomach. After helping the woman to her feet, the third was sent forward. That opponent showcased agility equal to the troops from Verona and fought until she dripped with sweat.

Meanwhile, Coura felt properly warmed up. She noticed the Mintelian retreating after the fourth meeting of their wooden blades and pursued to continue pushing. This fierce manner seemed to be more than the woman could handle. Her weapon bounced around between Coura's until she lost her grip, causing it to be sent flying. It landing on the ground with a thump just after the tip of Coura's sword pointed at her throat.

"That's enough," called their lead spectator.

Coura lowered her weapon and found her opponent smiling weakly, as if relieved.

"We're done for today," the sage added. "You are all dismissed."

Harriette appeared before Coura could follow the others, who left their leader where he stood, and led her to a nearby stream. The pair strolled beside it in silence until they came upon a pool broad enough for a dozen people to swim comfortably. A gentle waterfall poured clear water down at the farther end, and a sandy bank lined the edge of their side. After taking in the scenery, Coura noticed piles of folded towels, extra clothing, and bars of soap laid out in an organized fashion behind on the grass.

"As you might have already figured out, mornings are for meditation," her guide started with a wave at the supplies. "After lunch, you will report to Sage Vidar. When he dismisses you, you're welcome to come here to bathe and change clothes, or do whatever you wish before the evening meal. Your assignment is to help clean up and wash the dishes then. Those working with you will offer instructions. Also, laundry is done along the stream, just in case you need to know."

Coura expected to be assisting with such responsibilities after considering how everybody else pulled their weight through similar chores. She nodded without needing additional clarification, so Harriette left her alone. After utilizing the water for a soak, she ate before finding the leader of that area to introduce herself. The Mintelian woman gave simple directions and supervised until the chores were complete. By the time she returned to her hut, Coura became mentally exhausted enough to sleep.

*

The next day, the same routine awaited her, though no one spared her any extra attention. Her meditation session seemed even less productive due to a stiffness from sleeping improperly on the floor, causing her to fidget and shift around. This resulted in the usual strikes and minor welts, which lasted past lunch.

Sage Vidar and the people from the previous afternoon waited for Coura to arrive, then he threw her into more matches. This time, she faced three of the four men who were all skilled enough to extend the fights for more than a few minutes. It wasn't tough to figure out their weaknesses and play on those until she either knocked them over or disarmed them before placing the tip of her blade at their throats. Once they finished, the sage dismissed her so she could bathe and continue her uneventful evening.

On the third day of her stay with the Mintelian people, Coura woke with an inexplicably bad feeling, like a weight bore down on her chest. She ate lighter than normal and trailed behind the others to the usual area in the grassy, enclosed field where the old woman stood beside Sage Vidar. Both wore sour expressions and stopped talking as she approached. When neither addressed her, she raised an eyebrow.

"Sit," the woman instructed in response.

She, along with the sage, descended into their meditation position, leaving Coura to do the same. During that part of the morning, it seemed as if they were going to proceed with their regular session. The Mintelian still punished her for getting distracted, and she couldn't assess her center of power without acknowledging the pit lurking in her chest.

"Stop."

Coura opened her eyes to find Sage Vidar frowning at her. Then, he turned to glance at the older woman with the same expression.

"Leave us," he ordered.

From what Coura could tell, the Mintelian supervising her until that point couldn't escape from the sage's gaze fast enough. She understood why when he pinched the bridge of his nose and shook his head slightly before fixing her with a disappointing stare.

"Do you always have trouble concentrating?"

"I can never focus," was all she could think to reply with a shrug to cover her nerves.

The sage inhaled through his nose, released a drawn-out sigh, and folded his hands together. "What is it you came here to accomplish?"

"I need you to help me fix my soul space."

"If that is what you desire, you may return to the people below because that request is impossible."

Coura narrowed her eyes. "What do you mean? You took me in knowing that's my goal."

"And you will continue to fail if you push for what cannot be accomplished."

Although she longed to lash out at the Mintelian, something about his choice of words suggested he was hinting at more. "If that's the case, why would you waste your time and supplies on me if it's impossible to fix my center?"

"You assume healing your internal source of power will return your world to the way it was, correct?"

"I don't know," she answered honestly. "I told you about my past. My life has been influenced by demonic power ever since I can remember, so I don't expect that will change."

The older man's eyes softened, releasing a few of the wrinkles around them. "Your soul has already healed. Once the demon's hold was severed, your center shaped into a new form in order to accommodate the energy used by the creatures, or what you were forced to take into yourself. A mage's power flows constantly; nothing is ever stagnant. The same is true for yours."

"You're saying there's no way for me to prevent myself from luring demons," she muttered. The weight on her chest doubled, and the previously dull energy in her soul space hummed in an attempt to comfort her.

Sage Vidar rose to loom over her while losing any sense of sympathy from his expression. "I mentioned your initial goal is impossible to accomplish, but I believe you were misguided. You need to learn to manage the pools of energy within in order to use the power successfully and prevent yourself from becoming more of a target. This begins with searching inward through meditation. See if you can progress by yourself."

Coura remained where she sat as he strolled toward the cave's entrance.

I think I actually belong here, was the first thought that came to mind. *He made it clear he would have dismissed me if I wasn't worth his time, or worth helping. I suppose all I can do is follow his instructions and try to channel my soul space.*

She spent the rest of the morning unsuccessfully attempting to relax her body before giving up in favor of eating lunch. The group of sparring partners and Sage Vidar were together again when she arrived at the dirt area.

Despite their numbers, she faced the final man and nobody else that afternoon. Once he charged at her, she understood why. Unlike the others she faced, he grew bulky through years of training which sculpted his body into that of a soldier. While he had muscle, she possessed speed and plenty of experience to dodge and tap at him until an opportune moment arose to clinch the victory. They both stood panting and sweating after the effort until the sage ordered them to go again.

After two more matches, the older Mintelian waved her away for the day.

*

"Prepare yourself."

Coura plopped down into the grass opposite Sage Vidar and sat cross-legged with both hands pressed to her knees. They were alone in the meditation area that morning, which left an eerie presence lingering around the space and gave her the impression that morning wouldn't be a repeat of the previous.

"I understand what is holding you back," the Mintelian began. "I'm curious to see if you can overcome this hinderance first, so proceed."

She released a breath, closed her eyes, and tried clearing her mind. Even though no stray thoughts disrupted her mentality, she began to notice the physical distractions and told herself to ignore them one at a time; however, as soon as she brushed the first aside, another took its place, and so on. Her energy also began pestering her, like a swarm of bees jittering within her center, but she remained firm in her efforts to eliminate the distractions before moving forward.

A wave of disappointment washed over her when the sage ordered her to stop, though his voice and expression sounded neutral.

"Did you figure it out?" he asked after.

Coura shook her head, letting the frustration creep forward. "I'm struggling to prevent myself from becoming distracted. There's always something…"

"You're overanalyzing yourself," he interjected. "Stop focusing on what is on the surface and turn your attention inward, to your center. Itches and aches never go away. Besides, you should never shut your mind or body off, as though you are asleep. If that's what you aim for, then whoever taught you about meditation was a fool. Now, do as I said and look inward."

Coura closed her eyes again. After spending a few minutes relaxing her muscles, she found it easier to access her soul space when she wasn't trying to do so. Her mind wandered until the Yeluthian energy stemmed forward to fill her body with its customary warmth, lulling her into a mental state of safety and serenity. She allowed it to pull her deeper into the trance until a second presence crept forward, one slumbering beneath that warmth.

The primitive nature of the additional tendril startled her, and she recoiled, coming to her senses in the process. Her eyes opened after. At first, she stared at the ground before tilting her head back to gaze at the overcast above. Although she expected the sage's scolding, she couldn't repress a wince.

"Why did you retreat?" the sage demanded without hiding his irritation. "You reached the point where you could recognize what lies inside your center!"

"How do you know?" she muttered while her cheeks grew warm, reflecting the shame she felt.

"My expertise deals with the flow of energy and consciousness, a practice I spent my life honing and you easily insult."

The urge to rise and abandon the Mintelian proved tempting, but Coura avoided doing so. Instead, she took several, deep breaths in order to calm down and shake off the jarring reaction.

When it became clear she wouldn't abandon him or snap a retort a second time, the sage continued. "Once you find a method for reaching your center, all there is left to do is practice. This lessens the time it takes, sharpens your focus, and eases your mind into a comfortable rhythm. The real results are not what I can show you, for they are found within. I am but a guide to assist with the basics."

Coura propped her elbows on her knees before resting her head in her hands. "I can only do *that* over and over again?"

The Mintelian studied her for a moment, then he countered her question with another. "What brought you out of the meditation?"

The uneasy sensation beneath the Yeluthian energy began to rise, though subtly enough to avoid distracting her entirely. "I started to feel overwhelmed."

"By what?"

"The power resting in my center."

"You mentioned your angelic heritage and your ability to wield light magic. Is that what started to suffocate you?"

Coura didn't answer.

"The demon who used you as a host also reshaped your soul in order to access the natural energy their kind manipulate. Is that what the negative feeling stemmed from?"

"I don't know," she mumbled while sitting straighter to cross her arms and glance away.

Unfortunately, the Mintelian man wasn't the type of teacher to back down. "Since you don't seem to understand, and aren't willing to attempt doing so, let me explain what's happening. You've been busy seeking answers from others to a problem only you can solve. You want to listen to them and hear their advice instead of acknowledging what is actually keeping you from assessing your center of power. You're scared of what you will find when you explore deeper within yourself. So, tell me what is so frightening that you refuse to return."

Coura dug her fingernails into her arms as she prepared to face what she had been dismissing for years. "I'm not a normal mage. Every aspect of my life has been planned by someone else. A demon stalked my parents before I was born, then she found and used me because I'm part Yeluthian. I traveled across Asteom to fight all sorts of enemies because of her, and now more are attracted to the energy I unwillingly carry. People viewed me as a weapon when I wielded dark magic, a monster when they learned it was actually demonic energy, and something blasphemous because of my wings. I'm not fully human or Yeluthian; the power I possess doesn't change the fact that I don't belong anywhere."

"No matter the case, what energy you possess does not define who you are as a person," Sage Vidar threw in before she could continue, as if he planned for her to go off on an emotional tangent. "Magic is a tool crafted by the manipulation of internal energy. Everybody's levels and abilities differ. Your lineage, friendships, and positions should be irrelevant when you look inside yourself and interact with what's there. The life you've led up until this point may have been influenced by others, but ultimately the choices you made shaped the person you are now. Unless you conquer the fears ahead of you, your mentality and abilities will continue to suffer."

Coura could only nod slowly in response. Her gesture seemed to be enough for the man, prompting him to rise to his feet.

"Spend the rest of the morning doing exactly what I instructed, though without abandoning the meditation. After the noon meal, return here to do the same through the afternoon. I will send someone for you tomorrow morning."

The Mintelian took his leave of her then, carrying all the tension hanging in the air away with him. Once that disappeared, the enclosed space grew rather peaceful, especially when rays of sunlight pierced through the cloudy sky above. Coura stretched her legs while releasing a hiss as the stiffness eased, then she lied flat on her back and folded her hands on her stomach. For a while, she remained in that position to consider Sage Vidar's words.

He's right, she admitted sometime later. *Whenever I'm reminded of my connection to demonic energy and remember how severely my center was damaged, I relive the hate and frustration I felt, as well as what people directed at me. I figured my life would be different and I wouldn't need to worry about demons again.*

The resulting thought had her cracking a sardonic smile. *That was my first mistake. Byron and Emilea often mention how they have had to deal with demonic creatures and possessions over the years. I was being ignorant in assuming it would all end with Soirée...*

After pausing to reflect on what that meant, that there would always be demons and their creatures in Asteom, Coura sat up and returned to the meditating position.

"Fine," she grumbled, as if responding to the sage. "My soul space is what it is, so I'll remain a target for the rest of my life. Maybe there's another way I can protect myself and those around me. I'll never find out if I can't understand the power inside my center. At least, I think that's what he's getting at."

She took several, deep breaths before beginning the exercise again. After the third attempt, she avoided losing focus and could ignore the physical distractions; however, upon brushing against the second presence once more, her instincts kicked in, causing her to retreat. This went on until her stomach growled too loudly for her to dismiss, and she left for a lunch break.

Food following such a motionless morning left Coura desiring a nap, which added another interference she needed to push away during the early afternoon. As the sun slipped behind the mountainside, the area cooled considerably before she made any progress. In response, her teeth started chattering. She swore to herself after and rubbed her arms and legs in an attempt to warm up.

I'm not getting anywhere, she thought while recognizing how disheartened the notion left her. *I can't stop myself from recoiling when I encounter that presence. It feels deadly, especially with the Yeluthian power there.*

A second later, a sudden realization struck her.

Light and dark energies normally reject each other. The irritation I experienced with the Yeluthians when I discovered Soirée, and vice versa, were all too real. If that's the case, why isn't my light energy reacting in a hostile manner toward the underlying presence? Was I mistaken when I assumed it to be demonic in nature?

With a clear goal in mind, Coura eased into a relaxed state and reached within her center again. Her eagerness cost her precious minutes, but ultimately her Yeluthian energy welcomed her like a close friend. The power's warmth enveloped her when she let it, as though she would wield it into a spell; however, it led her deeper to where the frightful presence waited.

Coura's resolve wavered as the second source stretched toward her, yet she managed to remain focused. The sensation reminded her of a knife being slid along her skin, and she soon recognized it from her time manipulating dark energy.

Is this what happened when I was connected to Soirée? she wondered as both tendrils of power guided her deeper into her soul space.

Like a memory from a dream, the vision took shape to reflect her center, though she could never experience the state after her recovery from fighting in the demons' realm. What was once an all-white, endless void under her control possessed splotches of grays varying in shade. A visible haze also floated above, pulsing with life and flowing on a steady course.

The energies lingering with Coura separated from her then to soar toward different locations. Her Yeluthian power circled around the darker waves in more of a dance than a means of avoiding the opposite presence. Meanwhile, the other power merged with the shadowy fog. It continued to hang higher in the air while steadily floating toward the inky, unmoving patches.

For a while, she became lost in her observations.

Only the demonic energy seems interested in the darker holes, so that must be where it exits, like the Sie-Kie witch explained. On the other hand, my Yeluthian power isn't bound by a set path. It remains within me as a part of myself, but it adapted to the second presence. There is no conflict.

With nothing more than her will, Coura beckoned the light energy to her. A tendril branched off again to surround her while radiating its characteristic enthusiasm, filling her with a sense of comfort.

This is supportive, but that feeling can be dangerous. Should I choose to cave into my fears, I know I will never lose this power since it is engrained into my being. It would make giving up tempting.

She released that part before repeating the mental gesture for the opposite presence. Although the menacing sensation returned, the tendril of demonic power waited for her to direct it. She allowed its chill to penetrate the sense of safety her Yeluthian energy radiated; however, instead of spurring fear, it filled her with a sense of confidence.

It really is like a knife, she noted while savoring the stability from such emotion. *Dark energy is intimidating because of the potential for disaster. When it is wielded by someone who can control and understand the threat it poses, it becomes a useful tool. Without that authority or proper training, it remains an unfamiliar weapon.*

Upon releasing the energy, it returned to the matching flow while avoiding the Yeluthian power. Coura continued to watch what took place in her soul space with a sense of awe.

The shalma *told me demonic energy flows into and out of my center like a cracked pot meant to contain water, and it will continue doing so because Soirée manipulated this place in order for me to wield her power. What I inherited as a Yeluthian has always been present, but she repressed it, meaning I couldn't learn how to use light magic unless she permitted it. That must be why I could manifest my wings after I realized she was inside me.*

When Coura figured she had enough to contemplate for the time being, she withdrew from her center. Her eyes opened first before the aching of her limbs followed when she moved to stretch her legs and back. A groan escaped her then, and she looked up in an attempt to gauge the hour. Unfortunately, the overcast sky prevented her from knowing just how late the evening grew.

Because of the lack of lighting, she was forced to stumble toward the cave's entrance, through the tunnel, and into the field beyond before she finally reached the meal area. A pair of women washed dishes in the back to signal the end of the service period; however, they noticed her hovering at the entrance, waved her inside, and soon set a bowl of porridge in front of her without a word.

Still, Coura thanked them for the food. It proved to be enough to repress her hunger, and she offered to join them in finishing the chores before being rejected. With nothing else to do, she returned to her hut, dropped onto the floor, and fell into a dreamless slumber.

The Hunt for Answers

King Arval's visit continued to linger in Grace's mind even days later. His support of her actions in Asteom, as well as his mention of her parents' unreasonable behavior, lightened her spirits; however, she truly wished to aid him in his search for the ancestral weapons.

How can I prove I belong here as Yeluthia's ambassador if I do not attempt to assist my king or Aaron? she wondered that morning as she ate. *Perhaps I should reach out and inquire about what assistance I can offer, especially since the members of the nobility I often spend time with are either attending to personal matters or…*

"My Lady, is there a problem with your meal?"

Grace lifted her eyes from her plate after realizing she began pushing her food around instead of eating. "N-No," she stammered before clearing her throat. "Sorry."

Dianne, the guard who escorted her to breakfast and lunch every day, still appeared concerned from her seat across the table but didn't comment. She learned the woman was three times her age yet looked much younger, mainly because of a well-honed figure and high cheekbones. After she introduced herself on the second day, she held a casual air about her to ease some of the tension Grace felt at being monitored.

"The flowers in the queen's garden are in season," Dianne added after a moment of silence. "You haven't left the palace since I've been on duty. I don't want to give the impression you aren't free to do so."

The soldier's consideration spurred a smile. "I appreciate that. Perhaps we can visit this afternoon."

She left the conversation there since she planned on returning to her room. Still, her guard continued to press the subject.

"My sister always says fresh air helps a meal to digest. It also prevents a person from being tempted by a nap."

"She's right, but I would prefer to go later."

Dianne tilted her head. "Are you sure nothing is bothering you? Forgive my bluntness, but you seem distracted, my lady."

The part of Grace raised in a household under her entitled parents' authority longed to scold the soldier for acting so informally in order to cover her internal conflict. Fortunately, that piece of her personality dwindled over the years, and ever since she made friends in Asteom, she learned to trust others despite the risks.

"If you must know, I am recalling King Arval's unexpected visit." The memory had her involuntarily glancing down at her half-eaten plate again. "He requested my assistance with an issue, but I refused because it meant using my magic in an unfair manner. I wish to help, yet I am not sure how I can."

"You'd prefer to avoid using magic," Dianne muttered and rubbed her chin. "Did you discuss this with your king?"

Grace shook her head, yet the question gave her an idea. "He might not consider another method, but for the time being, perhaps I can ask Aaron."

Her guard raised an eyebrow. "Aaron?"

"*King* Aaron," she clarified while her cheeks grew warm. Sometimes she forgot to use his title due to his dislike of such formalities among friends. Dianne's startled reaction caused her to giggle in amusement after.

"I suppose you two converse often enough," the woman replied with a shrug. "In any case, would you like to head to the meeting chamber now?"

Grace considered what she intended to ask before agreeing once she recognized how casual the discussion with her friend would become, as it always did. The pair returned their dishes, wandered through the hallways, and eventually wound up at the council's meeting chamber within the following hour. After a brief wait, the door opened and several individuals exited.

"King Aaron has a recess, then the council reconvenes," one of the men guarding the entrance explained when Dianne inquired about the king's availability. "Please, try not to spend too much time inside, or I fear he will never see the day's light or eat a decent meal."

His blunt remark caught Grace by surprise. *I never realize how work often distracts from what is necessary to stay healthy. For his sake, I will not become an additional burden.*

Despite the warning, nothing about her friend appeared weak or bothered, though he definitely was not expecting her visit. He rose to stand, offered a greeting, and began to mention if something troubled her until she raised a hand in a motion for him to stop speaking.

"I came with positive intentions," she prefaced. Then, she summarized her conversation with her uncle, including his half-hearted request, and her decision to decline.

Once she finished, Aaron crossed his arms and shot her an appreciative look. "Your consideration for others never ceases to amaze me, Grace."

His compliment caused her to blush, though she chose to dismiss it in favor of using as little time as possible. "Thank you, but I still wish to help however I can, which is why I am here. Has your council heard more about the ancestral weapons?"

"I'm afraid not. No one's having any luck except for rumors. Given the passing years since they were last needed, it's not surprising."

"I see."

"If I'm being honest, I believe King Arval is focused on that task," he added as his lips curved into a frown. "The conversation involved myself, my council, and him, yet he seems to be managing this assignment. I have yet to receive an update from your people."

"Does it worry you?" she decided to ask. Her uncle would most likely prefer to oversee matters related to Yeluthia, but she could not understand why he felt the need to carry that burden alone.

Aaron released a sigh in response. "He earned my trust and respect, so I know he'll inform me of what he finds. This entire subject just makes me feel lost in a sea without answers."

Silence stretched between the two until Dianne cleared her throat from where she lingered by the door, signaling the end of their meeting. Grace thanked her friend, promised to do what she could to assist, and departed for her quarters; however, as they reached the staircase, she hesitated to ascend.

"My Lady?" her guard commented after a few seconds.

There must be something I can do without using my goddess gift, Grace told herself while staring up at the next level. *Without magic, I am just as ordinary as some of the citizens in Yeluthia and most in Asteom. What would they do if they were in my shoes?*

Dianne continued to attempt guiding them on, but she remained in place before realizing her best option in that position was probably the most obvious. She spun around and let her feet bring her to the grand hall before her guard slid in front of her, halting her steps.

"Where do you think you're going?"

"You said I have yet to leave the palace," Grace teased as she raised her chin. "Maybe somebody in Verona will has information about the ancestral weapons."

She hadn't revealed the entire story to Dianne, though she expected the soldier paid attention to her conversation with Aaron, and she couldn't see a reason to dance around the goal.

"Who do you expect to ask about such legendary items?" her guard countered. "I've lived and worked in the capital city my entire life, and I haven't heard of them. That's not to say they don't exist. I'm just concerned about you roaming aimlessly with no clues to go off of."

"My guess is no one actually knows what they are, or at least what they are capable of. Their golden color is the most obvious characteristic. I will begin by describing their physical appearance, then depending on where that leads me, I should feel its power through touch."

Dianne scratched her head, shifted on her feet, and glanced around the space for a minute. Still, Grace avoided pushing the woman who would act as her escort.

"I suppose my job doesn't end until later in the afternoon," the soldier muttered. "Before then, we can cover the central or eastern main road. I know several blacksmiths who tend to my comrades' weapons and armor, so they would be excellent resources."

Grace's heart leapt when her guard shot her a wink. "Thank you, Dianne!"

"Don't thank me yet," the woman replied and began leading the way toward the palace's entrance. "This is only the beginning of your treasure hunt, my lady."

*

For as optimistic as she felt when Dianne offered to aid her search, Grace soon learned a unique obstacle stood in her way. It started when the pair departed from the palace together to begin questioning what shopkeepers and craftsmen the guard had connections to. To Grace's relief, the woman did most of the talking; however, one mention of the Yeluthian ambassador threw the conversations off course. Each individual or group they faced seemed to note Grace's lady-like outfit and demeanor, but her title had them groveling for attention.

This happened until the entire eastern main road became aware of her presence in their district, and her questions were soon ignored in favor of offerings, compliments, or inquiries about affairs in the palace, most notably the massacre. Every time somebody brought up the private dining hall, her body grew tense, and the faces of the victims flashed through her mind.

Thankfully, Dianne recognized both the rising stress Grace experienced and that their purpose for visiting the area was lost. The soldier hurried to usher her back to her room, joined her inside, and promptly locked the door. Then, the two discussed the situation before abandoning the attempt.

The following morning, Grace's determination returned, though mainly because an idea came to mind.

Having a guard escort me draws attention, especially when I dress formally, and once people recognize me, they raise their defenses in order to appear good-natured, she noted while filing through her outfits for the least conspicuous clothes. *I would imagine the ancestral weapons are not being kept out in the open, which means I need to dig deeper.*

After another few minutes, she settled on a plain, gray dress she hoped would blend in with the subtle colors of the regular citizens. Next, she tied her hair into a bun at the top of her head without using a brush, allowing slight bumps to form and single strands to hang around her head. She expected the carefree nature of her updo and lack of makeup to help her seem less distinguished.

A knock on the door reminded her of the final, loose thread.

Dianne may be able to protect me should trouble arise, but she will ultimately appear as my guard and take the lead on the investigation. Besides, she is more formidable-looking, which could cause the civilians to avoid sharing details.

Despite her heartbeat picking up its pace, Grace composed herself, answered the door, and gave the soldier a polite smile. "Yes, Dianne?"

The woman standing at attention didn't seem to care about Grace's casual appearance. "Lady Ambassador, are you ready to head to breakfast?"

Although her stomach protested her decision to depart that morning without a meal, Grace shook her head. "I am not hungry at the moment."

Dianne raised an eyebrow but didn't comment, allowing Grace to continue.

"I would like to request a favor, if you do not mind returning to Verona."

"Does this have to do with yesterday's adventure?" the guard asked while wearing an amused smirk.

Grace nodded. "I am afraid my presence was the reason we did not find success in locating the weapons, so perhaps you may have more luck alone."

Her guard paused to consider this before shaking her head. "We might be better off leaving this to the king's council. They're unaware of our attempt, and they probably have their own plans in motion."

"I believe so as well, but I also understand their situation and what is taking place around Asteom."

She prayed the genuine sympathy she projected for Aaron, her uncle, and the rest of the council got through to Dianne. *They are already under enough stress; I hated adding more as a victim of the attack, and I wonder if my goddess gift may help identify the ancestral weapons as opposed to relying on just the humans' observations.*

That thought prompted her decision to venture into the capital city without her guard, though she needed to sneak out unnoticed.

"I suppose it couldn't hurt to ask around the eastern main road again," the woman finally said in a reluctant manner. "The people I'm familiar with acted so awestruck around you I couldn't get a word in. That must be what you meant."

Grace dipped her chin and lowered her eyes. "I often forget how many humans have yet to meet me, or even meet a Yeluthian."

"Don't worry. I'll see what else I can dig up around the city. In the meantime, I'll send my comrade to assume my position as your guard."

"That would be wonderful," Grace added while trying not to sound too cheerful about the change. "I may just remain in my room until the afternoon."

Dianne's resulting smile and salute almost caused her to abandon her ruse due to the woman's upmost loyalty to protecting her while assisting with her goal. Still, she wished the soldier well, closed the door, and released the sigh she had been repressing, which eased part of the pressure on her chest.

*

Throughout the afternoon, Grace reveled in the freedom of exploring Verona while unattended. She only ever wandered through the city during public events, and with at least one guard escorting her everywhere. This time, nobody paid her any attention as she roamed along the main road while avoiding the route Dianne would be on.

Once she found herself alone in her room, she selected the most worn cloak she owned before slipping out into the hallway. The soldiers posted at the front of the palace would recognize her, so she used another path on the southern side, which she remembered from when she tagged along with Commander Detrix, Emilea, and their chosen group to stop the former high priest. Although she did not recall each direction, she eventually followed several servants carrying laundry to hang, leading her through the exit where they hung clothes and sheets. She let her instincts guide her around the city after.

Asking about a golden weapon directly might raise suspicion. I must not be too forward with the subject then.

The words echoed in her mind as she visited each blacksmith, armor shop, and even the jewelry merchants with the intent to scope out her targets first. Nobody gave her more than a curt greeting or a wave, which she accepted as a sign that her disguise hid her position, and when the opportunity arose, she inquired about any unique or colored blades. Her question caused every person she interacted with to raise an eyebrow, scoff at her, or chuckle in response. At first, the dismissals stung, and she grew offended; however, she soon realized she could attribute the peculiar phrasing of the request to her ignorance.

At the next metalworker's booth, Grace approached the stand, removed her hood, and gazed over the weapons on display as though she were a noblewoman searching for a new toy.

"These look so dull," she commented after receiving the expected, half-hearted greeting. "My apologies, but I am looking for a gift to give my nephew. He enjoys collecting the most unique weapons and armor. Do you have any other items, perhaps one in another color or shape?"

She hated how she talked down to the blacksmith and worried he would turn her away for acting so entitled, but she became familiar with the nobility's way of behaving and knew she would have to commit. To her relief, the burly figure just crossed his arms, looked her over, and shook his head. She thought to press the request until another customer appeared, so she thanked him before departing.

The morning soon stretching into an uneventful afternoon filled with similar encounters. Nobody took her questions seriously, at least not entirely, though the merchants humored her by offering to check their entire stock until she inspected each piece and showed her appreciation for their time by purchasing a trinket.

Maybe the ancestral weapons are not even hiding in Verona, she mused on her stroll back to the palace. *In that case, I should confess my actions to Aaron so he is aware.*

The guards at the front gate let her pass without issue once she removed the hood masking her face and hair, and several individuals offered polite greetings as she made her way to her quarters. Part of her felt too drained from the day to climb the flights of stairs instead of going straight to the dining hall. Still, one reminder of her decision to abandon the guard posted at her door roused the sense of guilt she suppressed until that moment.

I pray they did not bother to knock or investigate the silence coming from my room.

Her hopes were soon dashed when she reached the hallway where her quarters lied. Instead of the regular soldier who monitored the space during the evening, Dianne stood glaring at her. The sight almost caused Grace to spin on her heel and flee in the opposite direction.

"Lady ambassador," the woman addressed her in a tone suggesting she was about to be scolded. "Would you care to inform me of your whereabouts this afternoon?"

Grace's shoulders involuntary slumped forward as she slowly trudged toward her room, like a child being summoned for a tongue lashing by their parent. Once the two stood face to face, she considered an excuse before resigning to admit the truth; however, Dianne opened the door and motioned for them to discuss the situation in private.

"How could you run off like that?" the soldier demanded when they were alone. "Because I offered to investigate for you, my replacement went straight to Assistant General Ceris when he couldn't find you, and our entire company searched the palace grounds! If I didn't return when I did to cover your actions, we both would be licking our wounds."

"What did you tell them?" Grace asked at a lower volume.

Dianne paused to inhale and exhale twice before answering. "Once I heard the guard's story about how he checked on you after you didn't answer his knocking, I figured you left right after I did in order to avoid being spotted. I told the assistant general I planned to go into Verona for the day, that I mentioned this to you and offered to escort you, and how you declined. Then, I shared how you met me at the gate after you changed your mind."

"Did he believe you?"

"Of course. My comrades and I have faith in each other, though they will distrust me more after this considering the final lie was that I forgot about those who would be rotating shifts outside your room. I'll be lucky if they don't replace me permanently."

When the woman crossed her arms and glanced away, the implications of Grace's carelessness dropped onto her shoulders.

"Dianne, I am truly sorry for putting you in that situation," she apologized while lowering her eyes to stare at the floor. "After all you have done to help me, I let you take the blame for my impulsive actions."

Another minute of silence passed before the soldier spoke. "At least tell me where you went."

Grace welcomed the change of topic, yet she wished she could offer better news. She explained her intent to visit the shops along the main road alone in order to avoid drawing the unwanted attention they experience during the day prior and ended with her findings. By that point, her guard appeared to be more invested in her retelling than upset by her disappearance.

"So none of the blacksmiths would bite," the soldier concluded and shook her head. "The information, or lack thereof, might actually be useful."

"Really?" Grace perked up from where she sat on the edge of her bed.

"Not enough to provide answers, but enough to eliminate options."

"You mean to say we can dismiss searching along the main road?"

Her guard nodded before flashing a grin. "Now, it's my turn to recount my day."

"Did you-"

"Let's just say the hint I received from a friend of a friend is our best lead. In short, there's an underground market that takes place on the evening of a new moon when no natural light can reveal their shady deals."

"Underground market?" Grace repeated in disbelief. "You mean, they hide in a tunnel system under the city?"

Her question caught Dianne off guard. Then, the woman startled her by bursting out into laughter.

"Please, forgive me!" the soldier exclaimed while wrapping one arm around her stomach and using the other hand to wipe her eyes. "I wasn't expecting… That's not what I mean."

Grace tilted her head without comprehending her guard's behavior.

Finally, Dianne cleared her throat in an attempt to resume her composure, though a slight smile remained on her lips. "An underground market isn't literally under the ground like that. Think of it as a place where merchants, weapons dealers, and more come together to sell higher end or sometimes illegal items without the fear of being caught."

The idea of such a thing left Grace speechless. *Why would anyone wish to participate in a risky, tasteless endeavor? Surely the generals and Aaron are aware of this!*

Her expression must have revealed her displeasure since her guard attempted to reassure her.

"I believe the generals already monitor the event, but everybody must be discrete."

Still, Grace could not understand the desire to buy or sell items that might be too dangerous or outlandish to sit in a booth during the daytime. "In Yeluthia, money and possessions are second to contributions, which raise one's status."

"Well, that's the way the world works in Asteom," Dianne muttered before picking up where she left off. "As I was saying, this market sounds like our best chance if the main roads didn't reveal the ancestral weapons. I think somebody would've mentioned a golden object if one did."

"I agree."

The soldier scratched her arm and looked away from Grace again. "I just need to learn the location of this place before the next new moon."

"Your friend did not mention that?"

"No, which isn't surprising. He's not the kind of person to be involved with that business; however, I'm sure I can ask around for more information. The only problem is my position as a soldier. Not too many people want to air their grievances if it could get them in trouble."

"Well, what if I…" The rest of Grace's offer remained on her tongue as Dianne shot her an unamused look.

"Don't even suggest leaving the palace for a while, let alone your room." Her resulting frown emphasized her lingering frustration with Grace's actions. "You just let me figure out how to proceed."

"If you are sure."

"I am." The woman's expression lightened after a pause. "I'll inform you every step of the way, my lady. I just can't risk putting you in danger. I'd never forgive myself if you got hurt because of my recklessness."

Grace longed to mention it would be her own recklessness to blame if something happened to her, but she sensed Dianne's sincerity and chose to keep the comment to herself. Instead, she thanked her guard before her stomach rumbled, causing the soldier to laugh.

"You didn't eat in the city, did you?" the woman chided when Grace blushed.

"I tried not to interact with too many people who could recognize me."

"That's fair. How about we head to the mess hall then? I'll arrange for the evening guard to replace me while you're there, unless you plan on sneaking away again."

In order to draw less attention to her scarlet cheeks, Grace rolled her eyes and rose while acknowledging how the soldier would never let the day's events fade into obscurity.

***

A knock at the door interrupted Byron's unplanned rest. He had been sitting at his desk attempting to scribble notes for the council meeting the following morning, and his head eventually dropped into his hands. The next thing he knew, he dozed off.

The light tapping continued after a few seconds, so he stood, stretched, and brushed his hair down in an attempt to appear decent despite the stubble taking over the lower half of his face. Over the past week, his consideration for his appearance steadily declined due to his mind wandering elsewhere. He dismissed the notion before approaching and opening the door.

He already expected to see his apprentice Lydia on the opposite side, though her hand had been raised in preparation for another round of knocking. "Yes?"

"Hello Master Byron," she started with a hesitant smile. "I'm here for your report."

He scratched his chin, let his eyes stray upward to the top of the doorframe, then gestured for her to enter. "Right."

Without waiting for a reply, his feet led him back to his desk. Only a single sheet of paper contained writing, which was due in part to his nap, but he found he hardly cared and handed it to her without reading what words he added that afternoon. Lydia accepted it eagerly before staring at the lone page.

"Is there anything else?" she asked while returning her gaze to him and letting her smile all but disappear.

"Were you expecting more?"

During the resulting pause, he went to the window in order to gauge the time. *It's nearly sundown. I should leave before they drag me into more of this business.*

"Master Byron?"

He turned around and found himself mentally skimming the room to ensure it could be left alone until the next day. The bed remained neatly made due to its lack of use, and every other object, including

99

the items on his desk and clothing, were arranged just how he left them over the past two weeks. After acknowledging that, he shuffled to his wardrobe for a cloak.

"Master Byron?"

"What is it?"

Lydia stepped closer while wearing an expression of concern that accentuated her handsome facial features. "You won't be joining the council meeting tomorrow morning either?"

He shook his head in answer without considering the alternative. When she deliberately shifted her position to block the door, he released an exasperated sigh. "Is there a problem?"

Her lips curved into a frown, yet her gentle tone didn't hint at any anger, only disappointment. "I don't believe my presence at the council's meetings is an adequate replacement for you being there. The reports you've provided don't cover every topic they discuss, and the generals easily poke holes in the points you argue. I can't defend what I don't fully understand."

Although he used to never imagine their current conversation coming to pass, at least not for years, Byron found himself considering what to tell his apprentice when he contemplated his future on the council. Cintra's injury and subsequent dependence on him left no time for politics, though he found his interest in other matters waning with each passing day.

"If it's that bothersome of an issue, don't restrict yourself to my report," he said to hurry the discussion along. "You're the one who has been present and listens to their arguments. Add your own questions and conclusions."

"I-I can't do that!" Lydia stammered and pulled her head away, as if offended by his suggestion. "You're the representative of the dark mages."

"Perhaps, but not for much longer."

Lydia's eyes widened and her mouth fell open. "Are you saying…"

Byron never expected to retire until he couldn't physically perform the necessary duties of a master mage; however, after Cintra woke the morning following her near-death experience, he understood she would need him for the rest of her life. He held her when she wept over the loss of their friends, then once the shock resulting from the damage to her body spurred hysteria and nightmares. She wanted nothing to do with the palace after stomaching the details he provided about the massacre.

I didn't listen to her premonition, he couldn't help but recall. *She tried warning me and coercing me somewhere else so we could spend our lives together in peace. Now, even if she does recover mentally, I wouldn't blame her for never wanting to step foot in the capital city again. I have no right to request anything from her after my negligence led to this.*

While his apprentice continued to stare at him with a mixture of confusion, horror, and doubt, he brushed aside his negative feelings in order to settle into a calmer mindset. "I'll give you my formally written resignation tomorrow when I return."

With that, he ushered Lydia out of the room and left her gaping after him while he hurried toward the mess hall.

*

The healing sessions during Cintra's recovery managed to return some motion to her legs, but she would never be able to walk properly or without assistance again. As soon as the light mages in the medical station deemed her in a stable enough condition to be moved, Byron considered his options for a location where she could stay nearby, which proved to be more difficult than he imagined.

His initial idea involved asking Lord Donovan if she could live at the merchant's estate in Verona, then he would speak with Marcy about assisting her. Unfortunately, Lady Katrina's death, as well as the other noblewomen's, shook the foundation of the capital. Households mourned their own loses even after the public ceremony, and additional guards had been organized to monitor the city at all times. Nobody trusted their leaders or their neighbors anymore. Byron heard from Katrina's butler how the lord expected to sell his home before winter so he wouldn't own property in Verona. He also mentioned Marcy moved in with the man she had become involved with, but nothing more.

The second option was to discuss the matter with Clearshot. His friend's home's location wouldn't be ideal, yet Cintra felt safe there before. To his dismay, losing Emilea took a toll on the man to the point where he didn't leave his quarters in the palace. Byron tried visiting his friend on multiple occasions only to find himself talking to the locked door instead and wondering if the person on the other side even listened. After that experience, he arranged for a servant to bring a meal there three times a day in case Clearshot refused to eat.

In the end, Byron utilized an inn on the western side of the capital for Cintra. It lied away from the chaotic business of the main road, and when he discovered the older man named Aimes working in its kitchen, he naturally trusted the staff. One glance at Cintra hobbling on crutches, and probably Byron's dour expression, and the older man gave them his complete attention. They arranged for her to stay in a comfortable space, and as far as Byron heard, Aimes kept her company while he worked during the mornings and early afternoons. The palace cooks had been more than accommodating when he requested a pair of portioned, portable meals over the past ten days so they could share dinner together.

During the remainder of his days, nothing could distract him from her, not the council sessions and their updates, the problems people brought up needing solutions, nor any other matter. He had strained Cintra's faith in him by dismissing her visions of an attack within the palace and put his position above her safety, losing her trust as a result.

She has nobody else to turn to, he reflected while exiting through the front gate with their meals packed into his satchel. *I hoped to add her to my life instead of merging ours together, as it should have been. I offered no compromises on my end; I don't intend to make the same mistake again. The council, Lydia, the mages... Everyone can continue their business without me.*

Byron held a neutral expression as he hurried along despite the rush of people spurred by the dinner hour. Soon, he reached his destination and prepared to enter the inn when movement out of the corner of his eye stayed his hand.

"Who's there?" he demanded while lowering his hand and turning around with a fire spell at the ready in case of danger.

To his utter amazement, Clearshot lingered a few steps behind, fidgeting with his hands and darting his eyes around the area.

"Is this where you're keeping her?" the man asked and licked his lips like a starved dog.

Byron nodded before assessing his friend's shaggy appearance. Clearshot's chestnut hair grew oily from a lack of washing, and a matching beard already overcame his chin. Despite his body remaining hidden under the cloak he wore, his thin, hollow cheekbones revealed he hadn't been eating enough. Worst of all were his eyes, which appeared red rimmed and glazed, as if his mind wandered elsewhere.

"What are you doing here?" Byron asked and decided to ease up.

"I need to talk to you, but since everyone I've spoken with says you've been abandoning the palace during the evening, I figured I would hunt you down."

Byron raised an eyebrow, then he opened the door to the inn. "Come in for a drink?"

After a pause, Clearshot dipped his head in confirmation.

The pair spotted Aimes and Cintra chatting in the common room among several men and a couple women occupying the surrounding tables. Byron approached the two and set the packaged meals on the wooden surface.

"You're back," Cintra said by way of greeting. Her genuine smile upon his arrival warmed his heart, though her lips evened out when she noticed Clearshot standing behind.

Meanwhile, Aimes waved at them both while showcasing his signature, hearty laugh. "Good to have you back!"

Byron eyed the half-eaten plates of food in front of them. "I thought I told you I would be bringing meals from the palace."

"Well, it's no trouble," Aimes replied a bit sheepishly. "Besides, I would prefer you enjoy the food hot."

The older man had no reason to be so hospitable, so Byron considered pressing the subject; however dropping it would save him precious energy. Instead, he thanked Aimes, took his seat next to Cintra, and gestured for Clearshot to join them.

"Don't worry, we're used to the palace's meals," he added before selecting one, packaged meal for himself and setting the other in front of Clearshot.

For a while, they ate their fill and found nonsense to dribble on about until Aimes excused himself.

"He is such a kind man," Cintra murmured as they watched the older man head into a back room.

"Are you ready to retire for the night as well?" Byron asked her after.

She shook her head. "Not yet, but thank you."

He took her hand in his, squeezed it gently, and smiled once their eyes met. If Clearshot didn't clear his throat, they would have savored each other's company even longer.

"That's right, you came here to speak with me," Byron began while addressing his friend.

"I would wait until tomorrow, but…" Clearshot's gaze slid down to the table, then he wiped at his eyes with a frown.

Byron understood the man's pain from losing his wife and waited until he composed himself.

"I can't take it anymore," the soldier continued. "Being in the palace surrounded by my memories of Emilea is killing me. I also need to visit Mace and Lexie."

"Are they aware of what happened?" Byron whispered as he recalled the children at the Magical Arts Academy. "It's been just over two weeks now since-"

"I know," Clearshot snapped. He inhaled and exhaled a few deep breaths before picking up the conversation again. "I wrote to them and shared the news. I'm sure they're expected me to see them, but I needed time to… In any case, my future here is…"

Byron waited for a complete response, but after a minute, he pressed for an explanation for the mumbled comments. "What are you saying?"

When his friend looked up, the man's expression projected pure heartache. "Emilea's title kept her tied to Verona. I was the one who wanted us to live outside the city because of the noise and activity, and she agreed to travel for her duties and stay in the palace when needed. We raised Mace and Lexie together, I requested to be stationed here, and it worked for a while. Once the children moved to East Hoover for their training, we discussed selling our home in order to stay in a single place. Now that she's gone, there's no reason for me to…"

"You're thinking about relocating."

Clearshot nodded. "When I leave, I won't be coming back. I put in my request yesterday, and General Tont approved it this morning."

Byron's eyebrows rose in surprise. "That soon?"

"I'm certain the generals are aware of my situation." He followed those words with an uncomfortable chuckle.

"So that's what you needed to tell me," Byron concluded. "This will probably be our last night together."

Clearshot narrowed his eyes. "Not exactly."

"What?"

"I wanted to let you know you're welcome to join me."

Until that moment, Cintra remained silent. The offer caused her to gasp. "You intend for us to move to East Hoover too?"

"I hesitated to mention my decision until I learned of Byron's behavior, mainly that he stopped attending the council meetings."

Cintra glanced at Byron, who contemplated the opportunity. He told her some of what he was and wasn't doing but figured it would be shocking to hear he had been avoiding his responsibility to assist the king of Asteom, especially with their new threat.

When nobody else spoke, Clearshot went on. "Emiliea's relatives are willing to pay for the house and property and can support Mace and Lexie financially, should the need arise. I'll be meeting with them tomorrow morning to sign the paperwork before removing what items I need. Then, I plan to depart from Verona. If you don't intend to live here either, I could use company on the journey and a friend to lean on, especially to arrange for a job at the academy."

Cintra laid a hand on Byron's arm while saying his name at a lower volume, projecting her uncertainty.

The future I hoped to give her is gone, he admitted while staring into her gem-like, sapphire eyes, which reflected her concern. *What we prepared for can no longer be achieved without my role interfering. The truth of the matter is, I need to be here for her without distractions in order to give her the best life possible, and I'm not sure that will happen if we remain in Verona.*

Byron inhaled through his nostrils, faced his friend, and nodded. "When do we leave?"

Simultaneously, Clearshot grinned and Cintra frowned.

Demonic Scars

A pair of footsteps roused Coura from her sleep, but she remained unmoving after remembering the sage's comment from the previous day about him sending someone to fetch her in the morning. The person placed a hand on her shoulder to gently shake her awake, so she sat up and found Harriette kneeling beside her.

"Dawn is approaching," the woman shared at a volume just above a whisper. "If you would like to eat, there is time before I am to bring you to Sage Vidar."

The sudden offer startled Coura, and she thanked Harriette before rising. Once she was alone, she got dressed, tied her hair back, and stretched her limbs, hoping the extra motions would give her a hidden dose of energy. To her dismay, as she lumbered toward the meal area, it became evident the previous evening's meditation-turned-nap had interfered with her sleep schedule. Because she didn't know what to expect that day, Coura ate light and drank plenty of the fresh spring water carried over before each meal; the latter reminded her she skipped her duties the night prior.

I can offer to make them up when I get more free time, she decided as Harriette appeared in the doorway.

After returning her dishes to the basin, Coura followed the Mintelian woman outside, across the field, and to the space used for the combat exercises. Sage Vidar and the last sparring partner she faced, the one possessing enough skill to match a soldier in Verona, stood together conversing until they noticed her arrival.

So that's what he intends to work on today. I can't help but feel relieved we aren't focusing on meditating right now.

"Good morning," the older man greeted her with a nod to Harriette. "I expect you found success yesterday after I left you?"

Coura tilted her head at the question when they halted within the circle of dirt. Although she wondered whether or not he could actually sense how productive she had been with reaching and understanding her soul space, she confirmed it. "I did."

"Excellent. Now we proceed to the next step."

The sage gestured for the fighter at his side to step forward, which the man did while raising the wooden sword he carried. At the same time, Harriette swept away from Coura's side to stand behind her master.

"Today we will test your magic," Sage Vidar continued. "You met Rydar already, and as you may have guessed, he has formal training with the blade. He is going to attack you from all sides, so you need to use light magic to protect yourself. I intend to assess your progress with the Yeluthian power you inherited."

Coura noticed both Harriette and Rydar's eyes widen after that comment, displaying their surprise at her lineage. She ignored them in order to channel her light energy in preparation to follow the sage's instructions. It sent a course of stability throughout her body similar to sunshine on a spring afternoon, as it did every time she reached inward for that power.

"Ready?" she asked her partner when he appeared composed.

After nodding in reply, he poised his weapon and charged.

It became obvious from his initial, horizontal swipe that Rydar had been ordered to move slower than normal, allowing Coura to manifest shield after shield between sidestepping and ducking. Sage Vidar only called the exercise to a halt after her opponent managed to catch her forearm when the shimmer of magic hid her view momentarily. The spot hurt and a bruise already began swelling, but she planned to brush the damage aside.

"Your shielding is consistent yet requires additional strength behind it in order to avoid shattering so frequently," the sage critiqued once she faced him. "That comes with time, practice, and patience. Now, let me see your healing."

Coura stared down at the throbbing lump in dismay as she considered her greatest fault with magic. *Emilea once told me my healing ability is weak because it went untrained. She explained how it takes years to master due to a light mage needing to study the body and learn from experience more than textbooks. I have the potential, yet I never bothered to do much with it.*

After considering the knowledge she acquired from the master light mage, Coura placed a hand over the bruise, closed her eyes, and focused solely on the energy rushing to tend to the wound. Similar to the injury her Yeluthian comrade suffered in the Western Woods, the afflicted area underneath the skin extended, as if naturally pushing to spread every second her magic worked. Thankfully, the bruise proved minor enough, and she heal it in a matter of minutes. Coura opened her eyes once she finished, held up the arm, and balled that hand into a fist as a demonstration.

The sage released a displeased groan. "That will do for the moment, but it would be wise for you to keep a supply of light energy just in case. Any injury you receive from this point forward is your responsibility, with or without magic. Is that understood?"

She nodded before being thrown into another round of shielding and dodging practice against Rydar. This time around, when he struck her, Sage Vidar made no attempt to stop them. It wasn't until Coura's energy mostly depleted and her shields stopped fully forming that Rydar retreated, as if by an unspoken order. By that point, she earned a dozen welts and bruises and avoided wincing while she stood panting.

Sage Vidar's voice cut across the area to draw their attention. "We will break for the noon meal," he announced with arms outstretched in a friendly gesture.

In front of him, a blanket had been laid out and topped with bowls, plates, and silverware. Coura sighed with relief and followed Rydar over to where the older Mintelian man dropped to sit. Once they settled around the dishes, Harriette seemingly emerged from nowhere carrying wrapped bundles containing their food.

She must have returned to the dining space to bring all this here, Coura realized while the woman served them one by one. *I guess I should've noticed when she disappeared, but I'm sure I would have earned myself another bruise if I got distracted.*

The four ate in silence and broke apart after to let their stomachs rest, then Harriette cleared the area. Sage Vidar called for Coura to go back to where she and Rydar sparred earlier sooner than she expected. The man she worked with remained by the sage yet still held the practice blade.

"I've been able to observe your light magic and note what needs improvement. Fortunately, nothing requires immediate altering, just time and practice. Whoever taught you was no doubt experienced in their field."

She smiled at the memories of her time studying under Emilea. Despite teaching somebody who grew up learning the opposite style of magic, the master mage treated Coura as she did any of her other students: with patience and kindness yet a firm, disciplined hand. She voiced as much to Sage Vidar.

"I see. What about the man you grew up studying dark magic under?"

"Byron is just as intelligent," Coura shared without considering the question for more than a second. "It helps that he knew me on a personal level. He played on my strengths and weaknesses, both as a student and a combatant."

The Mintelian nodded. "In that case, it shouldn't be a problem for you to demonstrate dark magic at an expert level."

Coura's heart dropped, along with her smile. "What?"

"I would like to spend the afternoon working on your demonic energy, just as we did this morning with the light spells."

She shook her head before averting her gaze. The sting of losing the power she developed and honed for years lessened over time, yet recalling it still proved painful. "I thought I told you. When I sealed the demon away, I lost all her energy."

"Yes, and?"

"There's nothing left for me to use."

The older man paused, rubbed his chin, then pierced her with a glare that sent a shiver down her spine. "What you claimed to manipulate is gone, and what you possess will never reach the heights of what once was. Still, if you were successful after I left you to meditate yesterday, you should be aware of the second power in your center. What flows through you is dark in nature."

Although she had an idea of what he hinted at, Coura's denial prevented her from agreeing. "So what if it is? All it means is I carry the energy. That's why the demon is after me and why I need to heal my soul-"

"No." The single word Sage Vidar uttered echoed around them, leaving a haunting silence in its wake. When he spoke again, he lowered his volume but kept the venom in his voice. "Commit these facts to memory: Your center naturally healed into the form it is now and will never return to what it once was. It adapted to be able to possess demonic energy and now does so freely, drawing the power into your body. Once you accept it, consciously or not, it belongs to you. Why then do you deny your ability to manipulate it into a spell?"

Coura said the first reason that came to mind. "That energy makes me a target for demons and their creatures."

"Any being with dark power will be tantalizing to their kind."

"Even so, wielding it will deliberately attract them to me."

"Not if you mask your presence. Surely your mentor taught you such a basic concept."

It wasn't Byron, she recalled. *Soirée did before I left the academy*.

"It's been years since I could use demonic energy," she muttered, unable to fathom how she could do so after Soirée's defeat. "Even if I could, I can't wield both light and dark magic."

"Why not?"

Coura opened and closed her mouth while racking her brain for an answer. "Each requires a different method for spellcasting."

"That is correct. You proved your abilities with light magic earlier, so all we need to do is aim to relearn those associated with dark energy. The knowledge is there; you just have to remember. Then, we can practice going between the two."

The idea of using light and dark energy in tandem was unheard of and left Coura with mixed feelings. *It makes sense, but it's not natural for humans, Yeluthians, or demons to possess both types of power. That's the reason why no one could ever do it. Besides, the skills take a lifetime to learn. I can't... That's insane!*

Despite exclaiming this in her mind, her heart believe it to be true.

"What is holding you back from accepting?" the sage went on while ignoring her hesitation and fixing her with a disgruntled stare. "You aren't the type of person to take failure or issues lying down. From what you told me about your life, you continued pushing forward in order to protect those you care about and defend Asteom. Why do you refuse to accept yourself the way you are?"

Coura bit her lip before answering. She had a sinking feeling he wasn't going to like her ill-conceived explanation. "It's dangerous. Demonic energy has always been a burden and is against the law because it leads to people getting hurt or being killed. I became an outcast because of my involvement with it and the demon it stemmed from. Now, another is attacking the country because of me. As much as I would love to be able to use dark magic again, I would rather be weak than put others' lives at risk."

A pregnant pause stretched between them before the Mintelian responded.

"You're afraid."

She crossed her arms and kept quiet; however, that seemed to make the sage grow even more upset.

"You're behaving like a coward!" he shouted at her as his face flushed a deep scarlet. "What happened in the past was the result of your bonding to that demon, and your center of power reflects this. The dark energy you take in will never go away or stop coming to you just because you brush it aside. Your ignorance is what will get people killed, not what you do with that power! The demon manipulated you before, claiming you as its own. Now, any being can come after you. Your best option is to keep that trail of energy hidden, though it will always be available for you to use if you build the courage to do so."

Coura contemplated this for a moment before shaking her head regretfully. Memories of the demonic creatures, those slain on the battlefield by the possessed Nim-Valan soldiers, and her fight against Soirée came to mind. In each, she felt like a different person, someone she feared becoming again. "I'm sorry. I just can't do it."

Sage Vidar didn't respond right away. His face steadily calmed into a stoic expression, yet the anger still remained. Suddenly, he raised a hand to point at her.

"Rydar," he began in a controlled, neutral tone. "We *will* continue for the afternoon."

During the entire argument, the younger man stood uncomfortably to the side. Evidently, he didn't appear to be expecting to do more that session, for his mouth fell open and his eyes went wide. "Sage Vidar," he started only to be hushed by a wave of his master's hand.

Coura's heart plummeted as the sword-bearing Mintelian approached to stand across from her. He wore a sympathetic expression, but that was the little solace she had for the next two hours when the combat started again. The sage expected her to tap into the dark energy resting within her center, yet she refused and instead called upon her Yeluthian power for shielding.

That lasted until she depleted her light energy. Then, the session fell into a beating.

Although her skills allowed her to avoid a majority of the strikes, those that landed hit true. By the time the sage stopped Rydar, cuts and bruises covered her limbs and face. The older man dismissed them for the day, so she hurried to the bathing area where she stripped off her sweat-covered clothes, sat in the water, and allowed herself to release the restraint on her self-control. She remained like that, breaths shaky, eyes watery, and body aching and shivering, until her hunger became too great to ignore.

Any blood from the open scratches washed away, and the swelling lumps across her skin eased slightly; however, given the stares she received upon entering the meal area, it seemed she still appeared worse for wear. The amount of whispers also increased among the typically quiet Mintelians who lived on the sage's property. Coura ignored them all, ate, and began her evening chores. When the older woman, the same person she first meditated with, dismissed her early, she knew they were somewhat aware of what took place and pitied her.

Because her body grew exhausted by the end of the day, the pain increased as she returned to her hut. There, she was startled to find a pouch of healing salve, a bowl of unnaturally cold water, and bandages soaked in a bitter-smelling solution.

What is this? she wondered while peeking outside. No one lingered near her location, so she accepted the items as a unanimous gift. *These people must always act indirectly. Could it have to do with the sage's temper? Maybe they're afraid of being scolded, or something along those lines.*

After applying the medication, placing a cool rag on the worst of the bruising, and wrapping others in the bandages, Coura relaxed to rest.

*

Harriette came to fetch her in the morning after she cleaned up and ate. The physical pain remained, yet the sharpness dulled thanks to the overnight, mundane healing techniques. Sage Vidar and Rydar stood together when they arrived, then Harriette broke away from Coura's side to join them, leaving her alone in the sparring circle.

"Are you going to cooperate today?" the older man asked. His voice sounded weary, though his tone and body language suggested otherwise.

Although she grew curious about his behavior, she decided not to press her luck by inquiring. "I'm not going to use demonic energy."

To her surprise, the sage nodded, as if expecting her response. "Right now, I would like you to focus inward on that presence instead. Walk me through your process, similar to how you mediate."

She tilted her head but decided the assessment wouldn't be harmful and closed her eyes. Unlike a meditation session, her body couldn't fully relax, and she needed to remain aware enough to share each step. That fact led her to consider noting what she felt when she reached out to each tendril of power. If she were to interact with one presence, it would ready itself in preparation for her to manipulate it into a spell.

114

The Yeluthian energy appeared first, so she welcomed and allowed it to fill her body with its characteristic warmth. She explained what she could in plain terms without leading it to an exit point, or where it would manifest.

Sage Vidar grunted to show his approval. "Next, locate the demonic power and interact with it, like what you did with the light energy."

Coura opened her eyes to glare at him. "I said I wasn't going to-"

"You won't be using it," the older man hastily interrupted. "In this exercise, I need to observe what happens when you make contact with it."

Despite her lingering hesitance after his explanation, Coura closed her eyes, retraced her steps to focus on her soul space, and located the restless tendrils of energy.

"Would you say the light presence detracts from the demonic one, or vice versa?" the sage asked when she returned to that point.

"No. It's like they're each following their own, separate paths."

"So, there is no hostility?"

"Not that I can sense."

"Good, now reach out to the dark energy."

The fear she felt during the previous meditation session had steadily been rising and finally caught up with her. "I can't…"

"Stay focused," Sage Vidar ordered. Unlike the day before, he didn't seem upset with her for her reaction. Instead, he acted as if this were an urgent matter requiring her utmost understanding. "Try again."

Coura pushed herself forward until a shiver slid down her spine and the sensation of a blade against her throat returned. "I can't," she admitted, ashamed of both her anxiousness and fear.

"Try again."

If it wasn't for the Mintelian's gentle manner of speaking, she would have abandoned the attempt in order to save what dignity remained. She managed to extend her internal presence toward the demonic energy until it brushed against her. Immediately, the intoxication of such power, and her memories of working with Soirée, returned.

Coura's eyes flung open as she recoiled from the dark energy. Her body grew cold, causing her hands to tremble, and her forehead became coated with sweat.

"There," she spat while wiping her head with the back of one, shaky hand. "Was that good enough?"

The older man's lack of an immediate response had her turning away with arms crossed. Dealing with the situation stirred unsettling feelings, especially since nothing seemed to be helping.

At last, Sage Vidar spoke. "Your instinct to shy away from that presence derives from your past experiences with demons and their creatures, not to mention your lineage. Notice how neither presence in your center rejects you; they are willing to act on your behalf. From what you described, interacting with the dark energy creates a sensation where your fear stems from. When you overcome that, will you be able to fully manipulate it?"

He paused for a moment, though she didn't reply.

"The answer is no, I don't believe so. You worry you won't be able to maintain control over the power even though yours is the only presence in your body. Without confidence in one's skill, a mage is helpless to their potential."

Coura listened intently before facing the Mintelian. His explanation proved to be painfully accurate and brought reality to the forefront.

"That's not entirely the problem," she admitted. "Whenever I used demonic energy, the connection to Soirée remained, even after I was stabbed with the ancestral dagger that tore her presence away. I soon figured out how much of a different person I became when I wielded her power, with or without her attached to my soul."

"Ah!" Sage Vidar exclaimed, as if she revealed a piece of information he didn't catch before. "You're afraid of losing yourself to that power."

Coura didn't respond, but that seemed to be enough of an answer for him.

"That can be overcome with time and practice as well," he said before ushering her through the exercise again.

*

When they paused for lunch, Coura felt exhausted. Even though she didn't do more than repeat the process, the consistent exposure to demonic power wore on her mental state, reminding her of what Grace, Emilea, Evern, and others possessing light energy experienced when they sensed the unnatural presence. The only difference seemed to be how interacting with it didn't disgust her.

Sage Vidar was right though. Because she remained in control of the energy resting within her center, her original worry ebbed enough to where she wouldn't tear herself away from the power when it approached.

I expected it to act like a mad dog and lash out at me for simply reaching toward it, she noted while staring into her bowl of untasted porridge. *Instead, it behaves just like the Yeluthian energy and waits for me to utilize it. That means it won't take over if I were to try wielding it into a spell, right?*

Coura became so distracted by her thoughts that a gentle touch on her shoulder caused her to jump and glance over at the source, which proved to be Harriette. The woman bent forward from where she stood in order to address Coura.

"You should eat what you can while you have the time," the Mintelian urged in an oddly sincere manner. "You will need your strength for this afternoon's lesson."

Although she wondered both what the session could entail and why the woman felt the need to offer a warning, Coura simply nodded before starting to eat. They paused to let their stomachs settle after, then the sage ordered her to return to the work area. Interestingly, Harriette occupied the spot at the older man's side while Rydar cleaned up after their meal.

"Since you are becoming familiar with tapping into the demonic energy, the next step is to establish a connection so it can be manipulated into a spell," the Mintelian began. "Before you argue, we won't be able to do much else until you overcome this dilemma."

117

She had opened her mouth to protest, yet she closed it upon realizing the truth of his words. *I need to trust him. That's the whole reason I'm here. Besides, I'm far enough from Verona and any other cities or towns that potential danger I attract will stay along the mountainside.*

When it became clear she was willing to accept his help, Sage Vidar relaxed his tight frown into a neutral expression. "What you must do is beckon the power, as if you are preparing to cast a spell. Don't worry about anything else. You must grow accustomed to the feeling once more."

Coura repeated those words in her mind while she obeyed his instruction. In an attempt to avoid considering the results enough to dissuade her, she reached into her center to seize the demonic tendril, like stretching an invisible hand. What she didn't expect was for the energy to practically leap when she gave it permission to act. Her Yeluthian power behaved the same, though comparable to a stream flowing throughout her body at a steady pace once she let it go; the demon energy shot like lightening through her veins. The thrill invigorated her from head to toe; however, the familiarity of the sensation shocked her the most.

"This is…" Her eyes widened while she stared down at her hands, which didn't tremble for the first time that day.

"That's enough," the sage called as she wrestled with her mixture of emotions. "Dismiss the energy."

This confidence and stability reminds me of her. Our bond always left me feeling like I could conquer any obstacle because I had complete faith in myself and my abilities.

Sage Vidar repeated his order, bringing her back to the present.

"Why?" she asked while raising her eyes to meet the man's, amber pair.

The Mintelian only stared at her with an unreadable gaze.

"You're going to tell me to do it again anyway. If you wanted me to wield dark magic a few hours ago, why the hesitation now? We can skip to the next step."

"You need to practice control."

Coura scoffed at his words. *I remember how to cast shielding and elemental spells, so that's not the issue. In fact, he preaches about how I should be practicing...*

The Mintelian began to scold her until she raised her right hand, placed the palm upward, and decided to test what power she possessed. Utilizing nothing except the memories of her classes at the MAA, she released the energy while shaping it into a spell, producing a flame in the middle of her hand. Although the fire's size was comparable to one of the village's pear-like fruits, Coura still felt a swell of pride and elation that spurred a smile.

I did it! The part of myself I lost for years has returned...

Those precious seconds ended in an instant when both of her arms snapped to her sides, and her legs pressed together, as if by the pull of an invisible rope. Her body went tense at the sudden, uncontrollable movement and dropped to the ground before she understood what happened.

Is this a binding spell? she wondered as she tried and failed to break free from the magical ties.

Coura looked over her shoulder to glare at Sage Vidar since she expected him to be the source; however, it was Harriette who extended her arms in front of her and radiated light energy.

"Dismiss the demonic power," the sage ordered for a third time.

With a final wiggle followed by a displeased huff, she released her hold on the energy. The tendril returned to her center like normal, and a few seconds later, the binding spell vanished. As soon as she could move without the restraints, she climbed to her feet.

"What was that for?" she demanded without hiding her irritation toward the situation and the sage's behavior.

The Mintelian man gave no indication her reaction bothered him. "Do you feel the difference in your attitude?"

Coura's temper simmered while she opened and closed her mouth twice, unable to comprehend how he could have guessed the dark power's influence on her mentality.

"I thought so," he continued matter-of-factly. His lips stretched into a thin yet proud smile, the first she had seen since she came to the village. "From my experience in dealing with mages, the abilities they possess play a part in shaping their character. The same is true for you, though you must face three, different personalities: one influenced by the demonic energy, one shaped by the Yeluthian energy, and your own when you are not using magic."

The nonsensical explanation left Coura bemused. "What does that mean? How am I supposed to function in multiple ways?"

Sage Vidar paused to consider the questions before holding up two fingers. "How I understand it, there are a couple options. The first is to continue on as you've done for your whole life by accepting each when you cast various spells. The second and healthier option is to establish a neutral ground of sorts. Whenever you act as a mage, you must not give in to the changes in your personality. Doing this requires complete concentration on the task at hand. You must focus instead of reacting based on your emotions."

Coura found herself wishing she kept the confidence from minutes ago. *That's insane! Nobody can ignore their emotions, especially during a fight. I guess that means I'm doomed if I continue trying to wield the demonic energy. Then again, I never had trouble in the past.*

"The time to discuss this further will come soon," the sage added to move the afternoon along. "For the rest of the day, you are going to practice reaching into your center for each type of power, masking both internally to prevent anyone from sensing what you possess, then holding and dismissing them on cue."

Reluctantly, Coura shoved the doubts aside in order to make it through the session. It took longer than they wanted for her to be able to seize the demonic energy again, and every instance she successfully did so, she remained unable to give it up due to how secure she felt while maintaining the connection. This resulted in several binding spells from Harriette that sent Coura into the dirt.

When the sky grew dim and her hunger returned with a vengeance, Sage Vidar prepared to end the exercise.

"Unless you overcome the lust for power, as well as the fear of losing yourself to it, you will never be able to reach your full potential," he stated before dismissing her. "Keep that in mind, and we will continue tomorrow."

Returning Threats

Transitioning back to his previous responsibilities in Dala didn't prove tough for Marcus. Unfortunately, part of his heart remained in the capital city, though he could not keep up with the news, assist his friend and king directly, or offer suggestions to the issues he knew continued to arise. General Tio also kept his attention on the base and southern cities' protection from the onslaught of demonic creatures that seemingly appeared out of nowhere.

As the days stretched into weeks, the people in that area began following a similar routine reliant on their leader's decisions. Marcus had been ordered to assume a route with his own squad, like his last assignment in the area, and his fellow assistant general did the same in another direction. The two were not only tasked with protecting the towns and roads between the Yeluthians' patrolling but also collecting any information on the ancestral weapons.

General Tio made no attempt to hide their intentions claiming his openness on the subject would allow the citizens to contribute whatever details they became aware of. To Marcus, the idea sounded too lax, yet he kept the doubt to himself.

I understand having faith in the people we serve is admirable, but his invitation gives the less honorable citizens an opportunity to take advantage of the situation, he had thought after that meeting. *Besides, it might be dangerous for the more enthusiastic among them to go searching for items nobody has seen in decades. A request between the soldiers, mages, and Yeluthians we trust would be just as worthwhile.*

Still, Calin hadn't complained, so Marcus refused to either. In fact, the Dalan assistant general began keeping him at arm's length ever since his return to the base a couple days prior.

I would believe his reserved behavior is due to the amount of stress we've been under, Marcus considered on his way to his room after the evening meal. *Everyone looks like they would rather continue their regular lives instead of the excitement the demonic creatures spurred at first. Then again, I imagine I had similar fantasies of grandeur when I first became a soldier.*

He reached his quarters, dropped onto his bed, and released a deep breath in an attempt to ease the tension in his shoulders, which he picked up throughout the course of the afternoon. It returned as soon as his mind wandered to his first encounter with the golden blade and his involvement in ending the demon's reign in Verona. With a grunt, he rolled onto his side in order to stare at the stone wall and picture the sunset he expected took place on the opposite side.

I hate this time of year. The evening seems to overstay its welcome, leading to shorter mornings and afternoons. Once it snows, the chill permeates the walls, and evidently through my boots. The general would call me soft for becoming so accustomed to the warmer temperatures in Dala. That's one positive aspect of being sent south instead of staying in Verona.

He hoped the comment would cheer him up, yet it only succeeded in reminding him of how useless he had been during his time in the palace. Before he could begin to connect his personal conflict with his father's impression of him, the increase in demonic creatures, or the attack in the palace, distant shouting from the hallway caught his attention. The sound grew louder and projected additional voices, which prompted Marcus to jump to his feet, retrieve his sword, and follow the source.

Others in the area caught on to the trouble as well. Soon, he found himself in the middle of a stream of soldiers heading toward the nearest exit. Their direction provided an explanation for the noise.

The base is under attack, Marcus noted as soon as he stepped outside. *Probably the creatures again, though they never raised this much of a fuss before.*

Light from the sunset gleamed in the distance to bathe the southern field and city in a golden glow. Those around him shuffled closer, as if uncertain where the threat could be; however, every head turned to look at the open area while the voices quieted and low growls became audible.

Stagnant, shadowy figures crouched within the tall grass, which didn't surprise Marcus given his experience fighting the demonic beasts. What did startle him was the appearance of a single, human-shaped silhouette among the creatures.

Who is that? he wondered while pushing his way in that direction. Instead of concern, he recognized how the stranger's lack of movement unnerved him.

His uneasiness continued to rise even when he recognized the general and Calin standing together apart from the nearby group.

"What's going on?" he asked to alert them of his presence.

The general growled before answering. "The mages claim that man possesses demonic energy and manipulates the beasts."

"Why not approach them?"

This time, Cain responded. "They advised us to rally our forces before taking action, mainly because it doesn't look like the enemy will attack right away. The city also doesn't seem to be aware anything is amiss yet."

Marcus understood their frustration and apprehension well enough to stifle his remaining questions. The past skirmishes with the demonic creatures never involved a leader of sorts. Some behaved by coordinating their strikes with others, yet this situation would be completely different.

Since that was the case, the Dalan troops waited anxiously for their commander to issue orders based on the enemy's movements. The minutes ticked by as they stood in defensive lines, and Marcus only considered an alternative strategy when the evening approached, effectively diminishing the sunlight.

Then, an unexpected voice reached them from the field.

"Who is the leader of this base?" The stranger's deep pitch couldn't mask the sense of arrogance beneath the question.

Marcus noted shuffling behind him to show how the newcomer shook the troops, though that ceased when Calin raised a fist as a warning. When silence filled the area again, General Tio stepped forward while puffing up his chest.

"Who's asking?"

A pause followed the man's words before the figure began sauntering forward. The movement caused the creatures in the grass to rise from their crouched positions and stalk behind their master in an eager fashion.

"Get ready," Calin announced over his shoulder in a controlled manner.

In response, those bunched up behind the trio prepared for combat.

Marcus drew his blade and gripped the hilt tighter than normal. *This stranger summoned the creatures, so his mental state might not be fully responsive. That is, unless we're not dealing with an ordinary human...or a human at all!*

He opened his mouth to share the potential danger with his superior when a sword appeared out of thin air in the figure's hand, leaving him to mutter a curse instead. *I've never heard of anyone manifesting a weapon using magic except for Coura. We're either facing somebody like her or the real creature.*

"Stop right there!" General Tio shouted before surprising everyone by plunging his blade into the ground in order to cross his arms.

Both Marcus and Calin stepped closer to guard their leader despite the stranger and its creatures halting.

"Are you responsible for the attack on Asteom's capital and the slaughtering of innocent lives in the palace?" the general asked. The intimidating quality of his voice hinted at a suppressed rage.

Marcus hadn't expected to be considering such a connection until that point, so he anticipated the reply.

"What are you babbling?" the figure responded, though his tone suggested the change of subject irritated him.

"Answer the question," General Tio pushed at the same volume and with the same amount of ferocity. "One month ago, a group slipped into the palace, massacred women, guards, and servants, and attempted to flee. Are you responsible for that?"

"I am not," came the immediate reply. When he continued, Marcus realized how offended the stranger became by the accusation. "When there is something I desire, I fight for the right to possess it. I do not sneak around in the shadows like a coward. No, my pride stems from my ability to best any opponent and claim their life and land."

General Tio plucked his sword out of the ground before scratching his chin in a rather casual manner. "Fine, but I take it you're controlling the creatures wandering around the southern half of Asteom."

"Now you're giving me my due credit," the figure boasted while his lips curved into a gleeful grin. "Would you care to see them up close?"

"If you're so fond of those beasts you'll keep them away from us, demon."

The general's final word hung in the air between them, and Marcus' stomach sank when the stranger didn't react right away.

If he doesn't deny the accusation, that must mean he really is a...

"What a pity." They caught the silhouette raising its shoulders and arms in a shrug. "It wasn't my intent to reveal my presence this soon, especially after masking my trail so well."

"Is that why you emerged with your creatures?" Marcus longed to throw in the being's face, yet the question remained on his tongue while his mind wrestled with the idea of fighting another demon.

"Humans are fickle and weak," their enemy went on in a new, weary tone, as if to feign exhaustion. "You denied the account from one of your own kind, and all it took to quiet your hunt was a decoy."

"What do you mean?" the general snapped to show his impatience.

"Emotions are easy to manipulate, which is how I convinced a mourning man to serve me those years ago. Then, when you abandoned my scent, I spent some time building my forces for the day when I rightfully claim this land as my own."

In response, the shadowy beasts flashed their teeth with growls and snapped at the air. General Tio and Calin also leaned forward, anticipating the enemy to bound forward. The noise caused Marcus to grip his weapon tighter in preparation for a charge.

"This is exactly how the previous demon behaved," he decided to warn the pair. "It used words to discourage us before attacking, though that one possessed the strength and speed to back up its claims."

His superior grunted to acknowledge the comment before the creatures sprang toward them with their master remaining in place.

The dim light didn't help their situation considering how well their enemy blended into the grass; however, most of the troops gained experience from the past couple years. What creatures Marcus took on alongside General Tio and Calin proved to be as ferocious as those he previously faced, and a brief glance at the bulk of the soldiers and mages showed they retained their coordinated combat skills too. This let him focus on each animal-like shape in front of him.

Once those in his area had been vanquished, he glanced around to ensure his comrades could still manage the remaining beasts. Calin approached to his right and placed a hand on his shoulder.

"That felt too short," the assistant general began before wiping his sweat-covered forehead with the back of his empty hand. "I've endured longer bouts with half as many of them."

Marcus nodded, yet he already reached the same conclusion. "This wasn't meant to be a serious attack."

"It was a warning," Calin finished for him.

Instead of replying, Marcus knelt next to the nearest creature's body, wiped his fingers against its teeth and claws, and rose while waiting for a stinging sensation. When none came, he addressed his comrade. "This batch doesn't possess venom."

"We should still tend to the wounded and dispose of the corpses. I'll organize that part. See what the general would like to do about defenses for the evening."

Marcus agreed and turned away while Calin jogged toward the mass of people beginning to huddle together. At first, his eyes struggled to adjust to the surrounding darkness, but he soon recognized his superior standing farther ahead and hurried to the man's side. His mind immediately went to the demon since it lingered in that spot minutes ago, and a sense of fear struck him at the thought of leaving their leader alone. Still, Marcus noticed General Tio's weapon at his side, and the man's expression scrunched into a scowl. Together, the pair surveyed the empty field in silence.

The demon was nowhere in sight.

***

From the previous fall and winter spent in Muld, Will had some idea of what to expect when he ventured outside the inner circle in his search for Finn. Yukin seemed more than accommodating, providing him with travel clothing consisting of leather padding and boots, a storage bag filled with plenty of food to last him through the journey three times over, and a special, oil-coated cloak that would keep it dry by preventing any liquid from being absorbed.

Once he trekked beyond the city walls, Will became extremely grateful for the preparations the young lord took to ensure he would be fine on his own. Rain fell every day after, and with the dropping temperatures his body felt freezing cold all the time. The dirt roads soaked up the water to form muddy, puddle-filled hazards, leaving him to find alternate routes where he would be able to continue safely. Somehow, he managed to make headway over the next week and a half until he practically stumbled into the southernmost town.

Its familiar sights after the lonely, arduous journey brought tears to his eyes, and he approached the medicine woman's home with his breath held. He pounded on the door, hoping Geneva would hear him over the pouring rain, and a minute later, the wood swung inward a bit. After a pause, he heard her voice.

"Will?"

He couldn't help but smile awkwardly at her disbelief. "Can I come in?"

In response, she ushered him inside, demanded he remove his cloak and sopping boots, then ordered him to sit while she prepared fresh tea. As soon as she shoved a mug into his hands and draped a blanket over his trembling shoulders to steadily warm him up, the questioning began.

"What are you doing here?" For as kind as her actions were, her voice teemed with irritation. "What happened at the capital? Is Finnley in town too?"

"Give me a moment to catch my breath, please!" he begged before chuckling to show he meant no ill will. "Finn isn't here. Actually, I'm looking for him…"

Over the next hour or so, he recounted the months spent in the inner circle with Finn and Yukin, including treating the sickness plaguing their people, their spying on the suspicious advisor, and finally their decision to send him after Finn. By the time he finished, no sunlight came from outside, forcing the old medicine woman to rise and light the lamps before commenting.

"So you'll be heading to the border then?"

Will nodded, too weary to use his voice. Geneva caught on to his fatigue, retrieved the empty mug, and shooed him toward the spare bedroom he had been staying in ever since she took him in.

"I have more questions," she assured him. "However, they can wait until you get a decent night's sleep and breakfast in the morning."

*

As promised, his caretaker laid out an assortment of bread-based items with cheeses, jams, butters, and syrups to compliment them. She offered to make eggs or tea too, so he accepted the latter before she picked up the conversation exactly where they left off.

"You're saying one of the king's advisors is wielding dark magic, the kind you recognize from Asteom?"

"I'm afraid it might be worse than that, but it could have been my imagination. In any case, this Lupin is a serious threat to both countries."

"And Finn chased after him," the woman concluded. She rubbed her chin while her concern strained the wrinkles at the corners of both eyes. "He was never the type to sit around when work needed to be done."

Will didn't respond. He ate more than his fill before leaning back in his chair to savor the warmth brought about by a full stomach. *I don't believe I've ever been unappreciative of anything in my life, but I'll be thankful for every meal, bed, blanket, and roof over my head from now on!*

Geneva sensed his lethargy and frowned. "Don't think you're out of the woods yet, young man. I would like to hear your plan for finding Finn and your intentions after that."

He paused to consider what he would tell her. Over the past few days, he put together a few manageable ideas for the near future based on what Yukin and Elena requested. "Locating him isn't going to be easy. Because of that, I'll be camping out on the border."

"Good, good. Wait for him to come to you."

"I also know it would be worthwhile to listen to what he has to say. If the Nim-Valan troops already crossed and are causing trouble, we may return to Asteom instead of the capital in order to report the issue to their generals and king. Otherwise, we might end up spying on Lupin first."

The older woman produced a long, displeased hum while shaking her head. "I hate the idea of you two being out there alone. What about the mages who traveled here with you?"

Will bit his lip. *It's one thing to risk my own life and another to request my friends do the same…*

"I can't," he replied timidly despite anticipating how Geneva would react.

"Why not?"

He didn't answer.

"Are you saying you dismiss the abilities of your friends? Is it because they aren't trained fighters? Do you not believe they are capable of handling such a task?"

"No, that's not it."

"Then what is?"

Will released a sigh while his insides twisted. "I care about them. They saved my life once already; I hope they never have to be put in that position again. I don't want anybody getting hurt."

Why he chose to express his protective feelings to the least sympathetic person he knew, he couldn't guess.

"Bah!" Geneva exclaimed as she threw up her hands. "Sensitive boy! You're not forcing them along, are you? It is only a simple invitation to aid you and Finnley."

Will dipped his head when his cheeks blushed.

"Yes, they are your friends," she went on in a slightly calmer manner. "However, you are also their friend. You worry about them just as they worry about you, so doesn't it make sense to say they will wish to protect you too?"

He considered her argument. "I suppose it's worth asking."

"Yes, it is. Their magic is useful to your endeavors, and if you do get the opportunity to return to Asteom, I believe they would take you up on that."

At those words, he recalled Clara's confession from months ago. *She sounded so distressed because she needed to keep part of herself hidden, a piece of who she is. I think Geneva is right.*

Once the pair cleaned up after breakfast, Will took his leave of his host, who packed two sacks' worth of food for him to bring along.

For the first time since he departed from the inner circle, the sun peaked out from behind the partly cloudy, almost blue sky. His first destination would be where Clara stayed, both because he trusted her to communicate more efficiently with the others and because of his personal feelings. The household she served had her acting as their front counter attendant, a task that reduced her from the skilled mage she was and drove her insane months ago when Will spoke to her for the last time before his journey north.

As soon as he stepped into the produce shop, he heard a gasp before spotting his friend at her position.

"Will, you've returned!" she practically cheered when he opened his mouth to offer a greeting.

He smiled in response.

Clara hadn't changed at all aside from re-dying her hair to a raven color, and her eyes appeared even brighter thanks to the glimmering, unshed tears they held. In a swift motion, she slid around the counter in order to meet him by wrapping her arms around his neck. When she lingered for longer than he considered normal for the friendly gesture, his arms tightened around her waist.

"I'm glad you're still doing all right," he mumbled.

"I missed you."

Her soft, gentle voice accompanied by the unexpected words caused Will's cheeks to heat up, which in turn made him thankful they were alone at the front of the building. Only when she released her grip did he break away.

"Tell me all about your assignment," she began eagerly. "What is their capital city like?"

"So Geneva told you where I was?"

Clara took a piece of her hair and twirled it around her fingers to avoid making eye contact. "A little. One way or another, everybody in town found out you had been asked to go to the inner circle to help combat a sickness spreading there. Because you were with Finn, no one seemed worried. They trust him a lot, I suppose."

Will recalled Finn's account of rescuing Geneva from across the border and figured most of the townsfolk wound up in Muld in a similar fashion. The reminder of his Nim-Valan associate led him to focus on the task at hand again.

"We can discuss my time in the capital later. Right now, I need your help."

At his change of tone, Clara's eyes widened. She nodded in response, so he proceeded to inform her of the situation in as few words as possible to save them time.

"We should leave immediately," she concluded when he finished.

Will glanced around the empty shop then at the back door where male voices conversed in tandem with the kitchen's noise. "Can you come along without causing trouble?"

If anybody tossed the light mages away when they found out about their trip to the border and the possibility of not returning to Muld, he hoped to avoid raising ill feelings in the area; however, Clara laughed at the question.

"These people are more understanding than you give them credit for. Head around town and find the others. Tell them to meet us at the eastern entrance where we won't be easily overheard."

Will contemplated this before shaking his head. "We can meet there, but I plan on utilizing the cabin Finn kept us in when we first crossed the border."

When he gave no further explanation, she accepted the notion, and the two parted for the time being.

Locating and informing the rest of the light mages took more time than Will expected because of the busy lunch hour approaching, prompting people to wander around the main road. Those familiar with him stopped to discuss his adventure to the city, which they imagined being luxurious and separated from the rest of Nim-Vala. He tried his best not to come off as rude while entering the handful of buildings hosting his friends.

Mary-Ann and Bryn had been selected together by a seamstress who taught them the technique to exploit their nimble, slim fingers. Both girls glanced up from their work, leapt over to embrace him, and agreed to go despite not hearing the entire situation. With a promise to meet the others later, they pushed him out the door. Their excitement at an opportunity to leave the northern country perplexed Will until he considered how unfitting their current lifestyles were.

I can't keep forgetting about their magic, he chastised himself. *Although I can never understand how it feels to wield energy, after years of living around mages I should know better than to assume they would accept hiding their power.*

Lissa, the youngest of their group, acted composed compared to Mary-Ann and Bryn and even slipped him a fried dough ball as he departed from the bakery where she worked. His final goal was Zelma, who ended up being taken in by a farmer and his family as an extra hand around their animals. She fed, watered, and collected the produce, which didn't sound terribly difficult, but Will assumed she received a heavier workload compared to everyone else. Despite this, she appeared the most reluctant to leave yet agreed to go with him after informing her caretakers.

Clara, Mary-Ann, and Bryn were waiting when Will arrived at the opposite end of Muld. A few minutes later, Lissa approached with red-rimmed eyes. He would have been concerned about the bakery owners reprimanding her except for the sad smile she wore.

I suppose I shouldn't be surprised they developed attachments to the townsfolk. Geneva might not be the perfect image of a sweetly grandmother or aunt, but I consider her something like that. She was kind to me and took me in as a student. It's a shame after all this time I still think of these people differently than I would anybody in Asteom.

The notion soured his mood, even after Zelma appeared. The five mages stared at him with hope shining in their eyes, so he focused his attention on their next goal.

"Once we reach the cabin, I'll explain everything," he promised.

Thankfully, they were already aware of that and kept a steady pace while he guided them into the woods beyond the fields surrounding Muld.

Test of Courage

The next day of Coura's training became a repeat of the previous afternoon until she chose to remain lying on the ground after Harriette dismissed the binding spell. She made reasonable progress before the group ate lunch, or at least enough to where Sage Vidar trusted her with casting minor, controlled spells, yet ultimately the demonic power proved too enticing to dismiss. Part of her savored how free she felt when the energy spread throughout her body, and the remainder honed in on her memories of how comfortable and confident she became while wielding that type of magic.

Only then did the Mintelian sage attempt to try another exercise.

When she began to rise again, the older man called for Rydar, who responded by approaching Coura in the sparring area. From the lone sheath hanging off his belt came a knife, and he assumed a stance afterward in preparation to fight.

She raised an eyebrow at the sage. *Real blades already?*

"I would like to test your commitment to what I am working to accomplish with you," he explained. "This seems like an appropriate time to begin shifting between spells. Treat this as a regular sparring session using only dark magic until I say to stop."

After those words, Rydar charged. Coura knew from how battered she had been when he used a wooden sword that a knife could end up deadly if she didn't act serious. Her opponent treated their match the same too, slashing for her midsection to start before swinging wide for her limbs. Despite her initial hesitation, she reached inward and triggered the demonic energy before recalling her past lessons and experiences in order to fall into form.

Coura focused on defensive maneuvers first, blocking his attacks by using a shield until the euphoria of exercising her muscles and magic led her to consider taking the offensive. Her eyes followed Rydar's movements, which allowed her to catch when he repeated an earlier tactic involving a swipe from the left, then an upward, diagonal line in the opposite direction before finishing with a downward slice to complete the triangular shape. Because she could predict the final motion, she prepared a retaliation.

As soon as his arm raised above his head, she extended her left hand toward his exposed side and released a suppressed lightning bolt. She only utilized a fraction of the power she normally expended for that spell to avoid harming Rydar; however, he still stumbled backward upon impact and landed squarely on his backside. The successful attack and what control she demonstrated prompted a smile, though it faded when her opponent jumped to his feet a second later, as if the bolt did nothing.

He must be used to dark magic or else he would be more traumatized by being struck by lightning.

The two continued their match, and she identified another opening while remaining on the defensive. This time, she countered with a fireball to send the Mintelian stumbling away. Rydar switched his fighting style after that. He created no opportunities because he quit following a pattern, making each swing unpredictable. In addition, he lunged forward whenever she crept ahead in preparation for another elemental spell, leading her to retreat.

Coura enjoyed the game they created, even after her opponent landed his first mark on her left bicep: a slice that dripped blood down her arm. To her dismay, Sage Vidar called the spar to an end immediately following Rydar's attack.

"That's enough for today," he then startled her by saying.

While Rydar cleaned off the blade on his shirt and sheathed the weapon, Coura noticed Harriette lean closer to the sage so the older man could whisper in her ear.

Why cut our session short? she wondered while ignoring the urge to groan in displeasure. *Neither of us are tired, and I didn't hurt Rydar enough to warrant a break.*

Out of nowhere, Coura got the idea to urge her partner into continuing the fight. She raised her hand and sent a minor lightning bolt across the space between them, striking the ground at his feet.

Rydar leapt backward in alarm, yet it was the sage who shouted at her in a heated tone after.

"Dismiss the demonic energy," he demanded.

She shook her head. "What happened to testing my dark magic?"

The question had been meant as a jest, though it did reflect her desire for combat. Still, Coura expected the older Mintelian to blow up on her, or at least order Harriette to cast a binding spell until she submitted; however, he moved to stand beside Rydar before facing her again.

"If you are truly willing to continue today's lesson, I will oblige you. Switch to your Yeluthian energy and heal that scratch."

He pointed to her arm where the cut's bleeding had steadily slowed, yet she wasn't inclined to do so and voiced as much.

"I've dealt with worse than this," she replied while placing a hand over the spot. "Besides, I'm becoming familiar with wielding the demonic energy again. This is good practice."

"That's not the part of this exercise I'm worried about," he countered before ordering her to use the light spell.

"What's the point of doing that now?" she asked instead of following his instructions. "You saw me heal my wounds already. Why are you being particular all of a sudden?"

Sage Vidar opened his mouth to continue the argument, closed it, and pressed his lips together in a displeased manner. A few seconds later, he extended a hand toward Rydar with the palm facing upward. The younger man evidently understood the unspoken request, for he drew his knife and offered the hilt to his master, who accepted. In the silence of the field, the sage flipped the weapon over to inspect both sides of the blade before turning and plunging the metal straight into Rydar's chest.

The strike was so fast and unexpected that Coura stood stunned until her sparring partner's body dropped to the ground where he clung to the hilt of his own weapon. Sage Vidar stood over him with an unreadable expression and met her eyes.

"Heal him."

Coura's heart dropped and her mind went numb until groans from Rydar brought her out of that state. She hurried forward, threw herself to her knees beside him, and examined the wound underneath what crimson liquid already tainted his clothes.

"Once he's taken care of, you are dismissed for the day," Sage Vidar concluded.

He walked away after those words, presumably to return to the village, though Coura didn't raise her eyes from the injured Mintelian. Her trembling hands hovered over the knife, but she couldn't bring herself to touch the weapon.

What should I do? she thought frantically. *If I remove it, he could bleed to death before I can close the wound, but I can't do anything with it there. His face is growing pale.*

Her indecisiveness cost them precious seconds, punctuated by a pained moan from Rydar. After gripping the hilt from under his hands, she yanked upward in a straight motion in order to cause the least amount of damage before dropping the weapon to the side. Then, she placed both hands over the spot, applied pressure, and focused inward on her light energy, though not before she remembered two, similar situations from her past.

A memory from years ago came to the forefront first. It had been her second encounter with an angel, one out for revenge for his slain sister. Marcus showed up to protect her in the MAA's training ground when she felt alone and afraid. In the process, he got stabbed and left to bleed out. Coura took care of their enemy, knelt at her newest friend's side, and in an image mirroring her current situation, tried to stop the bleeding by pressing her hands on his torso. That entire experience became a nightmare she had been helpless to prevent.

Come on, she cried in her mind to the Yeluthian power, which seemed to be waiting behind the demonic presence. *He's going to die!*

At that, she recalled needing to dismiss what she used earlier and did so before clinging to her light energy. The healing began, yet it proved too weak to act as efficiently as she needed. In her trance as the wound refused to close, she was reminded of her Yeluthian comrade Jerik and their encounter with Terran. The demon punctured her companion's throat right in front of her before disappearing into the Western Woods around them. No matter how much she poured into the spell, she couldn't save him on her own. Without his brother's arrival and assistance, he would have surely died.

I can't do this by myself, she realized while the scenes flashed in her head. *This is all my fault… I'm not strong enough…*

Tears slipped down her cheeks to tickle her face and distract from the healing. Absentmindedly, she rubbed her face with the back of one hand, stared down at both, and involuntarily repeated the words in her mind. Every part of her body started trembling while her short breaths reflected a sense of panic.

Hurried footsteps from nearby caused Coura to glance up in time to see Harriette throw herself to her knees on the opposite side of Rydar. The woman's hands already glowed before they fell on the wound, and within minutes she sat back to relax once she completed the spell. Meanwhile, Rydar seemed to be sleeping except for his shallow breathing.

The entire scene happened in a rush, leaving Coura to stare at Harriette in disbelief. "Is he…"

"Rydar is going to be all right," the Mintelian assured her in a voice much gentler than any time they spoke before. Even her expression as their eyes met was one of genuine kindness. "He won't stir for a while, and it might take a few days for him to recover completely, but he should be-"

A weak groan from the man in front of them startled Harriette, and she lost her composure when he cracked an eye open and attempted to sit up. Coura reached out to assist him even as Harriette put her hands on his shoulders.

"What are you doing?" the woman asked with none of the compassion from earlier. "Rydar, you must rest!"

Even against the protest, he managed to rise, though it cost him, as displayed by his panting and sweat-coated face. "Stop it, Harriette."

"You mustn't push yourself!"

"I'll be fine," he replied while giving her a crooked smile. After, he turned to glance at Coura, who dropped her eyes to avoid his.

He almost died because of me, she reminded herself. The same had been true for Marcus and Jerik in both memories. *He has every reason to hate me*.

"I would like to wash off in the stream," he said to Harriette instead of confronting Coura. "Can you help me stand?"

The Mintelian woman appeared displeased with the request, yet she agreed. "I won't be able to carry you by myself," she added.

Both heads looked toward Coura.

"It's the least I can do," she muttered in response to show how ashamed she felt of her behavior.

Harriette secured one of Rydar's arms around her shoulders while Coura did the same with the other so he could lean on them as they walked in the direction of the stream. Instead of going to the pool possessing the bath items, they stopped short of it in order to avoid tainting the cleaner space used by everybody else. Rydar refused to remove any clothing besides his shirt in the presence of the women, so they kept quiet before placing him in the shallowest part, allowing the moving water to pass over him.

Both Harriette and Coura scrubbed the dried blood off their hands before the former left to fetch towels and clean clothing for Rydar. When she returned, they helped dress him, then the three sat on the sandy bank as the sun began to set.

No one spoke at first; however, Rydar soon addressed Coura, dragging her away from her depressed mindset.

"Where did you learn to fight like that?"

"I started at the Magical Arts Academy and moved to Verona to train in their army," she replied halfheartedly.

"No wonder you move so fluidly."

She dared a glance at the man and found him staring across the water with a slight smile, as if he were remembering a pleasant memory. "What about you?"

"Everything I learned came from my father. We used to live in Lyrt before my mother died."

When he didn't go on, Coura prepared to drop the subject until Harriette chuckled.

"Rydar has been the only trained fighter here for years."

"That must be why nobody is used to seeing someone with bruises and injuries," Coura added without considering how the pair would respond.

The Mintelians shared an unreadable look before Rydar sighed and spoke again.

"The people moved here to live free from stress, even the potential for it. In the mountains, their problems are simple things, like whether they will get enough rain for their crops or if they should kill the chicken that stopped laying eggs. It's a basic way of life, which is exactly what they desire."

Coura couldn't help herself from raising an eyebrow at him. "They, not you?"

He appeared surprised by her question, as if he didn't realize what he revealed, then shook his head.

"You must remember, people venture to the Mintelian villages for healing as well, not just to make a quiet living," Harriette commented from Rydar's other side.

"Most of us end up staying, though," he added.

Coura's curiosity grew when they didn't expand on their reasons for serving the sage, yet she didn't feel like pressing for answers. *It's their business. I have no right to intrude. Still, there's something I need to know if I plan on remaining here.*

"I'm not going to pretend I enjoy being pushed around by Sage Vidar," she prefaced to draw their attention again. "If it helps me in the end, I'm willing to tough it out; however, I won't allow him to hurt innocent people. I'm not following someone who thinks he's above ending another person's life for the sake of teaching me a lesson."

A pause stretched between them before Harriette replied.

"I felt the same when I first began serving Master Vidar. Even so, I cannot hold him responsible for what happened today, or for any of his actions."

"Why not?" Coura asked without hiding her bitterness.

"The results are not only worth more than the means but also stem from an individual's choices. He is merely a guide. Hopefully, you can understand that one day."

How can she refer to herself and Rydar as disposable? It sounds like they're willing to give everything for the sage's methods.

As if reading her thoughts, Rydar shared his input next. "When somebody cares to learn about your life, view the darkness in your soul, and still find a person worth rescuing, it changes your perspective."

Coura bit her tongue to keep from continuing the conversation despite her impulse to do so. She realized how sensitive the subject was for the pair, and the man's words resonated with her shortly after.

"By the way, don't worry about me," he said to break the silence. "I would never hold you responsible for Sage Vidar's decisions. Harriette and I serve him with the knowledge that our lives belong to him."

The Mintelian woman peeked around to offer a smile. "He's right. We don't expect you to agree, but it's true. If we can contribute to your healing and the strengthening of your resolve, it will be worth the risks."

Coura's cheeks heated into a blush as a fluttering sensation rose in her chest. "Thank you," she felt compelled to say. "You're both so selfless."

By that point, the sunlight faded enough to signal dinnertime, so the trio moved to the meal area and ate together before breaking apart. Coura finished her chores with a new sense of assurance while reflecting on the day. Then, she returned to her tent to rest.

Despite what took place, Rydar's injury forced me to switch from the demonic power to the Yeluthian energy under pressure. That just shows how much effort I must put into keeping a grip on my mentality and not becoming overwhelmed by my emotions.

Before she let her mind relax, Coura vowed to trust Sage Vidar's direction without complaining while reigning in her reactions to wielding the various types of magic.

***

"Are you sure about this?"

Byron glanced over his shoulder to where Cintra sat at the table nearest to the inn's entrance. Although she could walk for a short time with crutches, standing created pain in her lower back where the initial wound had been, so he ordered her to remain seated while he watched for their ride.

"Not this again," he chided with a smile as he moved to kneel beside her and take her hands in his. "I would tell you if I didn't agree with our decision."

He wasn't convinced by her resulting frown, but he dropped the subject when she didn't continue.

The pair stayed awake later than normal the night before and discussed the journey to East Hoover with Clearshot, as they had done on numerous occasions since Byron agreed. He believed his friend Symon would welcome them with open arms and uphold the authority as headmaster to find positions for him and his friend, thus allowing him to officially retire as the MAA's representative.

To his dismay, Aaron and the king's council weren't behaving as sympathetically as he hoped. The group sent Lydia to him with a message, one demanding he return to the meetings and explain his behavior; however, Byron had already accepted his future at that point. His apprentice voiced her disapproval as well, even after he handed her his resignation letter. From then on, he stayed with Cintra and only returned to pack his belongings for the trip.

All I want right now is to wipe the slate clean, for Cintra's sake, he continued to tell himself whenever he considered remaining in the capital. *She needs me, and I owe it to her after the incident.*

Still, his partner didn't seem as keen on his plan.

"You aren't abandoning the people here, right?" she asked multiple times over last two weeks.

"They should learn to manage without me. Besides, my protege has been filling in for me and is doing fine."

"Clearshot said you stopped attending their meetings. Why is that?"

"Cintra, please…"

"It's not like you to give up on others."

Byron had pushed aside the comment and kissed her forehead. "I'm not giving up on *you*. This is what we imagined our future would look like. We have the opportunity to live away from the dangers surrounding Verona, and my duties won't get in the way of our time together. I can even ask the master light mages to look at you and test if they can repair the damage to your body. They're more skilled than anyone in the palace."

"I don't want you to regret this decision."

"Don't worry about me," he had answered and repeated as he knelt in front of her. "The carriage should be here soon."

Clearshot handled the details of their transportation, at his own request, so Byron didn't pry. He figured his friend would use some of the funds from Emilea's family to purchase or rent what they needed, and he planned to pay the man for that later. He also expected Clearshot to visit his children at least once before the trio finally moved, which led to a month's wait for Byron and Cintra.

At long last, we can put the past behind us, he reflected and returned to staring out at the empty street.

A few minutes later, the promised carriage rolled in front of the inn with a filly pulling the cart and a coachman holding the reins. Byron stepped outside to wave at the older man while Clearshot exited to greet them.

"Not too shabby," his friend commented and offered a smile, though any Byron saw were mere shadows of his former, playful grins. "Are we ready?"

"I'll fetch our bags," Byron replied before returning to the inn's lobby, holding the door open for Cintra to hobble through, and retrieving the four packs they decided to bring. Neither seemed to possess much they deemed valuable or important enough to need, and he promised to take her through East Hoover to purchase additional clothing, personal items, or trinkets for their new home.

Clearshot helped Cintra into the carriage, then he and Byron arranged the bags with the rest of Clearshot's belongings.

"I visited Mace and Lexie after our last conversation," the man began without removing his eyes from his work. "They agreed it would be best for me to live near the academy."

Even though his friend acted indifferent, the news startled Byron. He prepared to inquire about their responses to learning of Emilea's death; however, he realized the questions would be insensitive and dismissed his curiosity.

"These other packs must be some of their belongings," he said instead.

To his relief, his comment seemed to ease a nervous tension hanging between the two, and they faced each other after completing the preparations. Clearshot patted one of the bundles before meeting Byron's eyes.

"They each provided me with a list of items they left at the house when they moved to the academy. I like to think they aren't holding back, but part of me wonders if they plan on returning the next time they're in the area. Emilea's relatives are the type to hold onto the children's belongings. If it's not to avoid disposing of somebody else's valuables, then I imagine it will entice them to visit."

Byron chuckled at the remark before pointing at the carriage door. "We can continue this discussion on the road."

His friend nodded, prompting the two to join Cintra before the coachman started them on their journey. A few minutes later, he noticed her staring out the nearest window with an unreadable gaze, so he took her hand in his, drawing her gemlike eyes.

"Are you ready?" he asked with a smile that contradicted the sense of impatience he attempted to conceal.

Her resulting nod didn't ease his spirits as much as he would have expected it to.

Part Two

Crossing the Border

As unfamiliar as the land to the south of Muld remained, Will and the light mages managed to keep heading toward Asteom in order to find the border. They agreed to cross together then locate the troops who would be able to deliver the message about Advisor Lupin. Whether or not he actually was a demon, possessed by one, or acting as a dark mage in the northern country, Aaron and his council could use the warning going forward. The only piece of information Will purposefully neglected to share with Clara and the others involved his intent to return to Nim-Vala once they fulfilled their duty.

I made a promise to Yukin, he told himself while remembering Finn's assignment and dual role. *His mission is already dangerous, and magic will complicate the matter. It always does.*

"Aren't you hungry?"

Will shook his head to dismiss the thought before accepting the chunk of bread Lissa held out to him. Before their group set out, the youngest of the mages revealed a bag full of baked products gifted to them by her host. With what Geneva gave him too, they wouldn't go hungry for a few days. He thanked his friend before tearing off a mouthful of the stale loaf. After the first night, they collectively decided against starting a fire in order to avoid distractions that might cause anybody nearby to notice them. It made sleeping at night uncomfortable, but they could handle being chilled until they reached Asteom.

"You better hurry and eat," Bryn warned him as she rose to glance upward at the sky. "The sunlight is fading fast. If we don't leave soon, there won't be enough to scout ahead."

At the reminder, Will jumped to his feet. "I can eat and walk."

She raised an eyebrow with an unamused expression but said no more.

The two were responsible for checking the perimeter that evening and did so without fuss until they trekked south. It was then the air grew thick with the scent of smoke, prompting the pair to pause their steps.

"It's not much farther," Will noted, though his stomach began to twist from his nerves.

Bryn leaned closer to speak at a lower volume. "Could it be an enemy camp, or perhaps from Asteom?"

"Most likely the former. Remember how many days passed until we reached Muld? We should still have at least three to go, and as far as I know, Asteom hasn't encroached on Nim-Valan land."

"What should we do?" the light mage asked in a wavering voice.

Will peered into the trees ahead to no avail. *Either we attempt to circle around the camp or wait until they move on. The problem is there's no telling how established they are in their location without snooping.*

"Stay here," he instructed while steeling his nerves. "I'm going to see if I can gain any information from exploring in that direction."

She grabbed his arm, frowned, then released it and dropped her gaze. "I don't *want* to let you go, especially alone, but I understand. Please be careful! Clara will kill me if I let anything happen to you."

"I will," he answered despite her additional comment startling him a bit.

Although he felt like a fool, he crept forward until he could no longer spot his partner. The gravity of his decision weighed on his shoulders as he neared the next area. What voices he could discern spoke in the Nim-Valan language, which already helped distinguish the strangers, and metal clattered every so often to signal they wore armor.

Will waited to debate whether or not he should pursue additional details before pulling his hood over his head. *If I can hear their conversations, I might find useful-*

A noise, just the brush of leaves, sent a jolt through his body. Seconds later, someone grabbed his shoulder and yanked it backward to spin him around. Before Will could make a sound, whoever found him pressed a hand against his mouth, leaving him to stare at the cloaked figure.

"What are you *doing* here?" came a familiar voice, though the question had been growled through clenched teeth.

The hand lowered, so Will ventured a peek under the other's hood. "Finn? Is that you?"

"We don't have time for a reunion."

Those words confirmed his suspicion, raising his spirits even as the Nim-Valan seized his arm to lead him away. "I can't believe-"

"You have a *lot* of explaining to do," his friend interrupted.

Will had never seen the spy this livid, so he remained quiet until they moved far enough to speak at a normal volume. In the back of his mind, he wondered if he should search for Bryn since she would be nearer to their camp than he and Finn were.

"I'm glad I found you," he admitted with a weak smile to show his disbelief once the grip on his arm released.

"You should be. Did you realize you stood within their scouts' range? If somebody had been at that point on their route, they would have discovered you."

Will's face fell before his cheeks flushed. "I didn't know I was that close."

"Obviously." Finn upheld his disappointed glare as the silence between the two stretched. "Will, why are you here?"

"Yukin and Elena sent me," he admitted.

From the way the Nim-Valan's eyes slowly widened, he either wasn't expecting news from the inner circle, realized how serious the matter was if his masters asked Will to find him, or both.

"I'm guessing you didn't come alone?" Finn asked next after reflecting on the situation.

Will shook his head. "The mages you rescued with me are back at our camp."

"We should return to them to discuss our next steps in a safer location."

The two soon found Bryn pacing where Will had left her. At first, she seemed relieved when she learned Finn was the stranger; however, his grim expression stopped her from questioning his previous whereabouts. The others behaved similarly upon the trio's return.

After accepting his share of food, the Nim-Valan listened while Will recounted the discovery of Lupin's identity as a dark mage, Yukin and Elena's decision to send a messenger to the border, and finally the group's intent to cross into Asteom and warn their leaders of the potential danger. Judging by Finn's lack of an immediate response, Will sensed the spy's mixture of emotions.

"What I can tell you is that there's already conflict along the border," the Nim-Valan shared while glancing over each person in their circle.

One of the girls gasped, yet nobody interrupted with an outburst.

"It hasn't spread far enough south to cause major trouble for either side," he added as a bit of reassurance. "What I have been able to tell is the Nim-Valan troops secured the border at various locations and are encroaching to settle in the nearby towns. There, they appear to be waiting because their scouts are searching in every direction."

"Could they be waiting for reinforcements?" Mary-Ann asked during the following pause.

"Based on what I overheard and the lack of soldiers moving south, I doubt it."

"Then, what could it be?" Will pressed. During his work with Finn over the months, he picked up on the man's preference for thoroughly considering a situation instead of discussing the issue aloud. This meant if anyone else longed to hear his thoughts, he needed to become aware of their interest.

"The worst scenario is they have inside help, most likely in Verona, and are expecting to attack on cue. I can't predict the conflict ending well for either country though. It would take a major distraction to draw away the Asteom troops already positioned to block the Nim-Valans from marching farther south."

"What's the best scenario?"

"They're intimidated by the defense and are debating whether to retreat or follow through with their orders, whatever those may be," Finn answered with a humorless smile.

Zelma cleared her throat. "In any case, what you're hinting at is that it's impossible to cross the border now."

Will noticed the downcast expressions around the circle and tried not to show his own disappointment. *I suggested this. I gave them the idea and made it seem as though this would be when we finally return to Asteom together.*

"Not impossible, per say," Finn commented while rubbing his chin. He appeared to be contemplating the method, but his words already piqued their interest.

"What do you mean?" Clara asked.

"At this point, crossing the border isn't the problem."

When he didn't elaborate, Will realized what the Nim-Valan hinted at. "You've been doing that recently, haven't you?"

Finn stared at him and nodded but didn't appear surprised Will pointed it out.

"Then, what's the problem? Are the troops planting traps or monitoring the entire area?"

"No. Actually, the Nim-Valan soldiers are the least of my problems. It's Asteom's troops."

Will's eyebrows rose in alarm, and his friends appeared just as perplexed; however, the spy went on before they could grow too concerned.

"I memorized the routes for the scouts in each Nim-Valan camp and slipped around when I could until I reached Asteom's main camp led by a general and his assistant. Unfortunately, my appearance doesn't suggest I'm trustworthy. Their scouts claim I could be tied up and gagged until their leader has time to talk. Otherwise, I'm…"

"A spy for Nim-Vala?" Lissa finished and was rewarded with an unamused glance from Finn.

"To put it in plain terms, yes. I focused my attention on searching for the king's advisor instead since I heard rumors regarding his return. At the moment, I'm empty-handed."

"That's probably for the best," Bryn added after a moment with her arms crossed. "If this Lupin really is using demonic magic, you wouldn't recognize it."

Even in the darkness, Will noticed Clara point at Finn.

"Can we go back to what you mentioned earlier?" she demanded. "You found a way to reach Asteom's troops across the border, but they rejected you. What if we accompany you?"

Finn grunted. "That was going to be my suggestion. If somebody recognizes any of you, or at least your names, then they should be willing to allow you into their camp."

"I'm sure they could use the additional healers," Mary-Ann muttered loudly enough for everyone to hear.

"We can tell them about Lupin," Will concluded while meeting Finn's eyes.

The Nim-Valan dipped his head in confirmation, reinvigorating their group's spirits.

*

Sneaking around the Nim-Valan camps proved to be less thrilling than Will imagined, though this was positive news. Because of the layout, overlapping gaps or entire trails remained unsupervised, so they could follow without concern. He became impressed by Finn's observant nature as the man led them south until they found a spot to rest for the evening.

It must have taken him days of simply hiding and stalking the scouts in order to figure out what paths are available. No wonder he never seemed bored at Yukin's estate; this level of methodical observation doesn't allow him to be impatient.

Their group faced a couple close calls where the Nim-Valan spy held out a hand for them to stop moving and pressed a finger to his lips in a gesture for them to be silent; however, nothing came for them from the trees, so they continued on. Will didn't keep track of the distance, so after another day of straight hiking, he was startled when Finn circled their group up again and stopped for the evening.

"The Asteom scouts I encountered search the area ahead. We can either go over there so they notice us or wait until morning."

We're already across the border? Will wondered, both awestruck by their pace and disappointed by his inability to tell when he entered his home country.

154

Either due to the longing to sit around a fire with warm food or be surrounded by armed soldiers for protection, their decision seemed unanimous.

"Let's go meet them now," Clara announced on behalf of the light mages.

When she looked at Will, he nodded to express his agreement.

"Fine. I suggest one of you act as the spokesperson. They might interrogate each of us separately, so be honest." Finn crossed his arms with a gaze toward their goal.

Will lingered with him at the rear of the group when the rest continued forward with the intent to inquire about what would happen to the Nim-Valan once they reached the camp. When he couldn't find the appropriate words, he decided to abandon the attempt.

A shout in warning from farther ahead alerted them of the scouts and halted their steps. Two men wielding bows with nocked arrows crept forward: one from the trail they followed and another from the bushes off to their right. When the first demanded they identify themselves and their business, Clara stepped closer to begin recounting their tale. At the mention of missing light mages from General Casner's company, the bows lowered.

"You can't be serious," the man from the bushes muttered in disbelief. "That happened over a year ago. Where have you been hiding since then?"

"We escaped to a town across the border named Muld and remained with their people because of the fighting," she explained. "The Nim-Valan man with us is a spy from Asteom. When he learned about our situation, he decided to help us reach your camp."

Will glanced at Finn with concern since his secret had been revealed, yet he only saw the usual mask of indifference.

The scouts huddled together to discuss what to do in hushed voices before facing the group once more.

"Nim-Valan, are you the same person we sent away a few days ago?"

"I am," Finn answered without hesitation.

"Is what this woman says true?"

Will heard a displeased huff from Clara as the scouts dismissed her and her title while Finn answered.

"The light mage is correct about my loyalties and their journey across the border. They seek refuge in your camp while I wish to discuss the situation with your general."

The first soldier released a groan while the second rubbed the back of his neck, giving Will the impression they weren't certain what they should do.

"If you need additional proof, bring Assistant General Marcus here," he offered without fully committing to speaking up. "He was with the general when the enemy attacked our camp and can vouch for us."

"Assistant General Marcus?" the scout from the bushes replied with wide eyes. "He's been in Dala for months."

Will's mouth hung open while he tried to come up with another solution; however, his friend's name already earned them some credibility.

"He's right about that," the first scout explained to his partner before elaborating. "I traveled with the company when we set out for the fort in Nim-Vala. After the ambush and upon our return, we found no evidence to prove anybody escaped the attack at our camp. General Casner ordered us to return to the capital then."

"Ambush!" Bryn exclaimed, causing the man to nod.

"It was a trap from the start," he admitted while lowering his eyes to emphasize their past troubles.

Their group fell silent for a few seconds, yet the second soldier gestured for them to go along.

"The least we can do is offer you a chance to present yourselves to the general. I'll lead the way, but if you try anything funny, you'll regret it."

As they followed behind the man, his partner remained behind to continue the scouting duties.

*

Entering the soldiers' camp brought Will back to the horrific night when he, Clara, and the rest of the light mages watched the Nim-Valan barbarians slaughter their friends and comrades. He remembered the lone stranger's ability to destroy the remaining mages' shielding spell and felt his stomach knot.

I was so close, he thought while recalling his encounter with the king's advisor. *The man who ordered the attack walked right in front of me…*

Fortunately, the camp thrusted him into enough activity to keep his mind away from the unpleasant subject. The troops eyed their group suspiciously until a middle-aged woman recognized the missing mages and dropped what she had been doing in order to hurry over and embrace Bryn and Zelma while crying out their names. Will believed she was a fellow mage based on her behavior and familiarity with each, and this sparked more interest. He found himself offered handshakes or experiencing claps on the back by soldiers who apparently remembered him, or at least understood who he was, until General Casner stormed into the mix to demand what was going on. He listened without a hint of emotion, nodded once Clara finished explaining, then ordered everybody except Finn to find seats around a fire and eat before resting. The evening became filled with warmth from the fire, decent food, and plenty of company as questions and gossip began tying their absence to the current events in Asteom.

Will didn't see the spy before he fell asleep nor the following morning while the group ate breakfast and discussed their next steps.

"Now that the excitement is over, what should we do?" Zelma asked to initiate the conversation.

He hadn't considered that until he woke and found he didn't want to abandon what he'd become invested in. Evidently, Clara felt the same.

"Each one of us is free to return to the capital," she began and met every single set of eyes before landing on Will. "I don't blame you if you do, given what we went through, but I'm going to request a position here under General Casner."

If her response surprised anybody, they didn't show it.

"I'm staying too," Mary-Ann added, then Lissa.

Bryn laughed at their eagerness and shook her head yet copied the statement before Zelma did too.

Will's lips curved into a smile at their shared dedication. "I don't feel too silly now for hoping to remain here."

The young women beamed at him to show their amusement, which spurred a blush, and they agreed to visit the general. Along the way, they caught Finn being escorted across the camp by two soldiers. Will wondered what the Nim-Valan would do and broke away from his companions.

"I'll catch up," he told the mages with a wave before jogging over to the spy.

Neither soldier appeared bothered by Will stopping their walk, though Finn gave off the faintest hint he would prefer to keep moving.

"What's going on?" Will asked after nodding to the other men.

"What does it look like?" Finn countered in a neutral tone.

"You're not leaving so soon, are you?"

"I must. There are those across the border who need my update."

At the thought of the Nim-Valan returning to the northern country, Will bit his lip. The sinking sensation he experienced was one he had felt in the past when his friends would go off on their own, making him realize just how much he valued their relationship.

"What did General Casner say? Did you share what we know about-"

"Yes," Finn interrupted. "He is aware of our common enemy and the suspicions Asteom has. I would imagine he plans on informing you and your companions if you wish to stay."

Will couldn't think of anything else to say. *I can't keep him from his responsibilities to Elena or Yukin. I don't know what I expected to hear, but seeing him go off alone reminds me we live in two, separate worlds despite his allegiance to Asteom.*

"I understand," he replied before stepping aside. "Thank you for everything."

He expected Finn to walk away without a word, as was the man's nature, yet the Nim-Valan surprised him by placing a hand on his shoulder.

"I should be thanking you. You put your life in danger to save Yukin and countless others without owing them a reason or demanding anything in return except to have your friends guided home. I had almost forgotten what true kindheartedness is until we met."

The compliment hung between them for a moment, then Finn's hand dropped before he turned away. Will internally preserved the words while addressing the Nim-Valan one, final time.

"I'll wait here until you need me again. Just try to stay safe."

Finn looked over his shoulder with a genuine smile to express his confirmation.

A Thief's Prize

Grace didn't know what to expect from Dianne based on the woman's previous explanation regarding the capital city's underground market; however, as the days turned into weeks, she wondered if she should restrain the sense of hope that kept her optimistic.

Her uncle never returned with additional information or another request, and she heard nothing from Aaron or anybody else about the ancestral weapons, leading her to believe the council had no luck locating the items. Despite the lack of updates, Grace began to imagine herself as the hero who found a golden sword and presented it to her friend with Dianne at her side. She even considered using the weapon as a gift before proposing her idea of an arranged marriage, which still lingered in her mind.

The humans could use a boost in morale, especially before a war with Nim-Vala, she told herself to justify her decision to continue pushing for a way to strengthen the alliance while preventing herself from being hauled back to Yeluthia. *Part of me wishes their people were actually behind the attack in the palace, if only to motivate Asteom's citizens toward the same cause. Still, I am being selfish. I could never forgive myself for spurring trouble when Aaron and plenty of others are working to resolve multiple issues and better the kingdom.*

One afternoon about a month after Grace last ventured into the city, she contemplated bringing up the subject to King Arval until a loud knocking at her door caused her to nearly jump out of her chair near the window.

"Come in," she called while recovering and rising to brush down her lavender-colored sundress.

The door swung open to reveal Dianne, who looked normal except for an eager expression sharpening her features. "Lady ambassador, do you have a moment to talk?"

At first, Grace didn't understand the urgency, but she nodded and tilted her head. "What is it, Dianne?"

"It's about the underground market," her guard hurried to explain after closing the door. "I found out when it's going to be taking place and where."

The news spurred a gasp from Grace before her lips stretched into an enthusiastic grin. "That is wonderful! Will it be soon? Is it somewhere we can access? What should we wear to-"

"Let me explain," Dianne cut in before chuckling at her excitement. "The friends I mentioned living on the eastern main road started digging for information after my last visit. By that point, we needed to wait for the next new moon anyway. I've been to see them several times since then, and they finally got a lead.

A series of houses line the farthest end of an alley off the main road and lead into a basement that must have been built during Verona's founding. I heard the directions and code word they'll use for entry, though my contact didn't know what lies beyond. I'd guess the people will set up tables or spots and showcase their wares like normal, but the validity and legitimacy of the items is where there can be trouble. I also can't imagine they allow potential customers to bring weapons inside."

"We should take precautions then," Grace added as she considered the situation. When the following pause stretched long enough for her to notice, she glanced up to find her guard frowning with crossed arms.

"My lady, you don't honestly expect to join me."

"Why not?"

Dianne released a begrudged sigh. "I wonder if you forget you're the ambassador for Yeluthia sometimes. If anything happened to you…"

"My life is no more valuable than yours or anybody else's," Grace stated matter-of-factly. "I also do not plan on revealing my identity. The disguise I used before seemed to work just fine."

"That was around ordinary citizens. These people are slimy lowlifes who will attempt to swindle us, steal from us, or harm us if we look at them funny."

"You forget about my goddess gift. I can act oblivious or stare at the floor the entire time while scanning those in attendance for information relating to the ancestral weapons. That should be just as useful as observing the wares on display."

The woman contemplated that information before shaking her head and placing a hand on her chest. "My career is on the line! I'm sorry, but I can't take that risk."

Although she longed to argue for her competence, Grace forced herself to consider the soldier's side of the approach. *She will be distracted because of her obligation to protect me, regardless of what does or does not take place.*

"I trust you will fulfill your duty as my guardian," she began a minute later when she put together her thoughts. "Believe me when I say I do not wish to go along simply to observe or because I assume you need assistance. My value is as a mage, specifically one with a unique ability which will benefit our cause. That is why I wish to join you."

She fully expected Dianne to dismiss the notion again, though she hoped for a better outcome. When the soldier didn't respond right away, she raised an eyebrow.

"I want to let you come along, but my gut is telling me this may cause trouble," her guard admitted with obvious reluctance.

In a final attempt to get through to the woman, Grace utilized her past experiences. "I witnessed the attack on the capital and faced the former high priest beside the master mages. Although I may not possess the combat skills of a soldier, I am a trained light mage. If my goddess gift does not protect us, you can rely on my magic."

"That does make me feel better." Dianne paused for a moment while looking Grace over with a critical eye. "You'll be under my authority then, which means you follow my orders."

Grace beamed while nodding. "Of course!"

"I'm serious," the woman warned, though the tension hanging in the air dissipated when she physically relaxed. "The new moon is in two days. We should plan our approach, discuss the expectations, and prepare for the worst."

"I agree!" Grace cleared her throat when Dianne shot her an unamused look, presumably due to her lingering enthusiasm. "I will let you lead and offer suggestions."

"Fine, now let's start with assessing the location…"

*

"I sense dozens of individual presences below the building, just as you said." Grace opened her eyes after retracting her mind before glancing at Dianne, who stood off to the right.

The pair agreed to scout the area before wandering into what could be an empty building or a trap, which led them to their current hiding place in one of the shadowy alleys nearby. Each draped a cloak over their shoulders, though the soldier recommended they leave the hoods down to avoid drawing attention to themselves, and their clothing consisted of ordinary, dark-colored shirts, pants, and boots.

"If anybody suggests we're involved with the palace, you can bet they'll throw us out," Dianne warned that afternoon while dying Grace's hair black using an ink-like substance. "That would be the best case scenario too."

To the woman's credit, she had meticulously planned each step of the evening. Grace didn't know where her guard procured the ordinary clothing, cloaks, or hair dye, but she refused to question or doubt her partner. The two snuck out through the training ground as soon as the sun set and after they reviewed how they would be behaving.

I must not look at or speak to anyone, Grace reminded herself while waiting for Dianne to signal when it was time to move. *My job is to scan the minds of those present and let her know if I overhear details relating to the ancestral weapons.*

For as dangerous as the entire situation seemed, she found she grew anxious instead of afraid. Part of this related to her reasoning involving supporting her uncle, Aaron, and the kingdoms; however, her confidence had increased over the years, making her realize how much she matured since she departed from Yeluthia.

I became a victim, know what it is like to be helpless, and let fear overwhelm me before understanding how my power can not only protect myself but also aid others. I developed the necessary skills, so my weaknesses stem from my mentality.

"We can go now," her guard whispered to bring her mind back to their goal.

Both straightened before Grace followed closely behind the disguised soldier as the woman wove through another alleyway until they halted in front of an ordinary-looking door. Dianne knocked twice, then the wood cracked open enough for them to hear the man on the opposite side without seeing him.

"Dinner's begun," the stranger informed them in an expressionless tone. "What have you brought for the feast?"

"An herb-stuffed duck and four plums," Dianne replied in the same manner.

Grace assumed their exchange had to do with the secret code her guard mentioned, which proved true when the man opened the door wider so they could slip inside.

Even in the dim light of an oil lamp hanging behind him, she noted his stocky frame and how neither she nor Dianne would be able to resist him for long should he attack. Fortunately, he acted more professional than she gave him credit for.

First, he asked for their weapons, so they removed what they carried without issue. The soldier told Grace they would appear suspicious for not possessing them despite assuming they would need to turn the items over upon entry. She didn't quite understand, but she agreed to do so. After, the man claimed he need to search their bodies for hidden weapons. Grace noticed Dianne frown and grew nervous at the thought of a stranger placing his hands on her, yet he merely patted their sides, arms, and legs without suggesting he held additional motives.

"If you're caught with what I didn't collect, you'll be punished," he added while pointing a thumb toward the lone hallway beyond the door. "The same goes for misbehavior or stealing. We take the side of the sellers, so remember that if you plan on bargaining."

Grace kept her eyes on Dianne and went along when the woman continued forward without offering a response. She wondered what her partner thought about the place and if the cool persona reflected worry.

The lamps at even intervals remained the only objects in the stone hallway, and the pair soon reached a descending set of stairs. From it came a chorus of voices to signal their destination. Each step they took gradually revealed light and noise until they reached the bottom. Then, Grace's anxiousness spiked.

There must be hundreds of people down here, she realized before testing the space with her mind.

While she did so, Dianne led her past a second, bulky man monitoring the stairs and a third blocking a doorway. He sidestepped to let them pass; then, Grace didn't need to use her goddess gift to comprehend the amount of guests.

The basement area stretched farther than she expected, easily underneath the houses of that district, and dozens of bodies occupied any open room. In an odd way, what she saw reminded her of the festivals in Verona with merchants huddled behind tables or crouching over blankets holding their wares, which ranged from the expected trinkets and weapons to clothing, pouches or vials of powders and liquids, and even caged animals. Their customers spoke in hushed voices, and all wore some sort of cloak or wrap around their heads to prevent others from identifying them.

As if in response to this observation, Dianne casually pulled her hood over her face, prompting Grace to do the same a second later.

I need to avoid staring or making eye contact with these people.

The reminder seemed simpler to repeat in her head than to put into practice, especially when they began walking around and perusing the selections. Many of the people stood alone or smoked from pipes in a circle, filling the air with a haze that made Grace long to cough, though she refrained from doing so. The foul scent of dirt and sweat also mixed with the atmosphere, which grew worse because of how everyone pressed together in the closed space. At the far end of the area, several tents had been lined up, and strangers sulked with their faces covered while holding up various items for sale.

Grace grimaced from underneath her hood at the scene. *This place is like a rats' nest. I cannot imagine accepting a life like this, though I am sure plenty of people have no choice.*

Because she kept her head down to avoid tempting somebody into interacting with her, she focused her attention on Dianne's feet in front of her. The two didn't enter so close together; however, as they crossed from one section to another, she began to lessen the distance due to the humans who would bump into or brush against them. This also made her thankful she had been advised against bringing any belongings or money since she didn't doubt the likelihood of thieves wandering amid the group.

The pair also dealt with men and women who peddled items in their faces or stood in their way to showcase different products. To Dianne credit, she never acted bothered by the interruptions and even went so far as to touch or hold the objects before dismissing the individuals with a grunt. If anybody looked at Grace, she never noticed since she averted her eyes.

As the evening wore on, she grew uncomfortable in the toxic environment and considered letting Dianne know. Physically, her boundaries had been crossed from the beginning, yet mentally she began losing her patience.

According to her plan, we should be stopping for a few minutes at a time so I can scan the area, Grace recalled after holding her temper when a man unintentionally stepped on her foot before stomping away. *I only hope we get lucky and locate a weapon right away. The air is becoming too much to tolerate.*

Their next break came when Dianne approached a weapons dealer and began looking over the items on display. The soldier had inquired multiple times about decorative swords, daggers, or bows after they entered to no avail and plenty of snickering, seemingly at the ridiculousness of the question.

Meanwhile, Grace got to work. Like a breeze floating through the smoke and stink, she triggered her goddess gift and let her mind drift throughout the space, focusing on that particular corner for the time being. Each person's thoughts echoed around her, though softly enough not to overwhelm her own presence.

Too many voices are crowding this place, just like I expected, she reflected. *Perhaps a bit of prodding may yield more fruitful results, and at a faster rate*.

Only on one other occasion did she ever utilize her gift in such a way. During her time with the Dalan troops when they struggled to fight the possessed Nim-Valans years ago, she located Will's contact in Verona by whispering a word or two to the citizens in order to listen for a reaction that would reveal their familiarity with her friend. At the moment, she did the same, though at a much slower pace due to the amount of bodies crammed together.

Both she and Dianne found no success for a while, so they continued to blend in and stop wherever the soldier deemed appropriate. Grace repeated the process and noted only mild confusion at her quiet voice in their heads or no sort of acknowledgement. The hour grew late, which she felt despite the lack of any means to gauge the time, and she wondered how long the event lasted.

Dianne halted beside a tent where a frail man possessing a shabby, unkempt beard tested a short spear by swinging it dangerously close to his gathering of onlookers. For a minute, Grace watched too with concern for their safety before forcing herself to try using her goddess gift again.

Golden weapon... Gold sword... Gold dagger... Gold bow...

The words rang like a chant while her presence slipped over dozens of minds at once. Suddenly, a jolt of fright froze her in place, as if the source had pierced her with an arrow.

{*Who found out?*}

Grace's shock at the panic that struck her turned into hope. She hurried to trace the link, opened her eyes, and reached over to tug on Dianne's cloak without revealing her excitement. In response, her guard leaned over so she could share the directions in as casual a manner as she could muster. The pair lingered where they stood for another minute or two before heading straight for their target.

It took a couple extra pauses for Grace to identify the individual clearly, though she only listened for their voice instead of pushing with words. Once they reached him, the two spent a moment surveying the stranger and his wares.

The man appeared identical to most of who they saw considering he donned a worn, brown cloak, waved a hand at the weapons on his table, and loudly chattered to anybody who passed by. Nothing suggested he felt afraid of being addressed, so Dianne approached to inspect the items.

"What fine ladies to bless me with their presence!" he exclaimed while taking notice of them. In a single, sweeping motion, he gestured at what metal he had on display. "My selection is fitting for the king himself! Go on and pick one up if you don't believe me."

Grace longed to glance up at the man in order to assess his features but thought better of it. *A weasel in human skin. I am not a blacksmith, but I know he is lying.*

Each blade looked dull, and several bore chips to reveal their past, but Dianne humored the man by giving each a thorough inspection. Grace didn't bother touching them, instead remaining attentive of their surroundings.

"These are all worthy of the soldiers in Asteom's army," Dianne commented without sounding as facetious as Grace knew the woman would otherwise express. "Unfortunately, it's not what I'm searching for."

In a move that startled Grace, the woman turned to begin walking away. Before she could question her guard's motives for abandoning their lead, the man held up a hand and begged them to wait.

"Why didn't you tell me you had an idea in mind?" he pretended to scold her before laughing in an obnoxious manner. "Let's hear it. I brought many other weapons surpassing what're on display."

Grace's urge to scoff at the merchant's fake mannerisms and façade rose with each passing second, yet Dianne returned to the table and wore a curious expression.

"You'll laugh like the others," the woman added. "Nobody understands my taste."

"Only a thug raised with poor manners would mock such a pretty lady. Now, what is it you are seeking?"

Dianne proceeded to repeat the description Grace had heard dozens of times that evening: a decorative blade or bow crafted with a unique material. She perfected a story about her desire to show up a rival whose lover designed a bronze sword and embellished it with gems, which sounded as ridiculous as she intended. The entire time, the man held a dramatically sympathetic frown.

"Perhaps I am a fool for pursuing revenge," she concluded with a downcast gaze at the weapons on the table. "I should be paying a blacksmith, not buying less than I deserve."

Grace commended Dianne's acting and wondered if the soldier ever interacted with the nobility enough to pick up on their behavior. Then, she chanced a glance at the merchant. His expression faltered when his jaw tightened, and his eyes darted at the people nearby.

Why is he nervous? Does he not wish to sell the ancestral weapon, or is there a risk?

The three seemed to be waiting for another to speak until Dianne released a sigh and turned to walk away. This time, the merchant didn't stop her, so Grace trailed behind, albeit at a slower pace. Her heart dropped with each step.

This is our chance, she realized before planting her feet. *I refuse to abandon our hard-earned opportunity!*

In the middle of the stream of people, she closed her eyes, triggered her goddess gift, and called to the man again.

Golden weapon... Show them what you-

Her thoughts abruptly went silent when a hand dropped on her shoulder.

"What's wrong?" came Dianne's voice at a lower volume before she opened her eyes. The woman kept a grasp on her, though she struggled with an answer.

While Grace contemplated whether or not to discuss the situation there, the pair heard the man shouting and glanced over. He waved his arms in an urgent manner, drawing plenty of attention to his table, but a broad grin covered the lower half of his face.

Dianne left Grace then in order to investigate, prompting her to trail close behind.

"Ladies, my apologizes," he began with a bow. "I tempted you with the promise of more yet needed a nudge to muster the effort. Forgive my foolishness. Now, wait one moment."

The merchant ducked under his table to begin rummaging through whatever he kept there. As he did so, Grace noticed Dianne turn to her and winced at the woman's resulting, suspicious look.

She knows I pushed him with my ability. Well, we would not be getting anywhere without it.

"Come closer," the man called to them before rising and hunching forward over the weapons on display. His slick persona morphed into one similar to a conniving thief, though he maintained his grin.

Grace felt put off by his discrete behavior; however, Dianne leaned over the table, leaving her to do the same in order to observe what the merchant held underneath his cloak. Her anticipation rose while he glanced around at those passing by, as if he needed to avoid anybody else noticing their business. Then, he pulled back his cloak steadily to savor their privacy.

Could it actually be… She peered at his covered hand with bated breath until she could make out the shape of a dagger underneath. *The light is too poor to confirm its color.*

"This piece is special," the merchant grumbled in an attempt to keep his voice down. "My source became involved with the previous owner in Clearwater, though it lived in the capital for years. Nothing more is known about its history."

Grace continued to stare at the item and consider its validity while Dianne and the man discussed its possible uses, color, material, and other details. She expected her partner to express doubt and need to clarify if the dagger was indeed an ancestral weapon, so she decided to test the blade herself. At first, she called forth her goddess gift but only sensed the merchant's mixture of greediness, concern for his safety, and a surprising amount of hostility against Dianne.

The longer they lingered, the greater his patience dwindled.

In spite of the potential danger, Grace raised her hand to reach over and touch the dagger's hilt without hesitation. She purposely avoided grabbing it in order to receive less of a harsh response, yet the man slapped her hand away, recoiled while keeping the weapon under his cloak, and glared as he snarled.

"Do you understand the value of this item?" he snapped at her. His attempt to keep the volume of his voice at a controlled level resulted in an odd sort of growl, and he stepped backward when she didn't reply.

It didn't matter to Grace, for the effects of her actions revealed the truth. Once her hand connected with the metal, her Yeluthian power blossomed to life, like a ray of sunlight breaking free from behind a cloud. Its resulting warmth filled her body during that brief second and proved without a doubt the item's purpose.

"How much?" she asked before remembering her position as Dianne's shadow. Internally, she prayed the soldier would realize what the question meant for their cause.

A pause hung between them while the man seemed to freeze in place. His expression continued to showcase his distrust, yet the proposition of a purchase more than likely held his attention. After a minute, he cleared his throat, stood straighter, and offered a sly grin akin to his previous mask.

"My apologies. I thought your appearance had been for show and not a keen buyer of such unique weapons. This is valuable for that reason: No others exist throughout the entire country. I'm sure you probably assumed that beforehand."

"Enough riddles," Dianne interjected with none of the vulnerability she showed earlier. "How much for the dagger?"

Grace began to regret acting so thoughtlessly and demanding the price once the merchant raised his chin and tapped a finger to his cheek, as if contemplating an answer. Because they expressed obvious interest, she figured he would draw the deal out to collect the most amount of coins. Her anxiousness returned when his lips stretched into a wide grin.

"This is the grandest item I ever owned," he prefaced before holding up a hand and wiggling his fingers. "Five hundred gold coins."

His price caused Grace to go ridged.

"You're insane!" Dianne exclaimed, though she managed to keep her voice at a whisper. "Only the king himself would be able to afford that."

The man shrugged, visibly savoring their shock. "This is an item befitting a king, don't you agree?"

When Dianne didn't respond, Grace figured the woman was biting her tongue.

All this nonsense is *for Aaron and his council*, she muttered in her mind. The notion sparked her drive to leave with the ancestral weapon in their possession and forget the rest of the evening. *I doubt Dianne dared to carry that much with her, even if we collected enough.*

That seemed accurate when the soldier began bargaining to no avail.

"You may take me for a crook or a con man, but I know when I own a piece worth more than the rest combined," he bragged. "Five hundred gold coins. No more; no less."

Perhaps I should use my goddess gift again, Grace wondered when Dianne didn't argue a second time. Before she could make a decision, the merchant rebuffed them with a wave of his hand.

"Be gone. That is a small price to pay in this place. If you can't cough up the funds, then you should return to your humble abode with your dignity."

The pompous laugh following his comments tipped Grace over the edge. *Enough games. I am tired of stepping around obstacles in the way.*

Her hands clenched into fists while she projected her mind once again. This time, she preyed on his current emotions in order to stun him for a precious moment when she could act.

Your selfishness will cost this kingdom, she sent and enveloped his mind with the words. *Relinquish the weapon!*

As she hoped, the direct order affected him visibly so she could time her next move. The man's confident expression fell flat to reflect his utter horror, and even across the table she saw his entire body stiffen in shock. Once she caught that, she locked her eyes on the dagger, lunged over the table, and seized it from his hands.

Got it!

Immediately, the weapon's presence lifted her frustration away, and she yanked it free from his clutches before spinning around without hesitating. She expected the merchant to pursue her or call for someone else to do so, which meant her next steps would need to either be efficient enough for her to escape or clever enough for nobody to find her.

"Stop her!" the man cried after seemingly recovering from her mental shout. He repeated the words and several others, though they became lost in the noise from the crowd.

Grace held the weapon tighter in her hands and glanced around. The people who heard the merchant stopped or went over to investigate while everyone else dismissed what chaos she started.

I do not possess the knowledge of this place nor the skill to hide for long, she concluded while fleeing in the opposite direction. *My only option is to reach the exit with Dianne…*

At the reminder of her partner, she began to slow only for a hand on her back to push her forward.

"Don't stop," came the woman's voice from Grace's right. "We need to find a place to lie low until we form a plan."

Despite the order, Dianne guided them to a hurried walk at the end of the space before halting between a pair of tents so they could catch their breath. It was then the repercussions of Grace's impulsive action dawned on her. She began apologizing only to shut her mouth when the soldier leveled a glare her way.

"I'll scold you for that later," Dianne promised while panting and standing straighter. "Right now, we need to get to the exit. Crossing the area without paying attention caused me to lose track of our location, but I would rather take our chances on this side than wander back near the merchant."

"I agree," Grace added. "As for our location, my goddess gift should allow me to find the exit."

"Perfect. Let me know when you're finished."

After a brief, mental survey of the layout, she reported her findings. "The opening is along the far wall to our left, but many bodies are traveling against the shortest route. We will head straight into that mass if we go there now."

Dianne contemplated the update before holding out a hand. "First, give me the dagger. I can't let you remain in danger any longer."

Although she hated the idea of potentially throwing her partner's life into jeopardy, Grace obeyed.

"Second, and I'm extremely reluctant to admit this, we should split up."

"Really?"

"I won't be able to protect you, yet I'm sure the guards will recognize a pair of women over two, single figures with their faces hidden. You can use your ability to check on me anyway."

The suggestion startled Grace given her partner's protective instinct, but she didn't disagree. "Just tell me where to go."

Dianne tilted her head a bit before nodding. "I want you to exit as soon as possible while following the leftmost wall. Hopefully you can circle around the busy area you sensed, and I will do the same on the right side. Call to me if you run into trouble."

Grace could feel the woman's concern hanging in the air, especially when loud voices began drifting their way.

"Go," Dianne instructed as she slipped the dagger into a hidden part of her clothes underneath her cloak. "Be careful, my lady."

With that, the pair split apart. Grace didn't look back once she committed to her direction and expected Dianne did the same. Her attention remained on the ground while she forced her body to move as casually as possible in order to avoid seeming hurried, which she expected would lead the guards to her.

Just keep moving, she told herself. *I must not worry about Dianne. She trusts me enough to leave me on my own in a place like this, and I owe her that level of respect after what I did. I only pray nothing hinders our exit.*

The main opening came into view far sooner than she anticipated, leading her to release a sigh of relief as she wandered nearer. Then, she passed through under the watchful gaze of a hulking man befitting his position. Nobody else exited at that time, so she alone ascended the dimly lit stairs while holding her breath.

At the front gate, a different man grunted as she approached. He began by asking her for a purchase ticket, which she informed him she didn't possess because she had not bought any items. In response, he searched her by way of the previous pat down before returning what weapons she entered with and letting her go.

That was too close, she cried in her mind and hugged herself in the alley beyond. *If they recognized me, I would not be getting away so easily. Speaking of which, I wonder how Dianne plans to leave without that ticket. Should I reach out to her now? I may not be in the safest position to do so.*

It took all her self-control to continue toward the main road instead of linger in the area until the soldier returned to her side. Only the idea of the burley guards learning of her actions and hunting her down spurred her onward.

Once she merged into the populated areas closer to the palace, she started to relax. Nobody looked at her with any sort of recognition, proving her disguise still held, and she stopped outside the training ground's side entrance to wait for Dianne.

We were supposed to meet here together, she thought against a wave of fear at the possible punishments her partner might face. *All this trouble for an item the royal family should possess anyway. Is one person's life worth that risk? What if something happened to her?*

The minutes ticked by into an hour, but Grace remained outside. She eventually moved to sit with her back pressed against the stone wall. This earned her several glances from the soldiers on duty, and a pair even approached to inquire about her business. She considered lying to hide her ploy; however, given the recent attack by strangers pretending to be servants, she decided the truth would be a better option and mentioned waiting for a friend. The soldier looked to want to question her appearance, yet he merely vowed to keep an eye on her while she remained there.

*

This is hopeless, Grace admitted with a glance up at the lightening sky. *The sunrise is almost here, and she is still gone. I should not have left her behind. What was I thinking? Stealing from a weapons dealer... And in a place like that! She might be in danger.*

The notion led her to rise and begin pacing, both in an attempt to ward off her weariness and express her anxiety. Then, the sound of footsteps nearby reached her before a familiar voice did.

"Lady ambassador, were you harmed?"

She spun to face the silhouette she knew to be Dianne and inhaled a sharp gasp. "You made it back!"

The soldier approached while shushing Grace, though her expression projected a sense of relief. Despite their differing statuses, location, and fatigue, Grace hurried to wrap her arms around her partner.

"I worried what befell you," she shared and stepped back to break off the embrace. A broad grin stretched across her face. "What happened after-"

"Nothing as exciting as I'm sure you've been imagining," her guard interrupted. "I needed to spend some time observing our pursuers and figure out how to smuggle out our prize."

"You mean..."

Dianne reached underneath her cloak before removing the ancestral weapon. This spurred another gasp from Grace, and she shook her head in amazement.

"You did it! How did you manage to escape?"

The woman didn't respond right away. When she did, she fixed Grace with a disapproving stare. "I assume the man at the front asked you for a purchase ticket?"

"Yes, he did."

"Well, I learned about that while hiding among the crowd and observing their interactions. All I needed was a ticket, so I purchased a cheap dagger, pocketed the one they gave me, then disposed of the extra weapon. They're not too picky about details, which is probably due to the merchants' managing their own business and most likely just paying a fee to be present. When I figured I would be safe since nothing else took place, I snuck out behind several other people. It's dark enough in there to lose track of the time. I'm sorry if I kept you here."

Grace shook her head. "Please, I should be the one apologizing. You became caught in that predicament because of my rash decision."

"About that. Expect a respectful tongue lashing when we meet tomorrow. I'm too tired to put the energy into a lecture."

"I figured as much." Grace yawned at the thought of the hour, which teetered between being both too late and too early for bed. "I promise to listen when you are ready. Then, we can deliver the dagger to King Aaron together."

Defending the Base

Marcus found himself in plenty of scrimmages and life-threatening fights over the years; however, he didn't have experience with drawn-out battles. The closest he'd come had been among the Dalan troops when they marched to Verona in order to rescue those in the palace from the former high priest and original demon. For days, they struggled to make progress against the possessed Nim-Valans under the madman's control and needed to ration their resources, plot out their next steps every hour or two, and keep up morale despite their own uncertainty. He learned plenty about acting as a leader in dire circumstances, but the end always remained in sight, even if it involved retreating.

The southern base stayed on constant alert because of the new demon and its creatures. It never showed itself after approaching General Tio, yet the beasts eager to maim, kill, and consume were ready to attack when the sun set. Those driven off the night before returned without their previous wounds while others took the place of the slaughtered. It became a never-ending cycle that steadily wore down the Dalan base's troops, though the combat distracted their enemy from the city, which fortified its defenses during the day.

In order to be prepared for the inevitable onslaught, General Tio assigned scouts from the defensive squad to survey the surrounding area whenever the sun was up, allowing the rest of his soldiers and mages to rest until a horn sounded, alerting them of the beasts' arrival. Switching sleep schedules took a toll on many people, as did the relentless fighting. Instead of the upbeat personalities and humor usually present in the base, a sense of exhaustion and worry hung in the air.

Throughout their fatigue and concern, the general remained a firm foundation for his troops, never hinting at any intent to change their routine. Calin and Marcus tried their best to keep up with the man's seemingly limitless confidence, yet they often conversed about the worst-case scenario and what the rest of the country dealt with since they couldn't continue patrolling their routes.

As he finished donning his armor that evening, Marcus heard the warning horn sound, right at its regular time.

When will it end? The question sent a pang of despair through him and made him hesitate to leave his quarters. *How can we expect to hold off these creatures while building the strength and courage to face a demon possessing power we haven't even seen yet? Our chance of success dwindles every day.*

He stared down at his metal-clad body until footsteps on the opposite side of his door hurried to exit the base. Only when the noise quieted after a few minutes did he lock his feelings away and depart.

The troops formed an arrangement throughout the passing days where the weak, weary, and injured too stubborn to stay inside were positioned closest to the doors with everyone else across the bridge in order to meet the oncoming attack. As Marcus emerged and walked over the bridge above the moat, he learned the fighting had yet to begin. He noticed the soldiers shuffling in place while muttering to each other and caught mention of the demon, which caused his heartbeat to pick up as he jogged toward the front and joined the general and Calin.

"What's going on?" he practically demanded, startling his fellow assistant general in the process.

Calin shot him an annoyed glare in response before facing the field again. "The creatures haven't shown up, but our mages sense the demonic power stirring. General Tio ordered us to remain at attention until the presence is gone."

"That could take all night," Marcus mumbled, though he stated a fact rather than complain.

Calin nodded in response, then the two kept quiet as a hush fell over the troops. For a while, they gazed forward in preparation for a trap or trick until stars decorated the darkened sky beneath the light of the full moon. The general's gruff voice interrupted the silence just when Marcus started to shift from one leg to the other in order to keep the muscles from growing stiff.

"I've heard plenty of superstitions about drawing blood when a round moon hangs high in the night," the man nonchalantly shared without addressing them.

He paused, as if waiting for an answer, but Marcus and Calin could only glance at each other without understanding. So, he continued.

"They say spirits of the dead become active because moonlight is like how sunlight works for us: It allows them to view the world clearer. The scent of blood reminds them of when they had flesh and bones, and they long for that sense of familiarity. People perform rituals during a full moon due to that belief and offer sacrifices or cast curses. I'm not interested in those practices. As far as I'm concerned, evenings are for drinking and sleeping, not mindless bloodshed. I say, let the dead enjoy their rest."

Those nearby had leaned in closer to hear the explanation, as though they all sat around a campfire sharing stories. Marcus didn't intend to question the general's decision to speak; however, some mumbled responses until a low rumbling sound reached them from the field. After a moment, he realized it was chuckling resonating from deep in somebody's throat comparable to a powerful gale approaching in the distance.

A figure emerged from the tall grass, though they knew it had to be the demon. It stood just above Marcus' height, and with the light of the moon, they could spot additional features they didn't catch before. The muscles along its arms looked defined, a wide grin stretched across its pale face, and violet eyes glimmered as it observed the troops. Other than a pair of short horns sprouting from above its ears, the creature appeared frighteningly similar to an ordinary man.

"Your species' imagination never ceases to amuse me," it announced before laughing and shaking its head. "I can't say I've heard stories like that one before, with spirits and whatnot wandering in search of blood."

Did the general know the demon was there? Marcus wondered while ignoring the urge to glance at his superior.

General Tio didn't reply, yet he didn't seem surprised by the intruder.

"Your tale makes my venture here worthwhile already," the demon went on with a shrug before its smile vanished. "Shall we return to business?"

"What exactly is your goal?" the general asked in the same, unbothered manner.

"Didn't I mention this before? Once I find something I desire, I claim it. In this case, I seek to rule your base."

"You plan on attacking all of us on your own?" General Tio added while jerking his chin over his shoulder in a gesture to the structure. "What's the point?"

"That's my secret."

Marcus noticed the general straighten. "Why the creatures then? You think you'll *earn* this? Don't make me laugh! You're using mindless beasts to weaken your opponents before sweeping in to finish them off, then you pat yourself on the back for a job well done. I'll be the first to enlighten you on how pathetic that logic is. A coward relies on cheap tricks to snatch victory without even testing the limits of their mind or body. If you hope to continue with your plan, get out of the way so we can repeat another night of slaughtering your pawns!"

Those who heard the general's proclamation cheered to express their agreement, prompting additional support from farther behind where the troops assumed there was a reason for the positive noise.

Meanwhile, the demon seethed at the taunting. Its lip curled into a snarl, it hunched in a brooding manner, and both hands clenched into fists. Marcus placed a hand on the hilt of his sword in preparation for a strike or spell in retaliation, yet nothing happened. When the sounds died down, the figure replied.

"I hate being labeled as weak," it grumbled before turning its face upward to the sky. After a pause, it returned its gaze to Tio and went on without showing emotion. "If you view my strategy as trickery or a waste of my skill, I'd prefer to settle this in a simpler fashion."

A glint shone in the silhouette's left hand as it summoned its weapon, which proved to be a charcoal-colored sword that reflected the moonlight as it moved. The sight remined Marcus of the first demon, as well as whenever Coura manifested an identical blade in the past.

The general groaned. "And just what do you mean by that?"

"Why don't we settle our dispute?" The creature held its sword horizontally at eye level and brushed its fingers along the blade's surface. "One on one. Send your best combatant against me in a duel. If your soldier wins, I'll leave the base alone; if I win, this place belongs to me."

Marcus scoffed at the proposal. *Humans are physically and magically inferior to demons. It would be suicide to send somebody alone.*

He expected to hear Tio reject the offer, and probably include a jab at the creature's thought process, yet when his superior did speak it wasn't to dismiss the proposal.

"I assume the perimeters for victory will be adjusted for each combatant?"

The demon's grin widened. "Of course."

"General!" Calin interrupted in a fierce whisper. "You can't seriously be considering this."

Without removing his eyes from the field ahead, Tio nodded before addressing their enemy again. "Let's hear it."

"I win if I kill my opponent," came the chilling, calm voice of the demon. "They win if..." It appeared to be contemplating its next words until it outstretched its arms to both sides. "They win if they can land a scratch on me."

Instead of hopelessness or irritation, Marcus felt disgusted by the terms. "It's toying with us," he said to the general at a quieter volume.

Both he and Calin faced the general to wait for their next order; however, neither were prepared for Tio's follow-up question.

"Do either of you believe a single soldier or mage among our troops can manage a successful strike?"

"No," Calin answered first, as if appalled by the idea.

Marcus shared his matching sentiment after.

"Are either of *you* confident you can mark the creature?"

"You know I can't," his assistant snapped.

Perhaps Calin is waiting for Tio to realize how ridiculous the demon's challenge is. We can't trust it to keep its end of the deal either.

"What about you, Marcus?"

Despite how pessimistic he felt, he eyed the lone figure. "I fought against the previous demon in the capital with six others and it bested us. This one doesn't seem much different. Even though my skills increased since then, I wouldn't stand a chance by myself."

"I see." The general began walking forward.

"What are you doing?" Calin demanded while scrambling to the man's side with Marcus closely behind.

Tio shot them an amused smile. "You two don't believe anybody can land a scratch, not even yourselves. Well, where does that leave us then? This seems like the perfect opportunity to shut that demon up and drive it and the beasts away."

Calin reached out to seize the general's arm, halting their steps. "No one can fight that creature and survive, including you!"

"He's right," Marcus added. "We have other options, like the ancestral weapons and our Yeluthian allies in the area. The base and your troops are still able to fend off the attacks every night."

"What we don't have is time," their superior began in the most patient tone Marcus had ever heard from him. "If the demon decides to strike the base on its own, you agreed on our inability to stop it. How many will die in the process?"

Neither assistant general could offer a satisfactory rebuttal.

"We don't have any leads about the ancestral weapons, none of the angels are here to use their magic, and it gave us an opportunity to end the fighting. I'm sure I can manage better than anybody else. Why not try?"

As he released his grip to return his arms to his side, Calin cleared his throat. "If you die, we lose the base."

"That's true." Tio scratched his chin, as though the notion hadn't occurred to him. "I'm defeated, I die and the base is compromised. I don't accept the challenge, the demon and its creatures continue to persist and we risk losing more lives. We sure are in a real mess."

Against his willingness to put their leader in harm's way, Marcus found his voice again. "Or you win the duel."

"Or I win the duel," the general repeated with a sharp nod. "We only get one opportunity. If I'm the only person possessing the confidence, I'll wager my life. Besides, my two underlings can manage the base and troops anyway."

When the man turned away from them, the assistant generals locked eyes with a shared understanding of what Tio hinted at.

"Well?" the creature pressed to interrupt the moment. "Which human is brave enough to accept my offer? Unless you're too scared..."

Tio's sudden, hearty laugh made Marcus jump, and the general drew his sword before taking a pompous stance.

"Hurry up, monster! There's enough of the night left for me to drink with my men, and I don't intend to waste it."

Nervous muttering replaced the previous cheering from the troops when they heard their leader's declaration. Marcus and Calin remained where their superior left them, unable to do more than look on as the general approached his opponent.

The demon scanned Tio up and down before shrugging. "Your boasting piques my interest. I'm curious to find out if your actions will do the same."

It threw up a hand to the right, and before Marcus understood what was happening, a magical, violet shield circled the two combatants. He charged toward the spell with Calin on his heels and slid to a stop in front of the glimmering wall. The additional cover forced them to squint in order to make out the figures on the opposite side, though they could hear the voices clearly.

"Ready yet?" Tio asked while resuming his stance.

In response, the demon pointed its black blade at him for a moment before charging to initiate the clash. Their weapons met with clang after clang as the creature took the offensive by swinging for the general's sides in a controlled yet chaotic manner. Tio managed to block each strike until he found an opportunity to try a vertical slice, prompting his opponent to retreat with as much poise as a dancer. Without offering a break, it leapt at him again.

This isn't fair, Marcus thought as the darker blade knocked the general's away, forcing the man to raise his right arm and accept a blow meant for his chest. *General Tio needed to relearn how to wield weapons with his left hand ever since he lost his right one. Although he's more experienced than most of us, his age is showing because of the demon's inhuman speed. I shouldn't have let him go.*

He longed to mention this to Calin and share his guilt, yet he sensed his fellow assistant general felt the same about their situation, if not worse.

Tio chanced a swing for the creature's torso and attempted to sidestep away from a follow-up strike, but his opponent ducked under his blade instead. This provided an opportunity for it to throw its body forward and shove Tio backward. The man dropped to a knee and managed to muster enough energy to thrust his sword forward in retaliation. To their dismay, the demon stepped out of range, though it allowed Tio to push himself to his feet.

"Don't be going easy on me," the man yelled while pounding the end of his right arm against his chest plate.

Despite the shield marring his view, Marcus could hear the general's characteristic smile in the comment. Evidently, the enemy did too.

"I sense no fear from you," came the demon's reply before it chuckled. "That means you're either hiding your astounding skills or bluffing. In any case, you're a fool to overestimate your abilities."

"I never claimed to be anything more or less."

With a smirk still plastered to its face, the demon charged again. Their next bout lasted longer, though blood poured from slashes on Tio's left bicep and thigh at an alarming rate soon after. Marcus grew tense when the general attempted to back away while panting as beads of sweat covered his body and glistened in the moonlight before his opponent pursued.

"This ends now!" the creature cried with a lunge to stab forward.

Tio slid to his right, causing the weapon to graze his left side. He jerked that arm across the air for a horizontal slice in response; however, instead of retreating, the demon ducked under his sword, pulled its own back, and slid its blade straight through Tio's torso.

For a moment, time seemed to freeze as both combatants remained unmoving. Marcus' throat closed when the blow landed, preventing him from calling out or making a sound. Still, he kept his eyes glued to the scene beyond the shield.

Their enemy pulled the black blade back at an agonizingly slow pace to remove it from General Tio, producing a sickening gush in the process and allowing blood to spill onto the ground. As soon as the weapon left his body, the man pressed his right arm on the wound, bent forward, and began coughing up more of the crimson liquid.

"You were right," the creature began in a mocking tone as it stood straighter and observed its unclean sword. "You *are* a fool. I suppose I shouldn't expect much from-"

The gloating abruptly ceased when Tio pointed the tip of his blade at his opponent.

"You're acting like this is over," he grumbled and spat in the demon's direction.

Marcus expected their enemy's amusement to fade after that protest. Without a word, it stalked forward until its chest nearly touched the tip of the general's sword.

"At this point, all I need to do is wait," it commented then.

"Except you're not that type of fighter." The man's voice projected to the surrounding area and with such authority it didn't sound like he'd suffered any wounds. "Someone who truly takes pride in combat and values it as highly as you wouldn't settle for such an end. Would you feel you earned your prize by standing around until I keel over? I'm a man with a duty to defend his home. If I don't give it all I've got, no matter how many holes you put in me, I'll die a disgrace to my troops and the citizens of Dala. *That* I promise you, but if you plan on giving up on a proper duel, then it'll be easier for me to mark you with my blade."

The demon's eyes widened while Tio spoke, and the general charged and swung at his opponent before it could respond. Instead of using its sword, the creature dodged each of the wild attempts by leaning to either side, ducking, or circling around, as if the match turned into a warm-up exercise. Despite the obvious, the general let out a cry with each motion until his opponent finally raised its weapon to block his blade. A grunt escaped its lips as it pushed with enough force to send Tio stumbling backward.

Marcus' breath caught when the man fell flat onto his back where he coughed and struggled to sit up. The demon stepped closer to tower over him for a moment before poising its sword above his midsection.

"Although your skills proved to be far from the best I've encountered from a human, you managed to impress me. Your tenacity is unlike anything I experienced among your kind, and you understand the nature of a fight as well. Don't be discouraged; you are worthy of a proper death."

It raised the black blade straight up in a deliberate motion before plunging the metal into Tio. At the same time, the man lifted his sword to knock his opponent's weapon away. As the demon's hand lowered, the general seemingly missed his swing when no sound signaled the blades connection, though it appeared to pass close to the demon's arm.

Marcus' body began trembling with rage and terror, yet he avoided the urge to strike the shield. Calin held no such restraint. Dala's assistant general shouted their superior's name as he pressed both hands against the barrier and pounded on the magical wall. A few seconds later, he stopped when the creature released its sword, leapt away, and cradled its arm.

"You!" it roared with a glare aimed at Tio.

The man coughed weakly in the resulting silence before pointing with his stubby, right arm. "Let's see…the damage."

"He marked it?" Calin asked in a whisper. "Did he really?"

The demon remained motionless. Marcus swallowed his emotions once he realized what its hesitation meant.

"Yes," he replied at a volume the creature could hear. "I saw the general cut your hand."

The violet eyes found him and sent a nasty look.

"He's the victor."

The matter-of-fact statement sparked laughter from Tio, reminding Marcus of the limited opportunity for a rescue.

"Bring down this shield," he demanded. "According to the terms *you* set, you're obligated to leave us forever."

The creature hissed a curse, waved a hand, and dismissed the shield and its weapon, leaving them to shatter into shards of energy. Calin bound ahead as soon as the barrier broke apart while Marcus held his pace to a walk in case their enemy chose to ignore the deal. To his relief, it didn't seem inclined to do so.

"I spent years putting together a collection of pawns," it grumbled in a bitter manner, directing the words at Marcus. "None of that effort shall go to waste; that I promise you, humans."

Marcus stayed on his feet next to Calin, who threw himself beside the general, pressed both hands on the newest wound, and shouted for a healer. The creature's threat unsettled him even though they appeared victorious, yet it closed its eyes, inhaled a deep breath, and released a sigh as it seemingly shed its rage to don the pompous persona.

"Your behavior taught me another weakness associated with your kind. You obey a leader without thinking for yourselves then become helpless when said leader is gone. Such is the way of humans, I suppose."

The demon's resulting snicker prompted Marcus to grip the hilt of his sword tighter. Before he could offer a retort or draw his weapon, Calin startled him by responding to the comments.

"You're wrong about us."

"Is that right?" the creature teased.

The assistant general raised his eyes from the bloody mess and stuck his chin up to display his defiance. "Dalan troops don't rely on one person or a handful of people. Each soldier, mage, servant, and healer is expected to act as an individual member of our base and the team they are placed on. General Tio makes sure of it. You'll never understand because demons don't possess the capability to show respect. He's our leader. We don't follow him blindly; we serve him because he earned our loyalty."

The creature's smile faltered before twisting into a bitter frown.

"We're not helpless," Marcus added while turning away to look at the awaiting troops. Then, he raised a fist in the air. "Back up!"

The resounding cheers after his order were exactly what he hoped for, and the soldiers at the front began leading a charge. When he faced the demon again, it began retreating toward the trees. By the time the additional men and women reached Marcus, it disappeared in the foliage.

The general's coughing brought his attention back to the injuries. After selecting a pair of healers to tend to their leader, he ordered the outer squad and any volunteers to remain in position through the rest of the night while everybody else returned inside. Although admitting the results of Tio's challenge at the risk of losing his life hurt, the eruption of support for their superior eased some of the emotional pain.

With matters settled regarding the troops, Marcus knelt beside Calin and looked from the bloody torso to one of the healers. "How is he?"

The light mage met his eyes and shook her head slowly while the other rose to help his partner to her feet. Silence filled the area when the two left the unmoving figure on the ground.

Dala's assistant general bowed his head and placed a trembling fist on his chest. Marcus mirrored the respectful position a minute later when he looked upon the general's peaceful expression complete with a slight smile.

Borrowed Hope

Shall we assess the situation again, Your Highness?"

Aaron glanced up from the most recent report in his hands to stare at the representative for the dark mages named Lydia. The urge to toss the paper aside and bury his face in his hands was enormous, but he decided to set the document on his lap while shaking his head instead of making a scene. Emotions continued to rise throughout the day, so witnessing him overreact would cause more trouble than they needed at the moment.

"No, thank you. We've all been briefed on what's happening here and around the country. Perhaps resting for the night will provide us with ideas and better news."

He intended for the words to act as a polite dismissal, and fortunately those gathered around him in the meeting chamber understood. King Arval rose first and departed between his three commanders after offering their people's salute. Then, General Tont and General Garvish exited while mumbling to one another, and General Terrell continued shuffling through the documents scattered across the table. Finally, Lydia and Jenna lingered in their seats to cast concerned glances his way, prompting Aaron to stand, gesture for his guards, and follow them into the hallway.

"I'll be returning to my quarters," he decided.

A pause followed his words as the six, armored men and women shuffled to properly surround him before the group moved toward the nearest staircase. A few minute later, Aaron walked into his room, closed the door behind the soldiers, and dropped onto his bed to stare at the ceiling.

I wish Marcus were here, he thought absently when the desire to talk with somebody outside the council meetings grew. *He'd put me in my place and tell me to stop worrying so much. At least, that's what I hope he would say. Then I could pretend what's going on isn't as serious as it actually is, even for a brief minute.*

With a groan, he placed an arm over his eyes before unintentionally reflecting on what took place across Asteom.

To the north, the barbarians playing soldier began spreading east along the border. General Casner's reports suggested they did so to provoke his troops into attacking, though no one could figure out why or who led the groups. The most prominent issue related to the number of troops from Nim-Vala and the threat the enemy posed if they decided to charge at once. Without the same amount of soldiers or a level of magical power equal to the individuals, the entire northern section remained in danger.

Normally, sending additional troops wouldn't be a problem, he noted against a looming headache. *The real issue is Dala needs help too.*

To the south, the base already stretched their soldiers and mages thin in order to protect the towns the demon and its creatures continued targeting. King Arval arranged for his angels to monitor the area with the hope of catching and eliminating the source, but it seemed to have vanished after appearing to taunt General Tio.

Aaron trusted the man to handle the city, which was why he didn't feel concerned about their lack of communication recently. He also believed Marcus would be the first person to send a message should any harm befall the area. In a way, he had to hope for the best and place his faith in others because those in the palace, specifically certain members of his council, needed him.

Lydia and Jenna are learning how to behave during our meetings, but they weren't officially appointed as master mages. Acting as a representative takes leadership and confidence, which neither picked up due to the urgency of their situations. It's not my responsibility to promote them either.

He paused to focus on that particular issue, which he never made time to seriously consider.

I should ask General Tont for his input. My father installed a dark master mage on the council with the addition of the Mage Service Law, and Emilea had been selected by her mentor, Califer. Without a prior relationship to Lydia or Jenna, or any of the mages for that matter, I assumed they were the best replacements because Byron and Emilea chose them beforehand. The decision is left entirely to the person seated in the position, which has proved to be both helpful and harmful. On the one hand, the master mages act as mentors and delegate to provide experience, then they'll ease out of their role while remaining present to supervise until their participation isn't necessary. The problem is, as we're experiencing now, an emergency doesn't allow the luxury of time.

His mind soon moved in the direction of his friend's experience as an assistant general. *Another issue is preference. General Tont refuses to promote Marcus because he believes his son doesn't meet his grand expectations. I considered intervening, but it wouldn't sit right with Marcus. The decision to assign a replacement falls to the individual who should have the most say. Perhaps the council can establish a system of recommendations and voting in order to avoid favoritism and allow all the members to become familiar with the newcomers. Even the master mages could use assistants for the same reason.*

The longer he elaborated on the concepts, the more confident he grew in the idea of detailing perimeters for each assignment on his council. Spending energy on something other than the current problems also lightened his sour mood.

With the outline of a discussion in mind, Aaron went to sit at his desk and scribble various notes so he wouldn't forget later. He reread what he put on the page with a sense of pride until knocking at his door forced him to set it down for the time being.

"Your Highness," one of the guards began while cracking the door open. "Lady Zelnar and her guard request an audience with you."

"Grace?" Aaron muttered before realizing what his hesitation meant.

"My apologies. I informed them you have been resting, but they are rather persistent."

He cleared his throat and began to brush down his tunic and comb through his hair using his fingers to appear somewhat presentable. "You may let them in."

When the aforementioned duo entered seconds later, Grace's surprisingly eager expression took him back. Meanwhile, the unfamiliar guard escorting Yeluthia's ambassador placed a fist on her breast while standing at attention.

It's been weeks since I've had a chance to see Grace, Aaron reflected and offered a smile. *I hope she's recovering from the traumatic experience. I should probably avoid that topic altogether considering the outcome, though I wonder if she worked on the problems stemming from her parents' expectations. Perhaps if we get a moment alone, we can catch up.*

He opened his mouth to offer a greeting; however, his friend began speaking as soon as the door closed.

"We finally have an opportunity to meet with you! I worried you would be attending council sessions the entire day after we tried reaching out in the morning."

"I'm sorry," he apologized and allowed his smile to fade. "I didn't know, or else I could have scheduled time for us. What's the matter, and how can I help?"

The last reaction he expected in that moment was for Grace's lips to stretch into a grin. Even her guard attempted to hide a smile while fidgeting in place.

"You have it wrong," the Yeluthian replied, giggled, and held out a wrapped bundle to him with both hands. "*We* are the ones who are here to help *you*."

Aaron raised an eyebrow before glancing at the item she offered. He hadn't noticed her holding the object and wondered what she hinted at, so he accepted, albeit with some uncertainty.

"What is it?" he asked after a pause when he began peeling away several layers of fabric.

"We needed to make sure this remained secure," the soldier added in place of an answer.

Grace looked to her guard then back at him again. "Dianne did most of the work. You should thank her."

"Lady ambassador!" the woman beside his friend whispered in a shocked manner the Yeluthian dismissed.

"It is the truth, and you deserve praise for your efforts. Right, Aaron?"

"I deserve nothing, Your Highness. I was only fulfilling my duty to the kingdom, as a loyal servant should."

Grace continued their banter, but Aaron stopped listening by that point. His mind went blank when he finished unraveling the item underneath the wrap, which proved to be the farthest thing from his mind.

Judging by the weight, he assumed it to be a piece of metal, yet he didn't understand the significance of what his friend and the soldier delivered until a hint of gold poked through the final layer of fabric. Then, every muscle in his body froze.

Is this what I think it is?

The room fell silent as he peeled away the remaining cloth to reveal a dagger beneath. The polished surface held no fingerprints, and the simplistic design showcased the high quality of metalwork used to craft such a piece. He hated the idea of marring such a perfect weapon; however, the temptation proved too great to ignore.

"Where did you find this?" he asked without hiding his disbelief as he seized the golden hilt and lifted the item above his head to marvel at it from a new angle. Part of him expected to feel a surge of power or divine presence when he touched the metal, yet nothing seemed different.

"A merchant in the underground market kept the dagger in his possession," the soldier replied.

"The underground market," Aaron muttered before returning the weapon to its cloth and carefully rewrapping it. "I'm not too shocked by that actually. I would bet it cost a fortune."

When neither woman commented, he returned his attention to them and found both averting their eyes.

"Surely I can pay you for what you spent," he added after considering the potentially massive amount they sacrificed.

"That isn't necessary, Your Highness," Grace's guard replied while shaking her head.

Aaron sensed more they kept hidden and narrowed his eyes slightly. *Why do I get the feeling there's a chapter of their story they neglected to mention.*

The thought spurred him to press for additional information, though he prayed their explanation would not be a lengthy one.

"Since we've been blessed with an opportunity to converse, I'd like to hear exactly how you obtained this weapon?"

*

The chamber felt stuffier than it had in days, though due to an anxiousness combating their previous frustration. Every council member arrived within the hour after he sent a messenger to summon them, which took place once he finished his discussion with Grace and the guard named Dianne. The pair willingly shared what led them to the dagger, and despite his gratefulness for their unprompted plotting, he couldn't help but lecture them on the importance of being cautious, acting as representatives of Asteom and Yeluthia respectively, and informing others of their intentions in case the two found themselves in a dangerous situation they couldn't escape.

However, their success more than made up for the commotion they stirred, and he made a mental note to send somebody to compensate the merchant they stole from.

Five hundred gold coins is a steep amount, but an ancestral weapon has proved to be priceless. If they reported back to me or one of the generals before sneaking into the underground market, I would have preferred to request the seller's presence so I could discuss this with him in person. The situation is what it is now.

Aaron began by thanking the group for returning to the meeting chamber before diving right into business and sharing the positive news. He took pleasure in observing their expressions lighten as frowns flipped into wide smiles when he held up the golden dagger. Many questions followed the reveal, yet he shortened Grace and her guard's story while omitting a few details.

"The off-duty soldier who visited the underground market did so after weeks of investigating and interrogations," he explained while handing the item to King Arval. "She located the weapon with some help from Ambassador Zelnar's goddess gift, and the pair brought it to me this afternoon."

"This is certainly our people's handiwork," the Yeluthian leader commented while inspecting the metal with a proud smile. "My niece must have sensed the sealing spell placed upon its surface, or perhaps the presence which heightens our light energy."

The king's commanders each took a turn marveling at the dagger before it circled around the table to the generals and mages. Only Jenna seemed to react like the Yeluthians; everybody else complimented the craftsmanship until it reached Aaron again. Then, he wrapped the item into a bundle with the same cloth and set it on his lap in order to address his council.

"Now that this is in our possession, what should we do?"

They tossed around several ideas in the past should one of the ancestral weapons turn up, yet the subject seemed to have been swept under the rug while they focused on more pressing matters.

"If I may speak first, I recommend we keep it in the palace for our protection or send it to the southern base to use against the demon there," High Priest Jurek offered.

General Terrell voiced his agreement after, followed by Jenna and Lydia, though those who remained silent didn't appear to dismiss the suggestions. Aaron waited for additional comments from the generals before responding.

"My personal preference is to deliver the dagger to Dala with a Yeluthian soldier in case the demon shows up again to intercept the messenger. We are on high alert because of the previous attack, so I assume it will avoid making itself a target in this area. The troubles to the north could use the aid from the south once the creature is taken care of or intimidated enough to go into hiding. We are also training the light mages so they know the necessary spells to contain beings possessing demonic energy. King Arval, do you believe that will be enough?"

"I do," the majestic-looking figure replied and nodded. "I would not claim the demon shall keep to a single location, but Asteom is becoming more adept at handling the threats it poses. Perhaps informing the general in the southern base and requesting his input is the wisest route. After all, he alone understands the capability of his troops. I will spare Commander Detrix to deliver the message since he possesses the necessary knowledge of the area already."

Aaron found his spirits rising with the Yeluthian king's support. "Thank you for your honesty. Does anybody else need to discuss the next steps before we arrange for the weapon's transport with General Tio?"

He didn't expect an answer due to the purpose of the meeting being fulfilled; however, Lydia raised a hand, as if waiting for the cue.

"Your Highness, I wish to bring up another item for the council to discuss."

Aaron gestured for her to continue, so she stood with her hands clasped behind her back and kept her eyes on him as she began.

"We need to be utilizing our best resources given the current state of the country. Our issues require a variety of skill sets to resolve, and I don't believe we have enough."

"What do you mean?" he asked without hiding his genuine curiosity at the new topic.

She bit her lip in a hesitant manner. "I would like to request someone be sent after Master Byron."

Startled gasps and grunts from around the room followed her statement, though nobody interrupted.

"His experience involves leading the mages, fighting inhuman creatures, and plotting ahead, which I feel might just be the key to finding and eliminating the demon. I'm not who this council needs right now, but I will serve as well as I can."

Aaron noticed Jenna glance down at her hands and longed to comfort the women by assuring them of their own abilities and knowledge. Still, he understood Lydia's reasoning and found himself leaning in the same direction in regard to Byron.

"I appreciate your selflessness," he responded before opening the floor to the rest of the chamber. "I agree with Lydia. Losing our master mages so unexpectedly left us at a loss. I'd like to hear what the rest of the council has to say about this."

General Tont raised a hand. "I second her idea to bring him back. Byron's sharp intuition contributed to the palace's safety over the years, including the defeat of the first demon."

A majority of the participants nodded in agreement.

"The issue isn't whether or not he'll contribute to a solution," General Terrell added. "Rather, the question becomes whether or not he will agree to return."

"That's right," Aaron muttered while rubbing his eyes, as if remembering the sights after the massacre in the dining hall caused them to burn. "Byron left for personal reasons. If we go to him, it's with a request, not a summons."

The resulting murmuring projected their discouragement since the master mage needed to join them of his own volution. To Aaron's surprise, King Arval was the one who pushed for them to try.

"The reward will be worthwhile, and not much is at risk. Divided or jagged leadership reflects onto the country. My commanders and I have sensed the disjointed mentality of the human mages ever since the master mage departed. Why not send a messenger with our proposal?"

"What's the worst that could happen?" General Tont asked those at the table. "The man says no, then we can say we reached out."

"We shouldn't go into it with a pessimistic mindset," Jurek chided.

As if the high priest's words sparked another idea, Lydia pointed at the man enthusiastically. "You're right! The goal is to convince him to return, at least until the demon is vanquished."

"In that case, we should send somebody who's familiar enough with him," Aaron mumbled. He began to consider their options but didn't get far before Commander Evern interrupted his thoughts.

"If I may suggest a volunteer, my daughter is close to Master Byron."

Aaron hesitated to agree, mainly due to his friend's current whereabouts.

"She was my first choice too," Lydia added. "I can't come up with another person among his former students who spent as much time with him."

The sapphire eyes of the Yeluthian commander drew Aaron's attention, and he sensed her father's desire to keep her involvement with the Mintelians between them and King Arval.

Coura's experience possessing demonic energy probably isn't part of her past their people are fond of. I would also hate to deal with the aftermath of Hendal's escape to the Mintelian village, so that situation can remain a private matter.

Since he also couldn't dispute his friend's close relationship with Byron, Aaron shrugged. "If she's willing to do it, I won't argue. Can you arrange for a scout to share our request?"

The commander dipped his chin and appeared a bit relieved. "I will assume responsibility and send one of my soldiers to inform her of the situation."

"Have the two visit Byron after. There's no point in bringing them here when East Hoover is along the way."

"Yes, Your Highness."

With nothing else to discuss, Aaron ended the meeting on an optimistic note, letting the group know they should be seeing the fruits of their labor soon enough. He returned to his quarters to find a hiding spot for the ancestral weapon, ordered two of his guards to stand watch despite their lack of knowledge regarding the dagger, then he decided to move outside to the queen's garden. There, he greeted the dozens of people wandering along the trail until he entered the private section.

For the first time in months, he looked forward to what the near future would bring.

***

The sheer determination with which Coura approached her training ebbed drastically over the weeks once she began shifting between using light and dark magic. The latter would never be as powerful as it had been, yet in a way, it forced her to decide on a course of action based on what spells proved necessary or more beneficial at the moment. Meanwhile, Harriette offered to teach her how to manipulate her Yeluthian energy after their evening chores. Although the Mintelian woman never developed their relationship beyond a student and mentor, Coura became confident in her light spells for the first time, strengthening her control.

What Sage Vidar reminded her every afternoon, and what she eventually engrained in her mind as the days blurred together, was to detach from her emotions and focus on what her senses picked up instead. This grew easier when she quit fighting the urge to dismiss the sage's instruction to switch between the types of energy. Rydar continued acting as a competent combatant able to adapt to whatever she tried. Despite her efficiency during their sparring matches, he consistently left cuts and bruises, which remained her responsibility to heal when the sage dismissed the pair.

After the first couple weeks went by, she stopped keeping track of the passing time. The villagers ignored her, the weather stayed bleak and cloudy, and she had nothing to look forward to except the next task at hand. The bland setting did help eliminate distractions, so she embraced it in order to successfully ignore her feelings and focus.

"Don't forget to mask your energy," the older Mintelian reminded her that afternoon while she practiced magic with Rydar. He sat beside Harriette across the field to observe her progress halfheartedly between chats with the woman.

Coura snuffed out the urge to respond that she already did so and figured he merely hoped to provoke her. *I won't give him the satisfaction*, she decided before sending a thin bolt of lightning past her opponent's right ear.

He had seen her use the strategy before to catch him off guard and didn't flinch, so she prepared another with the intent to land a minor jolt; however, movement out of the corner of her eye stayed her hand. Even Rydar abandoned his stance to face the two men approaching their location. Coura glanced over at the sage and Harriette as they rose to their feet.

"Did I order you to stop?" he snapped before circling around the dirt area.

The demonic energy in her center hummed slightly in response to her annoyance before she clamped down on the stray emotion. It still proved difficult to dismiss the bloodlust and enjoyment from combat stemming from that power, but she did so after Rydar raised his weapon again.

He charged with a grunt, forcing Coura to weave together a shield constructed from the light energy, which always seemed ready when she beckoned it. Thanks to Harriette's meetings and individual practice sessions, she kept the spell tied to her center and fed it while concentrating on manipulating the power. Because of this, she couldn't readily use a new spell, especially one consisting of the opposite type of energy.

Whatever she planned on attempting next fell through when a familiar voice said her name.

"Coura, I need to talk with you."

She stepped away from her shield yet kept the spell going. If she brought it down, Rydar would come after her, according to the sage's order; this way, he had an excuse to not pursue. She turned away while placing her faith in that assumption and saw Lavine alongside the same guide from Kercher who escorted her before. The Yeluthian wore his bronze armor, except for the helmet which rested under his arm, and stared at her despite the lack of a warm welcome, which consisted of Sage Vidar scolding the two for trespassing while Harriette cowered behind the older Mintelian. The guide whose name she didn't remember appeared bewildered by the intrusion, yet the Yeluthian's sapphire eyes remained on Coura.

When he didn't address her, she walked over to meet him. "What are you doing here?"

"Commander Evern sent me to find you. He requires your assistance."

When he didn't elaborate, the sage took the opportunity to continue berating them. "What right do outsiders have to demand entrance on my property? You claim to be soldiers who follow the law, yet I never received a request. This is a private lesson, now leave!"

The man from Kercher attempted to apologize only to be interrupted and insulted for his lack of manners.

Lavine eyed the Mintelian with an unreadable gaze before directing his next question at her. "Will you help us?"

Coura opened her mouth to respond before closing it and averting her eyes. "I shouldn't leave. At least, not yet."

The Yeluthian hesitated before continuing. "I am afraid the country and its people's safety are at risk. Your king's council, as well as King Arval, hope you will be able to bring Master Byron back to the palace."

"Byron?" Coura's head snapped to Lavine. "What happened to him?"

"He retired from his position on short notice and moved to East Hoover. I can provide the details once we are on our way."

Although she wondered what additional information he kept secret, Coura felt conflicted between remaining in the Mintelian village or returning to the world beyond. To her amazement, the sage stayed quiet throughout the limited explanation and waited for her answer.

If I go, I might regress to my old mentality, she thought against a rising fear of the unknown. *It seems as though I just arrived too. Then again, I'm now successfully meditating, practicing both light and dark magic, and self-monitoring my energy. My original goal focused on healing my soul space, yet I learned that isn't possible because it changed. Would it be worth it to stay and abandon Byron, Aaron, and the rest of Asteom then?*

The unanimous response to that unspoken question arose from a wave of guilt at the idea of turning her back on her home and friends.

"Let's go," she replied with a nod.

Lavine perked up while the guide from Kercher spun around and began hurrying away.

Coura chanced a glance at Sage Vidar since she expected backlash for her decision; however, the Mintelian pointedly put his back to her before walking away without a word. The outright rebuff hurt considering she prepared to thank him for the experience, though Harriette remained to offer a slight, awkward smile.

"Go," the woman urged before moving to meet Rydar in the sparring area.

When the combatant waved at Coura after, she dismissed her shield and raised a hand to return the gesture.

With nothing else tying her to the village, she led Lavine to her tent so she could change clothes and retrieve her few belongings before they exited the area. The two hiked for a bit until they stood alone in an unpopulated part of the mountain. Then, they took flight.

Because of the late hour, Lavine directed them to land as soon as they spotted the outside of the forested area bordering the eastern farming land. There, Lavine rationed their dried meal, built a fire, and revealed what drove Coura's former mentor to leave Verona.

She hadn't stuck around the palace long enough after the attacks to hear details about the massacre and victims, and learning about Emilea and Cintra's fates struck her like an invisible blow to the gut. Whether or not she agreed with Byron's decision to retire suddenly and dismiss his responsibilities didn't matter; the emotional toll seemed like enough reason, in her opinion.

Lavine purposefully left her after to scout the area nearby. Once she found herself alone, she let tears fall in memory of the master light mage until a sense of weariness drove her to sleep.

In the morning, the two moved on toward East Hoover.

Uncertain Steps

In order to avoid startling the townsfolk, Coura and Lavine agreed to land farther down the road from their destination, dismiss their wings, and enter through the main area. Despite the cautious approach, the Yeluthian's armor drew people's attention anyway, though he held a neutral expression that suggested the gawking didn't bother him. Meanwhile, Coura grew inexplicably anxious about returning to the place she once recognized as her only home.

Nobody should remember me, except maybe the teachers, she told herself for reassurance while focusing on her breathing. *Perhaps I'm afraid of what they heard from the palace. It's been a few years since I shed my reputation as a human weapon, but how long does it take for gossip to spread between the academy and the capital? Would people believe the lies?*

The walls surrounding the Magical Arts Academy loomed ahead, forcing her to consider the current issue instead of her personal feelings.

"I would imagine Byron and Cintra are staying here," she began as an excuse to spark a conversation. "Clearshot should be welcome since his children are students, and Byron's friends with Headmaster Symon. There's a wing available for guests they would be using."

"Is that so?"

"We'll need to visit the gatekeeper for entry and probably request our own rooms after a meeting with the headmaster."

"Are you excited to return?" Lavine asked in a startlingly enthusiastic manner. "You studied here, correct?"

She nodded. "I haven't been back since I left for Verona with the mages who graduated at that time."

Their conversation ended there since they drew near the gatekeeper's station, which lied in front of metal bars sealing the school away from the rest of the town. Because of his position and formidable appearance, Coura left the talking to her Yeluthian companion, who acted more than willing to take the lead on their assignment. He revealed their intent to speak with the headmaster first due to their arrival sparking interest from anyone who caught the bronze shining off his body. News of an angel in such an out-of-the-way town would cause a ruckus among the students and faculty, especially if they remained unaware of the reason.

To her relief, the gatekeeper understood. He instructed them to wait while he slipped away, then he returned a few minutes later with a younger woman bearing curly, brown hair and glasses. After introducing her as his assistant, he bid them well. Lavine thanked the man before he and Coura followed their guide into the building beyond.

For the most part, the hallways looked and felt the same compared to Coura's days as a trainee. While she began recalling her time as a student in the various rooms, Lavine conversed with the young woman about what the academy taught and the career paths available to human mages. The area became familiar enough for Coura to recognize the route to the headmaster's office, reminding her of the numerous visits during her later years.

Everyone must be in class, she realized when nobody crossed their path. *Maybe finding Byron will be easier than we anticipated.*

The gatekeeper's assistant opened the door to the waiting room, ushered them inside, and informed the secretary named Jann of their purpose. With her role fulfilled, the younger woman directed a curt nod at Lavine in a parting gesture.

"Just a moment," Jann addressed them afterward with a warm smile. She rose to knock on another door in the space, which she entered a few seconds later.

In the resulting silence, Coura wondered if the secretary remembered her from the minutes they spent together before the headmaster would call her in for a disciplinary lecture. The woman emerged sooner than expected and held the door open while waving for them to go inside. As if in response to the previous thought, Jann shot her a wink when the two made eye contact.

"Welcome," came the man's gentle voice from the space. "Please, take a seat."

A pair of chairs had been positioned to face one of two desks at the far end of the wide room, which held books, papers, clay mugs, writing utensils, and an assortment of random items on its surface. Lavine accepted the offer, so Coura joined him as a figure rummaged through a cabinet near the lone window.

"There," the man punctuated and closed the wooden doors before turning to face his guests. "I apologize for the improper introduction. This afternoon was supposed to be a cleaning day of sorts."

"I assume a headmaster's free time is precious," Lavine added while standing to extend a hand. "Thank you for allowing us to meet with you under such unexpected circumstances."

Headmaster Symon stepped closer to accept the gesture while Coura rose and mirrored her partner. The man had aged more than anybody she'd seen since her departure. What was once a head full of hair now displayed only a few whisps, and new, square spectacles stretched the width of his face. He didn't look as thin as she remembered, though he hunched forward to display a permanent slouch. Despite the physical changes, his studious personality remained the same.

"My spare time is no more valuable than yours, I'm sure," he commented while breaking off the greeting.

When he glanced at Coura, she debated offering the same greeting until his bushy eyebrows rose and he leaned forward to inspect her face.

"Coura Galdwin? Is that you?"

"Headmaster," she said in reply while acknowledging his correct observation, though she hoped her crooked smile didn't come off too much like a wince.

The man adjusted his glasses then straightened, chuckled, and held out a hand. "Look at how much you've grown!"

She accepted the handshake and felt the building tension in her muscles ease before the three took their seats.

"Well, I know Coura," the man began and put his hands together on his desk while eyeing the Yeluthian. "You may call me Symon or Headmaster. Whatever you prefer."

Lavine introduced himself after and prepared to mention their purpose for the visit until the headmaster released a discouraged sigh.

"You're here for Byron, correct?"

Coura crossed her arms and tilted her head. "Was it that obvious?"

"Based on his behavior, I figured some sort of issue drove him from the capital."

"He is not in trouble," Lavine added to reassure the headmaster.

Still, the man shook his head. "Byron? Trouble? When are *those* words ever spoken together?"

She couldn't tell if he was joking until a smile stretched across his lips, and Lavine took the opportunity to summarize the incident in the palace and Byron's guilt at Cintra's injury, leading the master mage to leave Verona. The Yeluthian omitted the council's issues and their desire to ask for Byron's input as soon as he would return, which Coura thought was for the best.

When Lavine finished, Headmaster Symon snatched a cloth from one of the desk drawers and wiped his spectacles. "As much as I wish to become involved for Byron's sake, I'll keep my nose out of it. Jann should be finished arranging your rooms, and I trust Coura remembers where the laundry, bathing, and kitchen spaces are. All I ask is that you don't cause problems for the instructors or our students."

"You have my word," the Yeluthian answered as he rose and bowed.

Coura did the same, though she had a feeling the headmaster directed the request toward her. *It's been how many years since I lived here and he has to warn me to behave?*

Despite that, he mentioned how glad he was to see her again before the pair exited the office and conversed with Jann.

*

Lavine suggested they split up and search the academy for Byron once they located their rooms and he removed the distracting armor. Coura agreed, though exploring became difficult between the scheduled classes. People flooded every hallway until the next session when they all scattered in various directions. She decided to visit the mess hall then for a brief meal before heading outside to the training ground used for magic.

Groups of students ranging from pairs and trios to a class of sixteen practiced both offensive and defensive spells, which she halfheartedly monitored. As she circled the wide area, she sensed her former mentor wasn't around.

If Byron intended to return to acting as an instructor, I would've found him by now. He's not in the populated spaces, and Headmaster Symon didn't mention where he's staying. Perhaps he isolated himself in order to avoid drawing attention to his appearance or Cintra's injury.

Coura considered her next move before opting to consult Lavine in case the Yeluthian had better luck with the search. In the meantime, she strolled toward the nearest, wooden bench, sat, and soaked up the sunlight she had been deprived of during her weeks in the Ghurun Mountain Range.

Throughout the afternoon, clusters of trainees ambled in and out of the building. She found herself content simply observing their progress while making internal comments on their technique. The sun sank until it disappeared behind the westernmost wall to shade the area, and her stomach growled, signaling the evening hour.

I suppose I should meet Lavine so we can eat before the dining area grows too crowded, she noted while rising and stretching her stiff limbs.

As she began walking toward the metal door that led inside, Coura let her gaze wander over the remaining students for a final time. Her steps automatically slowed when she noticed a group of girls on the far eastern side practicing shielding magic. From that distance, she couldn't discern much about them physically; however, when the faded, gold-colored wall they constructed crumbled, she believed one of the trainees looked familiar.

They tried their unified shielding spell again, so she went closer while staring and waiting for another break. When they did stop and the air cleared, the blonde mage she studied cracked a smile when another praised their control, cementing the girl's identity.

"I'm sorry to interrupt," she began as she approached, alerting the group of her presence. "Can I borrow Lexie for a minute?"

Each of Clearshot's children enrolled at the MAA when they came of age, which the man had bragged about endlessly after his daughter left the previous fall. Their admiration for Coura matured into them viewing her as a resource to improve their abilities, so Mace and Lexie eagerly shared what they learned whenever she visited over the years. Hearing they would be experiencing a similar education warmed her heart, though she often missed their casual lessons outside their parents' home.

Lexie didn't appear to have changed much from their last encounter, yet her naturally outgoing behavior seemed reserved as she gaped before closing the distance between them. "This is a surprise!"

"Can you spare a moment?" Coura asked with a glance at the onlookers who lingered behind their fellow classmate.

At her question, Lexie snapped out of the dazed mindset, took her by the hand, and dragged her toward the wall where they could be alone. "I wasn't expecting you. Why are you here?"

"I'm in East Hoover on an assignment," she explained when the mage trainee released her hand. "I'm hoping you'll be able to help."

"Me?" Lexie squeaked as her eyes wide eyes.

Coura nodded yet hesitated to share the purpose for her visit. Until that point, she hadn't considered what memories mentioning Clearshot, or even Byron, would stir. This, coupled by her own guilt over Emilea's death, left her in an uncomfortable position.

"I'll do what I can," the light mage added, as if noticing the slight tension hanging between them.

"I'm wondering if you can tell me where your father or Byron are," Coura ventured in a neutral tone in order to avoid sparking negative emotions. "I explored all the main areas inside and sat outside for hours, but I haven't seen or heard any hints."

The young trainee raised her eyes and considered the request. After a minute, she snapped her fingers, then the smile returned. "Father agreed to tutor archery lessons when he first arrived. If he's not in his room, he must be in the secondary training ground. Let's go together!"

"You don't need to accompany me," Coura interjected before Lexie grabbed her hand again to lead her inside. "I didn't plan on disrupting your afternoon."

"That's just an extra practice session."

"Are you sure?" No matter what Coura said after, the girl had her mind set on the task. Part of her appreciated the offer, but the haunting reminder of what their family endured hung over her head as they entered the building, crossed through the busying hallways, and moved outside to the opposite area.

Emerging into the second space used for combat was like traveling back to the days when she had been a novice with weapons. One of her former instructors, a hefty man named Robin, monitored several trainees while they worked in pairs to disarm their partner. She recalled his many attempts to slow the steps despite her overeager attitude, which often resulted in bruises or minor cuts for her opponents.

As Lexie led her around the space, Coura considered what lessons she had been placed in before the headmaster removed her so she could work one-on-one with Byron. She averted her gaze from the group in response, though nobody paid them any attention. Aside from Robin and the trainees, another class consisting of older students sparred at the farthest end, and a boy practiced solo maneuvers on a straw dummy. Finally, where Lexie went stood a dozen or so bow-wielding trainees positioned in a row and aiming for a single bale of hay. The two came to a halt and admired the accuracy of each archer as they released their arrows individually down the line. All hit the target though in various spots.

"Not bad," Coura heard the first man comment before lowering his bow. "Actually, I'm impressed, especially since we just finished our session."

She hadn't noticed Clearshot among the students until he turned and addressed each person to offer tips on improving their skills.

He looks exhausted, she noted with a sinking heart, forcing her to recall how she didn't see him since before Emilea's death.

Normally, a wide grin stretched across his clean-shaven face, reflecting a cheerful demeanor, and his behavior never hid his true emotions. He did smile as he spoke, but it and his words held no joy. His cheeks developed a grayish tint, his eyes were slightly sunken, and he let his facial hair grow into the start of a beard. His entire personality changed as well since he spoke calmly and without any sort of passion.

I suppose we're all becoming different people.

Lexie stepped forward after the thought, prompting Coura to follow. Clearshot noticed their arrival immediately and offered a brief nod before finishing his conversation and dismissing the trainees.

"How was the lesson, Father?" his daughter asked while wrapping her arms around his slim waist.

"My aim is as accurate as ever, but my muscles need strengthening," he replied while returning the embrace.

"You say that every day!"

"It's true," Clearshot argued with a more genuine laugh.

Coura put her hands on her hips until they broke apart and Lexie gestured to her.

"Look who came to visit."

The man's expression showed no surprise at her arrival, yet he crossed his arms and said otherwise. "I'm amazed you're here, Coura."

"It's been a while," was all she could think to reply. The guilt stirred again when she couldn't figure out how to start a subject without it becoming related to the massacre, Emilea's death, or her immediate disappearance.

To her dismay, Clearshot wasn't willing to continue the conversation. She even caught his eyes narrow a bit.

I bet he harbors resentment toward me for disappearing that night, Coura admitted to herself when she remembered interacting with him, Emilia, Byron, Cintra, and Katrina mere hours before the incident. *Either that or he figures I'm involved somehow. I can't really blame him given I was a target too.*

"You seem like the perfect fit to teach archery," she threw out when the silence grew unbearable. "During my time as a trainee, we only had a single instructor for distance-based weapons. He knew the basics of using a bow and arrows, but when it came to how we could improve, he couldn't offer more than urging us to practice."

Clearshot's lips dipped into a slight frown. "I'm having fun, or as much as I can. Recovering from the physical damage an enemy inflicts is easier than when they attack the heart. I'm sure you can attest to that."

With a deep breath, Coura dropped her arms to her sides, dipped her head, and abandoned her attempt to dismiss the shame she felt. During her time with Sage Vidar, Harriette, Rydar, and the other Mintelians, she learned they didn't disguise or repress their emotions as she expected. Instead, they grew accustomed to a simple life, so they expressed what they felt as soon as they experienced it and moved on. Nobody questioned whatever she bottled up, and no one showed concern until she warranted it. The minimal emotion she allowed to permeate her mentality also strengthened her spellcasting without distraction. She called upon that self-control before addressing Clearshot and Lexie.

"I'm sorry about Emilea," she started at a quieter volume. "I only found out about her death and Cintra's injury a few days ago. I abandoned Verona to find a solution to a personal problem instead of helping track down the culprits who are responsible. You two, Mace, and the victims' families deserve more than my apology. That's why I agreed to work with the Yeluthians. If I can do anything else to-"

Clearshot stepped forward until he stood directly in front of her; the sound caused her to stop speaking and glance up. She expected some sort of physical backlash, yet he merely laid a hand on her shoulder with misty eyes and a gentle smile.

"Thank you," he offered in a voice choked by unshed tears. "You're acting so mature about this, especially compared to us older adults. Nobody places any blame on your shoulders. The enemy has a plan, and I'm sure you're as much of a victim because of your magic."

"Well, I should have-"

In an unexpected gesture, he pulled her in for an embrace before mumbling more. "Emilea trusted you too. She wouldn't wish for us to wallow in the past."

He released her after and stood straighter. Although the pain of the master mage's passing still remained, Coura felt willing to accept Clearshot's words in order to ease her stress.

"Now, why are you here?" the man asked next when Lexie went to his side. The trainee took her father's hand in an expression of comfort before the two shared a look, making Coura wonder how much the children's love and attention healed his grief.

Without distress mucking their conversation, she could discuss her assignment without feeling guilty. "I need to find Byron. Apparently he abandoned his position. The king's council is hoping he'll return and assist them with figuring out what to do about the issues to the north and around Dala."

"You sound calm even though you're referring to such major dilemmas," Clearshot muttered while scratching his beard.

Coura just shrugged. "My partner and I spent the afternoon searching, but I didn't find any signs to indicate that he's here."

"That's because he probably isn't."

She raised an eyebrow, prompting him to elaborate.

"I'm not entirely sure since I haven't explored the area too much, but Byron disappeared as soon as I received a room and a job."

"What do you mean?"

"I haven't seen Master Byron around the academy," Lexie added. "We can ask Mace too."

Coura crossed her arms and contemplated where else they could look. Ultimately, the evening crept over the training ground by that point, and she needed to meet up with Lavine. "Thank you, Lexie. It seems like I'll be here for at least another couple days, so I'll try again tomorrow."

Clearshot and his daughter agreed to wait, ending the conversation there.

Once the three returned inside, she mentioned her partner and split from the pair to head toward her room. A few minutes later, she found Lavine in his quarters wiping the previously worn armor with a clean rag. The two shared their lack of results before deciding to eat with the intent to begin a serious search for Byron the next morning.

*

East Hoover's size wasn't comparable to Verona or Dala, but it possessed enough shops and eateries to keep somebody busy for a full day. The MAA purchased most of the town's produce and hired those who lived in the area for various tasks, making it fairly self-sufficient. Coura hadn't considered how the place functioned since she remained inside the academy when she was a trainee. To her, the buildings and homes became the extent of what she saw of Asteom.

Headmaster Symon led the way along the single main road lined with businesses and cheerful citizens who waved at the trio or greeted the man. The headmaster had offered to escort Coura and Lavine to where he figured Byron might be hiding when the two went to meet with him that morning. He didn't seem bothered by their second intrusion and claimed he had the time to spare.

Fortunately, his hunch proved correct. Despite the brief pauses, they only stopped when they reached their goal. Near the edge of town stood a populated building, and the three slipped inside amid the lunch rush.

The tavern looked as ordinary as any she ever visited, if not cleaner than most, and smelled of burning firewood. Headmaster Symon continued across the space with nods and waves at those occupying the nearby tables, and at the back sat Byron with an arm around Cintra's shoulders. While her former mentor appeared normal, Coura could sense a sadness emanating from the woman beside him.

Then, Byron noticed the trio, and his expression hardened.

Just like Clearshot, she noted.

"We found you at last," Headmaster Symon said by way of greeting and dropped into an empty chair at their table.

Lavine remained standing, so Coura did too. Meanwhile, Byron stared at the Yeluthian first before lowering his eyes to meet the headmaster's; he ignored Coura completely.

"This must be important if *you* left the academy. I take it you're not just here for a meal?"

"Afraid not, my friend."

"We would like a moment of your time, Master Byron," Lavine explained with a slight bow.

Coura refrained from scoffing at his manners considering the unnecessary formality in such a casual setting. To her surprise, Cintra responded and placed a hand on Byron's arm.

"I'll be fine. Go ahead."

"I'm not leaving you alone," he commented at a lower volume akin to a grumble.

"Allow me to keep you company," Headmaster Symon offered, addressing Cintra specifically.

She immediately accepted, forcing Byron into a corner.

"We may speak outside," Lavine continued and flashed a polite smile.

He allowed Byron to exit first before following with Coura behind, then her former mentor chose an alley close to the building where they would remain away from prying eyes. Once they settled into place, he crossed his arms, straightened, and glared at the Yeluthian soldier.

"What's this about?"

"Commander Evern sent us on behalf of King Aaron's council," Lavine began while letting his smile fade. "The members offer a plea for your return in order to combat the current issues along the northern border and-"

"I already resigned from my position," Byron interrupted in a calmer tone of voice than his expression suggested. "Lydia should be equipped to take over."

"It is not so much about the title. King Aaron and those on his council suggested we reach out because of your prior experience and knowledge regarding demons and their creatures."

"We?" Byron shifted his eyes to Coura, as if he just realized she was present too. "You're involved in this?"

She tilted her head. "I'm here, aren't I?"

"The fate of your kingdom is at risk," Lavine cut in. "You proved to be a valuable asset for your country in the past, and that is why your king requests your presence."

At the Yeluthian's comment, Byron showed his temper. "That woman with Symon is depending on me right now, and she's safe far from the capital. That should be all the reason His Highness and the council need to accept my decision."

"Master Byron…" Lavine fumbled for an appropriate reply before glancing at Coura for support.

Throughout their argument, she found herself conflicted by both sides, as well as her personal attachment to each. Byron became valuable to Asteom, more so than her, yet comparing him to a useful tool reminded her of the many times throughout her life she had been regarded as a weapon. The notion didn't sit right with her.

"This isn't an order," she explained. "Aaron, King Arval, and the others sent us to request your return. You're free to decline."

Lavine looked baffled by her lax attitude while Byron's annoyed expression eased into a suspicious, albeit slightly confused, stare.

I guess I'm supposed to convince him to join us. The fact of the matter is exactly what I said: He doesn't have to leave East Hoover if he truly wishes to remain here. There's also the matter of Cintra's care and where she'll stay.

"I hate to say you wasted your time by coming to East Hoover, but I won't be returning," Byron concluded, though with a sense of relief instead of a defensive attitude.

Lavine released an irritated sigh before sending her a disappointed look.

"If you feel like this is the place that needs you the most, then you should stay," she added and hoped her honesty would reach them both.

When the discussion ended and Lavine announced he would be returning to the MAA, her former mentor volunteered to walk with them while the headmaster watched over Cintra.

A Master's Responsibility

Symon had been the first person to question Byron's decision to leave Verona with Clearshot and Cintra in order to live a quieter life in East Hoover. Initially, his friend believed the trio planned to visit; however, once he explained what took place in the palace, the headmaster acted sympathetic. He offered Clearshot a position as an archery instructor, allowing the soldier to stay in the academy where his children could look after him for the time being. Byron still believed his mourning companion would abandon the capital instead of request a permanent reassignment, which would allow his friend to escape the chaos.

He desired that with Cintra too.

Nothing hindered that dream until the Yeluthian and Coura interrupted their lunch. As soon as the two entered after Symon, Byron's frustration rose, mainly because he'd been avoiding the headmaster's attempts to convince him to properly announce his retirement.

It thought it would be obvious by my dismissal of what current events surround Asteom that I have no interest in serving the kingdom anymore, he reflected as he exited the tavern with the angel. *I devoted my life to combatting the country's problems because the transferred trainees, including Coura, needed me. King Hernan, and now Aaron, sent me away from the capital, often against my own will or because they trusted me to combat their issues. Now, Cintra is relying on me, and I promised to be there for her. This is my choice. Unfortunately, no one seems to understand.*

The council's decision to send somebody after him wasn't surprising based on his accomplishments and involvement with the palace's dilemmas over the years. Lydia and those with her knowledge could manage the training and responsibilities required by the position, yet they lacked his experience, which translated into valuable insight. The recent mention of a demon also warranted careful consideration. Because of that specifically, he assumed everyone who participated in the previous battle in Verona would support his return.

Of all the people he expected to argue with him, Coura sat at the top of his list. The fact that she returned to East Hoover startled him given he hadn't considered how she fit into the situation in the dining hall; however, he figured it pertained to her various relationships in the palace. Part of him hated the idea of her falling in line just to please her friends and father, which led to a building sense of resentment.

Then, she left him stunned.

"If you feel like this is the place that needs you the most, then you should stay," she said after clarifying their orders.

Byron wondered what prompted her to make such a passive comment and longed to ask, which was why he volunteered to return to the academy with the pair after. *Symon will keep Cintra entertained, if he doesn't talk her ear off first, so I have time to speak with Coura. Out of everyone I encountered after the massacre, she seems to have distanced herself the most. Has she spoken with Clearshot or his children yet?*

He contemplated how his friend would react to seeing her after the incident considering she only appeared to coerce him into returning to the capital. Along the way, he realized he hadn't seen Coura since the chaotic evening, and before the ball even began at that, leading him to wonder why she shut herself away.

Meanwhile, Byron recognized the Yeluthian who introduced himself as Lavine from multiple encounters during the construction of the additional training ground and dormitory, though the two didn't speak to each other. The angelic soldier didn't attempt to hide his displeasure with the outcome of their request, nor did he bother to make conversation while they walked along an empty path toward the main road. This left an uncomfortable silence hanging between the three.

When the tension became too heavy to ignore, Byron inhaled a deep breath, released it in a drawn-out sigh, and prepared to apologize for his short-tempered behavior until a surge of energy struck him like a splash of cold water to the face. He instantly identified it as demonic in nature while the wave of power continued rolling over his body. Each limb froze when his own energy hummed in distress, a sensation within his center he'd grown accustomed to over the years of fighting the unnatural creatures.

Coura and Lavine halted as well, and the three glanced to their left at the same time.

"One of the beasts appeared," the Yeluthian confirmed before sprinting in that direction.

Coura chased after him a second later with Byron close behind, though he remained attentive enough to note how his trained instinct encouraged him to move toward danger instead of away from it.

As the trio hurried across town, the ground gradually began trembling at inconsistent intervals, causing people fleeing the area to stumble or lean against nearby buildings. Not everybody who lived near the academy possessed the necessary power to be trained as a mage or learn spellcasting, but those who did began filing closer order to launch elemental projectiles or craft a shield and protect those around themselves.

Byron looked beyond the crowd before sliding to a stop when he could study the intruder in question. Unlike any demonic creature he'd seen before, this one assumed the form of a black-haired bull, though it only showcased a single, blunt horn on the right side of its head, like a leafless branch. It stomped its thick legs in an impatient manner at the edge of town and swished its whip-like tail from side to side, producing a faint whistle. What proved most problematic was its enlarged size, which looked comparable to a single-story home.

The muscles can back up its menacing presence, he observed when the beast snorted. Without a weapon, Byron had no other option except to rely on magic, so he dove into his reserved pool of dark energy and carefully masked his presence in order to avoid concerning the innocent civilians.

Lavine and Coura donned the proper attire of the soldiers, which meant they hadn't forgotten to come equipped. Each drew slim, steel blades from the sheaths clipped to their waists before the Yeluthian charged to initiate a fight.

"I'll support you from here," Byron shouted to his former student before she ran ahead.

Without considering what the two would do, he assumed the role of a defensive mage first in order to prevent both unnecessary damage to East Hoover and voluntary individuals or trainees who might attempt to join but would ultimately get in the way. He spun around, raised his arms, and released a shielding spell. The energy left his hands to stretch across the area in front of the buildings and streets in a violet glow. Although his power would act as a transparent wall, he planned to monitor the flow until support from the academy met them.

When he completed the spell, Byron put his back to the shield in order to observe the strategy Coura and Lavine devised. The Yeluthian became the distraction by keeping to the creature's front side and waving his sword for its head. At the same time, Coura continuously slipped into its blind spot, allowing the pair to swipe and stab from both ends. The beast's bellowing filled the air as it lowered its oversized head to swing the massive horn or lunge at one of the two. Fortunately, Coura and Lavine's speed and skill kept the duo out of danger, and Byron noticed how well they coordinated their attacks. His concern only returned minutes later when the creature came within range of his shield.

They should lead it toward the woods, he thought, though the warning sat on his tongue since he figured they already knew that. *The creature's hide is too dense for their swords to successfully produce serious injury. Our best bet is to keep it contained until other dark or light mages arrive to manage the shielding spell for me.*

From where Lavine and Coura circled the beast, he sensed its demonic power growing and considered what prompted it to build such a reserve of energy. The Yeluthian must have felt the same, for he started backtracking farther from the buildings. To Byron's dismay, instead of following, the creature lashed out at his shield with its misshapen horn. The direct strike produced a ring that echoed in his ears, yet the magical wall didn't budge.

He tensed when it reared its head for another blow until Coura aimed a blast of fire at its eyes before it could follow through with the motion. It seemingly roared in pain, yet the lack of visible damage hinted that her magic didn't do any harm; however, the spell did succeed in shifting its attention.

When the beast lunged to stab her with its horn, she leapt out of the way and continued sidestepping in the opposite direction. Lavine took advantage of the moment to slice at its tail and back legs, revealing his intent to switch roles with Coura. Unlike earlier though, their opponent didn't change its focus from its current prey.

The hoofs slammed into the earth, causing it to shake enough for Coura to stumble in place. In an attempt to rid herself of the attention, she spun on her heel, sprinted toward the main road surrounded by the trees of the forest outside East Hoover, and resumed her stance. Lavine adjusted his position during that time and wound up at the creature's front side again.

The shift in their fight led Byron to glance over his shoulder at the shield. *This should hold if the beast manages to strike it again. I'll keep an eye out for reinforcements while supporting them. The townsfolk already evacuated the area, so we can plan on killing it here.*

As his eyes returned to the same scene, he managed two steps before a second flood of demonic energy poured from a new location to fill the space. He abandoned his subtle approach in favor of racing ahead when a second creature identical to the first emerged from the woods near where Coura stood. He caught her raise an arm, as if blocking a blow, and the air around her glowed briefly before the additional opponent swung its head to connect its horn with her body right through the minor shielding spell she mustered.

The sudden attack swept her off her feet, knocking her weapon out of her hands and sending her tumbling across the ground. When her body rolled to a stop, she faced away from Byron, who shifted his charge to go to her side. Before he could reach her, the first creature stomped over to put itself in between, preventing him from continuing.

"Get out of my way!" he growled and clenched his hands into fists after sliding to avoid barreling into the beast.

While that one hindered his progress, the other targeted Lavine since the Yeluthian inserted himself in its path in order to keep it from harming Coura any further. She still remained unmoving, and ruby blood trickled down her arms and back.

I shouldn't have left those two alone, a tiny voice whispered in Byron's head. *I didn't learn from what happened in the palace. Katrina, Emilea, and so many others lost their lives because I dismissed Cintra's vision. I ruined her life because of my carelessness, and now Coura's hurt, East Hoover is in danger, and this Yeluthian...*

His internal scolding paused as the second creature knocked Lavine aside when the Yeluthian refused to be herded away from his unconscious companion. The soldier caught himself from falling over and didn't appear phased by the unfavorable shift of the fight.

Still, recognizing how his lack of assistance meant the people he cared for would be at a greater risk lit a fire under Byron.

I'm tired of falling short and letting beasts and enemies hurt others when I possess the abilities to stop them. Even if it takes my entire being, I will make sure these creatures die!

***

A painful throbbing in Coura's head dragged her out of unconsciousness. Every part of her burned or stung, and she found herself lying in the grass. A warm liquid covered her arm and torso, which she soon realized was her blood, while noise and tremors worsened her headache. When she opened her eyes, the light did the same, so she squeezed them shut.

I remember... a demonic... creature...

The second, bull-like beast appeared following an unexpected blast of energy within the woods beyond the road where she stood. There hadn't been time or space to scramble out of its range, so she crafted a shield as best as she could given the emergency.

That spell probably saved my life, she noted as her mind became less muddled.

Sitting up sent sharp stabs along the right side of her body, but she managed while attempting to move her injured arm. The fingers twitched, though it became apparent bones were broken in multiple places. Fortunately, her head cleared enough so she could process the situation.

She wound up to the side of the road closest to the current fighting. Lavine engaged with one of the demonic creatures while it circled around him before charging and swinging its horn. Because he remained the beast's only target, her Yeluthian comrade couldn't wear it down or attack without putting himself in danger.

A glimmer in front of the town showed Byron's shield still held; however, Coura sensed light energy being poured into another spell behind the glass-like wall. It took her a moment to realize dozens of mages gathered at the edge of East Hoover and presumably crafted another shield for additional support.

Finally, she thought with a hint of bitterness, though the sight eased some of her concern.

When she spotted Byron nearby, her worry returned twofold.

The master mage wore an unamused expression while launching all sorts of elemental projectiles at the creature's legs and the ground, forcing it to slow in order to avoid losing its footing. Coura grew tense when she steadily sensed greater amounts of dark energy slipping through his control.

He's expending more power than he can mask, which doesn't look necessary. That means he's purposefully disregarding how much strength he puts into the spells. He's being reckless with where he casts them too.

As if in response to her observations, one of Byron's lightning blasts missed the creature and struck a tree behind it, starting the branches on fire. A second bolt scattered toward Lavine, though it dissipated before it could reach the Yeluthian. While she considered what she could do to assist either person, the master mage shot a spear-like icicle through the first creature's leg where it stayed and caused the bull-like beast to stagger.

Byron can handle himself right now, Coura decided and turned her attention to Lavine.

With a grunt, she ground her teeth, climbed to her feet through a pain-induced haze, then plotted out how to safely creep closer. Before she could even take a single step, another of Byron's stray spells in the form of a fireball blasted in front of her. A curse escaped her lips at his careless behavior, prompting her to glare in his direction.

Instead of continuing with individual spells, he began sending multiple waves by extending both hands toward the creature, which roared since it could not escape the onslaught. Coura watched as its wounded leg caught on a chunk of upturned earth, sending it onto its side. Its resulting, alarmed cry abruptly cut off when Byron launched another oversized icicle through its skull.

Without pausing to survey the results, the master mage stalked past the twitching body to where Lavine danced around the second creature's attacks. The Yeluthian's movements kept the beast's back to Byron; however, he remained hidden from Byron's line of sight as well. Coura held her breath when her former mentor raised his hands without offering a warning and released a blast of fire at the second creature.

What is he doing? He's going to kill Lavine too!

The grass burned away, leaving patches of charred earth while minor flames crawled along the drier spots. Lavine didn't expect his support and stumbled backward from the wave of heat. At the same time, the beast trumpeted in a frightened manner, spun around to face Byron, and charged.

Somehow, Coura predicted what the master mage planned to do in response and jumped into action in order to defend her clueless, Yeluthian comrade. Her goddess gift triggered as soon as she acknowledged the ability, producing a portal she threw herself through in order to appear at Lavine's side. Despite the minor disorientation and his expected confusion, she committed to raising her unharmed arm toward the creature and casting a shielding spell using whatever light energy she possessed.

A heartbeat later, Byron's lightning slammed against her magic in a deafening clasp of thunder.

"What is he planning?" Lavine shouted above the noise. "Does he not see us?"

Immediately after the lightning came shards of ice, though they struck the transparent wall less forcefully. Coura ignored the questions in order to maintain her concentration since the spell required her to continue adding power until the ground shook once and the elemental projectiles ended.

A few seconds of silence passed before she dismissed her shield. A cloud of smoke hung in the air and hindered their sight, yet soon they could spot the second creature lying on the ground with multiple, icy spears lodged into its head and neck. Most of the flesh on its side had been stripped away or charred into ashy scabs as well. Beyond the mangled remains stood Byron. His chest rose and fell while he panted, and sweat darkened several spots on his clothing. As soon as he noticed Coura and Lavine lingering farther behind, his eyes widened, as if he just realized the position they had been in.

Raised voices from the town drew Coura's attention before she saw the additional shield disappear. Somebody began issuing orders to dispose of the creatures' bodies, put out the spreading fire, and inform the citizens of the conclusion. As she looked between the approaching faces, the toll from using her magic and forcing her body to move while injured returned, causing her to sway. Lavine wrapped an arm around her shoulders in response.

"You lost a lot of blood," he commented with a glance at the puddle forming in the grass.

Coura groaned while trying to keep still until a mage spotted them and called for a healer. A group of five hurried to surround her before guiding her into a sitting position where they began repairing her damaged head, arm, and torso. They worked diligently, so she avoided the urge to interrupt with questions and tried locating her former mentor instead.

Despite the effort, he was nowhere in sight.

***

All the excitement remained on the outskirts of East Hoover as Master Gage, a dark mage instructor, took control of the situation, allowing Byron to remove himself from the area. The scent of the burned carcasses brought him out of the slump he wound up in once he spotted Coura and the Yeluthian on the opposite side. Before that, he had dropped into a satisfying, albeit disgraceful, showcase of his unrestrained desire to release his power in order to quell his own strife. There would be time to discuss what happened with Symon and the academy's faculty, the soldiers stationed as guards around town, and Coura and Lavine, but he needed a break to clear his head.

He trudged through the streets before leaning on a building in a quieter section near the tavern where he left his friend and Cintra. Then, he shifted to press his back against its warm surface.

I don't know how many years it's been since I fought without thinking about anything other than killing; probably when I was a trainee or first starting out in the army.

He hated acting only on instinct for many reasons, yet the most prominent related to his reputation to stay levelheaded in stressful situations. It became a goal, a state of mind to achieve and prove he could manage the responsibilities he accepts as a capable leader.

Maybe my self-control slipped because I don't live a life in the palace anymore. Without a reason to restrain myself, I figured the consequences wouldn't affect me.

Byron slid to sit while continuing to press his back against the stone structure and let his mind wander. For the first time in weeks, he reflected on himself and his decisions as the morning stretched into early afternoon. The sun continued on its route west across from his position, shining golden light on his entire body. He struggled to find the motivation to rise despite knowing Symon would be needed after the incident and leave Cintra alone. Then, he sheepishly realized he had to mentally prepare for her scolding.

Pretending I'm not responsible for her isn't going to stop her berating, he thought with a smile while using a finger to trace lines in the dirt.

"So, this is where you've been hiding."

Byron raised his eyes at the familiar voice and saw Coura standing farther down the path. Her right arm rested in a sling and bandages covered that side of her head and body, but she appeared otherwise unbothered. Still, his stomach dropped when he considered how close he had been to accidentally hurting her and Lavine.

When he didn't respond, she strode over to lean against the building, just as he had done earlier.

"Headmaster Symon and the instructors are looking for you," she began at a lower volume. "Lavine explained what took place, but I imagine they want to regroup and make sure you're all right. I offered to keep an eye out on my walk."

Byron could tell how exhausted she was despite her feigned lack of interest in his sulking, prompting him to release a tired sigh. "I'm sorry. I shouldn't have-"

"Don't."

The forcefulness of that single word struck him as though she'd thrown an actual rock at his head. He craned his neck to look up at his former student and found her staring straight ahead, purposefully ignoring his gaze.

"Don't apologize," she continued in a calmer tone. "You did what needed to be done in order to stop the creatures."

"I acted carelessly," he admitted.

"No, you were angry."

Byron dipped his chin. "Those are quite similar."

"Maybe." A pause followed her response before she added more. "Everyone expects powerful mages to be perfect, I guess. If we're not, then we become a threat. They believe we help because we can, not just because we care about those we protect. Most people don't consider that mages and soldiers are human too."

He didn't comment. Coura's blunt honesty reflected his own feelings, and she called him out on it after.

"That's why I don't care what you decide to do. People, even friends and family, ignore what we want because they value our input too much, whether its magic, opinions, or skills. I can't blame you for being frustrated."

Byron continued watching his former student, who avoided meeting his eyes, before understanding her behavior acted as her attempt to cheer him up. The support, as indirect as she made it, lightened his spirits, so he figured sharing his personal concerns couldn't hurt. "You know, I never thought I got a choice in the matter."

"Of course not," she interrupted. "That's because you never reject an offer to help."

"It comes with the title."

"No, it's your fault for accepting whatever you're asked to do."

A smirk tugged at his lips. *I wonder what's gotten into her. Coura never shied away from standing up for what she believes in, but I haven't heard her deliberately lecture someone before. Still, her support in my decision to leave the palace means more than she knows.*

"It was my choice," he muttered in response to her previous words. "In reality, nobody forced me to do anything. I had my mind so set on breaking free because of what took place that I overreacted. I put everyone else ahead of my own desires for so long, and Cintra's injury narrowed my view."

They lingered in silence for a while until the sun dipped behind the nearby structure.

Coura pushed herself away from the building with a wince, though she met his eyes for the first time since they began talking. "Did you speak to her yet?"

Byron shook his head, rose to his feet, and dusted himself off. "I'm sure Symon arranged for her to return to the academy."

"Let's go then."

*

Strolling through the town had been his favorite pastime when he lived in East Hoover because it provided an opportunity to be around ordinary people in a peaceful setting. Those who recognized him often shared their appreciation for his position as an instructor, his work to defend the area, and more recently, his service to the kingdom. As he returned to the MAA with Coura, just about everybody expressed how grateful they felt for how he handled the demonic creatures, and many commented on his showy way of doing so.

Over the years, he perfected a response consisting of a balance between acknowledging his actions and maintaining modesty while avoiding lingering on the event. To his side, Coura would offer brief nods if anyone addressed her, but she didn't stop moving toward their goal until a woman's voice called for Byron farther down the main road. It took a minute for him to recognize the figure as Cintra, who approached at a hasty pace with the assistance of her crutch. At the sight, he began jogging to meet her. She said his name once more as he slowed to halt so the two could wrap their arms around the other in a casual embrace.

"I'm sorry I left you at the tavern," he started before they broke apart. He held her shoulders and attempted to explain what happened only to be interrupted.

"You ran off!" she exclaimed and lightly punched his chest continuously until he released her to back away.

"A pair of demonic creatures showed up and…" His excuse faded into mumbles then silence when the woman shook her head, placed a hand on her hip, and pointed an accusing finger at him with the other.

"I mean *after* the fighting," she clarified before easing up on him. "Symon was kind enough to return to the academy with me when we heard the news. We waited for you, but you didn't show up, so I decided to search the area."

Byron frowned at her response. He could only think to offer another apology, which didn't appear to fix the issue.

"What happened?" she asked next and tilted her head at him.

"I needed some time alone," he admitted before remembering Coura. He glanced over his shoulder to find her lingering behind, though the pause gave her an opportunity to excuse herself from his company.

Her sapphire eyes darted between Cintra and Byron before she looked beyond at the academy. "I'm heading back to rest."

Byron nodded as she passed them and made a mental note to speak with her later. Meanwhile, Cintra sent her a polite smile yet said nothing. Without any distractions, he decided to reveal his concerns and prepared to do so until his friend stepped closer, seized his hand, and pulled him forward to begin moving along the road.

"You're a generous man, Byron," she startled him by saying. "Whether it's time, power, or whatever energy you can spare, you never hesitate to step in. I always admired you for that, but I'm afraid I abused it too."

"What I chose to do with my life has always been my decision, especially staying here."

Cintra fluttered her eyelashes, and her lips curved into a coy smile. "I hope my charm has something to do with it."

Byron felt himself blushing. "Of course."

"After my injury, I needed time to mentally recover from what took place and accept my physical limitations," she continued in a more serious manner. "You've been my strength, reminding me of what there is to live for when I was fully certain I would die."

She squeezed his hand during the following pause, so he did the same to reciprocate his feelings.

"Byron, I never requested much of you, but there is a favor I must ask."

"Anything."

"Go to Verona and do what you can to help resolve their issues."

"I won't leave you alone."

"But I'm not alone," she replied while raising her chin a bit and flashing a bold smile. "You introduced me to Symon, Cornelius, his children, and most of the light mages. Plenty of other people live in the academy as well. I'm recovered enough to move around on my own and prepared to open up to those who are willing to listen. Besides, I believe I'm finally able to face my fears about learning to control my ability."

Byron's eyes widened. "Really? You're certain you can handle wielding your light energy?"

Cintra nodded without a hint of concern. Her newfound confidence proved to be a positive surprise, one he hadn't been expecting or considering when he agreed to go to East Hoover.

"However, I will only continue if you return to Verona," she added. "You should do whatever your heart desires, which knowing you means weighing your options then going wherever you are needed the most. The kingdom needs you more than I do right now; I'm sure you realize that."

Byron anticipated a resulting sense of guilt to leave him feeling as though he should decline. He prepared to be overcome by an urge to protect his dearest friend and lover above all else, yet hearing her admit her trust in him led him to become more sure of himself than he'd been in months.

I suppose hearing her give me permission to leave was the reassurance I subconsciously searched for. Because I ignored her warning and brought her to the capital, I believed I owed it to her to give her the best life and keep her safe, especially since she relied on me for so much until now. How could I ever expect her to hold a grudge against me for what neither of us could prevent?

"Thank you," he found himself replying. "When I return, I promise we can start our life here together."

Her resulting smile warmed his heart.

"That's all I could ever dream of."

Unity

Byron found Coura chatting with Lavine after his and Cintra's discussion, explained his desire to accompany them, and ignored their unspoken intrigue relating to his changed mind. The trio planned to depart as soon as possible, so Symon made the preparations for them and Cintra, who would be tended to by the staff and students.

Unlike the previous days of sunshine and warm temperatures, the following morning began with low-hanging clouds to signal an inevitable rain shower. He and Cintra arrived to meet Coura and Lavine as the two gazed up at the sky. The former didn't wear the previous sling and had the bandages removed while the latter donned his people's bronze armor. Symon was already present alongside a mare, leading Byron to assume he would be riding horseback while his companions flew above. About a dozen people joined them outside to say their goodbyes to him, including Clearshot and the man's children; however, his friend dressed in travel clothes as well and shouldered a decently sized pack.

"What are you doing?" he asked without hiding his suspicion.

Clearshot still looked grief-stricken, yet a sense of determination came through in his expression despite the smile he cracked at the question. "What? Is this a private party?"

Byron narrowed his eyes. "No, but are you sure you're ready to leave?"

"I wouldn't be here if I wasn't."

Part of him wondered what the Yeluthian thought since the blond soldier glanced over at the sound of their voices. When neither the angel nor Coura addressed the request of an additional person on the journey, Byron assumed they felt comfortable with it.

I'd like to decline, if only to allow him more time to recover, yet Clearshot isn't an impulsive man. He must have some reason for joining, though I believe I already understand.

"Tell me why you wish to return to Verona?" he countered at a lower volume in order to avoid drawing further attention to their discussion.

His friend's smile faded, and an anger shone in the brown eyes, yet Clearshot answered in a neutral, controlled tone. "I'd like to help capture the creature responsible for Emilea's death."

Byron figured as much and nodded. He believed it would be disrespectful to deny the widower due vengeance, even if the role would be minor, so he stared past Clearshot to where Symon watched them. "We'll need another horse."

"You don't *need* another," the headmaster added while patting the mare's rump. "You'd just have to get comfortable with each other. This girl can carry two, you know."

Byron's sardonic glare spurred a laugh from the man, and Clearshot appeared to relax into a laidback attitude reminiscent of their years together.

"Are we prepared to head out?" Lavine asked while approaching.

As the trio faced the Yeluthian, Symon cleared his throat and resumed his professional demeanor.

"Pardon the delay. I must fetch a second horse for your additional rider."

Lavine raised his eyes to the sky again. "Would you expect the weather to hold, or do the storms here grow fierce?"

"We don't get much of a downpour at once, though it often stays consistent."

"I see."

Byron tilted his head. "Does rain hinder your flight that much?"

Lavine shook his head, then he scratched the back of his neck in an uncertain manner. "Yes and no. Our wings will not be affected if there is less than a downpour, and we can always stay above the clouds. The problem is visibility, both between us and to keep track of you on the ground. Unless we coordinate stopping points, I am afraid there is a possibility of accidentally splitting up."

Byron paused to consider that.

"We have mounts available if it would be easier to travel together," Symon offered.

The Yeluthian's calm expression faltered. "I have never ridden before," he mumbled while his eyes widened. Then, he glanced at the mare, as if assessing the animal's physicality. "Is it safe?"

"Yes," Clearshot reassured him. "It'll make your legs and back sore for a few days though, especially if we're in a hurry."

Lavine's lips curved downward into a frown while he considered their options. In the resulting silence, Coura's voice chimed from where she still stood monitoring the sky nearby.

"You all talk too much."

Byron shifted his gaze to his former student with mixed feelings. Ever since he saw her again, her behavior remained reserved, which he thought had been due to her returning to East Hoover. Many of his fellow master mages and instructors interrogated him about her over the weeks since they each heard varying degrees of what took place during his time in the palace.

Healer Clara wondered about her unnatural power, Master Gage questioned her sanity considering the demon's influence, Master Eva couldn't believe we kept her around after the suspicions, and others seem curious or doubtful of her contributions. Perhaps being in an environment that holds such negativity leads her to close herself off in order to avoid reflecting on the past.

In any case, he decided to include her in their planning. "What would you prefer to do, Coura?"

"Are we set to go?"

When everybody voiced their agreement, she strolled over, faced away from the group, then raised her left hand. Byron didn't sense any energy, yet he understood she intended to cast a spell. Before he could question it, he noticed the air in front of her hand shimmer. The light it radiated grew brighter in the dim morning and expanded into an oval shape stretching above Byron's head and twice the width of his shoulders. Within seconds, an image formed to replace the light, and he could vaguely make out an open field with several, blurry figures beyond.

I completely forgot about her goddess gift; however, I was under the impression she never wanted to use it again.

The last time he witnessed this unique side of her Yeluthian power had been when she demonstrated it in front of a selected group including him, though he hadn't volunteered to test the portal. The idea made him inexplicably nervous.

Mumbles and gasps from the shocked onlookers rose around him, including from Symon and Clearshot, yet she addressed them without a hint of concern.

"This will take us to the magical training ground outside the palace. I should be the last person to pass through and can probably keep it open for just one minute, so hurry up."

Lavine was the first to step forward with their bags and didn't hesitate to enter into the spell. His body rippled as he did so before blurring into the image, like passing under a waterfall to the opposite side.

"Time to go," Clearshot announced, shaking Byron out of his daze. The man hugged each of his children, wished them well, and accepted their orders to stay safe and take care of himself before jogging through the portal.

Meanwhile, Symon approached to clap Byron on the back. "We'll catch up when you return," the headmaster promised. "Just be sure to keep this country from falling apart."

"I'll do my best."

Cintra took his hand after, squeezed it, then kissed his cheek. "I will be here when you return."

Byron nodded since he couldn't express the heartfelt words that came to mind without wasting additional time. After, he readjusted the bag on his shoulder and walked toward Coura. She hadn't turned around or spoken to anybody, so he figured their business was finished.

In order to pass into the spell, he pictured the magic as a doorway and stepped through; however, unlike a normal opening, the world felt as though it dropped from beneath his feet, leading him to stumble forward into a new setting with different sights and sounds being thrown at him.

It became too much for his spinning head to handle. He dropped to his knees, squeezed his eyes shut, and focused on breathing until he became grounded. When he could look around, he discovered he hadn't been the only person to take the sudden trip poorly. Clearshot sat cross-legged nearby with his head in his hands, and Lavine mirrored the position except the Yeluthian could address the dozens of confused soldiers, mages, and servants who were in the area during their arrival.

Behind Byron, Coura remained on her feet but bent forward with her hands on her knees and panted heavily. The lone remains of the portal appeared like fragments of light that shattered into nothing, disconnecting them from the academy.

I bet creating and holding that spell drained most, if not all, of her energy, he realized. *How incredible. It would have taken us days to get here instead of a matter of seconds! No wonder she's exhausted. Why did she decide to use it now? Doesn't casting it bother her considering its use against the first demon?*

"Master Byron, are you all right?"

A trio of dark mages he recognized hurried over to kneel beside him and inspect his condition.

"Yes, I'm fine," he answered the individual who asked. "We just need to catch our breaths. I'm sure our Yeluthian companion mentioned this, but we returned from East Hoover using one of their people's spells called a goddess gift. You should check on the wielder. She could use something to eat and drink after expending her reserves."

"I'd be better…if you didn't use up…the *entire* minute I gave you," Coura scolded him from where she remained gasping for air.

The mages looked between her and Byron before rising to assist the former. After a few minutes, he managed to stand on his own just as the crowd began to disperse.

***

As the council gathered together for the first time since Grace and her guard procured the ancestral weapon, Aaron glanced around the table at each face and sensed the hopefulness they projected. Part of the mood had to do with the attained method to combat the demon and its creatures, but mostly he felt Byron's presence at their meeting made a difference in their morale. The master mage's assistance seemed to be the first positive outcome of their recent efforts.

The council's additional member appeared the previous morning out of thin air thanks to Coura's Yeluthian magic. After hearing the news, Aaron scrambled to put together what would be necessary for their unexpected meeting while attempting to control his anticipation. Byron acted as a point of fortitude for him ever since they worked together before his parents' murders; the same proved true with Coura, though on the personal side rather than the professional. He contemplated visiting her once he learned of the group's arrival, yet the portal spell left her in need of sleep for the remainder of the day.

Despite the limited participants in the meeting chamber, part of him hoped to see her among those at the table.

Don't get distracted, he told himself as the members looked to him to initiate the session.

"Thank you all for being here," he began before pointedly glancing at Byron. "It's nice to view a glimmer of light at the end of this tunnel we've seemingly been wandering through."

The master mage nodded to acknowledge the comment.

"Everybody should be caught up on our current affairs. General Casner sent a messenger to deliver an update from the northern border, and Commander Detrix returned from Dala with a report on the patrol routes. I will turn the discussion over to you two."

The Yeluthian rose first, leaving Casner's soldier to slouch forward and wait.

"Thank you, Your Highness," Detrix added with a bow. "I am afraid I might hamper the mood because of the dilemma the Dalan base is facing. Allow me to start with what we are already aware of. The demonic creatures still appear consistently across the south, keeping our soldiers and your light mages occupied. I deemed the situation severe enough to continue monitoring, which leaves us at a loss since they cannot leave or be replaced; however, they are capable of maintaining their assignments. We will not need to send additional troops at the moment."

The information didn't seem to affect most of the table, but Aaron figured worse news awaited them when the Yeluthian avoided meeting anyone's eyes.

"As for the base, I regret to inform you of General Tio's untimely death at the hands of the demon we have been searching for."

Aaron's heart dropped, and the rest of the council members' faces fell. Some even muttered curses or punctuated their disbelief with gasps.

"How could this happen?" Byron asked at a lower volume akin to a growl.

"According to the assistant generals, the creature challenged them for possession of the area after wearing down their forces by attacking every night. The general thought it best to take advantage of the opportunity by wagering his life on the people's safety."

"What a fool!" General Tont exclaimed through a mixture of anguish and disbelief.

Detrix merely tilted his head at the interruption. "Fool or not, he bested the demon."

"Him? How could that happen? The man's-"

"General," Aaron interjected sharply to silence the premature rant. "Allow the commander to finish his report before commenting."

Tont's face had already been flushing, yet it seemed to grow a deeper scarlet after he crossed his arms and pressed his mouth shut.

Detrix shot Aaron an appreciative look before continuing. What followed included an account from Calin and Marcus about the demon's defeat and disappearance, as well as the base's attempted recovery. They performed the pyre ceremony with the city's priest present, but the creatures returned after the first night.

"Of course a demon breaks its promise not to go after the base again," Commander Isan muttered loudly enough for everybody to hear.

"Is that all from the assistant generals?" Aaron asked Commander Detrix when the angel didn't add more.

"Yes, Your Highness."

"Then we should focus on combating the creatures there-"

"Excuse me!"

Aaron's mouth hung open when the messenger from Casner's group cut him off mid-sentence. Although the man appeared uncomfortable under the scrutiny from those around the room, he managed to stand.

Still, Aaron trusted the soldier wouldn't interrupt if the news wasn't important. "Well?"

After bowing to recover some of his composure, the messenger dug a piece of parchment out of his jacket's inner pocket. "Forgive my interruption, but you may wish to hear General Casner's update before beginning this discussion."

Instead of feeling annoyed, Aaron grew intrigued. After permitting the man to continue and listening to the report, he appreciated the soldier's determination.

Casner shared the appearance of a group of light mages who had been presumed dead during the Nim-Valan's first ambush over a year ago, as well as their guide: a spy from Asteom. Like the troops stationed at the border, Aaron took pleasure in hearing about the survivors' arrival and huffed a laugh out of sheer amazement. Then, in the blink of an eye, his joy turned sour.

"According to the mages who returned to Asteom, the Nim-Valan king's advisor, the man leading the enemy on their tirade, is a dark mage wielding demonic power at best or a demon in the guise of a human at worst."

A stunned silence followed his words until both Tont and Garvish exclaimed their disbelief, Lydia requested the messenger repeat the report, and one of the Yeluthian commanders commented on the improbability of the latter. Aaron listened to their voices since he needed time to process how the news shifted the direction of their dilemmas.

"Are we actually going to accept two demons appearing to attack Asteom?" Garvish asked the room while throwing his arms up into a dramatic shrug. "The likelihood of more than one is rather poor."

"Why do you say that?" Lydia countered.

The general scoffed at the question. "Nobody noticed the creature holds a position within their king's home? I could understand if it blended in among their people through possession, but I doubt this could go unnoticed."

"Actually, it would make the most sense," Byron commented.

"Why?"

The master mage's mouth had twisted into a frown, though nothing else showed his displeasure. "After the recent incident within the palace, let alone one manipulating the former high priest and rogue Yeluthians, I believe we shouldn't assume the Nim-Valan royalty are able to detect the presence of a demon under their noses. In any case, even if it isn't a demon, the group claims the advisor wields dark magic, possibly demonic in nature. As far as I know, their people never had the ability to manipulate any type of energy."

"That has always been correct to my knowledge, but times may be changing," King Arval shared. His words riled the council again.

Handle one problem at a time, Aaron thought while pondering how Casner's report would influence their decisions going forward. *If we are dealing with two demons, we need to consider all angles, like if they're working together or not.*

The chamber devolved into various conversations between the generals, mages, and Yeluthians as Aaron, Casner's messenger, and the high priest juggled their attention in order to listen to each. By the time everybody quieted and glanced at their leader, he felt prepared to move forward.

"I suppose this can't get much worse," Jerek threw in to reflect the concerned expressions around the table.

Despite their pessimism, Aaron refused to let their mentalities sink so low. "I believe it would be better for us to assume there are multiple demons. That seems to be the most beneficial explanation."

The high priest tilted his head to show his lack of understanding. "Your Highness?"

"Consider what's taken place so far. One demon revealed itself to Coura when she accompanied Commander Evern, then it reappeared in the Western Woods a couple years later. I think it's safe to assume that being is responsible for the creatures multiplying to the south and challenged General Tio to the duel. On the other hand, Nim-Vala's conflict began when they ambushed General

Casner's troops after luring the troops across the border with the promise of an alliance. Ever since then, they have been encroaching on our territory."

"Are you saying the demon or dark mage hiding in Nim-Vala orchestrated the massacre?" Tont asked as his widening eyes projected his understanding.

Aaron dipped his head. "I just don't believe a single creature would have the necessary connections in Asteom to cause trouble over such a vast distance."

"I agree," King Arval added a moment later. "With this in mind, the problems should be addressed as two, separate conflicts instead of one ranging across Asteom and Nim-Vala."

"Exactly."

Tont grumbled a curse before turning in his seat to face Casner's messenger. "You're going to be recounting a lot of information to your superior."

Although the man blushed, he upheld a professional expression.

Tont opened his mouth to continue speaking; however, Garvish shared his input first.

"I suggest we focus our troops on Nim-Vala. If we spread out along the border, they won't be able to cross. The soldiers can communicate between groups in order to locate the demon or dark mage in charge."

"I second that idea," Terrell added.

"What about the south?" Byron countered. "We shouldn't leave the Dalans in a state lacking leadership."

"Why don't you go there? You're familiar with their assistant generals and the base's layout."

Byron paused to consider this until King Arval cleared his throat to draw everybody's attention.

"If it may aid in your decision making, I will share my intentions regarding Yeluthia's troops."

Garvish and Terrell mumbled their approval while Byron raised an eyebrow and remained silent.

"If the council plans to use a dual approach in opposite directions, Commander Detrix will return to the southern base and its surrounding area alongside half our remaining soldiers in Verona. It seems the late general made an impact on that creature, so pressuring it into revealing itself might work."

"Keeping it and its creatures in that area also prevents them from moving north," Byron added, to the Yeluthian's approval.

"Commander Isan will stay with me here, along with the rest of our troops. Finally, I would like to recommend Commander Evern to assist in your efforts along the Nim-Valan border. He would be a reliable messenger and patrol scout in case the combat reaches farther into Asteom's territory."

Aaron avoided the urge to complain at the lack of support for General Casner, yet he understood the king's motives. *Their responsibility is to support us, not become involved in another country's affairs. In fact, I believe I feel the same. Besides, they already spread their troops as thin as possible.*

"I find your assignments acceptable," he shared before directing his focus to the others seated in front of him. "What about the rest of you?"

His question was met with a murmur of agreement.

"Our Yeluthian allies have their positions, and we will fan our troops out across the northern border for the time being. I refuse to invade their country, even though there may be a demon or dark mage involved. The support to the south will allow us to keep our attention solely on Nim-Vala."

"We'll also need to wait and see what that demon chooses to do," Jenna added in a timid manner. "No one trusts their kind, but it may not show up again after the oath to General Tio."

"I doubt that," Tont muttered.

Most everybody nodded in agreement, then Byron picked up the conversation again.

"Despite the possibility, I would prefer to resolve one problem instead of tackling two at the same time. Because of this opportunity, I request to accompany Commander Evern to the northern border with whatever mages can be spared."

It took a while for him to convince the council that the capital would be safe with the Yeluthians present and the mages would act as a means of intimidation rather than combatants, yet Aaron trusted the master mage's intuition from the beginning.

Some part of this mess needs to end soon, he reflected after dismissing the meeting. *Our people and King Arval's can't hold out while we wait around for the enemy to tire. Their lives, and the lives of those fighting for Asteom, deserve more respect than our indecisiveness has shown.*

***

Although using her goddess gift expended her reserved energy, Coura found she didn't regret doing so once she recovered and learned what took place at the council's meeting. Both Byron and her father visited at various points during the third day after their return to inform her of the news regarding their reassignments, as well as the discovery of an ancestral weapon and General Tio's fate. They would be sent to the northern border together, and each requested she accompany them alongside the hundred or so mages making the journey. She chose not to mention how the other made the same request, but she agreed to join.

Two days later, they prepared to depart. The atmosphere in the grand hall filled with the dozens of mages' eagerness and anticipation as the additional troops lined up, though Coura ignored everybody and passed through the front entrance. As she expected, Evern and Byron stood on the bridge with Lydia, Clearshot, and the new master light mage named Jenna.

"What's going on?" she asked after the five greeted her.

"Commander Evern requested to fly ahead in order to alert General Casner," Byron explained. "I'd like to go with on horseback while Lydia and Jenna lead the mages, so Clearshot agreed to assist them with the move."

"I don't like the idea of splitting up; however, you and Commander Evern would reach the site to report on the council's plan a day before the messenger," his protégé added while crossing her arms. "The general can organize the placements beforehand so there isn't dead time between our arrival and the repositioning."

"I plan on assisting him with organizing the placements too," Byron shared.

Coura eyed her father. "And?"

Evern held a controlled, neutral expression. "Lavine insisted on joining us instead of guarding the palace. So, we are now waiting for a horse and my subordinate."

She figured he grew displeased with Lavine for disobeying his orders and Lydia with Byron's impulsiveness, so she figured her best option would be to stay out of their personal disagreements.

A few minutes later, a stable hand approached leading a chestnut-colored stallion that fidgeting in place. She instructed Byron on the animal's care given its stubborn behavior while Coura observed his mount and marveled at its muscular build honed from years of training. Lydia and Jenna went closer to inspect the creature, and even Evern studied it closely. When Byron held the reins, the stallion began nuzzling the girls for affection. Coura noticed her father turn away then and did the same to see their final companion strutting over.

"Forgive my tardiness," Lavine apologized to the group. He appeared relieved when nobody commented on it.

"Shall we go?" Evern asked Byron.

When the master mage nodded, Clearshot, Lydia, and Jenna wished the four well before returning to the grand hall and their company waiting inside. Without the extra attention, the stallion huffed and decided to come closer to Coura before shoving its head against her shoulder despite her attempts to push it away. Of course, Byron found this entertaining and let the animal continue while Lavine chuckled. Only when she moved out of the animal's reach did her father intervene.

"If you have had your fun, we should get going," he chided to no one in particular yet with an amused smile.

*

Their flight to the northern border split into three days where the fliers landed at designated locations to meet Byron, who kept up despite being grounded. The fourth morning proved to be bitterly cold, and the chill clung to their clothing and armor, sending shivers throughout Coura's body. They reached the camp around the middle of that day without stopping for a break.

Those who spotted them warned the rest of the troops, so nobody seemed alarmed by the Yeluthians' appearance. Instantly, she noticed how lean the men and women looked and noted their sunken cheeks accompanying the hopeful gazes. What surprised her most was how the people treated Byron and Evern. The former already built a reputation among the mages and soldiers, leading his presence to bring a sense of relief since the troops knew he supported them. On the other hand, her father stood as a pillar of light, representing the Yeluthians and their alliance with Asteom. The people surrounding them practically worshiped the pair because of their statuses, as well as the camp's desperation. Meanwhile, Lavine savored the attention his appearance drew, which didn't seem like less than what Evern experienced, yet his raised chin and confident smile highlighted the people's current need for support.

Coura ignored the stares and comments directed at her. As far as she was concerned, there would be time to relax when they eliminated the main threat. Byron had been the first to mention the possibility of a second demon leading the lowest class in Nim-Vala. Although she didn't care about the northern country's politics, he explained their kingdom's system for identifying their citizens and how thousands were practically left alone while the nobility and royal family lived a life of luxury in their secluded, fortified inner circle.

"The place seems ready for an uprising," he had shared days earlier. "The only question is, why is the lower class targeting Asteom instead of their leaders who hold the power?"

They briefly discussed reasons for this but ultimately figured it wasn't their responsibility to come to that conclusion on behalf of the kingdom.

At any rate, a demon wouldn't care about something as petty as ruling Nim-Vala, Coura thought as she scanned the camp. *Terran wishes to conquer, Soirée desired to test her magic, so what does this one want?*

As she considered this, their group reached the center of the area where Casner waited with a pair of soldiers. Byron clasped hands with the general before the man ushered their group inside the nearest tent, which proved to be wide enough to hold everybody comfortably.

"Well, isn't this a pleasant surprise," Casner began. His face radiated the same enthusiasm as his troops, though Coura noticed the general avoided looking in her direction while addressing them. "We've been waiting for the backup King Aaron promised, but I expected more than this. I'm sure you'll fill me in on the situation in the capital and to the south."

At the invitation, Byron shared the council's decision to send the mages north and King Arval's decision to split his remaining forces. "The threat of another demon or a dark mage assisting the Nim-Valans is reason enough for us to strengthen our defenses along the border," he concluded.

Casner sat in silence for a moment before scratching his head. "I understand, and I won't question the extra troops, but we're not certain it actually is a demon we'll be dealing with. Their leader isn't exactly someone I'm familiar with."

"It is still best to remain as cautious as possible," Evern added.

"You're right. I trust your insight." The general looked from Evern to Byron, then at Lavine. When his eyes landed on Coura, he appeared to be trying not to curl his lip.

She dismissed his behavior in order to quell a rising annoyance, which he always seemed to spur whenever they interacted in the past. *I suppose my relationship to Soirée is difficult to forget, especially when her involvement led to so much trouble.*

Their discussion continued for at least an hour since the general wasn't in favor of separating his soldiers in order to cover the entire border, even with the additional mages on their way to the site. In a way, Coura agreed with his trepidation as splitting up also left weaker points for the enemy to strike, yet Byron and Evern assured the man of their ability to monitor the areas in need of supervision and target the Nim-Valans' leader.

Casner leaned back, crossed his arms, and gazed upward at the tent's ceiling. "If your aim is to go after the demon or dark mage in charge, I suppose there's no harm as long as it doesn't provoke their troops into attacking."

"Even if they do, Asteom will be prepared," Evern replied. "Besides, we do not intend to enter their territory. Every action can be on your soil in order to avoid providing a reason for them to retaliate."

"Right. You mentioned that earlier."

"So, I assume you would like to wait for the mages before dispersing your soldiers?" Byron asked.

Casner nodded. "Let's talk over dinner."

At the cue, the two others present with the group exited and returned bearing bowls of a grain-filled porridge. Coura found it similar to the Mintelians' simple meal and slurped down her portion instinctively before anybody else finished.

For the remainder of the evening, the general, Byron, and Evern plotted where to send what soldiers along the border while staring at a map laid out by one of the assistants. She kept quiet yet remained alert enough to study what she could. When the main troops' positions had been assigned, Evern suggested he and Coura set out in the morning to patrol the east while Byron and Lavine did the same at the halfway point.

"It would be wise to search ahead in case the enemy intends to cross at another point," he summarized.

"I should be able to inform the newcomers of their positions and delegate leaders on my own," Casner decided. "I'd appreciate the help, especially since we've only been able to spare a handful of scouts in those locations."

"I'd like to suggest a change," Byron startled her father by adding. "Lavine is probably more familiar with you, Commander. Coura should come with me on foot instead."

"I can vouch for my subordinate's abilities."

"Of course, but I'm referring to your relationship. You two probably work better together, and I with Coura."

"Are you suggesting I do not know my own daughter?" Evern countered and raised an eyebrow.

Byron shook his head, yet he didn't answer the question. "We have combat experience together. If it should come to a fight, I believe that's more important than getting along. Don't you agree?"

Coura's father didn't respond right away. Their indirect arguing made her uncomfortable since they never seemed hostile toward each other in the past. Even Lavine appeared taken back by their behavior.

"I understand," Evern replied at last with a dip of his head. "You should not feel the need to avoid your real concern."

Byron's eyes narrowed to show his impatience. "Which is?"

Her father's lips curved into a slightly arrogant smile. "The flight across Asteom would be easier for an experienced flyer. You wish to avoid potential exhaustion befalling my daughter when Lavine is better suited for the journey. It is a considerate and accurate assumption, so I accept."

Based on Byron's controlled expression, Coura got the impression that wasn't his intent. Night fell upon the camp by that point, prompting the general to conclude their meeting and order the four to rest in a set of tents nearby.

In the morning, packs with dried rations had been set beside leather armor and plain tunics, pants, and boots matching every other soldier in the camp.

"What is this?" Lavine inquired and held up a flat piece of the protective padding which acted as a breastplate.

Byron explained the item's purpose before waving over a woman carrying supplies in their direction. "Excuse me, but would you happen to know who provided us with these?"

Although she shook her head, the soldier then pointed at the pieces and answered. "I don't, but I would guess they're meant to replace any metal armor."

"Replace our armor?" Evern commented. "Why would we abandon our best method of defense?"

"Cold and metal don't go so well together. If you plan on staying, I'd leave yours in that tent and forget about putting it on until summertime. Otherwise, you risk freezing to death." With that, she walked away.

"How interesting," Coura heard her father mutter after.

The four donned their new clothing and leather plates and strapped on their weapons. Once they felt prepared and ate breakfast, their group set off for their assigned positions.

*

Coura remained in the sky with Evern and Lavine until they reached the first destination where she and Byron would stay until the soldiers and mages arrived to take over. The land didn't appear any different from the other forests in Asteom since the trees grew sporadically within grassy fields, so the duo set up a basic camp after the Yeluthians departed.

The following morning, they decided to explore in order to become familiar with their surroundings before hunting and foraging for enough to make a suitable dinner. Then, the two switched shifts throughout the night to keep watch. Coura volunteered for the earlier hours since she'd grown accustomed to rising before the sun, and her full stomach sent her straight to sleep without issue.

Their rations provided a decent breakfast, allowing Byron and Coura to split up and continue their search without distraction. She found nothing noteworthy to the south while the east proved to hold denser woods. The approaching winter stripped whatever branches possessed leaves, shading the scenery in grays and browns. Fall also promised lower temperatures, as the woman from the main site had mentioned. When she returned to the camp during the afternoon, Byron already sat around the start of a bonfire, and his mount nonchalantly munched on the grass it could reach from where its reins were tied up.

"Did you find anything?" he inquired after she hurried to drop down across from him, huddle closer to the flames, and wrap her cloak tighter around her body.

"No. The forest looked and sounded normal."

"I wish I could say the same."

Her interest piqued at his comment. "Did you see the Nim-Valans?"

"There's a group settled near the border," he explained while rubbing his hands together. "I hid and waited so I could count their

250

numbers and wound up with around fifty men. They didn't seem to be doing much aside from patrolling, though I believe they just crossed into Asteom's territory."

"Are you sure?" Coura had no indication of what separated the two countries; without a proper map, they wouldn't know for certain.

Byron mirrored her thought. "Even if we don't have an accurate way to tell, their movement is enough of an answer. Our arrival is perfect to keep an eye on their behavior. I feel comfortable approaching that many in a fight."

She raised an eyebrow at that. "You're assuming they aren't trained and the magic wielder isn't among them."

"True. I didn't spot or sense a hint of dark energy to signal their leader's presence, and it appeared as though they were stationed there to defend the border. Let me rephrase my comment: I like our chances if the situation leads to a confrontation."

Since Coura trusted his intuition, she decided not to pursue the subject, though part of her hoped they wouldn't need to resort to violence until their reinforcements arrived.

Aiding a Friend

Will didn't refrain from releasing a frustrated groan when Clara finished revealing who ventured north to join General Casner's troops the previous afternoon and departed early that morning. "Why didn't anyone tell me Coura and Byron were here?"

Clara's immediate answer didn't console him much. "I tried finding you as soon as I heard, but you didn't tell me where you ran off to. I fell asleep before you returned, and they already left by the time I woke up."

Her tone suggested his disappearance annoyed her, which made Will feel worse. "I'm sorry. It's not your fault."

Because of the unfamiliar location, the healers avoided experimenting with new plants around the area, forcing them to use only what they brought from the capital. Will learned how limited their supplies became and offered to forage for what they could find while internally thanking Geneva for her instruction during the months he spent in Muld. After giving a brief lesson and concocting the potions and remedies he perfected in Nim-Vala, he stayed with them to restock the items until after midnight. The light mages from his original group slept around their fire when he returned, so he joined them. When he rose and prepared for the day, his friends were away on their own tasks, and Clara pulled him aside to reveal the news.

I can't believe I missed them, he thought against a welling sense of regret. *According to the general's report, I either went missing or died over a year ago...*

"It's going to be fine," Clara reassured him after noticing his glum expression. "They won't be far considering they were ordered to remain along the border and patrol the enemy troops. Assistant General Mattias informed us of the decision last night. He also mentioned additional mages are traveling from Verona to support Asteom's forces."

"That's a positive update," Will mumbled. Before he could consider what else to say, she looped her arm around his elbow and dragged him toward the mess tent where the two merged with a line of men and women who yawned or rubbed their eyes to show their weariness. Until they received their portions, she kept her arm hooked on his. Neither sparked a conversation, yet he found comfort in her presence.

I have nothing to be worried about anymore. We're in a fortified location surrounded by allies, and more are on the way. Then again, such a decision means Aaron and his council are expecting the conflict to continue. I wonder if Finn will be safe. The reminder of the Nim-Valan spy ebbed his hunger, so he pushed his half-eaten breakfast aside.

Meanwhile, Clara finished the rest of her meal before leaning back with a content sigh. "It's not the best food in the world, but after living off stale bread and berries like we did across the border, I'll never not be grateful for a full stomach. You know what I mean?"

"Sure."

She raised an eyebrow at his dismissive response. "What's the matter?"

Will glanced away. "I'm worried about Finn."

"I see."

"It's silly. He's a grown man, and I barely know him, yet…"

Clara reached over to touch his arm in a sympathetic gesture. "He's your friend. There's no shame in admitting that or being concerned. Who knows, he might even return soon since the general accepted him. All we can do is wait and do our best with what we can control."

He placed a hand over hers and smiled. "Thank you."

They talked further until he cleaned his bowl, then they split apart to assume their responsibilities. For the most part, the general and his assistant assigned their newest recruits to mundane tasks benefiting the whole of the camp, which everybody accepted willingly. Bryn had commented on how she would rather perform basic chores for the time being than be thrown into potential conflict where she would maintain shielding spells against the enemy or heal injured comrades. The rest of their group felt the same.

Before Will realized it, he was staring up at the cloudy, night sky while attempting to fall asleep. The temperature plummeted with an overcast, prompting them to wear extra layers of clothing, as well as hats and scarves. His last thought as he drifted into sleep consisted of a scene where he crept into a bed possessing several quilts and savored the heat of a fire across the room.

*

At one point during the night, Will heard a commotion taking place somewhere on the opposite side of the camp. It hadn't been enough to rouse him fully, so he ignored it in favor of falling back into his slumber. In the next instant, he woke to the sound of shuffling feet before somebody shook his shoulder.

"Wake up," came Clara's voice at a lower volume.

He grunted to show he heard her then debated rising against the lingering chill.

"Come on, it's almost noon already. Don't make me pull your covers away."

Her words sounded menacing enough. "I'm getting up," he responded, though he knew he was whining.

Fortunately, Clara laughed instead of following through with her threat. "Hurry! I have a surprise for you."

Will steadily began his morning routine after she left him. Only when he felt refreshed and properly dressed for the weather did he return to where his friend sat in front of the fire.

"It's about time," she muttered to reference his lack of punctuality. "Maybe if I told you the news, you would show a little more urgency."

"News?"

Clara pushed herself to her feet, dusted off her pants, and fixed him with an impatient look. "Finn entered the camp early this morning."

Will's eyebrows flew upward. "What? Why is he-"

"Let me finish," she practically snapped. "The noise from the scouts woke Mary Ann and I, and when we went to investigate, we saw Finn being dragged to the healers' tent. Apparently crossing the border into Asteom has become dangerous. He claimed he needs to speak to the general but passed out right after."

"Was he injured?"

She dipped her head. "Four arrows were embedded in his body, and he bore minor bruises. It's nothing we couldn't handle, especially since the wounds were fresh."

Will released a shaky breath. *Finn... What drove him to head south in the middle of the night?*

"Anyway, General Casner just went to meet with him about an hour ago," Clara continued. "I figured they would be finished by the time you stirred."

"Thank you for thinking of me. I wonder why he would suddenly return."

"I don't know, but his reasoning can't be good."

With the somber notion in mind, the two hurried to the healers' section.

Clara and the additional light mages had been put to work ever since they agreed to remain in the camp, so only a handful of patients rested within that area and for minor injuries. She moved directly past the bedrolls and fires toward the centermost tent where the worst patients were kept. As they approached, the opening flap flew aside, allowing the general, his assistants, and four other soldiers to emerge before separating to march in different directions. No one paid Clara or Will any attention as they entered to find a pair of women beginning a recovery spell on the shirtless Nim-Valan, who seemed to be sleeping.

"We already told you to leave us," the older of the two began while picking her hands up from the man's torso and glaring in their direction; however, upon spotting Clara and Will instead of the general and his subordinates, her irritation vanished.

"Forgive us for intruding," Clara replied in her most sincere, respectful tone. "May we assist?"

"I thought I ordered you to rest. You've done enough."

Instead of accepting the dismissal, Clara stepped closer to kneel beside the woman. Will followed suit on the opposite side and assessed Finn's body. He saw no puncture wounds, blood, or bruises, to his relief.

Meanwhile, the older healer released a long breath through her nostrils in resignation before elaborating on their patient's condition. "He's stable. The earlier spells took care of the worst, and we plan on inspecting what's left. I only threw a fit because General Casner won't stop pestering us about when this stranger will wake."

Clara and the additional healer chuckled at that comment, then the latter glanced at Will.

"I'm sure *you* understand the impatience of the men and women who claim every conversation has a deadline."

His lips curved into a slight smile to show his support. "I do, but I'm afraid I belong in that category now. This man is a friend from our time in Nim-Vala. I worry he intended to bring a message about the conflict along the border."

The women glanced at each other before moving to stand.

"I'm sorry about your friend," the older of the two began. "Since that's the case, I trust you and Clara to look after him. I expect he should come alive around sundown, but there's no certain answer. When the time comes, please find me for an inspection, then I'll send for the general."

"Yes, ma'am," Will and Clara responded in unison. They watched as the women exited the tent, and some of Will's worry followed the mages out.

"I'm glad to hear Finn is safe," he muttered as his eyes lowered to his hands. "I just wonder what drove him to return after all that has happened."

His friend shifted to lie on her side with her head propped up by one hand in order to observe the Nim-Valan. "Right now, we just need to wait. There's nothing else to do but be patient."

*

The time crept by during their quiet conversations until the sun dipped below the trees to darken the space. Will's stomach growled in response, so he offered to grab them something to eat while Clara lit the tent's only lamp. The scent of food over an open fire drew him to the line of troops waiting for their portions. He accepted two bowls of the usual, oat-based porridge from a tired-looking man before returning just as the evening chill swept in.

"These should be cool enough now," he explained, prompting Clara to reach for the one he offered.

She thanked him but didn't attempt to scarf down the meal like he prepared to do. Will dropped to sit across from her and tipped the bowl back only to jump and spill precious drops upon hearing a grumble.

"Of course you would be here as well."

"Finn?" Will leaned forward while ignoring the porridge completely to find the Nim-Valan staring at him with an unamused expression. "You're awake!"

"Where is the general?"

"I'll go fetch him," Clara responded.

After she set her bowl aside, stood, and hurried out of the tent, Will opened his mouth to launch into a series of questions until he noticed how bothered Finn appeared.

"What's wrong?" he decided to ask instead.

He figured the Nim-Valan would ignore him and expected the silence between them to stretch until Clara returned with General Casner, yet the reply came immediately.

"There's trouble."

"What does that mean?"

Finn licked his lips and averted his eyes, showing more vulnerability than he ever had in front of Will. "I overheard a meeting with Advisor Lupin and a few of his soldiers, presumably those leading the troops. They mentioned a mission in Verona failed, leading the advisor to begin verbally lashing out at their incompetence."

The mention of Asteom's capital startled Will. "What happened?"

"From what I gathered, they focused on three targets, including the king and Yeluthian ambassador, but nothing seemed to go as they planned because of somebody named Terran."

"Who is that?"

"This Terran inadvertently meddled with who would be in the palace, leading them to improvise. The soldiers scattered in order to reconvene and plan how to finish their business."

"Why would-"

"Before I fled that area, I learned Advisor Lupin is going to order his troops to cross the entire border in order to provoke Asteom into acting. He intends to give King Syrus a reason to go to war while creating a distraction for those hiding in Verona. If this doesn't motivate the king, he'll turn the outer circle citizens against their ruler."

"When do they plan-"

"If that's the case, I doubt I can return to the capital in time…"

Will gave up on questioning Finn as the Nim-Valan's voice faded into mumbles. *If what he said is true, we need to warn General Casner as soon as possible. Aaron, Grace, and the people in the palace are in danger, and the northern section of Asteom needs protection. Clara mentioned additional soldiers and mages are supposed to be arriving soon. On the other hand, if Lupin's plan fails, Nim-Vala's king and the inner circle may face an uprising.*

In that moment, he realized why the situation troubled the spy. *If the advisor orders the outer circle citizens to go after their capital, Finn wouldn't get there in time to warn Yukin and Elena. He chose to return here and trust in Asteom's forces instead.*

"They'll be safe," he stated without considering the likelihood of the statement.

It didn't seem to matter. The Nim-Valan raised his eyes to meet Will's, and some of the concern reflected in them eased. A minute later, Finn attempted to sit up, so Will assisted him before offering the remaining bowl of the untasted meal. His friend accepted without a word and cleaned the dish in a matter of seconds.

"Where could Clara be with the general?" Will wondered aloud to distract from his looming hunger.

As if his words were a summoning spell, the tent's opening flap parted before the group of soldiers from earlier filed in with the light mage trailing at the rear. No one addressed him, so he remained where he was. Even if he hoped to leave, the limited room prevented him from moving without becoming disruptive.

Whatever compelled Finn to show his emotions disappeared as soon as they were no longer alone. The Nim-Valan resumed a neutral expression and tone of voice while informing the newcomers of what he overheard, though he spent less time on the report. Will imagined the ability to present concise updates without being influenced by personal conflicts became a feat only somebody trained to do so could pull off. In a way, his friend's sudden change of behavior felt jarring.

I'm glad he considers me trustworthy enough to reveal such reactions, but I hate thinking about how he must hide behind a mask in front of everyone, Will admitted while General Casner and the others accompanying him began asking for specific details on certain aspects of what they heard. *Then again, Finn is a spy. If he can't control himself, I doubt Elena, or even Yukin, would allow him to wander freely.*

"Let's start by sending a messenger to the palace," a soldier suggested, drawing Will's attention. "Even though our troops are prepared to depart with the mages once they arrive, I believe we shouldn't wait to march east."

"I concur," the general added. "I'm sure the capital is already aware of trouble since the previous attacks failed. Until I know we can't handle the Nim-Valans and this advisor on our own, we must manage with what we have."

Through some, unspoken cue, the assistant nodded and exited the tent, presumably to organize a messenger and alert the camp. General Casner turned to Finn again after.

"What do you plan on doing?"

The question didn't hint at an expected response, which Will assumed meant the general had no particular use in mind for the Nim-Valan.

Finn paused to contemplate an answer. "For the moment, I need to recover my strength."

General Casner's eyes narrowed slightly, but he didn't comment. With nothing else to discuss, everybody except Will, Clara, and Finn exited the tent.

"I should go too," the light mage said after a moment of silence and without looking at Will.

Despite that, he nodded before she departed.

I wonder if Clara and the others received assignments alongside the troops. Although he tried not to let it bother him too much, the idea of his friends being sent onto a battlefield while he remained behind made him feel useless.

"Where will you be stationed?" Finn asked a second later, unintentionally adding to the sting.

"I wasn't given any orders."

"So, you'll stay here?"

Will grunted in confirmation.

"It's a relief to hear that."

The unexpected statement had Will glancing at the Nim-Valan and raising an eyebrow.

"I can't imagine you lined up in the middle of armor-clad soldiers," the man added. "Combat is especially brutal without the comfort of a fortified shelter or companions to lean on for support."

"I appreciate the sentiment," Will muttered before rising. "I should have sent for your caretaker earlier, so I'll go find her now for a follow-up session."

Finn lied down, released a drawn-out sigh, then closed his eyes; Will accepted that as a dismissal.

*

The following morning, the camp echoed with sounds from the soldiers and what light mages prepared to travel along the border for their new assignments. As the general mentioned, most of the troops already packed and readied themselves for when the additional magic users arrived from Verona, allowing them to depart sooner. It seemed as though the camp became empty by the time Will rose and headed toward the medical tent.

"Are you awake?" he called before pulling the opening cover away. Seeing the Nim-Valan on his feet, dressed, and shouldering a bag startled Will enough to hesitate.

"Judging by the lack of noise, I presume everyone moved out," Finn commented in his usual, tactical manner.

"Few of us are in the camp now. I thought you…" He ended the sentence prematurely when he considered the man's allegiance and commitment to being a spy.

"You figured I would stay," Finn finished with a slight, amused smile.

Will avoided admitting the truth by deflecting the topic. "Are you going to return to Yukin or Elena and warn them?"

The Nim-Valan paused to consider an answer. "Not yet."

"Then where will you go?"

The second moment of silence told Will his friend internally considered how much information to reveal. This led him to guess it would be a choice he wouldn't support, which only left a single option. "You want to find Advisor Lupin."

If his assumption surprised Finn, the spy didn't show it. "He should be easier to track down once the border is fortified on Asteom's side."

"And after you locate him?"

"I believe the men under his watch won't know what to do if he's killed. Nobody among their ranks has shown they possess the knowledge or skills necessary to lead and strategize."

"Meaning they might surrender or scatter back into Nim-Vala," Will concluded.

Finn dipped his chin. "That would be the best-case scenario. Slice off the serpent's head, and the body will crumple."

Still, it means going up against someone using dark magic, Will noted while chewing on his bottom lip. *I agree with the approach, just not the execution.*

Movement from the Nim-Valan had him glancing over as Finn walked toward the opening. Instinctively, he sidestepped to prevent his friend from exiting.

"Why do you stop me?" the man demanded with a hint of irritation.

Before he could comprehend the action, Will gave an honest answer. "I won't let you go alone. It's too risky, and Yukin and Elena wouldn't want you to be so hasty."

"Are you sure it's not because you're displeased with my decision?"

"I am too, which is why I'm coming along."

For the first time Will could recall, Finn appeared dumbstruck, though the Nim-Valan recovered a few seconds later. "I would be a fool to remove you from this camp when it's vulnerable."

"The people who remained behind will be fine," Will insisted. "Unless you see a reason for it to be fortified, I'm just going to sit around until we receive news from the groups placed along the border. With you, I can act as a scout or report your attempt in case you fail."

He hated speaking so bluntly about their poor chance of success, but in order to get his desire to contribute across, he needed to be honest and say what would convince Finn. Fortunately, he chose the correct words.

The Nim-Valan scratched his head at Will's suggestion. "If you have your mind set on accompanying me, I won't stop you; however, I refuse to let you do more than observe."

"If anything happens to you, I'll return to Asteom and inform the general or one of his assistants."

Finn huffed a laugh, as if to end their conversation. What neither expected was a third voice to chime in from the opening behind Will.

"I suppose I can tag along in case you *both* get yourselves killed."

He spun around to catch Clara poke her head inside with a grin as her blonde hair fell over her shoulders.

"I thought you accepted an assignment with the rest of the troops," he admitted while she entered to stand beside him.

His ignorant comment had her placing her hands on her hips and replying in a matter-of-fact tone. "We were given the option to watch the camp and guide the support mages when they arrive from the palace. I'm not letting you two scurry off without a healer though. It's dangerous; you made that much clear. There's no reason to reject my help."

Will opened his mouth to protest before remembering Geneva's words. *I planned to give Clara and the other light mages the opportunity to remain in Muld where they would stay safe from the ongoing fighting, yet I didn't realize how I offended them by assuming they didn't want to protect Asteom too. They deserve to choose if they want to be involved or not.*

He nodded and looked at Finn. "She's right."

For some reason, Nim-Valan culture valued women differently than men, as he learned over the year and a half spent in the northern country. Mainly, men considered themselves as the laborers. For their mother, sister, wife, daughter, or another female to accept such a burden meant they were not worthy to care for the more level-headed creators of life. Finn's behavior reflected this mentality ever since their first encounter when he refused to involve the light mages in his business but let Will know the details. At the moment, the Nim-Valan pressed his lips together in an obvious attempt not to appear too disagreeable.

"I promise not to interfere with your duty," Clara added in a gentler manner, as if to reassure Finn. "My responsibility is to act as a healer."

"If that's what you wish, I thank you for your selflessness," the man replied and bowed his head.

Will smiled at the respectful gesture that spurred a slight blush from Clara. "Let's hurry before anybody has a chance to question us."

His companions agreed, so the three set out with Finn in the lead.

Master and Student

The sound of Coura and Byron's breathing filled the air, along with puffs of white, as the pair hid behind the largest boulder in the area. A Nim-Valan scout passed by moments ago on his regular route, which they tracked the day before, and disappeared into the woods once more.

"I don't like this," Byron grumbled while relaxing his body to lean against the stone. "They're behaving as though they expect to encounter Asteom troops at any time."

"Wouldn't that benefit us?" Coura countered. Unlike her former mentor, she didn't want to ease into a false sense of security while in an unfamiliar location. "If they remain on their guard, they won't consider crossing the border unless they're sure it's safe."

"Either that or unless they're assured of victory."

The ominous silence after his words left Coura considering the enemy leader's position. *I haven't sensed a foreign presence, light or dark in nature, ever since we left the palace. That alone gives me a bad feeling about who we're dealing with, especially if they understand how to hide their energy from us.*

After another minute, she abandoned observing the trees ahead to sit cross-legged next to Byron, who removed a pouch containing dried oats. The limited rations the main camp provided acted to fend off their hunger until they could hunt again later in the afternoon. Their isolation meant plenty of animals wandered around without a primary predator, and the pair wouldn't remain long enough to establish themselves as a regular threat.

"What do you suggest we do now?" she asked when Byron made no attempt to rise once they satisfied their stomachs.

He ran a hand through his hair twice before answering. "Honestly, I'm worried."

"Why?"

"Part of me hoped to encounter their leader right away or learn of his whereabouts in order to stop him before he has a chance to strike. Since we didn't find this mage…"

"He could be preparing for an attack somewhere else along the border," Coura concluded. "If the Nim-Valans entered Asteom before, they can do it again, so they most likely know about the support being sent from the palace. At least, that's what I think."

"Me too. In any case, our responsibility is to manage this area." Byron stood, offered her a hand, then pulled her to her feet when she accepted before continuing. "Let's head back to the camp."

With that, they turned to begin backtracking through the tall grass surrounding their hiding spot. About a dozen steps later, they picked up the faint noise of rustling leaves and spun around to see shadows of the Nim-Valan men multiplying beyond the nearby bushes.

"Hide!" Byron ordered and dove for one of the many boulders scattered throughout the field.

Even as the words reached her, Coura slid behind the trunk of a nearby tree and pressed her back against its tough bark.

Where did they come from? she wondered while controlling her internal surge of panic. *We should have heard them approaching long before now. They can't possibly be able to move without creating so little sound!*

Despite the thought, she peeked at the opposite side with bated breath as the enemy troops proved her wrong. The scout they previously followed led the way before two others fanned out to monitor the sides. She counted a dozen first, who meticulously stepped like alert hunters trailing their prey; then, two groups filing in a line proceeded ahead. That second batch created what noise warned Coura and Byron of the men's approach, though it still proved to be less than what she would have expected.

If I was paying attention to that spot, I would have caught their movement earlier. We're not as accustomed to the land as they are, and they intend to use their knowledge to their advantage. I hope they didn't spot us already.

The scout she observed gave no indication he had, so her thoughts revolved around whether or not to wait, potentially preventing the enemy from crossing the border. Her next instinct was to look toward her partner for his signal; however, she found him holding out a hand for her to remain in place while his eyes assessed the lay of the land.

The rocks adorning the tall grass and the uneven terrain limited their range and speed, especially if the Nim-Valans fought as mindfully as they hiked. Byron and Coura possessed magic, which proved to be their main advantage. In addition, she couldn't discern a way to separate the two countries, meaning anybody could be trespassing before they realized their mistake.

Despite the opportunity to surprise them, she knew her former mentor didn't like to take unfavorable chances. Still, the encroachment from the troops didn't slow.

When the nearest scout prepared to stroll past their location, Byron hurried to gesture for her to follow him before springing into action. He rose to his full height and extended both hands in order to cast a shielding spell. The Nim-Valans looked alarmed by his sudden appearance, yet they recovered at a startling pace. Men farther back launched arrows at the master mage only for the projectiles to bounce off the violet wall of energy. Byron stood firm on the opposite side in a show of intimidation.

Coura emerged from her position after a second round of arrows attempted to penetrate the shield, prompting those in front to begin muttering to one another. Somebody shouted in an authoritative tone, then the projectiles ceased before the men conversed and pointed fingers between her and Byron.

"I'm guessing they're going to try surrounding us," the master mage commented in the meantime. "If they didn't want a fight, they would retreat instead of lingering to plot their next move. No one came forth to explain their trek into Asteom's territory, so I doubt any of them speak our language."

Coura placed a hand on the hilt of her sword but didn't draw the weapon. "How should we handle this?" she asked, expecting her former mentor to have already taken their abilities into consideration.

"I believe the best option for us and the kingdom is to force them back without pursuing. Once they're aware of the strength Asteom possesses along the border, they might think twice about attempting an invasion here or elsewhere."

"At least for the time being," Coura added. What she didn't mention was how highly he valued the pair's magic and combat skills; his expectations made the corners of her lips turn upward.

Two sword-wielding mages against fifty or so tough-looking brutes. If they're well trained and disciplined, we could be in serious trouble. This is risky, even for Byron.

He glanced over at her, as if hearing his name in her head. "Ready?"

She responded with a curt nod and drew her blade.

The shimmering wall of energy faded and dispersed into fragments, which floated to the ground. Although the magic became harmless after its release, the Nim-Valans froze, studied the remains, and only continued marching forward once there were no visible traces. Their behavior revealed their lack of experience regarding the spell, and most likely light and dark power in general. Coura filed that piece of information away as she prepared to face the four men who took her on first.

They seemed hesitant to raise their weapons until she did so. Then, they treated her like an enemy and charged at once. In order to avoid their swings without losing her footing, she relied heavily on her blade to knock their swords and clubs away and remained planted where she stood. Either they weren't expecting her lack of movement or they didn't believe her capable of dealing with more than one opponent. The shifting of their weapons caused them to lose their balance, and evidently the strength behind the strikes, so she countered with slices to the torso and legs.

Based on Byron's strategy to force them into retreating, they wouldn't be able to say much about the protection along the border if they don't receive a few wounds, she figured, prompting her to focus on incapacitating the majority.

Years of self-control when sparring with comrades kept her from going too far, though another wave of six men targeted her after witnessing their bested companions writhing on the ground. These Nim-Valans also attacked as a single unit and managed to surround her, but the lunges and swings didn't carry as much weight or coordination, allowing Coura to parry them swiftly and earn only a handful of scratches along her arms and back.

During the next break when the Nim-Valans scrambled to face her again or drag the injured away, she caught Byron at work with a dozen or so bodies lying close by. He decided to take an all-magic approach to their situation, a tactic Coura found interesting given it required him to rely on spells without additional protection. Both his hands waved through the air, alternating between blasts of flame and ice directed at the enemy's feet. A few of the men's clothing caught on fire, leading them to yelp or scream and stagger, and nobody could get too close.

Her attention returned to her opponents. Their growing weariness prevented them from landing more than a handful of marks and revealed a lack of training, which would raise their stamina in addition to their knowledge of how to keep the combat steady. Another issue they faced and Coura took advantage of became their inexperience when working alongside their comrades. They hesitated to move when another would attack or bump into one who needed to backtrack. This provided enough openings for her to manage each attempt while reserving her physical energy; however, the activity riled up the power within her center. Memories of Sage Vidar's scolding when she couldn't control her magic returned in response.

I just need to be able to let go of my emotional hold on the energy instead of clinging to it once I use a spell, she reminded herself. *My skill with a weapon can fend off this group, so this might be a useful exercise.*

Without waiting to reconsider her commitment to the Mintelian's teachings, she searched for an opportunity to reveal her magic to their opponents. The men began retreating, though some took to the cover of the forest in order to sneak around Byron and avoid his waves of flames and ice shards. Out of instinct, she reached her left arm toward her former mentor and triggered a lightning spell. The bolt shot across the space between them to strike one of the shadows lingering behind the master mage, who craned his head around to see the smoking body lying in the grass.

Coura then took advantage of the burst of confidence the demonic energy spurred to ward off the remainder of her attackers. About a minute later, she couldn't help herself from sending another, less powerful lightning spell in the same direction, stunning her chosen target. Byron didn't react the second time, yet the Nim-Valans had enough. Their backtracking became a full retreat as those attempting to carry their injured or fallen companions to safety abandoned such efforts to save their own lives.

The energy humming in her center urged her to pursue until she noticed Byron stepping away from the scene while keeping his front side to the northerners.

We succeeded in protecting the border here, so we have no reason to stay, she concluded and began copying her partner. *I suppose he also intends to let them return for the rest of their comrades. That would avoid giving us a merciless reputation and worsen the countries' relationship.*

As soon as the pair felt comfortably under the shelter of a denser bunch of trees, Byron suggested they return to their campsite for the evening. The trek was uneventful, which Coura appreciated, and they snacked on their dried rations before venturing out to hunt.

Darkness enveloped every part of the forest outside their fire's glow due to the lack of a moon, so the pair kept vigilant as they skinned and ate what hares they caught. All the while, Byron's stallion remained calm, which eased some of their concern.

"I doubt the Nim-Valans will try ambushing us tonight," Byron began, uttering the first words either of them had spoken on the subject since their retreat.

Coura didn't respond until she finished licking her fingers clean while savoring the roasted flavor. "You don't think so? It's a perfect night to be sneaking around."

"True, but we also proved we can hold our own against dozens of their combatants. Unless they're willing to sacrifice more troops in order to enact revenge or open a path into Asteom, they shouldn't act so prematurely. Besides, General Casner informed us of their loyalty to the advisor using dark magic. I'd wager they'll wait to hear their next orders."

"It would be useful if the leader shows up. You were hoping to meet him anyway."

Byron didn't comment on that, so she shifted to lie on her back and gaze up at the starry sky. Her mind wandered over mundane tasks to complete in the morning, such as gathering firewood, possibly moving closer to their water source, and the successful trapping and hunting locations, in order to avoid staying awake to contemplate the danger ahead. Nothing seemed to help though.

She rolled onto her side to find the master mage sitting and staring off across the dim fire. "Would you like to switch shifts?" she ventured to ask.

"I can't stop worrying either," he surprised her by answering with a slight smile.

"You're the one who said the Nim-Valans won't attack."

"It's easy to say one thing and feel a different way. My instincts and logic are conflicted."

"So, you lied." Coura found it difficult not to grin when her partner turned his head to shoot her an unamused expression.

"I didn't lie. Rationally, it wouldn't make sense for them to cross the border just to find us before tomorrow. Despite the probability, I won't let my guard down."

She rolled her eyes, positioned herself on her back once more, then let out a sigh. Before she could try to sleep, Byron changed the subject.

"When did you plan on telling me you learned to use elemental magic? It would have been beneficial for me to know before we engaged with the Nim-Valan troops. Did Evern show you? Or, maybe Emilea..."

"It's not from my Yeluthian energy."

A pause followed her response. Her nerves rose at the reminder of why she decided to run away with Hendal toward the Ghurun mountains, as well as how she delayed revealing her ability to manipulate the demon's power flowing in and out of her center.

Byron broke the silence while she continued to debate a proper explanation.

"I would've been less startled if I could have sensed your energy when you released those spells. Is there a reason for your secrecy?"

"No," Coura answered, letting her weariness regarding the past experiences seep into each word. "It's a lot to revisit, and I felt miserable most of the time. When I agreed to travel with Lavine to get you, I had to readjust."

She understood how vague she phrased her reply and hated the idea of hiding behind her preference for being dismissive. Of all the people she met throughout her life, her former mentor had been the most understanding of the changes she endured, which was why she trusted him more than anybody else.

He also never felt satisfied with her half-hearted answers.

"Start from the beginning," he ordered. "The last time I saw you, we split apart the afternoon before the massacre in the dining hall. To be honest, my focus became narrow because of Cintra's injury, so I didn't even notice you left Verona."

After a minute to collect her thoughts and sort through the memories, Coura shared her side of the event and resulting journey to Kercher and the Mintelian village. Knowing what she currently did about the master light mage, Cintra, and the rest of the palace raised a sense of guilt at her lack of compassion and decision to abandon her friends during their time of need. That pain settled once she sheepishly admitted to breaking Hendal out of prison after visiting the man for months.

Then, she informed Byron of their trek to Kercher, including how the former high priest resolved to stay with his nephew at the church instead of joining her to visit the sage for their people's soul cleansing. The rest of the adventure regarding Sage Vidar's assessment of her reforged center and his training with both sets of energy at her possession sounded more coherent than she anticipated.

"I didn't learn about Cintra or Emilea, or any of the results for that matter, until Lavine and I set out for East Hoover," she added at the end. "Everyone else sounded adamant about your return, but I understand why you and Clearshot needed to leave the capital."

Throughout the evening, she stopped several times to ease her throat with drinks from her waterskin, and Byron had lied down after feeding the fire. The nightlife around them filled the air with noise and grew louder once Coura finished recounting her tale. She held her breath while waiting for his response.

As the minutes passed by, she worried how he would react until Byron's faint snores rumbled underneath the natural sounds surrounding the pair.

So, it matters that little to him. The realization prompted a smile, her tense muscles began to relax, and she huffed a laugh. *Perhaps he got me talking so I would put him to sleep. Well, I don't mind keeping watch until he's ready.*

Despite the unexpected outcome, a weigh dropped off her shoulders as she sat straighter to monitor the shadowy environment.

***

Sunlight warmed what started out as the coldest morning since they settled into their camp, at least in Byron's opinion. As he considered the weather and collected another branch off the ground, he scanned the terrain to his left for any sign of intruders. Nothing during his early patrol suggested the camp had been the target of spies overnight, which came as a relief, so he began to return with his armful of assorted, wooden pieces.

Upon entering the area, his horse neighed and approached until the rope around its neck couldn't extend farther.

"I know, I know," Byron grumbled with a sympathetic smile meant for the animal.

After dumping his bundle beside the firepit, he dug through his pack for one of two remaining apples he stashed away before departing from General Casner's location. The stallion danced in place at the sight then devoured the fruit when he came over and held the treat out.

"Hopefully we're not here too much longer," he muttered as he patted his mount's neck. It proved to be a beautiful creature desiring human interaction, which had been a trait Byron didn't associate with what he used in the past.

In any case, I want the rest of the soldiers and mages to arrive soon. Watching our backs drains physical and mental energy better spent on more productive tasks.

When the horse felt satisfied with his attention, it shook its mane, moved away, then began nibbling on a patch of fresh grass nearby. Byron looked on for a moment before returning to his belongings to procure the waterskin. His final duty for the morning consisted of gathering fresh water and purifying it using his magic; the thought reminded him of what he learned the night before and prompted him to glance over at his former pupil.

Coura seemed to have fallen asleep while attempting to keep watch since he allowed himself to drift off after her explanation. She sat up with her arms folded over her knees and her head leaning on them in an uncomfortable position that would result in a stiff neck. Despite that, he left her alone.

The second I touch her, she'll assume something's wrong and abandon the break, he reflected. *If she does believe I merely suggest she adjust herself, she would be on her feet once she realizes I began the chores and scouting.*

In a way, he needed the morning hours for himself to process her story. The news of her manipulating both her natural, Yeluthian energy and the demonic power streaming into her center because of the creature's experiment came as a shock. Not only was it unheard of for a mage to possess each type, but the sage she visited provided a believable explanation. Byron wouldn't argue with somebody who spent their life assisting people like Coura, especially since he couldn't come up with a reason to do so.

If she's accepted this, then I suppose there's nothing else to discuss unless she brings it up. I'll also leave it to her to share this with her father or anyone else who needs to know. I picked up on her trepidation, so she may not even plan on revealing this part of herself unless she has to.

He continued patrolling the northern section of the surrounding land once he completed his final task and let his mind wander before locating the place where they engaged the Nim-Valans the night prior. The upturned earth, scorched grass, and burning stench revealed the otherwise natural setting. Nothing stood out from what he remembered, but he crept nearer to the enemy's side before taking a seat in the same spot he and Coura occupied before the attack. There, he meditated while keeping an eye on the area.

To his surprise, his partner never ventured to find him. Byron's suspicion steadily rose throughout the late morning and early afternoon despite the lack of movement across the border. Soon, he decided to return to the camp to check on her. When he found nobody around, he called out.

"Where are you?" he heard her respond yet couldn't pinpoint a direction.

"At the camp. I've been monitoring the area where we fought the Nim-Valans."

The sound of footsteps to his left alerted him of Coura's location, and she jogged into the space while panting. "Any problems?" she asked between breaths.

Byron shook his head, raised an eyebrow, and opened his mouth to question her, but she cut him off.

"Great. Come help me." With that, she spun around to begin walking back the way she came, leaving him to catch up.

"Where are we going?" he decided to inquire when no explanation came during the following minute.

"I figured you went north, so I explored to the west. When nothing looked out of the ordinary, I decided to watch from the sky."

"That makes you an easier target."

"Not if I go high enough," she added and pointed upward. "You didn't notice me, so I doubt anyone else around here did."

The notion caught Byron off guard since he hadn't thought about somebody being above his location.

Coura took advantage of the opportunity to continue. "Don't worry. I didn't notice the enemy, even on their side of the border. When I circled around again, I found us dinner. Because we're supposed to be cautious, I decided not to fly near the camp, but I had to wait until you returned."

The pair eventually reached the destination of the aforementioned source of food located in one of the woods' rockier sections. At a glance, Byron couldn't identify the furry animal, which looked to be as long as his former student was tall.

"What is it?"

"I think it's a boar," Coura explained while they stood over the creature. "It must have gotten separated from its herd."

"What are these marks?" he asked after noticing several lacerations along its exposed side. When she didn't answer right away, he looked over to see her rubbing the back of her neck while averting her eyes.

"Well, I didn't bring a weapon along because I was in the air, and I didn't have time to hurry to the camp for my sword. The best option became using magic. I expected a minor lightning spell could do the job, but once it saw me, it squealed and charged. I didn't mean to-"

"I get the idea," Byron interrupted with a frown. He remembered her mentioning the demonic energy sparked negative emotions and reacted in turn, resulting in her rushed misfiring. "Then you went to find me?"

To his surprise, she released a tired sigh and gestured toward her right. A faint trail noticeable only by the bent grass led to the boar.

"You *dragged* it here?"

"I needed to make sure it wouldn't be disturbed until I could get you."

Byron left the conversation at that, even though he almost mentioned how a predator could easily follow the scent and pick apart the body before they arrived. Instead, they planned how to butcher the animal there to avoid luring scavengers toward their camp.

Despite the lengthy process, the two ate well that evening, and Coura chose to keep watch again as long as Byron promised to be up before she drifted off.

***

The meat the pair harvested could have lasted them at least another week, but as fate would have it, they didn't remain alone for much longer. A couple uneventful days passed before they heard the

275

thundering of marching feet beneath the noises of the environment. The wildlife quieted, yet the sound announced the arrival of the support Casner had promised.

While Coura ventured north to survey the border, Byron remained in the camp to greet the troops who would be joining them to continue guarding the centermost location along the edge of Asteom. Although she grew accustomed to working by herself or with a team over the years, her former mentor expressed his relief for the backup, so she agreed to leave the strategizing to him and whatever soldier with authority had been sent to assume responsibility.

The additional people also meant their meager camp needed to expand into multiple sections in order to accommodate the two hundred or so men and women. By the end of the first and second days, everybody looked exhausted, though their behavior never hinted at this.

The next week blurred together after that. Coura slid into place among the others in a daily routine consisting of the chores she and Byron had already been doing themselves. More company meant more conversation, so those who recognized her didn't hesitate to ask about her experience with the Nim-Valans. Any free time allowed for meditation sessions, practicing magic away from curious onlookers, or catching up on sleep.

Fortunately, the northerners stayed away from the excitement, which both relieved and concerned many.

Byron had been requested to join the assistant general, whose name eluded Coura, in order to update the troops' leaders on the situation. When he left her side then, she didn't speak with him again until he intercepted her on her return from a scouting assignment days later.

"Follow me," he ordered and gestured toward the opposite end of the camp.

"What's wrong?" she asked while hurrying to walk beside him.

"Commander Evern and Lavine are back. I thought you might like to be present for their update."

Upon hearing about her father and his subordinate, she nodded in agreement and didn't press for details. If he deemed the situation an emergency, he would give her all the information she'd demand before she could utter another word.

A firepit at the center of their original space served as the meeting area and appeared full already. The Yeluthians sat amid a dozen, standing soldiers and ate in silence while Byron and Coura joined the group. If they noticed her, they didn't give any indication or greeting. The commander utilized his position by beginning the discussion after setting his empty bowl aside.

"We appreciate your patience. Now, allow us to share the news from farther east."

For the most part, their experience sounded nearly identical to Coura and Byron's. A single incident forced the pair to engage with the Nim-Valans who tried crossing the border, but the skirmish ended abruptly once the enemy witnessed their opponents' strength and power.

"They fear our people, and presumably magic in general," Evern concluded.

"Did they attack again?" a man from the group asked.

"We had no other conflicts at that location. Once the expected troops from General Casner's camp arrived, we requested to fly here in order to explain the situation as it stands; however, we spotted signs of activity as we moved west. Abandoned firepits, footprints, and other clues suggest the Nim-Valans are either hiding from your soldiers or they already snuck into Asteom."

Someone behind Coura muttered a curse.

"They're aware of our plan," the assistant general announced and let his annoyance show. "Their troops came across while we got into position. We can't stretch ourselves too thin, but the entire border must be guarded."

"Not necessarily," Byron stated against a unified, rising protest from those around the firepit. His firm tone halted the arguing. "I doubt the enemy overheard the general. They would be foolish not to assume Asteom intends to fortify its defenses to the north. With that in mind, they may have trespassed after the troops marched east, and Commander Evern and Lavine just happened to notice from above."

"I believe your assessment is the likeliest explanation," Coura's father chimed in. "Their trail seemed to be fresh, or more recent than over a week ago."

The assistant general nodded while rubbing his chin, drawing everybody's attention. "Then, we shall extend our patrol routes to include these unwatched areas."

His order prompted debating once more, as well as various suggestions on how to handle the situation.

By that point, Coura regretted accepting Byron's invitation. *I'm not comfortable enough with these people or the enemy to predict their next moves, so I won't pretend like I know what we should do. This is also on a wide scale, involving more than just us and this camp.*

As she finished the thought, she gazed around those by the fire and caught Evern's eye. Even without a verbal cue, she understood he intended to speak with her once the fuss died down.

What now?

Extended Reach

The opportunity for Coura to talk with her father arose once the assistant general grew too fatigued to continue bouncing ideas around. Their group decided to meet again in the morning, then everyone separated for their bedrolls. Coura, Evern, and Lavine were the only people to linger. Byron noticed since she remained beside him, and he cleared his throat as a means of requesting an explanation.

"I do not intend to keep you long," the commander began and got to his feet.

Lavine mirrored his superior before they moved to close the distance between the four. Meanwhile, Coura crossed her arms and tilted her head.

"What didn't you tell them?" she asked at a lower volume. This earned her a crooked grin from Lavine and a frown from her father.

"As perceptive as ever," the former commented before Evern answered, speaking both to her and Byron.

"The humans do not bother me since I believe Asteom's forces are more than a match for their numbers and level of combat skill based on what we encountered. The real problem lies with the stranger leading their troops. If it truly is a magic user utilizing a demon's energy, we will be facing a dangerous opponent."

"What do you have in mind?" Byron pressed.

"I wish to request the ancestral weapon be brought here in secret. That way, we possess a means of ending the threat once and for all." He turned toward Coura as he went on. "I would prefer to send you to the capital in order to retrieve the dagger."

"Why me?"

"If you disappear for a while, it'll be less noticeable than them," Byron answered for the Yeluthians.

"I can agree with that, but I won't use my goddess gift," she stated after recalling the additional time spent recovering from the draining spell.

Her father nodded, as if expecting the response. "We can spare the time, especially if you leave soon."

The idea didn't bother Coura; in fact, she felt better about being nearer to an ancestral weapon when demonic power became involved and mentioned as much once she officially agreed.

"Are you going to inform the assistant general?" Byron asked Evern in a neutral tone.

The Yeluthians exchanged a look before the commander dipped his chin.

"It would be disrespectful not to." His reply revealed his hesitation, but nobody decided to pursue the reason for it.

Instead, they spent a few minutes crafting a message for Aaron and King Arval on Evern's behalf, then they split apart for the evening.

In the morning, Coura prepared what belongings she would need for the journey, met her father, Byron, Lavine, the assistant general, and a handful of other soldiers, and their group hiked south to distance themselves from the camp. They had her recite the message, adjusted a couple details, and added more before she took her leave of the northern border.

*

Two days of flying brought her within sight of Verona the morning of the third. Instead of heading straight to the palace, Coura decided descending outside the city would avoid drawing attention to herself. Her windblown appearance already emphasized how fatigued she felt since she hurried to her destination, so she attempted to fix her hair and clothing to look more presentable along the way.

"Head for the council's meeting chamber first," Byron had advised. "Technically, the royal family owns the ancestral weapon, so Aaron should be the one you address regarding our request. King Arval might give some suggestions as well."

That comment led to the general's assistant insisting she inform his superiors, then Evern mentioned his fellow commander.

It's as if they want me to share my update with every person I bump into in case somebody offers a useful thought, she complained to herself before brushing a stray strand of hair away from her face. *I just need the dagger, not an assembly following me around with questions.*

Once inside the palace, she climbed the grand staircase to the second floor. Plenty of soldiers, mages, and servants wandered aimlessly while conversing or seemed to be focused on their duties like Coura, which she appreciated. No one stopped her, but a few people waved or offered a greeting she halfheartedly returned. Soon, the chamber's entrance came within sight, though no guards blocked the door.

Is it empty? She tested the knob, found it locked, and refrained from muttering a curse at her poor luck. *Wonderful. Where could Aaron be at this time?*

After crossing her arms while considering what she remembered of his usual schedule, she decided to try searching the queen's garden.

The area proved to be popular, though Coura believed it had to do with the slightly warmer and sunny weather. Every section held two or more people either chatting or reading, so she figured she would start at the rear and work her way forward. Unfortunately, a lone guard patrolling the private space prevented her from entering.

"This is King Aaron's personal garden," he explained.

Coura couldn't help herself from rolling her eyes. "I know. Can you tell me where he is?"

"My position does not require me to keep track of His Highness' location," the man replied while letting his annoyance creep into his voice.

In response, she spun around without another word to cross to the nearest section and begin the search again. *He wouldn't be in either training ground, and I would've heard a commotion in the city if he left the palace, which means he's somewhere inside. I wonder if I'd have better luck looking for one of the generals or King Arval.*

That notion led her to explore the southern field afterward.

The space reserved for magical combat and spellcasting grew considerably over the last year or so due to the Yeluthians' involvement. A building meant to house their people neared completion during her last visit, a pair of stables stood on opposite ends of the fenced area to house practice weapons and armor, and she lost count of the soldiers and mages, both angels and humans, who spent the late morning outside.

Coura glanced around for a familiar face when somebody called her name. A younger man around the same age as her strolled toward her from the left. Although she couldn't recall his name, she recognized him as a Yeluthian from Detrix's company.

"I am glad to see you again," he began with a slight smile.

Coura tilted her head. "What are you doing in Verona? I was told all the commander's troops moved south."

The smile faltered a bit. "They reorganized how many scouts should patrol the skies. Some of us were needed here instead."

When he didn't elaborate, she decided to drop the subject in favor of her mission. Asking about the kings led him to bring her to a friend she didn't know, but the stranger apparently worked a regular shift guarding the palace's upper floor. He had no information about Aaron, yet he suggested she try visiting the library since Commander Isan often spent extra time researching in the quieter space. With no other leads, she returned inside, through the grand hall, and to her next destination.

The wide array of books and their musty smell greeted Coura as she entered. She never frequented the area enough to memorize its layout, forcing her to peer around each corner in the hope of discovering the Yeluthian commander. After a few minutes of searching, she noticed her target in one of the farthest corners with a pen in hand to scribble notes while glancing between a text and his page.

"Excuse me," she whispered to avoid disturbing the people nearby.

Isan looked up briefly, as though he didn't expect anybody to address him, then he straightened once she didn't go away. "What is it?"

The question didn't sound rude, yet Coura knew this particular commander didn't exactly favor her like his comrades. "I bring news from the northern border. Can you tell me where King Arval is?"

"Evern sent you?" he muttered while scratching his graying beard. "My king has been inspecting the new dormitory and will not return until the evening meal. Is it urgent?"

She nodded before offering a summary of their suspicions regarding the dark mage in Nim-Vala, ending with the request for the ancestral weapon.

"I see," he replied in a thoughtful manner. "Although I can understand your need to receive the dagger, it remains in the possession of King Aaron. We only share input regarding its use."

Coura refrained from groaning with displeasure as her goal continued to evade her. "I understand," she responded instead before thanking the commander for his time.

As she prepared to take her leave, Isan held out a hand in a gesture for her to wait and cleared his throat.

"I overheard a discussion at the end of our council meeting yesterday afternoon. High Priest Jurek and King Aaron needed to visit the private dining hall today to oversee some changes. That is all I know, but you might try investigating there first. I will inform my king of your message as well."

His insight raised Coura's spirits, and she expressed her gratitude again before returning to the library's entrance.

As the day wore on, she struggled to ignore her sore feet and shoulders while climbing the nearest staircase to the second floor. Noise and movement greeted her as people carried chairs, tables, lamps, and art supplies from the direction of the grand hall. The sight both confused and frustrated her, though underneath those emotions grew an inexplicable uneasiness. With each step, Coura assessed the men and women she passed until she slipped around a pair of servants hauling a wooden table out of the private dining room.

She hadn't ventured into the space since learning about the massacre, yet she imagined the horrific experience that cost dozens of women their lives. The floor shined bright when she entered to show no hint of the past, though the servants tracked in plenty of dirt. In stark contrast, the once-decorated walls showcased new designs sketched in chalk against a white background. The smell of paint hung in the air to emphasize how the previous art needed to be redone, presumably because the damage had been too much to mend.

Coura recalled the room's former beauty as she glanced around for her friend. *What a shame. This used to be one of my favorite parts of the palace.*

Across the private dining hall, she spotted Aaron engaged in a conversation with a pair of men who gestured at a section of the sketches. Grace stood at his side in a rose-colored dress and nodded at something he said.

Coura's lips curved upward into a smile as she watched her friends. *How many weeks have passed since I last saw them? Although it's been at least a few months, they look the same. I hope they'll be relieved I'm back instead of upset about my disappearance. Regardless, I need to know about the weapon.*

With her resolve set, she prepared to step farther into the room until a recognizable presence swarmed the air around her, causing her to freeze in place. Heavy footsteps thundered behind and signaled an attack; however, she became distracted by the dark energy filling the dining hall. Somebody struck her in the back of the head as a result, sending her to her hands and knees.

This is demonic power, she realized against the throbbing of her skull. *Who would possess such a frightening amount?*

Coura ground her teeth and began to rise only for a force from behind to shove her down. While she lied on her stomach in a momentary daze, the stranger stomped over to pounce, pinning her to the ground by placing their knee on the middle of her back and grabbing her shoulders. Another two appeared from her blind spot and held her arms.

Some people picked up on either the presence or her attackers and glanced that way. Their worried voices echoed around the room, along with the noise of furniture being scuffed on the floor or set down without care.

When a pair of worn, dirt-covered boots came into view, Coura decided to demand answers before lashing out and putting the onlookers in danger. "What's going on?"

Instead of a response, one foot pulled back and aimed a kick at her head. The worst of the blow landed on her left temple, though the sharp jerk of her jaw pressed her bottom lip against her front teeth, splitting it near the middle. The resulting daze made her stop fighting against her restrains for a moment. Then, her temper flared; in response, the energy in her center stirred.

"That's enough of that," a male voice warned.

Before she could consider if she knew the person, he raised his leg again. This time, she braced for the kick, which connected with her ribs to knock the breath out of her.

"What is the meaning of this?"

At the sound of Aaron's commanding voice, Coura ceased her efforts.

There must be a reason these people targeted me, especially since this isn't the first time I've been ambushed on palace grounds. It could be Terran's doing or a spy from Nim-Vala too. Whatever the case, I'm stuck here for now.

With nothing else to do except listen, she focused on memorizing what she could while repressing the urge to attempt another escape.

***

Lord Hempton's invitation to offer input on his art proved to be the perfect excuse for Grace to speak with Aaron. Her royal friend's business prevented them from meeting by chance, so she utilized her connections within the nobility to find an opportunity and seize it, even if it meant returning to the space that still haunted her.

This has gone on long enough, she thought while following the presenters around. *I need an answer to figure out where I belong, if only for my own sanity.*

Despite her previous confidence, she wished to mention the subject when she could be alone with Aaron and avoid distractions. This led her to request time to discuss the artwork with Asteom's king; however, his casual behavior toward her continued showing how he saw her as a close friend but nothing more. Acknowledging that didn't bother her until she wondered what he would say when she offered a proposal.

Would our relationship become awkward or distant? It does not matter if he accepts or declines; a change will likely take place. Is this what I truly want?

In the midst of her personal dilemma, a pressure steadily rose and added an extra weight onto her shoulders. Her first instinct would have been to brush the uncomfortable sensation away, yet she soon remembered the presence from when she tried relaxing in the queen's garden, though it felt weaker then and eventually faded.

This is the same energy, she realized before scanning the hall while memories of the massacre came to the forefront of her mind. *I experienced this with Coura when she possessed demonic energy too…*

Aaron and those closest to them noticed her concerned glances, but before they could react, a commotion erupted near the entrance. What workers began transferring the new chairs and tables dropped what they carried in order to scramble away as a trio of men in ordinary clothing akin to the servants' restrained somebody on the ground. A burlier figure dressed similarly stood next to the group, as if to supervise.

Without fully committing to becoming involved, Grace's feet pulled her in that direction before Aaron and his guards hurried to keep up and approach the strangers.

"What is the meaning of this?" the king of Asteom demanded as he halted in front of the group.

While his question hung in the air, Grace noticed a fifth man shutting the last of the entrance doors, presumably after closing the others to keep everyone inside. The familiar scene had her readying her light energy in preparation to defend herself, Aaron, and those nearby.

The man in front of those on the floor turned to stare at the king in response. His chestnut-colored, uncombed hair and beard seemed quite the polar opposite from his clothing, his dark eyes sunk into his skull to give him a menacing appearance, and a sword hung on his belt. At his feet, Grace soon recognized the figure being pressed to the floor by his three companions. Before she had the opportunity to reach out to her friend, the stranger drew his weapon and placed the metal tip against Coura's head. A heavy silence followed, as if the entire room collectively held their breath.

"Who are you?" Aaron demanded, though in a much calmer manner than Grace expected given the victim's identity.

The man grinned. "Is this all it takes to earn the ear of Asteom's king? I'll admit, this isn't really fair for you. This pest has been in my sights for a while."

To emphasize his point, he pulled his leg back to kick Coura in the stomach with an audible thump, causing the onlookers in the room to gasp. She tried unsuccessfully to free herself, prompting Grace to glance at Aaron. Her friend glared at the stranger, yet nothing else suggested he felt seriously concerned about Coura's life being in danger.

"Nim-Vala doesn't appreciate how you treated our request for an alliance," the man continued, allowing his expression to show his annoyance. "Your troops' positions along the border suggest you intend to go to war."

"Preparing a defense is not the same as starting a war," Aaron replied without pause. "Why don't you just admit you're here to provoke me and reveal the reason?"

While Grace listened, she triggered her goddess gift and honed in on the attackers. She fully expected them to be Nim-Valans given the previous incident; however, every mind seemed hazy except for the man speaking, and the unnatural presence she felt throughout the encounter stemmed from the other four. When she coupled that with what she learned about Coura in the past, her muscles grew tense.

Still, she stepped forward and raised her chin in an assured manner. "Tell us the truth. Why are you here, and why are you the only person not possessed by demonic energy."

Aaron's head snapped to her to display his shock while the stranger frowned.

"Clever, Yeluthian," the Nim-Valan grumbled. "I thought I was lucky when I spotted you since you escaped our capture last time. It turns out our sources were correct. You abandoned your palace in the clouds for us lowly humans…"

"Mind your tongue."

He chuckled at her response. "Don't worry, ambassador. Our attempt to kidnap you would have been at our convenience. You continue to only have value as a bargaining tool. If your people decide to support Asteom's oppression of Nim-Vala, then you should watch your back-"

"Guards, seize them!" Aaron interrupted while putting himself in front of Grace.

The soldiers around the room crept closer and readied their weapons. In response, the Nim-Valan kneeling on Coura's back grabbed a fistful of her hair in order to crane her neck in one direction. The group's leader then lowered his blade, pressed the edge against her exposed skin, and drew a concerning amount of blood.

"Don't act so hastily," he warned after. "Would you *like* me to kill her?"

Aaron paused before replying. "You never told us why you're here, but you revealed your intent to create tension between Asteom and Nim-Vala. I also assume you're allying with the enemy mage hiding along the border. Why else would your comrades not have control over their minds?"

"Am I?" The blade punctured Coura's skin farther, and she twisted her head with her eyes squeezed shut in an attempt to escape its painful touch. "What about the threat near the southern base? Is conquering the north more important than your own citizens?"

"You're shifting the blame," Aaron countered. "Is there a confidant you've been ordered to protect? Perhaps it's the leader of the Nim-Valans my troops are facing."

The stranger curled his lip to snarl at him. Instead of a verbal response after, he turned to kick his prisoner in the ribs. When the king didn't offer more, the man struck her again with a growl.

Why does Aaron not try to stop this man from harming Coura? Grace wondered and found herself longing to jump into the fight. *Does he not care that she is being hurt?*

She prepared to extend her mind to him and reveal her hope to use a spell until she noticed his hands. Unlike the rest of his composed appearance, they had balled into fists and trembled slightly, reflecting a repressed rage. When he continued attempting to discuss the situation and push for answers, she steadily began to understand his internal conflict.

Aaron will not sacrifice his kingdom's safety for one person, she realized as her heart sank. *Just because he has feelings for her does not mean he will dismiss his duties as Asteom's leader. If he did, the country would be at a greater risk. I...I had not considered how his loyalty to his kingdom outshines my own. While I sat by and waited for my chance to pursue my goal, he struggled to accept his role as a king. Meanwhile, I hoped to use marriage as a reason to stay because I have not been honest with my parents and myself about what I want.*

With that in mind, she embraced the comfort of her rising energy while it supported her, as it always did, and returned her attention to the verbal bout in order to assist her friends.

"You seem to be facing two problems," the Nim-Valan continued. "A war is upon you to the north, yet you possess the numbers to squash out the resistance there, and conflict remains around the south because of the demonic creatures. I would hate to be in your shoes."

While Aaron questioned the Nim-Valan's awareness of what took place in Asteom, a plan took shape in Grace's mind. Her power fluttered in response to the spell she prepared just as the man laughed and started offering a retort. Both arms extended in front of her in a single motion, and she released the light energy while focusing on weaving the tendrils together into invisible strings. Then, the magic acted based on her training with Emilea.

The attackers' leader shouted at her just as the spell crossed the distance between them to wrap around him. Grace tightened her hold by commanding the power to constrict, a feat requiring all her attention and resulting in the man's arms snapping to his sides and his legs sliding together involuntarily. The grip on his sword slipped as well, and the weapon clattered to the floor a second before his body.

At that, Aaron pointed to the remaining Nim-Valans. "Capture them!"

She ignored the resulting commotion while the soldiers apprehended the four others during the next minute or so. Then, her friend's voice pulled her away momentarily.

"Is your spell going to be enough to restrain him?"

When Grace nodded, he bolted forward and threw himself beside Coura, who shifted to lie on her side once the Nim-Valans were dragged off. She followed at a walk in order to avoid letting the spell slip by loosening her grip on the energy; however, by the time she reached her target, a pair of soldiers began binding the man's wrists. A minute later, she dismissed her power so they could arrest him.

I never used that before except during my sessions with Emilea, she reflected after the guards thanked her for her assistance and her vision went in and out of focus. *It took most of my energy just to keep him from breaking free, but I suppose it was worth the effort.*

A groan from nearby reminded Grace of Coura, and her heart dropped once she glanced over to see her friend attempting to sit up with Aaron's help.

"Let me heal you," she instinctively began while hurrying over and dropping to her knees.

Coura wiped away some of the blood coating her bottom lip and chin before wrapping an arm around her midsection. "That was an impressive binding spell," she commented through a wince.

"Don't talk," Aaron chided her. He prepared to say more until a soldier from behind addressed him.

"Your Highness, what should we do with these five?"

"Bring them to the prison for interrogation," the king replied. "Instruct the remaining troops to inform the mages so they can alert us if any additional spies are hiding in the palace or around Verona."

The soldiers who heard saluted him before hustling away, leaving only his guards and the remaining men and women who observed the entire incident. The onlookers started collecting their scattered belongings after and departed to spread the news.

Meanwhile, Grace laid her hands on Coura's arm, stretched her presence to feel for damage, and avoided gasping at the bruised organs and broken ribs. She assessed what energy she had at her disposal before admitting what little she could do since she chose to interfere and restrain the Nim-Valans' leader. The healing spell focused on mending the worst parts until she grew lightheaded.

Coura didn't seem to notice or dwell on what took place, to Grace's amazement. "Someone wielding demonic power possessed most of that group, and they admitted to being associated with Nim-Vala."

"Could it be the same demon terrorizing Dala?" Aaron asked without hiding his displeasure.

"I doubt it. The energy feels slightly different from what I experienced in the south, and Terran never mentioned working with Nim-Valans."

A pause followed her answer as Aaron seemed to be contemplating the situation, so Coura waved Grace away to rise.

"Wait," he ordered before Grace could. "Where are you going?"

"I came here to get the ancestral weapon. It may be our only way to stop the dark mage on the border before they attempt to harm anybody else here."

"You have not been fully healed," Grace protested while jumping to her feet.

"I'll be fine." Despite the words, Coura hunched forward slightly in a posture meant to ease pain in the torso before addressing Aaron again. "Evern and Byron said you can give me the dagger."

The king didn't respond until after he rose to his feet. "Let Grace finish her work."

"We don't have time for-"

"I understand. I'm smart enough to know we'll stand a better chance of stopping the Nim-Valans if we restrain the source of that power. I also believe you're hurt, and I can't imagine you fighting when you're not completely prepared." He waited, as if expecting another interruption. When none came, he continued in a more sympathetic manner. "I'll be right back with the weapon. Until then, just be patient."

Coura nodded without hiding her reluctance, so Grace picked up with the spell. Aaron turned away from them, signaled for his guards to follow him, and exited the hall. Grace used all her remaining energy to mend her friend's injuries before the king returned, yet she knew what hadn't been healed would still take days to recover. When she mentioned as much, her friend didn't look bothered by the warning, which concerned her.

"Please, do not push your body," she nearly begged in a final attempt. "You would upset plenty of people if you worked yourself to death."

Coura seemed taken back by the serious comment and dipped her chin before offering a rueful smile. "I'll try, but you know I've never been gifted at staying out of trouble. I envy you for that. You continue fighting for what you believe in without letting yourself be knocked down or put into a cage."

Before Grace could reply, Aaron and his surrounding soldiers returned.

"I'd like you to go to the southern base first," he began and held out a satchel presumably containing the dagger.

Coura snatched it from his hands, peeked inside, then shouldered her new baggage. "Why? The others are expecting me on the border."

"Based on Commander Detrix's report, we can confirm the demon's appearance and narrow its location. They're also weaker than the troops to the north. We need to end the conflict within Asteom first then deal with Nim-Vala."

"All right. Is there anything else I should be aware of?"

"Assistant General Calin is in charge of the base now. Find him or Marcus and go from there."

Grace noticed Coura frown, but she didn't argue, allowing Aaron to send her off.

"Leave as soon as you're ready," he advised with a faint sense of worry. "And be careful."

"I will."

The parting gaze the two shared left much to be desired, though Coura took her leave of the hall without another word. Grace watched her friend depart with mixed emotions; however, she found she held no resentment regarding the king's feelings.

I only desired Aaron's attention in order to enact my plan, which I figured had to be the best method to solve my problems. Instead of charting my own course in life, I pushed my parents away because I disagreed with their expectations. Perhaps I needed to explore my options, decide for myself, and stand up for the future I dream of instead of relying on others to influence what I do and do not want.

She released a weary sigh after resigning to rest and contemplate the topic later.

"Thank you for your help," Aaron startled her by adding in the resulting silence. Then, he shifted his eyes from the doorway to her and smiled. "I don't know what I would've done if you didn't intervene."

"It was nothing," she reassured him and returned the gesture. "I am just glad to be of assistance. I still wish I had enough power to fully heal Coura."

"She didn't seem like she's in the mood to hang around. Anyway, you should take it easy and recover your strength."

Grace nodded and prepared to exit when another thought came to mind. "Aaron, I could sense the demonic presence looming over those men. Perhaps I can be of use to the generals in their search for additional spies."

When he didn't reply right away, she looked back to find him wearing a pleased expression. She tilted her head in response, causing him to chuckle.

"Sorry," he apologized after. "I'm just thinking about how after all this, you're still willing to become involved in Asteom's messes. You've made such a positive impact, and I owe you."

The weight on Grace's shoulders lifted upon hearing his words, yet she merely attributed her support to her ever-changing role.

Dala's Stand

Given all that had happened since General Tio's death, Marcus didn't expect any positive updates from their troops, the Yeluthians, or anybody in the palace.

The demon they faced upheld its half of the deal, though that only pertained to the base. It continued releasing the monstrous creatures under its control upon the southern half of Asteom and targeted Dala, presumably as revenge for the late general's victory. In a way, Marcus and Calin viewed the attacks as a backhanded slap; the structure housing their troops never faced adversity, but the people suffered instead.

The following weeks consisted of reports from nearby towns who experienced an increase in damage to their homes and missing livestock. The Yeluthian and Dalan troops continued to handle what they could, yet their numbers became too spread out to manage as diligently as Marcus would like. Meanwhile, Calin had been thrown into the general's role and accepted the responsibilities seamlessly. This didn't surprise Marcus since the other assistant general understood what was being asked of him.

Their focus narrowed to the city soon after. The demon had yet to appear, but the beasts returned to invade as soon as the sun set. This forced the pair to station soldiers around Dala instead of the base and assign rotating shifts so the men and women could recover enough energy in time for the onslaught throughout the night. Marcus imagined the amount of enemies would decrease as the time passed; however, that didn't seem to be the case.

He also hadn't had a proper break in weeks, so he doubted his memory. Calin never restrained his temper-fueled comments on the subject either, which often soured Marcus' mood.

As he entered the meeting space to update his new commanding officer on the previous day's assault from those he met in the city, he froze at the sight of a bronze-clad figure cradling a long bundle wrapped in cloth.

"There you are," Calin said by way of greeting. "Get in here. Our scout from Clearwater has an urgent report."

Marcus frowned but obeyed. After shutting the doors, he dropped into one of the nearest chairs without a word to show his fatigue.

The armored Yeluthian glanced back at the additional guest and let his shoulders sag a bit. Still, Marcus noticed a sense of hope emanating from the angel before he returned his eyes to Calin. Their superior crossed his arms after.

"Go on then."

"Yes, Assistant General," came the immediate response. "As I mentioned, I hail from the group assigned to monitor Clearwater and its surrounding areas. The attacks became more frequent this past month, resulting in enough damage to concern the residents. Many felt the need to arm themselves with whatever they deemed a worthy weapon and join in the fight. My direct supervisor Gormel met with the city's leaders during this time to discuss the risks, mind you, but the humans feel entitled to protect their property, belongings, and loved ones. This led to debating before the-"

"Pardon the interruption," Calin cut in while rubbing his right temple. "Can you start by explaining why you're here, soldier? It's been a long few weeks, so we've become adept at understanding brief reports instead of lengthy explanations."

The Yeluthian's mouth hung open a bit, as though he couldn't believe somebody would dismiss what he had to say, while Marcus couldn't help but crack a smile at his comrade's impatience.

Although I want to comment on the impression General Tio made on Calin, I know the former's reaction would have been much less polite. His resulting swell of emotion from remembering the man subsided when the Yeluthian continued in a slightly offended manner.

"An individual in the city has been hiding one of the ancestral weapons."

Silence filled the space until Marcus and Calin processed what the soldier just revealed. Then, they both practically jumped out of their seats.

"What did you say?" Marcus demanded first without hiding his disbelief.

The angel stuck up his nose a bit. "I mentioned the citizens of Clearwater hoped to assist in fortifying the city's defenses."

"Sorry for skipping ahead," Calin apologized while rubbing the back of his neck in a sheepish manner. "I suppose we're also used to hearing less exciting information. Can you show it to us?"

At the request, the Yeluthian placed the bundle in his arms on the table and began unwrapping it. "The human who kept this claimed he purchased it during a visit to Verona nearly twenty years ago. He thought it a decorative piece, so it remained unused until the humans began collecting what items they could use against the demonic creatures. When my people noticed a golden blade being wielded, somebody inspected the metal and verified its origin."

Marcus huffed a laugh as he recalled his past experience with one of the legendary items. "Anybody who knows even the basics about weapons would admire the craftsmanship of an ancestral weapon."

The final corner of the cloth peeled back to reveal a glint of gold underneath, which shined brightly despite the limited light of the room's lamp. What designs adorned the hilt looked nearly identical to what Marcus remembered from the blade he wielded against the demon in Verona. He rose to reach across the table without the others' permission, grab the weapon, and weigh the metal in his hands before marveling at its unmatched artistry.

"It's just like the one I used," he muttered before passing the weapon to Calin, who performed a similar inspection.

"I wonder why the fool hid this," the other assistant general commented. "I'm certain King Aaron sent word to every populated area in search of these."

"The man acted unaware of the notice when my supervising officer confronted him," the angel added with a shrug. "In any case, the city's leaders decided to have it brought here since the demon last appeared in Dala."

Calin set the sword back on the table, took a minute to contemplate what the object's appearance meant for their forces, then asked if the soldier had any more information. When the Yeluthian claimed to have finished his business, their leader dismissed him.

Marcus made sure to thank the messenger before watching the angel leave. Part of him still indulged in the thrill of their discovery, yet he knew Calin's silence meant his comrade didn't entirely share that same elation.

"I wish I could confirm this will change our situation," the assistant general commented with none of the confidence he showcased earlier.

"Doesn't it?" Marcus countered and removed his eyes from where they lingered on the golden blade in order to meet the other's stare. "We have a way to stop the demon."

"What about the creatures? Their master hasn't appeared ever since the duel. Even if we kill it, the attacks will keep happening."

"Then we kill them one by one. At least they won't continue multiplying without their source of energy."

"When did you become an expert on how demonic magic works?"

Marcus narrowed his eyes at Calin's sardonic expression. "I'm not. We can interrogate the mages until somebody confirms or denies my assumption."

"Quit pouting; I was only joking. The main issue has to do with the demon's location since it's hiding. I don't want it to learn we possess an ancestral weapon. Otherwise, it might avoid coming near Dala."

"You're going to wait until it shows up again?"

The assistant general nodded.

Marcus couldn't disagree with his superior's logic, though he wished for the power to end the conflict on their own terms rather than the demon's. *Despite the odds, this news gives us a chance. I believe that's what our troops and the people across Asteom have been praying for.*

*

As the sun dipped to signal dusk, Marcus paused to enjoy the brief moment of contentment before following Calin into Dala. The two agreed to do whatever they could to lure the demon out of hiding, which meant challenging it to another duel; however, this time, they wouldn't go about it alone.

"You'll keep the ancestral weapon in its sheath until the time is right," his comrade decided. "When that moment arrives, I trust you will use your best judgement."

Marcus placed a hand on the golden weapon's hilt, which currently hung on his waist, after recalling the order.

People wandering through the city normally welcomed the troops with friendly smiles or verbal greetings, but ever since the creatures began damaging their property and claiming more lives, they hid inside where they would be safe when the conflict continued. Only the marching feet of the soldiers behind the assistant generals broke the lingering silence.

Calin split apart with his group after to assume their daily assignments until evening. That night, Marcus would meet his comrade at the outskirts of Dala in order to taunt the demon. None of their previous attempts to find the creature amounted to any results, mainly because they permitted no one to search beyond the safety of the established perimeter, so they figured they could directly confront the unseen source of their problems.

We have the element of surprise thanks to the ancestral weapon, Marcus reminded himself as he met Calin at the end of the day. *I worry our skills are not enough to defeat a demon though, especially since it overpowered General Tio without effort. I would suggest we form a team for this instead of volunteering, but we're all tired. The palace and northern border can't sacrifice the soldiers or mages, leaving us to fight this threat ourselves.*

While Marcus considered how long it would take to receive additional support from the capital, Calin turned around and scratched his head, as if confused.

"What's the matter?" he asked when the Dalan soldier scanned the area.

The assistant general tilted his head. "Do you hear that?"

"Hear what?"

Calin pressed a finger to his lips and glanced to his right. "I thought I heard cries from near the base," he explained a minute later.

Marcus paused to listen before shaking his head. "Perhaps your mind is playing tricks on you. I doubt the demon would go back on its word, at least not so soon. Besides, the base isn't completely unprotected either."

His comrade didn't look convinced yet didn't protest, so the two moved to the edge of the city closest to the open field that stretched before the moat. By that point, the city's lamps had been lit, brightening the area significantly.

"Now, we wait," Marcus muttered to confirm their plan.

Calin dipped his chin without a word.

The time passed as usual without revealing their enemy for a few minutes. A handful of demonic creatures gave away their locations by creeping through the grass or coming close enough so their violet eyes picked up a crimson glow from the lamps; however, none attacked until their master gave them permission, which usually took place around midnight.

Despite that knowledge, Marcus found himself keeping a hand on the ancestral weapon with a growing, inexplicable sense of anxiousness. He also didn't remove his eyes from the grassy area until he noticed the sound of footsteps drawing near and at a faster pace than a walk. The thought of an attack elsewhere had him spinning around, leading Calin to do the same before they could make out a shadowy figure approaching at a jog.

"Relax," said a familiar voice he hadn't heard in months. "It's just me."

Marcus' eyebrows rose and his mouth fell open a bit once he recognized Coura in the road. She wore no armor aside from basic, leather padding, and beads of sweat decorated her forehead. Otherwise, she appeared the same as he remembered, albeit quite pale.

Has it really only been a few months since we were in Verona? It feels longer due to the conflict.

Unlike Marcus, Calin didn't seem fazed by her sudden arrival.

"What are you doing here?" his fellow assistant general asked as soon as she stopped in front of them. "We didn't know you were coming."

"Wait, how did you get here?" Marcus added once he considered the distance she would have needed to traverse from the capital. "We didn't receive a notice for backup."

"Give me a second," she snapped while bending forward to place her hands on her knees in an exhausted manner.

I remember Aaron telling me about how she can use a Yeluthian spell to travel from one location to another, he noted when she spent the next minute catching her breath. *Does that mean she came alone? Why would she do that?*

With a final, deep sigh, she straightened, looked them each in the eye, and grinned. "It's been a while since I visited Dala. I'm glad to see you two again."

Her carefree greeting proved to be such a stark change from what Marcus and Calin experienced lately that they could only offer weak smiles in return.

"To answer your first question: Aaron sent me," she began and allowed her expression to reflect the severity of the situation. "I have a report from the palace and an update on what's happening along the northern border."

Marcus' heart dropped upon hearing her reply. *If Aaron ordered her to come here immediately, I assume his problems and those near Nim-Vala aren't much better than what Calin and I are facing.*

For the next hour or so, Coura proceeded to fill the pair in on what took place, including Byron's absence and return, what she experienced on the border and why they requested she return to the palace, and the enemy's staged attack in the dining hall before she left. Hearing of a second invasion in the capital city troubled him deeply given Aaron's position during both instances, yet he agreed with the conclusion regarding separate enemies.

"Even if the demon and dark mage aren't working together, their plans are benefiting from the other's results," he added once his friend finished her summary. "That explains why our troops must be spread so thin and why Nim-Vala has become such a problem recently."

Calin expressed his agreement with a grunt and crossed his arms. "I appreciate the news, but why wouldn't King Aaron write a notice beforehand? We aren't risking the lives of our troops by using messengers unless it's absolutely necessary, so why send you with information that doesn't impact us at the moment?"

"First, he didn't have the opportunity," she explained while counting the reasons on her fingers. "Second, I can get here without issue, and I need to head north next. Finally…"

Marcus watched as she removed a sheathed dagger from her satchel and held it out to Calin, who accepted with a curious stare. As he slid the weapon out from its protective cover, they saw an unmistakable, golden shine.

"Is this…"

"I don't know exactly how they found it," she continued while attempting to suppress a smirk at their startled expressions. "Aaron wants us to deal with the conflict here first, then he'll focus on the northern border. Casner and his troops seem to be able to manage on their own for the time being."

A pause followed her final statement when the assistant generals shared a knowing look.

We might actually stand a chance with both the sword and dagger, as long as we can keep the creature in range.

Coura glanced between them, and her smile faded. "What's wrong?"

Calin responded by raising an eyebrow at Marcus and nodding.

Without a word, he drew their secret weapon and laid it across his hands for Coura to admire. This time, her eyes went wide and her mouth hung open in disbelief as she leaned closer to inspect the metal without touching its polished surface.

"Our soldiers stationed in Clearwater procured this for us," Calin replied without sharing the details. "This is the first night we're going to use it."

"That's a relief." She stepped back without attempting to grab for the dagger she brought. "This changes the plan."

"Does it?"

"One ancestral weapon can seal the demon here, then I'll bring the other north to use against the enemy's leader there. We'll accomplish twice as much in half the time."

"So you're staying in Dala?" Marcus asked next. As optimistic as he felt about the additional support, both from his friend and the dagger, he didn't know if her presence made her a target or if she'd hinder their attempt to corner the creature.

When she glanced away without answering, he narrowed his eyes.

"Is it going to come after you again, like in the Western Woods? Because if that's the case, you would be better off in the base, unless we risk it following you north toward Verona."

"What if I choose to fight with you?" she countered, though her tone didn't sound as forceful as he expected.

"You'll be in danger."

That spurred a chuckle, and she looked at him again. "Is it any different for both of you? Besides, I'd make a useful distraction."

Marcus prepared to berate her for the suggestion since he hated the idea of endangering a person's life, especially after all she went through in the past, but Calin spoke before he could get a word out.

"We hope to taunt the demon into coming out of hiding tonight."

"What do you mean?" Coura pressed after a pause when the Dalan soldier didn't continue.

Calin shook his head and lowered his eyes to stare at the ground. "The general agreed to a duel and lost his life in the process, yet the deal they struck beforehand prevents it from harming the base. Well, it hasn't shown up since then, but its creatures attack the city and surrounding towns every night. The two of us want to lure it out and defeat it with the ancestral weapon in our possession."

"You have a better chance of interacting with the demon if I'm here," she added with a thoughtful expression. "He also wouldn't try to escape if I challenge him."

"You and your partner were almost killed before," Marcus pointed out. "What makes you think this will be any different?"

More reasons rested on his tongue, yet he managed to keep from snapping at her for her reckless behavior. *I trust her to do her best, but I also need her to understand what might happen if she decides to join us. We've dealt with the attacks for months and have an investment in the outcome. If the demon emerges, I'm afraid we'll only get a single chance. Otherwise, this becomes a hunt against a being who knows we hold its lone weakness.*

To his slight dismay, she didn't back down and even put her hands on her hips in a displeased manner. "I'm not stupid, and I'm not going about this alone. We'll be in control of the situation, you have two of the ancestral weapons, and I can use my magic. Our only concern should be preventing him from escaping once he learns what we're trying to do. I believe I can draw him to us too."

Although he wondered how, Marcus didn't comment on her response. She had been his comrade for years and saved his life on multiple occasions. If she was being adamant about participating in the fight, he would just waste his breath by arguing.

During his pause, Calin picked up the conversation to finalize the details.

"Our troops can prevent any interference during the encounter, but I'll need to reorganize our current defenses. Are you ready to act tonight?"

Coura immediately shook her head before slouching her shoulders a bit, surprising both assistant generals. "Getting here on such short notice took most of my reserved energy. I'd rather be decently recovered than attempt to challenge a demon how I am now."

Marcus frowned as the Dalan soldier agreed to wait until she recovered. He hated dragging the problem out, yet he'd grown to accept the necessary measures needed to ensure a better chance for success.

The assistant generals intended to stay at their location while Coura mentioned returning to the base; however, the threat of the creatures, as well as her wobbly steps when she turned away, prompted Marcus to offer to escort her toward the nearest inn instead. When she agreed and thanked him, he understood the severity of her weariness and allowed her to use him as a crutch while they moved through the city.

***

As expected, the demonic creatures began their assault later in the night, yet the casualties proved to be less severe than what the Dalans became used to. Everyone spent the next day resting and returned to their positions the following evening to prepare for a similar experience.

Coura slept through a majority of the combat, though not by choice.

It seemed obvious from the assistant generals' disappointed expressions that they wished to end the conflict as soon as possible, and she agreed; however, her body subconsciously protested her determination by abandoning her attempts to stay awake or move around until noon on the third day since she arrived. Even then, a lingering ache bothered her ribs to remind her of her previous impatience at the palace, preventing Grace from healing the damage she sustained despite the Yeluthian's limited power.

If I wasn't trying to conserve energy for tonight, I would mend them myself, she thought while dressing in what armor the people offered, securing her sword to her waist, and departing from the inn Marcus selected for her. *Then again, my reserves felt nearly drained when I arrived, so I shouldn't push my luck. I will need all the strength I can get when I face Terran.*

Despite her faith in her comrades and the blessing of the two ancestral weapons, confronting the demon stirred a sense of unease she never experienced before. Fighting Soirée had been personal, like she needed to rid herself of her past mistake; however, she knew nothing about Terran other than his resolve to conquer Asteom and spawn demonic creatures.

The same proved true with the second, unknown entity hiding within Nim-Vala.

Don't worry about that now, she told herself after spotting the troops closest to the field where her friend instructed her to go once she recovered. *Aaron is a capable leader with enough guards and sense to avoid another attack, Grace is safe in the palace, and Byron and Evern should be able to handle themselves. My main goal is to fulfill my role here.*

Some individuals appeared to recognize her and waved, yet no one attempted to hide their weariness as the sun sank closer to the edge of the earth with every passing minute. Finally, when stars decorated the sky and lamps were lit at their backs, the soldiers positioned themselves along the border of the city, and the area fell silent.

In that moment, Coura focused on the dual presences lying within her center. Each tendril ebbed and flowed in a unique rhythm, yet neither disturbed the other, reminding her of Sage Vidal's claim that her energies became balanced. What he didn't mention, and what she hoped wouldn't change that stability, was what could happen if she utilized her demonic power to attract Terran's attention.

"Are we set?" came Calin's voice from behind at a volume the entire group could hear.

A mixture of nods, salutes, and vocal confirmations followed in response.

Coura glanced over her shoulder after when footsteps signaled the assistant general's approach. Marcus trailed behind with a sheathed dagger in hand, and both paused to converse with her.

"Are you ready?" the Dalan soldier asked with a raised eyebrow. "If so, I would prefer to know what you plan on doing since Marcus and I will be relying on that trick you mentioned when you first arrived."

"We'll see," she replied as her eyes drifted up to the darkening sky. "It's not like I tried this recently, but I believe he'll come once he knows I'm here."

Calin scratched his chin before continuing. "Worst case scenario, the demon doesn't show up tonight and it's a repeat of the previous days."

When he paused, Marcus picked up the discussion. "Normally, we push the front line forward to put distance between the city and the combat, then the rest of the squad continues to monitor the border. This prevents a creature from slipping through. We'll stick to that trend today, except you'll be on the front line with us in order to lure the demon out."

"I should try to move farther ahead, just in case," Coura added.

The assistant generals shared a look before her friend went on.

"I'll be at your side then."

"And I can support you two from behind," Calin concluded with a nod. "Although the rest of the soldiers are well-trained too, I would rather they protect the city. I wouldn't put it past a demon to use the creatures as a distraction."

A call from the front for the Dalan leader had them glancing toward the field, though its lack of urgency didn't raise an alarm. With a final wish for luck to be on their side, he moved east through the squad, leaving Coura and Marcus alone.

She figured that would be the end of their conversation; however, her friend held out the weapon in his hand.

"Here," he directed, prompting her to accept the dagger. "I have the sword, so we should be properly armed."

Coura stared down at the weapon in her hand without attempting to unsheathe the golden blade. Still, it's warmth soaked through the cover, like a gentle touch to reassure her of its presence. That feeling offered a unique sense of comfort, yet she couldn't stop herself from considering whether or not it was the same one that wounded her in the Valley Beyond.

I used to be considered a potential enemy, and the angels nothing more than a myth. Soirée was able to do as she pleased because the country never focused on what they didn't believe could happen until it stood right at their doorstep. Now, the kingdom faces another demon, possibly two, and nobody became aware of the problem until I fell into the mix...

"What's wrong?" Marcus asked a second later.

"Is this ever going to end?" she muttered without thinking as a weight steadily dropped onto her shoulders. Instead of clarifying, she let the question hang between them until she realized how inappropriate her timing was and prepared to apologize.

Before she could do so, her friend placed his hand on top of the dagger, startling her enough to glance up and meet his eyes. In them, she recognized his strength and understanding, as well as a hint of his own worry.

"It will," he stated in a confident manner. "We can't help what the world is like when we're born into it or what life will throw at us, but we'll overcome our struggles together. If you don't believe me, look at how much progress has been made during our lifetime."

While Coura reflected on his words, Marcus removed his hand, stood straighter, and looked past her to monitor his troops.

"Besides, we would be bored without the need to stay on our toes, demons or not."

"Thank you," she offered while attempting to return her focus to their current goal.

Marcus responded with a smile. "You don't have to thank me. Let's just finish this so we can go home."

A Final Push

Despite the squad's preparation, nothing out of the ordinary appeared until after midnight. Coura needed to keep moving in place in order to avoid growing tired, unlike the soldiers surrounding her who became accustomed to the rotating sleep schedule. An initial hint of agitation spread through the area while she stretched until the entire field fell silent. Then, they heard growling.

"Here they come," Calin announced from the front, prompting everyone, including Coura, to draw their weapons.

She noted a lack of urgency in his warning, which intrigued her given the severity of the evening's plan; however, the shuffling of feet and armor forced her to concentrate on the enemy and stifle what apprehension grew after.

The snarling of the demonic creatures soon blended in with shouts and startled cries. What mages remained with the main group summoned balls of fire to cast the field in a glow reminiscent of the rising sun. Still, Coura could only catch glimpses of the beasts as they leapt and bound through the tall grass to pounce on or swipe at unsuspecting troops.

Don't get distracted, she reminded herself while gripping the sheathed ancestral weapon she held in her left hand and the ordinary sword in her right. *Separate from the mess with Marcus and call out to Terran.*

The instructions repeated in her mind as she hurried to her friend's side. He hadn't put much space between them, but he prepared to jump in and protect those around him from an unseen attack.

"I'm going forward," she told him above the noise. "Cover me."

Marcus nodded to show he heard her while his eyes continued to wander.

With her backup aware of her intentions, Coura jogged away from the city. She kept her attention on what shadows slid in and out of her field of vision before breaking from the safety of her comrades. A chorus of snarls pursued, but she continued to hold a consistent pace, trusting in her energy, as well as her friend's dedication to fulfilling his role as her bodyguard, for the time being.

When she put a satisfactory amount of distance between herself and the fighting, she slowed to a stop. There was no time to linger on her next task since the creatures on her tail breathed down her neck, so she dove into her center of power and seized the demonic presence. In response, the power engulfed her, as it always did, giving her a feeling of confidence and security amid the dangerous chaos.

Terran, she called in her mind while imagining her inner voice echoing throughout the area. *I know you're hiding out there. Come and face me!*

As the challenge lingered in the air, Coura abruptly released the hold hiding her power's essence. This allowed any living being nearby to sense her energy, including the mages, attacking beasts, and even those without the ability to utilize magic, though the latter group could not perceive much aside from an uneasy feeling.

The creatures ended their pursuit of her and Marcus after, yet she assumed they followed an order from their master instead of being intimidated.

"I take it this is your doing?" her friend asked while stepping up to her side.

Coura grunted in confirmation and decided to prepare her secret weapon for when she would inevitably need it. She slipped the covering off and tossed it aside before poising the dagger in her left hand, allowing her right one to continue wielding her ordinary blade. Despite the consistent support the Yeluthian item provided, she couldn't help but notice that arm growing numb within seconds.

I suppose the demonic power I possess would clash with a weapon projecting light energy. At least I can manage for a while...

Shuffling in the grass directly in front of them brought her attention back to the present.

"This is a surprise."

The deep voice sounded close enough to raise the hair on Coura's arms and put her on edge, mainly because the source stayed hidden. Marcus crept forward while she considered a response, so she ordered him to wait in a whisper.

"You were never the type to remain out of sight when I'm around," she began while addressing their unseen foe. "What makes tonight any different?"

Like a shadow stretching with the setting sun, a figure emerged from the grass farther away than she expected, though he appeared taller despite the distance. His entire head bore tuffs of hair similar to a mane this time, and his pale skin stuck out more than normal against the dark backdrop. To her dismay, his pompous expression came across clearly.

"We've met twice, yet you claim to comprehend my knowledge of strategy," he responded and placed both hands on his hips. "Besides that, I kept you alive both times because you are useful to me. You're a resource, nothing more."

"Then why reveal yourself at all?" she countered, though she already knew the answer.

Terran's prideful smirk twisted into a grin. "Did you not hear me? Soirée's power has always been alluring; all demonic energy is. When you released it just now, I couldn't restrain myself from investigating. Are you making an offering in order to join me in conquering this country? Perhaps you wish to experience the life of a ruler over the humans."

"Like I would ever turn my back on my home for a despicable creature," she spat back. To emphasize her displeasure with the idea, she raised the golden dagger and her sword at once.

Marcus did the same with his ancestral weapon a second later; however, Terran didn't seem phased by the items. They heard him scoff at the threat after crossing his arms and returning to a more relaxed expression.

"I suppose you believe you're above us," Marcus startled Coura by adding as he took a step closer to the demon. "If that's the case, why not prove it. This time, you'll defeat the leaders of the base and claim additional power if you succeed. The only thing standing in your way now is your own arrogance."

Although she knew her friend was merely goading Terran into initiating the fight, the truth of his words still came across clearly. *If we fail here, the base is as good as gone. This is our last chance to end the conflict to the south, as long as he doesn't flee again.*

In response to the assistant general's comments, a black sword manifested in the demon's hand before he stalked forward.

"I prefer to savor my opponents until they lose the will to fight," he growled. "The last man I faced was the most fun I've had in years, but if it is a swift death you wish for, then I shall oblige."

From Coura's side, Marcus charged forward as soon as Terran came near enough to strike. His sword connected with the demonic blade when he arched it into a horizontal swipe, and the resulting ring of metal echoed in her ears.

She immediately jumped into action in order to maintain a consistent barrage of attacks, which aided Marcus when Terran easily brushed the ancestral weapon aside. He followed by sidestepping her lunge, bringing up his sword, and attempting to catch her off guard with an upward slice; however, Coura angled the dagger in her left hand so it could deflect the otherwise detrimental blow.

Marcus picked up where she left off, though this time he managed to keep the demon between the two. The black blade acted like a shield since Terran moved swiftly enough to turn around whenever she jumped in and parry her effort to catch him with his back to her.

Let Marcus be the main target. The dagger is less conspicuous, so perhaps I can slip in with a sure strike.

Despite the endeavor, the idea proved impossible to act upon. She caught their opponent land several, minor cuts on her friend when the demon began to become more physical. At one point, he reached out and shoved her backward as she raised her sword, throwing her off balance. All the while, Terran wore a giddy grin, displaying his pleasure with his position in the fight.

The single-sided affair continued for minutes without changing, which made Coura start to worry once she remembered Soirée's unpredictable behavior. This led her to alter her tactic by retreating a couple steps in order to provoke the demon into pursuing, which he did by lunging. As she twisted away, earning her a deep scratch on the side, Marcus leapt forward to return the favor. The golden blade cut across Terran's arm just before he could dodge.

With a snarl, their opponent turned his furious gaze on the assistant general before focusing solely on Marcus. Coura decided to use the break to consider a new strategy.

His speed and strength are enough to overwhelm ours, she noted while watching her friend maneuver through the rage-fueled strikes. *We have the ancestral weapons, but they're useless if we can't get within range to stab him. He also hasn't used his magic.*

This led her to recall her own abilities and contemplate whether they would be beneficial, especially in the limited light. *My Yeluthian energy can't do much, and it would be risky and distracting to try my goddess gift, not to mention it would leave me significantly weaker. That leaves dark magic.*

While she began formulating a plan that wouldn't put Marcus in harm's way, Terran took control of the fight. His swiftness allowed him to catch her friend with a punch to the shoulder, then he plunged his sword through an opening around the armor protecting Marcus' thigh. The assistant general's resulting, pained cry motivated her to drop her sword, reach into her pool of demonic energy, and raise her empty hand to release a bolt of lightning.

The spell struck Terran in the middle of his back, sending him stumbling forward while Marcus sank to his knees and gripped the wound. Meanwhile, Coura closed the distance between the two and prepared for a follow-up attack.

As soon as the next bolt left her hand, the demon spun around to manifest a shield, blocking the lightning in less than a second. Its close proximity had her backtracking in order to avoid the smoke and sparks that filled the air. Naturally, she raised the dagger in preparation for a surprise strike since her vision grew hazy. None came, to her amazement given her momentary vulnerability.

Instead, Terran crept out from the gray cloud with a smirk and a greedy glint in his eyes.

"How astonishing," he began in an excited manner, like he enjoyed how the direction of the fight shifted. "You had me believing you couldn't wield Soirée's energy. Nonetheless, that power is too dangerous to remain in the possession of a human."

Coura flinched when he raised a hand suddenly, then she remembered their last encounter when he didn't attack. Unfortunately, she could do nothing against his command of his kind's type of energy. Her chest grew constricted while the power in her soul space reacted to the invisible leash by thrashing until she felt the Yeluthian portion shirking away; then, the demonic half began to slip. Despite the lack of pain, she wrapped both arms around her stomach in an attempt to ease the resulting, indescribable ache the pull spurred.

Not this again! He let me go last time, but Soirée managed to steal it all when she tried. He controls the connection to the demonic energy, so I have to get him to release me before it's too late. I need a distraction. An idea came to mind while more frantic thoughts had her on the verge of panicking.

Her first plan involved stalling until Marcus could join again; however, he appeared to be trying to stand with a determined expression as he watched her. His injury limited his movements, so she recalled what she previously noted about the ancestral weapons.

If I can't get close enough without this happening, perhaps he can. Or…maybe he doesn't need to get close at all!

The understanding that she would need to relinquish her remaining weapon didn't frighten her as much as she expected, though she winced at the only way she could think to get it to her friend. After inhaling a deep breath in anticipation, Coura straightened as much as she could.

"You're just like her," she grumbled loudly enough for Terran to hear.

To her relief, the demon took the bait and frowned.

"Are you speaking in riddles now?" he teased, yet his curiosity kept him interested in her response.

"I guess it isn't obvious," she continued while sending him a crooked smile. "Soirée resorted to taking my demonic power by force too."

She held her breath when his face settled into an unreadable expression. A moment later, he lowered his hand, abruptly cutting off the pull. Her body returned to normal, but the stress still left her panting.

"It's amazing," Coura continued with the hope of setting him off. "You two are so alike. Actually, she started her work in Asteom decades ago, which means you've been copying her ever since."

Even from a distance, she could hear Terran's growl as he bared his teeth at her. "Brave words for somebody in your position."

One more push...

"Why would I worry? You haven't done anything she hadn't already accomplished, so I know what to expect."

"Pathetic human!" he roared before charging with his blade pointed at her.

Coura mentally prepared for the retaliation and focused her attention on the demon's left shoulder. In order to assure Marcus would be able to collect the ancestral weapon, she needed her next move to be precise. Her lessons over the months came back to her when she took the rehearsed stance for throwing knives, swept her arm across her body, and released the dagger in time for it to soar through the air. She wasn't surprised when Terran noticed and ducked to avoid the blade, yet she released a sigh of relief upon realizing how difficult it would have been for her friend to find it if their opponent decided to knock the golden blade away.

All that was left to do was remain the distraction. The demon stabbed for her torso, so she crafted a shield with what light energy she could muster, which didn't prove to be enough to hold beyond the strike. Its shimmering fractals began descending to the ground after he shattered it; however, instead of his weapon, which she anticipated darting for her, his hand shot toward her head to seize a fistful of her hair.

"How pitiful," he commented while yanking her forward to stand toe to toe with him. "I imagined you to be more of a threat, but now I can see you are no better than the rest of your kind."

Coura's hands went to up to claw at his in an attempt to free herself. Because she became preoccupied with his grasp, she didn't notice him release his sword before he threw a punch that landed in her gut. The impact knocked the breath from her, though she couldn't slouch due to the hold on her head.

"Wait a moment," Terran started again with a bit of humor. "I forgot, you're a half breed! It's a shame neither your human nor Yeluthian blood blessed you with greater strength. You showcase the worst of each, sad race."

This caused him to laugh while keeping his grip.

Still, Coura didn't let his insults affect her and raised her glare to meet Terran's cold, violet eyes. "Soirée said that too."

His entertained façade slipped then. The empty hand shot for her throat, and once he seized it, his other released her hair to do the same. Coura clawed at them to no avail and lost the ability to breathe when they tightened.

"Soirée this, Soirée that," he snapped as he leaned closer. "Your obsession knows no bounds, but unlike my old rival, I won't let you walk away after I claim her power!"

Stars blotted her vision, and her lungs burned against the suffocating pain in her throat. Her last sliver of hope remained with her friend whom she prayed could utilize their last chance at victory.

***

Throughout the encounter with the demon, Marcus managed to hold his temper in check until he recognized the creature using its magic against Coura; before that, he earned himself a nasty puncture wound in his right thigh. Memories of the fight involving General Tio led him to attempt to be proactive instead of waiting to end the bout so he wouldn't become any wearier. His hastiness led him to disregard the possibility of a physical attack, which bruised his arm. Then, the enemy's blade cut through his armor enough to drop him to his knees. Before he had a chance to react, an explosion threw the creature off its balance, and he remembered his friend's ability to wield spells, though it had been a while since he saw it in action. That distraction drew their opponent's attention, allowing Marcus to catch his breath in between applying pressure to his bleeding leg.

I can still stand, he noted as more of a motivational comment than the truth. *Perhaps I can strike from behind.*

Only when the aftermath of their magical exchange settled did he spot the demon with an outstretched hand and Coura hunched over to wrap both arms around her midsection. Marcus attempted to rise but dropped down again with a grunt after struggling through a single step.

I need to get closer, he told himself and growled a curse. *She's completely vulnerable!*

What words she exchanged with the creature were lost when he recalled how he felt after losing Will. The ache still remained to remind him of the consequences of his carelessness despite his friend's persistence, and he tried standing once more.

To his horror, Coura decided to throw her dagger while the enemy charged, leaving her open for it to retaliate by grabbing her head. The strategical part of his mind couldn't comprehend her tactic since the demon dodged with little effort while the rest of him became numb from shock.

Stop gawking and go help her!

Still, his damaged leg wouldn't cooperate.

What should I do? Why is she so careless? The second question brought his thoughts back to the present. *That wasn't an accident. I know Coura and fought beside her for years. She wouldn't risk her life unless she intended for this to happen, and she wouldn't leave herself unarmed unless the situation called for it. Does that mean...*

He swung his head around in a frantic search for the dagger he assumed she recklessly abandoned until a glimmer of gold farther to his right revealed the ancestral weapon's location. Then, he understood.

My movements are limited with this wound, so the next best option is to use a long-distance attack. I'll only get one shot at a surprise strike.

Marcus' heartbeat increased while he frantically crawled over to the dagger with the knowledge that his friend continued to suffer every second he spent preparing. Due to the lack of additional projectiles, he would need to focus entirely on his stance and the snap of his wrist, though the dim lighting didn't help.

With as much force as he could muster, he climbed to his feet while keeping most of his weight on the uninjured leg, adjusted his throwing position based on that difference, and took a deep breath. Both eyes locked on to the widest part of the demon: its back.

This is no different than a day of training, he reminded himself to calm his nerves. *I clear my mind first, then the motions will carry me through.*

He caught Coura's arms drop to her sides and knew he had no more time to waste. Just like every occasion he dealt with regular knives and daggers, Marcus swiped his arm across the air, timed when to release the ancestral weapon, and watched as it soared toward his target. Crimson glimmers from the distant firelight caught on its metal surface before it sank into the demon's shoulder blade.

At first, the creature didn't move. The grip around Coura's throat loosened, leaving her to drop to the ground where she remained still. Marcus restrained himself from rushing to her side until he could be certain the creature would no longer pose a threat to them, though he hoped to ensure his friend's safety.

He hadn't noticed how humid the air grew until it began clearing seconds later. Then, the demon reached a hand over its shoulder to grab for the dagger inserted into its back; however, Marcus could see it trembling violently enough to demonstrate what effect the angelic weapon had on such a being. At the same time, it turned to face him. What was once an egotistical expression melted into disbelief, and the violet eyes darted around before landing on him.

The two stared at each other for what felt like an eternity before the demon fell forward onto its face where it stopped twitching. By that point, the pain and bleeding in Marcus' leg became too much to bear any longer. He dropped into a sitting position to again apply pressure to the wound while panting.

I...can't leave this unattended... As if to emphasize that point, his sight began going in and out of focus until he shook his head. *I can't pass out yet, not when Coura needs help.*

Footsteps in the grass from behind had him looking over, and two figures neared. Without slowing, they went to his side and knelt, allowing him to recognize one as Calin and the other as a light mage wearing a white cloak.

"You aren't dead," his fellow assistant general commented while placing a hand on his back. "That's good news."

Marcus instinctively smiled and huffed a laugh. "Maybe not yet, but I'll be there soon if you leave me to bleed out."

"Sorry, I'm not letting you off the hook that easily."

Calin nodded to the light mage, who seemed to be waiting for permission to begin a healing spell. Her hands replaced Marcus', then he felt warmth radiating to repair his damaged flesh amid a faint, golden glow.

"Where's Coura?" the Dalan soldier asked after.

A jolt of panic shot through his body upon recalling her until they could hear coughing mixed in with the nearby fight against the remaining demonic creatures. They scanned the area together until Marcus could make out the silhouette of his friend on her hands and knees next to their subdued opponent.

"She's alive," he mumbled. The realization relaxed his muscles, allowing him to feel how exhausted his body became.

Calin must have caught his words, for the Dalan soldier chuckled while the light mage ended her spell. "When I glanced over, you three dropped like flies one after the other."

"How's the rest of the squad?" Marcus inquired. Despite his optimism given the assistant general's appearance at his side, the resulting, deep frown hinted at a worse situation across the field.

"Not as organized as I would like, especially since the beasts targeted the city instead of what they usually do. Some slipped through, and I plan on following up with them when I'm done here."

"Go," Marcus ordered. As flattered as he felt that his comrade would abandon the fight to check on him after the demon fell, he knew the troops would benefit from at least one of them issuing instructions going forward. "I'll manage now that I should be able to stand."

"What about Coura?"

This time, he addressed the light mage. "Would you mind joining me?"

The woman, who already looked worn out, nodded, so the three rose before Calin left them alone.

Although he should have expected some sort of remaining hinderance from his injury, Marcus didn't believe he would need assistance until he practically tripped when his leg wouldn't raise. The healer acted swiftly to insert herself under his arm in order to act as a crutch. When they crossed the area to reach Coura, she still hunched over on her knees with a hand on her throat.

"The demon shouldn't be a problem anymore," he said by way of announcing his presence. "Calin went to support the troops, but he brought this woman here to heal us."

Part of him felt guilty for not requesting her name, yet the light mage didn't seem to mind. She helped lower him to the ground before moving toward Coura; however, his friend startled them by raising a hand to halt the woman from progressing.

"I don't need a healer," she explained, though her raspy voice and laborious breathing suggested otherwise.

Marcus opened his mouth to tell her not to act tough, but the light mage cut in before he could utter a word.

"If that's true, I'll be returning to the city. We don't have time to waste on heroics."

Coura dipped her head a bit, as if to reconsider, yet she met the woman's eyes after. "I appreciate the offer, but there are lives at greater risk."

With nothing else to add, the light mage spun around to jog back toward where the remnants of the demonic creatures' attack lingered. Marcus attempted to study what movements and bodies he could at a distance yet gave up when his disoriented sight began playing tricks on him.

We're in danger if the beasts turn tail and barrel straight into us, he noted while his friend started coughing again. *Besides, I know*

Coura's in pain. The demon strangled her into losing consciousness. That isn't an injury she can ignore.

He released a sigh and got to his feet, then he offered her a hand when she stared at him without comprehension. To his dismay, she shook her head.

"We should return to the city and find Calin," he pressed. "Our mission is complete, so there's no point in waiting for someone to drag us away."

Still, Coura didn't move. At first, she opened her mouth to protest his request, but she shut it a moment later before pointing at where the demon lied in the grass. It hadn't moved since it landed there, showcasing the ancestral weapon's potency.

"I guess we do need to figure out what to do about that," he muttered. "If you refuse to leave it, then I suppose you'll need a guard."

He followed his halfhearted comment by returning to a sitting position beside her. Although she appeared to want to make a jab at his remark, she only shot him a doubtful glance. Her silence reminded him of the severity of her condition and why he needed to remain at her side until they could both rest.

*

Marcus managed not to nod off while the pair waited in the field. Sounds from the distant fighting steadily grew fainter until he noticed more people in the area along the perimeter.

"Calin should be coming for us or sending somebody to fetch us any time now," he shared in the surrounding silence.

He didn't expect Coura to respond, though he wondered what she thought of the evening since she had encountered the demon multiple times in the past. When he glanced over to where she sat with her arms wrapped around her knees and her droopy eyes fixated on the ground, growing light from the approaching dawn allowed him to catch a glimpse of the creature's handiwork. Dark splotches decorated her throat to display bruises, and shallow cuts revealed how it dug its fingernails into her skin.

"Are you sure you can heal that?" he asked quietly without considering the question. That absentmindedness earned him an annoyed look from his friend.

"I'd like to…make sure I can…get back to my room before…using magic again," she explained through a broken whisper.

The multiple pauses, as well as the worn sound of her voice, let Marcus know the damage done to her throat would prevent her from speaking at length, at least not without worsening its soreness. He apologized for underestimating her remaining strength, then he had to scold her into keeping silent in order to avoid causing herself additional pain. To his relief, a group parted from those along the border a few minutes later, signaling the end of the conflict.

During the time he and Coura spent in the field, he planned his next steps carefully. First, he intended to instruct the soldiers to monitor the demon's body so it could be guarded until they knew what to do with it. While that happened, he would help his friend to her room before locating Calin for a debriefing. He had no idea what took place in or around Dala and refused to sleep until he felt confident the pair got the situation under control.

Spies on the Border

The lack of concern for his safety, as well as Clara's, bothered Will as he hiked through the woods behind the light mage, who followed Finn's lead. It had been days since the trio departed from General Casner's camp together, yet his resolve remained firm; that surprised him considering the danger they maneuvered around.

Ever since they returned to Nim-Vala's territory, an eerie silence hung in the air. They hardly spoke outside their evening conversations before two would rest and one kept watch, and usually those discussions consisted of brief acknowledgements about the area. The temperature continued dropping as well, forcing them to constantly move just to keep warm.

What drove the three onward and occupied Will's mind a majority of the time related to the enemy camps. On the second day of their journey, Finn had stopped them to point out a location ahead where about fifty Nim-Valan troops rested, so he circled the perimeter to progress south. This gave Will the idea to begin charting what dangerous areas the spy memorized from his treks across the border. They spent that evening and every evening since adding additional information to a crude map.

Even as Will recalled the layout while the trio tiptoed along the empty space, Finn held up a fist. He and Clara froze so they could listen for footsteps, then their leader glanced at Will and pointed northeast.

Another Nim-Valan camp so soon? he longed to ask in disbelief, though he nodded instead to acknowledge the new location.

His gesture acted as a cue for Finn to adjust their route before they crept at a cautious pace.

That makes eleven within a three-day march to the border, and we're not even that far east. If Lupin isn't hiding among the ones

Finn observed, then I worry how many more lie waiting for the advisor's orders.

After a few minutes, their leader halted and signaled for them to huddle close.

"This isn't a place I checked before," he shared, creating puffs in the air with each word. "I'll go alone now to do so. Stay here until I return."

"Are you sure?" Clara startled Will by adding given her silence throughout a majority of their time together. "It's going to get dark soon. We can wait for tomorrow morning."

Finn shook his head, yet his chestnut eyes raised to the sky after. "There's no time to waste, but I'll be quick. Start preparing our blankets, eat, and try to rest."

The order had Will rolling his eyes since he received it every night, though neither of his friends seemed to notice. Once he and Clara found themselves alone, they began setting up their spaces before dropping to the ground where they rubbed their arms and legs for what precious warmth they could generate.

"I don't like this," the light mage stated after a moment.

"It's not just you," Will responded absentmindedly. "I've never met anybody who enjoys being out in the cold."

She shot him an unamused look. "Not the weather!"

He stared at her without comprehension until a yawn snuck up on him. When her eyes narrowed after, he decided to humor her. "What's bothering you, Clara?"

"Doesn't it concern you how none of the Nim-Valan camps were doing anything?"

"I'm sure they're conserving their energy, just like the people with General Casner."

She paused for a moment. "I suppose so. It just seems…odd."

Will didn't have a response, so they sat in silence until footsteps in a steady rhythm alerted them of Finn's arrival. The man's voice reached the two before he emerged from the bushes they entered from earlier.

"He's not there either."

Clara waited for the Nim-Valan to sit before offering the bag of dried rations. Meanwhile, Will sensed tension stemming from the spy.

"Was there trouble?" he asked after Finn finished and returned their food to the light mage.

"It looked and behaved like the other camps."

A pregnant pause stretched between the three until Clara addressed the man.

"Nothing out of the ordinary, right?"

Finn shook his head and raised an eyebrow, as if expecting her to go on.

"The Nim-Valans aren't acting. Doesn't that seem strange?"

Will prepared to bring up her previous anxiousness until he noticed the spy staring at the ground to contemplate the question. "What is it?"

"She's not wrong."

"About the camps?"

Another minute of silence passed, though this one allowed Will to consider where Clara's concern stemmed from.

The enemy isn't moving yet, which means the attacks along the border must have stopped too. Finn hasn't heard a tip pertaining to Lupin, demons, magic, or any sort of indication to signal trouble. This momentary peace should help our forces prepare, and I believe we would catch wind of a plan in motion, like if their spies infiltrated Asteom.

He inhaled the crisp air before releasing a drawn out breath that caused the muscles in his legs to ache. "We'll just need to keep our eyes and ears open. Right, Finn?"

The man refused to remove his gaze from the patch of frozen earth in front of him.

"I don't understand what's bothering you two," Will finally admitted while glancing between Clara and Finn, who looked at him after the outburst. "They could be taking a break, waiting for orders, or revising their plan based on General Casner's forces. Let him handle the fight, and we'll locate our target."

The light mage nearly interrupted him by snapping her fingers. "That's it!"

"What?"

"She's right," Finn added with a serious expression, yet a fire burned in his eyes. "The issue is in front of our faces."

Will felt his lips curve downward into a frown. "I just outlined our situation and the enemy's behavior."

"Not only that," the spy interjected. "You also revealed what we're struggling to deal with."

"Well then explain it!"

Clara and Finn exchanged a look before the latter indulged him.

"You listed what they *could* be doing at this moment, meaning several possibilities are floating around, and all pertain to their leader."

Will scratched his head. "So?"

"Essentially, we can't predict their next steps. There's no telling if a plan is already in motion, if they are waiting, what Lupin is up to, or where the advisor is hiding. How can we report what the enemy is doing when we didn't gather evidence to guide us forward? The lack of information is what has been problematic, not necessarily the camps themselves."

"I see what you mean," Will muttered after a moment. During Finn's explanation, his mind started working to assess their days along the border and came up with nothing useful. "All we can do is continue with our business until you overhear an answer."

With nothing else to add to extend the discussion, the three soon resumed their evening routine.

*

The next two days of sneaking through the woods along the border revealed three more sites housing Nim-Valans, though Finn mentioned the lack of activity taking place in each. Will began to add notes on his crude map with possible suggestions relating to the enemy's motives; however, the same ideas came to mind and rotated on a loop in his head.

While he and Clara waited for their companion the next morning when the spy believed they reached a new camp, the two bounced what they learned back and forth in the hope of discovering a better plan than what they currently followed. In the midst of their conversation, a hurried pair of footsteps alerted them of trouble.

"What's wrong?" the light mage demanded before Finn burst through the nearest pair of bushes. Already she began packing their few items, prompting Will to do the same.

Their leader's next words had them stopping and snapping their heads in the man's direction.

"The enemy at that location is going to attack in three days."

"What?" Will exclaimed before starting to inquire about the news only to be interrupted by Finn.

"It's a new moon, so they can cross the border under the cover of darkness. Our position is far enough east to prevent General Casner's company from reaching them before they are able to-"

"Slow down," Clara ordered in a firm tone. "Tell us about the camp's location and numbers first."

"There's no time. We need to get moving, or else…"

When the volume of Finn's voice lowered into a mumble, Will took the opportunity to offer his input. "We can discuss this on the way."

His friends glanced at him before lowering their gazes, as if considering alternative options. The three ended up heading toward the border while the spy shared his observations.

"Although the camp's layout appeared similar to the rest, it held almost twice as many troops, though there didn't seem to be a leader managing the men," Finn explained while ducking under a low-hanging branch. "I found a comfortable hiding spot close to the outermost tent, and that's where I overheard those inside discussing the arrangements for an ambush."

"You said they're moving because of the new moon, correct?" Will added.

"Yes, though it will take at least a couple days to reach Asteom from this distance at a march."

"Perhaps they intend to draw near under the cover of darkness but wait to strike or sneak ahead," Clara suggested.

The trio paused their conversation in order to focus on crossing a fallen log that acted as a bridge, which allowed them to avoid hiking around a stream. During the break, Will attempted to consider the enemy's motives for acting so suddenly.

It probably isn't hasty to them, and going at that time hides them from Asteom's soldiers. Also, what is this group's mission if our troops will be able to meet them there? Could they be creating a distraction to lure General Casner away from the main camp? What would that succeed in doing?

He expected someone to pick up the discussion once they continued, yet neither Finn nor Clara seemed inclined to do so. Because of their silence, Will decided to follow behind and avoid distracting them enough to slow their pace.

They trekked through the afternoon and into the evening, but Will and Clara's inability to efficiently find their way in the dark led to the Nim-Valan stopping for the night, though with no shortage of reluctance. A late meal satiated his hunger for the time being, and he lied on his back in an attempt to rest. Still, his eyes scanned the stars above for answers.

"What's bothering you?"

Clara's question hung in the air until Will realized she addressed him. When he sat up to respond, he found both companions staring at him with concerned expressions.

"Why are you looking at me like that?" he asked and trembled from the chill.

Finn didn't comment, though he averted his eyes, but Clara tilted her head and shared her reasoning.

"You're just quieter than normal, and don't say it's because we're in a rush."

Will had opened his mouth to reply with just that, so he promptly closed it before shaking his head.

"I can tell you're distracted."

"The camp Finn spied on is bugging me," he admitted before digging through his bag for an additional blanket to wrap around his shoulders.

His response drew the Nim-Valan's attention. "Share your thoughts. You often find valuable insight in seemingly obvious situations."

"Thank you for the compliment," Will added. "It's odd how only one group out of the others you visited mentioned an attack. Why would a single unit move while the rest remain behind? That would be the perfect opportunity, unless that camp's troops are meant to act as a decoy. Still, General Casner would rally the soldiers and mages as soon as the conflict arises."

Despite the natural sounds of the nightlife surrounding them, a sense of tension began tainting the air.

"You might be right," Finn responded after a couple minutes and rose to stand. Then, he met Will's eyes. "The men in that last camp mentioned departing to reach the border by the new moon. Nothing about their words suggested they would be going alone."

A shiver slid along Will's spine. "You don't mean…"

"Every camp is going to strike at the same time!" Clara exclaimed and practically jumped to her feet. "Why didn't we learn about this earlier?"

Finn shook his head before kneeling to gather his items. "Nothing any of the troops said hinted at a joined attack, and they didn't appear to be preparing to march south."

"That's because they won't need to get ready for a while since they're closer to the border," Will summarized and mirrored the spy's sense of urgency. "The people you overheard are a day or two behind the rest, and who knows how many more groups are hiding."

The three finished packing and shouldering their bags as their leader selected a direction. Then, he faced Will and Clara while wearing his trademark, unreadable expression.

"We must warn the general and any additional soldiers in Asteom. Even if our hunch proves to be incorrect, the last camp's troops will be on the move and need to be stopped."

With that, they began a grueling hike through the wildlife, which didn't become spooked by their hurried steps, to Will's amazement. A final thought plagued him after a while, though he kept the comment to himself in order to avoid disturbing Finn and worrying either of his companions any further.

I imagine Advisor Lupin has a plan for the Nim-Valans once they cross the border, or maybe it's already in motion. Why am I feeling like we're missing a key part of this fight?

***

The aftermath of Terran's attack the previous evening remained a mystery until Coura motivated herself enough to rise, get dressed, and wander through Dala despite her sore muscles. Based on what she saw during that time, she figured the demon released his creatures into the city with an order to mangle whatever they could get their claws and teeth on. Her eyes were immediately drawn to various, dark splotches on the road and crimson smeared across several buildings she passed; however, nobody seemed shocked by the sights.

Next, she focused on what scattered items littered the streets and alleys. Tables, carts, booths, and other wooden structures had been torn apart to lie in fractured pieces, along with their decorations and belongings. Even houses constructed of stone or brick possessed damage in the form of missing chunks, chalk-like scratches, and shattered windows.

Despite the damage, Coura felt too weary to consider what befell the citizens. Her brush with death at the hands of their enemy shook her to her core, especially since she was willing to bet her life on an opportunity for Marcus so easily.

I would imagine the people were ready considering how often Terran and the creatures appeared, she rationalized in order to distract from her personal concerns. *It seems like the recovery is going smoothly too. Perhaps I won't find much to do to assist the troops.*

She departed that morning with the intent to locate Marcus or Calin and offer her help because of how faint the mages' energy became. The notion stemmed from her encounter with the healer after Terran's defeat, which prompted her to dismiss the offer to fix her throat. Although the bruises around her neck displayed what she endured and hinted at the pain underneath her skin, she opted to let the area recover on its own while her power returned.

I would rather build my reserves than push myself too hard, she decided when she reflected on the situation. *Who knows if Dala is out of the woods just yet. Besides, Evern, Byron, and the rest of the troops on the northern border are waiting for the ancestral weapon. I'll need to be able to fly there as soon as possible.*

When she found Marcus at the edge of the city near the eastern clearing, it didn't surprise her to see him issuing orders for the soldiers and mages who awaited a new task. Coura lingered nearby to give him time to do so before approaching when he finished and turned his attention toward the field.

Evidently, the sound of her footsteps alerted him of her presence, for he glanced over his shoulder with a hint of concern before offering a greeting. "You shouldn't be up so soon," he commented after she moved to stand beside him and gaze out at the empty space.

"You look like you can use an extra hour or two of sleep," she retorted, though her raspy voice didn't sell her attempt to reassure him of her stable condition. He even called her out on it after.

"I thought you could heal your throat."

She nodded and hoped her silence would be enough to end his reproaching. Unfortunately, it led him to shoot her a dubious glance instead.

"Where's Calin?" she asked to move the discussion in a different direction.

"Resting. We spent the night fortifying our defenses before splitting apart to manage other jobs. While he organized the remaining troops, took care of delegating mages to supervise the injured, and returned to the base to establish a squad there, I worked with the people to record the casualties, property damage, and rations necessary for the next couple days."

Coura raised an eyebrow. "That sounds like a lot to handle at one time."

Her friend paused and stared at the sky with a slight smile despite the circumstances. "It would have been much worse if we weren't experienced. The creatures' attacks over the past weeks forced us to learn what did and didn't work, along with what our troops and the civilians needed."

When she attempted to respond and mention she figured as much, the irritation in her throat threw her into a brief coughing fit. This led Marcus to begin searching for a healer until she calmed down enough to tell him to stop. The metallic taste of blood sat on her tongue, yet she remained adamant about not burdening the already overworked mages.

"I wish you wouldn't be so stubborn," she heard him mutter after a minute of silence hung between the two.

His comment caused her to smile. "You make your sacrifices, and I make mine. Speaking of which, where are the ancestral weapons?"

The shift in tone prompted a frown from Marcus, yet he answered without hesitation and at a lower volume. "Calin and I agreed to leave the dagger where it is until we can decide what to do about the demon. Several soldiers and a couple mages are guarding it on a rotation, but nobody seems that interested in investigating the area."

When Coura considered her first encounter with a golden weapon, perhaps the same one her friend used against Terran, she appreciated their caution. *When the rouge angel Drake stabbed me and removed the dagger during our fight in the Valley Beyond, Soirée's demonic power leaked into the world and created monstrous beasts as a result. We're better off just accepting our losses and leaving that behind.*

"What about the other weapon?" she pressed.

"I offered to keep it in case trouble arises again," he replied while placing a hand on the sword sheath buckled to his waist. "Why are you asking?"

His question hinted that he predicted her answer, so she didn't beat around the bush. She explained her plan to deliver the ancestral weapon to General Casner's main camp where Evern and Byron stayed in order to pass it along to somebody who would put it to use against the dark mage wielding demonic power. By the time she finished, her voice wore away, though she didn't worry him enough with her coughing for him to locate a healer.

"That's why you're here," he concluded with a thoughtful expression. "You're ready to leave."

"The flight will take a few days since I don't expect to go at a breakneck pace, so I would rather avoid wasting time."

Marcus turned to her and crossed his arms while his face set into a concerned expression. "Your mentality matches your words, which doesn't surprise me, but what about your physical condition? It took days for you to recover from your journey here, then we were thrown into a fight that could have easily resulted in our deaths. If you decide to leave when you're not fully recovered, you might wind up in a precarious situation you aren't strong enough to overcome, or doing so would take even more time."

Coura paused to consider his advice. *I'm too weak to use my goddess gift without the spell leaving me incapacitated, but with the ancestral weapon amplifying my Yeluthian energy, I should be able to manifest my wings and reach the northern border. Terran managed to steal most of the demonic energy I possessed, so I can't rely on that either. Still, there's one issue bothering me enough to look into personally.*

"I understand, and I appreciate your sympathy," she began after deciding to share her concern. "There's plenty of uncertainty surrounding the border, meaning I might expect a break but be thrown into another fight for my life; however, I need to find out who is wielding demonic energy alongside the Nim-Valans."

"Could it be this demon's involvement?" Marcus asked and gestured toward the empty field with his chin.

Coura shook her head. "No, that's the problem. I mentioned how the fake servants in the palace had been possessed until Grace intervened. Well, the power I sensed was demonic in nature, but it felt different than Terran's, like a separate presence."

"I take it it's hard to explain to somebody who isn't a mage?"

"Even a dark mage wouldn't be as familiar with the essence to tell the difference."

The two stood observing the clearing for a while in silence until Marcus released a sigh and unbuckled the weapon from his belt. Then, he handed it over to her.

"I'll look like a terrible assistant general for sending you off in the shape you're in, but I guess it can't be helped," he commented as she accepted the item. "Just make sure to send a messenger with updates. I plan on doing the same for Aaron and informing him of the news here."

"I will," she promised before meeting his eyes. "You have my word. Also, don't blame yourself for my choice to leave. You're a gifted leader who earned the Dalans' trust. Calin will need your knowledge and skills."

His resulting smile showed his appreciation for her comment, even though he rolled his eyes. "At this point, I'm just working so I can get a full night's rest once the commotion dies down. Thank you though."

With nothing else to say between the two, Coura stepped away and began to return to her room for her belongings while a soldier escorting an older woman took her place beside Marcus and requested his assistance.

An Unfavorable Sight

The atmosphere of General Casner's camp shifted with each passing day, giving Byron a sense of unease. After seeing Coura off so she could recover the ancestral weapon in the palace, he returned to the general's main base of operations with her father and Lavine in order to reconvene. There, they waited for additional orders; however, none came. It wasn't until Byron noticed the Yeluthians' disappearance that he sought answers.

He found Casner in the man's tent during a conference with several soldiers and lingered outside until the group dispersed. Then, he hesitated to interrupt what few minutes of free time constituted as a break for their leader.

"Who's nosing around out there?" came the general's voice, saving him from floundering any further.

Byron cleared his throat and pulled the tent's opening flap back to reveal his presence. "My apologies, sir."

"It's just you," Casner grumbled, though he gestured for Byron to enter. "Some people around here like to stand nearby in case I raise the alarm, like they don't have their own responsibilities. The shadows they cast along the tent make me think I'm about to be ambushed."

"That wasn't my intent," Byron added. He accepted a place across from the man, allowing him to gaze over the maps and paperwork while they discussed the situation. "I actually came to request an update and possibly see if you need me sent anywhere along the border."

Until that moment, Casner upheld an expressionless stare. His thin lips curved into a pleased smile at Byron's offer, and his eyes closed for a few seconds, as if he attempted to savor the moment.

"I've been trying not to burden you," the general admitted after assuming his usual gaze. "Your previous departure reflected your wish to be left alone, so I want to make sure you're not in harm's way too often."

The response surprised Byron, though he attempted to keep his feelings under control given it had been his decision to return to his duties, with Cintra's blessing. "I appreciate the sentiment; however, please know I am willing to act on your orders. My magic and experience are two characteristics many in your camp lack, so I can step in when you need me."

Casner inhaled a deep breath before releasing it through his nostrils in a drawn-out sigh. "I'm afraid that's the problem. Our scouts aren't reporting any activity from the Nim-Valans."

"Their attacks stopped so soon?"

"It's been weeks since the last incident, which is normally worth celebrating, except without information on their intentions, our troops are out there standing at attention. It's like staring into a cloud of fog and expecting an arrow to fly at any second. We can pray our reaction is sharp enough to keep us from getting killed, but the building pressure leaves room for weariness and mistakes."

"Why not send somebody to spy on their camps?" Byron suggested. "At least then they might be able to signal when the enemy marches south."

"I already assigned one to infiltrate the Nim-Valans' locations and report back with information on the dark mage leading them. Commander Evern and his underling volunteered to survey the border from above as well."

"They did? I had no idea."

"The commander claimed eyes from the sky would serve us better than watching on the ground, which I agree with," the general added. "Besides, those wings will bring them back faster than anybody on foot."

"Still, one spy and two angels can only get us so far."

Byron paused to contemplate that, filling the tent with silence until neither seemed to be able to come to a conclusion. Then, the general groaned in a bored manner.

"Despite the lack of activity, you have my permission to act in whatever way you see fit," the man shared with a grin. "You're sensible enough to know where you're needed and what should be done. Can't honestly say that about most people in the camp."

Byron returned the smile before raising his eyes to the top of the tent in thought. "I appreciate your faith in me. For the time being, I'd like to remain here until your spy returns. I'm curious what information their report will contain."

"You and me both. I'll send somebody for you when he returns then."

With an agreement in place, Byron thanked Casner for his time before departing.

*

The troops didn't need to wait long for an update despite the lack of movement across the border. Two days after Byron's meeting with the general, he woke instinctively when urgent voices called for the soldiers and mages to assume defensive positions. The sources of the noise eluded him, so he figured he would hear the reasoning when he found Casner.

Fortunately, the man hadn't made it farther than a few steps outside his tent.

"Let's get a shield in place all around the camp, reinforce the southern and eastern sides, and prepare for combat!" the general shouted to anyone in the vicinity. When Byron approached at a jog, Casner noticed and issued his next order. "We'll set you on the offensive with dark spells once the enemy starts entering through a break in the surrounding shield. Aim for the rear while the soldiers meet their front line."

"Yes, sir," Byron automatically replied before spinning to head toward the opposite end of their location.

Already, Asteom's forces appeared wide awake and poised their weapons to point at the shadow-filled woods. Byron set himself in line with the other mages who would fulfill the same role, though he knew he might need to abandon their plan at any moment. A minute later, those possessing light magic merged their energy to weave together a shimmering wall at the front of the soldiers, protecting those who would spot the enemy first.

337

It seemed their spell acted like a trigger for the Nim-Valans to appear, for dozens of men clad in dark clothing and leather padding leapt forth to strike at the shield with swords, spears, and clubs. The light mages' energy muted the blows; however, Byron realized some part of their attack came through when people near the middle and rear of their forces dropped to their knees or fell into the grass.

They didn't get through at the front, he noted and glanced from left to right. Both directions showed similar results from the other groups.

As he searched for the cause, several individuals throughout the area pointed upward, revealing the answer.

"Watch the sky!" he yelled to those around him, who responded with bewildered expressions until he raised both hands and prepared a shielding spell of his own.

The energy he mustered extended from his center to form above their group, like a roof blocking the rain. Instead of water, thin objects gently dropped onto his magic. After a moment, he recognized the tactic.

"Tell the troops at each side to watch for arrows being launched over the perimeter," he instructed for those standing around him without looking away from his spell.

Multiple voices accepted the order before he heard footsteps hurrying away. Soon, the familiar noise of combat met his ears, yet he refused to abandon his defense until he needed to. Clashing weapons, grunts, and pained cries echoed throughout the camp, yet none came close enough to concern him and draw his attention.

Casner's strategy to pluck them off one at a time by lowering the front line's shield must be working well, Byron reflected when the movement began dying down. *I haven't noticed any more arrows either. Could they be fleeing already? Why attack at all if they knew we possessed this level of magic?*

He raked his brain for answers to no avail. Fortunately, cheering to the south signaled a successful hold.

"The Nim-Valans are retreating," somebody announced, prompting more celebration.

Still, Byron focused on maintaining his spell. Due to the number of projectiles he observed, he figured offering a warning to the surrounding soldiers and mages would prevent a surge of panic when the arrows dropped from above. He began by requesting the assistance of those around him in order to alert their comrades and tell everyone to cover their heads or move away. Once he received their approval, he dismissed his spell. The arrows his shield held fell with little weight, though he miscalculated the amount, as well as the significance of his decision when he looked at the results on the ground. At least a couple hundred littered the camp, and after inspecting them, a chill slid down his spine.

They're a crude design, that's for sure, he noted from the uneven, whittled shafts; however, his eyes lingered on the arrowheads, which appeared to be covered with an oily liquid. *Poison tips? Were they planning on eliminating a portion of our forces from a distance? I see no other reason for their attempt.*

While those around him continued with the recovery and began retrieving the arrows, Byron searched for the general in order to inform the man of his observations. It didn't take long for him to find the camp's leader due to Casner's familiar voice barking orders near the center of the area. As soon as he caught Byron's eye, the general grinned and dismissed the soldier he had been speaking with.

"I owe you," the man began before clapping Byron on the back. "The south side would've been hit severely if you didn't come up with that trick."

"It was nothing," he replied before shaking his head. "How are the others?"

Casner's smile faded as he scratched his chin. "The southern side faced the bulk of the attack since the enemy's plan revolved around poisoned arrows from the front and circling behind to weaken the rear."

"You seem bothered by the results."

"That's because I am." The general paused and let his eyes wander over the surrounding faces. "The number of Nim-Valans surprised me. I didn't expect to face such a force here all at once, and despite our victory, I have to wonder why they chose now."

"This wasn't intended to be the final battle," Byron concluded, spurring a nod from Casner.

"Exactly. Your quick thinking saved us from a great loss, but were they actually attempting to lessen the number of Asteom troops, or did they have another objective?"

Without a clear answer, the pair decided to accept the outcome and focus on their next steps.

*

Although Byron recognized the impact of his shielding spell during the skirmish, the aftermath showed just how significant stopping the waves of arrows had been. He learned about the severity of the poison and how it immobilized the unfortunate victims at best and killed them within minutes at worst. Several met this fate, though the rest who had been struck recovered in the medical tent. General Casner ordered the projectiles the troops collected to be burned once the light mages began treating the injured. The excitement of the evening wore away then, leaving everybody exhausted. Byron accepted the opportunity to rest and left the scouting to the camp's leader and his assistants.

The next morning didn't seem any different than the others since his return, yet he made sure to keep his senses sharp in case their enemy took advantage of the peaceful atmosphere. Still, he began to relax once the environment remained undisturbed.

I wonder if it's too soon to bother Casner. Perhaps he heard from the spy across the border or the camp's scouts returned with useful observations. Whatever the case, it feels inappropriate to lounge around when the potential of another attack looms over us.

With that in mind, Byron mentally prepared to confront the general about their situation and potential options as he moved around the tents, bonfires, and groups of soldiers finishing their breakfast. Nothing appeared out of the ordinary until he approached the leader's area. Without warning, the opening flap flung outward, nearly hitting Byron in the face before General Casner's second-in-command stepped forward.

"Excuse me," the man named Mattias began in a hurried manner before pausing to assess the visitor. As soon as he recognized Byron, his expression reflected a sense of panic. "Forgive my rudeness, Master Byron! I didn't-"

"It's fine," he interrupted while dismissing the accident. "Is the general busy?"

"Actually, he sent me to find you."

The soldier's frantic behavior settled once he made the comment, so Byron accepted the offer to enter after him. Inside the tent, Casner stood facing the opening and waved before gesturing at another figure across from him.

"Excellent timing," the general said by way of greeting. "Come and join us."

Byron assessed the stranger until they glanced over their shoulder at the newcomer. Although his eyes needed a minute to adjust to the dimmer lighting, he immediately recognized Commander Evern's familiar face.

"You're back already," he commented and filled an empty spot opposite the assistant general.

The Yeluthian nodded. "Yes, though I am afraid I bring a troublesome update."

"Commander Evern just arrived, so I send Mattias to summon you while we got started," Casner explained as he crossed his arms. Then, he turned his attention to the Yeluthian. "Now that we're together, go ahead and share your report."

Evern inhaled through his nostrils before releasing a long sigh to emphasize a weariness the commander never seemed to show. "Thank you. Last night, the Nim-Valans ambushed the camp where my subordinate and I stayed. Their troops managed to eliminate our defenses to the rear; however, we swiftly dealt with the threat until the enemy decided to retreat. More were apprehended after when Lavine and I pursued."

Them too? Byron thought with no shortage of alarm in the resulting pause.

"I ordered my subordinate to guard the area while I returned to inform you of the details. On my flight here during the night, I noticed dozens of other spots where the Nim-Valans appeared to have instigated attacks. By the time I descended, the enemy was gone. Each location shared their experience, which sounded similar to what I participated in. I flew straight here after."

"So they planned to strike at once," the general mumbled. "None of our defenses fell, correct?"

"No, sir."

"Did the enemy happen to use poisoned arrows?"

Commander Evern shook his head, though Byron swore the Yeluthian's eyebrows raised slightly. He figured Casner noticed the intrigue as well, for the man went on to describe their experience the previous evening. Once the three were on the same page, the tent fell silent.

I'm getting a bad feeling about the Nim-Valans' strategy, he admitted to himself while lowering his eyes to stare at the ground. *Attacking at the same time would make sense if they possessed enough troops to severely damage our forces. Also, none of the camps encountered the dark mage leading the enemy. If I stood in the stranger's position, what would I be trying to achieve?*

The question lingered in his mind as he initiated the discussion. "It's obvious the Nim-Valans didn't expect to defeat all our defenses in a single night, so why move?"

"Not to mention the unique tactic they used on us specifically," Casner added and met Byron's eyes. "I already stated the significance of your shielding spell, but I believe it's worth noting that our camp would have been overcome by the enemy."

"Do you mean to say their focus was on this location?" Evern asked the general, who dipped his chin without confirming the assumption.

"A lack of answers is becoming our main hinderance," Byron picked up. "I for one would like to learn about their leader. Something tells me they used last night as a means of testing our forces. The enemy might be searching for a way to enter Asteom, or worse."

Commander Evern faced Casner and straightened. "If that is the case, I request permission to scout the border from above in search of the dark mage. Perhaps I will sense the individual's use of demonic energy and can track them from above."

"That could prove beneficial," Byron added when the general appeared to be contemplating the idea. "From what we understand, the Nim-Valans aren't coordinating on their own. Our best chance at locating their leader would be to scout along the entire border."

At the support, Casner nodded. "I agree. The risk is great, yet I won't order you to remain in one spot if you're willing to venture from the sky. If you spot the mage, I trust you to act in our peoples' best interest."

Evern thanked the man for his approval before spinning around to exit the tent without another word. After he did so, Byron addressed the general, who grabbed a pile of paperwork and began leafing through the documents.

"You wouldn't prefer him to report back if he finds the enemy's leader?"

"Of course I would, but who am I to say what the best course of action is in a situation I'm not part of?" the general countered. "The commander should understand when he can take advantage of an opportunity and when he needs backup. In my opinion, our alliance should reflect trust and competence on both sides."

"That's an admirable opinion."

When Byron lingered inside the tent instead of departing or continuing the conversation, Casner shifted his gaze away from the page in his hand. "Is there anything else?"

"Commander Evern mentioned his ability to sense demonic energy. The mages here should be able to do the same and alert you of trouble beforehand."

"I'll keep that in mind."

Byron hesitated to share his point until the general waved a hand as a gesture for him to continue.

"What else?" the man urged.

"I would also like to request permission to scout the border."

The general didn't look startled by this, which Byron hoped for considering the camp would lose its most powerful mage.

Commander Evern's reasoning is sound, even for me. We need to take out the enemy's leader in order to scatter their troops or push them back into Nim-Vala.

"I'm reluctant to do so, but I'm sure you expected that," Casner replied and offered a wry smile. "I do owe you for your work already. Besides, I just emphasized my trust in the alliance and our troops. What kind of leader would I be if I became a hypocrite?"

Byron returned the gesture. "Thank you, general. I can't promise I'll find the enemy's dark mage, but you can count on me to protect whatever camps I interact with."

"I appreciate that, and I'll hold you to your word. Now, you better get going if you plan on making headway before dusk."

After expressing his gratitude once more, Byron departed to procure the necessary rations and pack his few items for the potentially arduous journey.

***

The northern border appeared as bleak as Coura remembered, though she recalled the wildlife hiding within layers of bushes and needle-covered branches. Its environment differed from most of Asteom except the Western Woods, reminding her to keep her guard up due to her lack of familiarity with the area.

I should locate the camp where Byron and I stayed before my flight to Dala, she decided during the afternoon once she considered her next steps. Already, a chill from the dropping temperature penetrated what extra clothing she procured, leaving her shaking enough to become a concern. *If Marcus saw me like this, he'd scold me for leaving so soon. Once I fulfill my role and deliver the ancestral weapon, I plan on warming up in a bundle of blankets next to a bonfire and not moving until I can return to Verona.*

Despite her intent to use the promise as a means of motivation, the image of flames and the heat they projected seemed to worsen her physical condition. She instead focused on the land below in order to keep track of how far west she planned to travel. The golden sword strapped to her waist amplified her Yeluthian energy, like she remembered it doing in the past; however, she worried how much strength she would lose once she relinquished the item.

Worry about that later. For now, I need to find a place to rest, then I can continue in the morning.

What she thought to be an area she recognized came into view minutes later just as the sun touched the horizon and shaded the sky a deep hue of orange, yellow, and crimson. The uncertainty led her to hesitate before she started descending subconsciously.

I shouldn't push myself so hard until I can recover what energy I burned these past few days, Coura admitted when the aches in her limbs and ribs increased with the change in pressure. *Not to mention, I never completely healed my body after the surprise in the palace, using my goddess gift to get to Dala, and dealing with Terran.*

She managed not to groan at the memories while selecting an opening to drop to the ground near a stream of smoke signaling an ally's camp. Once she passed under the canopy, shadows met her on all sides, though the lack of bugs and snow raised her spirits enough to keep moving toward her goal. With each step she took, Coura steadily realized how quiet the forest had grown.

The woods to the north don't possess the wildlife to become loud, especially in winter, but I should at least be able to pick up noise from the group at the camp. Her heart sank at the notion.

Experience taught her to approach cautiously until she could assess the situation, so she slowed to a crawl while scanning the trees for any sign of danger. Every, weary muscle tensed in preparation to act should she wander right into an ambush. Meanwhile, her dark energy waited for a command, and a hand rested on the golden hilt of her sword.

Still, her senses didn't alert her of anything out of the ordinary aside from the silence.

If I didn't see the smoke for myself, I would have assumed the troops nearby hiked to another spot.

Soon, Coura reached the edge of the campsite and froze before peeling away a pine tree's branch blocking most of her view. Whatever parts of her that didn't expect the worst instinctively screamed at her to flee the scene then as her eyes were drawn to dozens of bodies lying motionless across the open area. The likeliest reason didn't strike her until she noticed the glow of the bonfire's coals and a thin stream of smoke rising to touch the sky.

The enemy attacked recently.

She backtracked away from the camp, releasing the branch she held in the process, before leaning against the nearest tree trunk in order to calm herself down by taking deep breaths. Her frantic heartbeat contributed to the minor pain in her torso, yet she began to process the situation without becoming overwhelmed by her emotions.

I'm sure this was where Byron and I stayed, though less troops occupied the camp based on the people there now. I need to investigate for survivors and clues before deciding what to do.

With an outline of a plan in her head, Coura mustered her courage, readied her magic again, then returned to the open area. Her feet led her around the perimeter and showed the scene from various angles; however, after a minute to get her bearings, she concluded the enemy had abandoned the camp.

I sense no unnatural presence to signal a demon or dark magic, she first acknowledged. *That means the Nim-Valans probably snuck into Asteom and waited for an opportunity to strike when our troops settled for the evening. The wounds are not fresh though, so this took place before sunset.*

After releasing a sigh, Coura looked around once more. No other observations stuck out, leading her to consider departing in order to warn General Casner. The longer she debated going, the greater the weight on her shoulders felt until she couldn't ignore the imminent threat. Her hand returned to the golden hilt, and she accepted the warmth the item provided.

I need to let someone know about what happened here, especially since the Nim-Valans are likely going south. Perhaps I missed more than this too.

Coura raised her other arm before summoning the Yeluthian spell while imagining her experience when she arrived at the border with her father and Lavine. No matter how often she called upon the magic, it felt enthusiastic as the power extended to form the mirror-like portal she'd grown accustomed to. Her circular frame of energy remained the lone light in the surrounding darkness, even on the opposite side, so she used that as a guide while stepping through. The sensation always threw her off balance, especially when she wasn't in her best condition, yet she managed to remain on her feet with only mild nausea and dizziness thanks to the ancestral weapon's ability.

As usual, the spell drew the attention of everybody in the area. Soldiers swarmed around with the tips of their blades pointed at her while she sensed mages crafting shields.

"Where is General Casner?" she demanded before anyone could question her sudden appearance. In order to seem like less of a threat, she straightened and decided to introduce herself. "I'm Coura Galdwin, Commander Evern's daughter and an ally arriving from the Dalan base. I need to deliver an update for the general as soon as possible."

Whether or not the people knew her didn't matter as soon as she mentioned her father's name. Various voices muttered about Yeluthia, the commander, and the southern base before their weapons lowered and the mages dismissed their spells. Finally, a middle-aged man with gray hair down to his shoulders shoved his way to stand in front of her.

"I recognize you from our initial meeting with General Casner," he began and gestured for her to follow him. "I'm Assistant General Mattias. How's Dala holding up?"

Coura attempted to hide how much effort it took for her to make up for her shorter steps compared to his strides, especially given her fatigue. "They're managing now."

She prepared to share Terran's fate until he turned sharply, literally cutting her off. Then, he continued speaking.

"I trained Marcus when General Tont first pushed him into being a soldier. After his reassignment, I didn't hear much until the demonic creatures started increasing the frequency of their attacks. Hopefully he's still doing all right."

"He is," she replied and offered a smile when the man glanced over his shoulder at her. "Marcus is one of my closest friends. I think he learned more over the last few months than he would have in Verona."

"I'm relieved to hear that. Maybe the general will finally promote him now."

The two reached the centermost tent before Coura could respond to his comment. Mattias entered to alert his superior of her arrival, so she lingered outside and waited for a signal to enter. A minute later, Casner practically stormed through the opening with his assistant trailing behind.

"What's this about a messenger from Dala?" the general demanded in a displeased manner that sparked Coura's dislike for the man.

"That would be me," she responded, drawing both his gaze and prompting a frown.

"You were supposed to return to the palace, not meander around the southern base."

Coura contemplated a retort, though she thought better of it when she remembered the remains of the camp she just arrived from. "I did. I have an update from King Aaron and news from Assistant Generals Marcus and Calin. Can we talk in private?"

The professional approach eased some of the tension between them, leading Casner to invite her and Mattias inside the tent where they each sat facing the other on worn cushions. To her surprise, the general asked if she needed food or drink, yet her appetite still hadn't returned.

"Let's start at the beginning," he urged to move the conversation along. "If you returned to the palace, then you should have the ancestral weapon we requested."

At his prompting, Coura dove into the recent events surrounding her journey across Asteom, including her arrival in Verona, the incident with the Nim-Valans, and Aaron's decision to send her south with the golden dagger instead of to the northern border. When the general interrupted twice to question the intruders' plan and the king's reasoning, she didn't repress her annoyance as she answered. He fell silent after when she described the encounter with Terran and Dala's recovery efforts.

"Marcus gave me this to bring here since the dagger isn't available," she concluded while drawing the golden blade from its sheath.

Casner muttered a curse under his breath in amazement, and she held it out with some reluctance; however, he made no attempt to reach for it.

"How such a weapon can inspire courage through appearance alone is beyond me," he startled her by commenting before raising his eyes to meet hers again. "I believe it's rather useful in the hands of a mage, or specifically a Yeluthian."

She nodded.

During the resulting pause, he let his eyes drift around the tent, allowing Mattias to speak for the first time since the three sat together.

"An ancestral weapon with such power should be in the hands of somebody who can best use it, don't you agree?"

"Yes," the general grumbled. "My thoughts exactly. I also believe the perfect person is already searching for the individual leading the Nim-Valans."

"You're referring to Evern," Coura added and sheathed the blade.

"I trust him to wield it properly once he locates the demon or dark mage. The issue is how we can get it to him since he won't be returning, at least not soon."

"What do you mean?"

Casner opened his mouth in a displeased manner before presumably remembering when she departed for the capital. Then, he cleared his throat and replied in a calmer tone. "The commander and Master Byron requested my permission to scout the border in search of the source of the demonic energy. Apparently, they felt more confident going on their own rather than staying with one of the camps."

An icy jolt shot through Coura's body at the reminder of the Nim-Valans' attack. *They didn't hear about the other locations yet.*

After inhaling a deep breath in preparation for the men's reactions, she released it in a long sigh. "I stopped at another camp just before sunset in order to spend the night and fly here in the morning, but it seems the enemy already crossed."

"What?" the general growled.

"The site's occupants were all killed."

Both Casner and Mattias looked at her with mixed emotions, so she went on to share her observations during the resulting investigation and her decision to head straight to their current location.

"It's just like what Commander Evern reported and what took place here," Mattias shared in a dejected manner. "The enemy attacked as soon as evening approached. We managed to hold them off, but it seems this happened to every site along the border."

Coura felt she should offer words of sympathy given how the news bothered the pair, but the general moved on before she could do so.

"With circumstances being what they are, we need to send a messenger to deliver this weapon to the Yeluthian commander while the rest of us reconvene about the recent fighting."

"Allow me to go," Mattias interjected and placed a fist on his breast. "I will visit the other camps and check on their statuses as well."

While his superior agreed and began issuing specific instructions, Coura rose to her feet, dismissed the sense of weariness pressing on her body, and looked between the two when her movement caught their attention. "I'll go."

"The assistant general is more than capable of this assignment," Casner snapped.

"Would finding Evern be easier from the ground or the sky?" she countered and met his resulting glare reminiscent of the man's past attitude toward her. "I'm not doubting Mattias' abilities. We don't have time to waste. He can also focus on checking each camp without hurrying."

He doesn't trust me, she realized when the general didn't offer a rebuttal. *Even though I fought alongside him and his troops over the years, nothing changed his original view.*

The notion spurred a sense of pity instead of the bitterness she expected. Fortunately, she earned enough favor from the assistant general to win his support.

"Monitoring from above would be better overall," Mattias added with a glance at his superior. "I'll focus on leading the remaining sites' recovery efforts and recording their current states."

"That sounds like the most beneficial use of your skills," Casner responded. "The weapon's delivery is key to our success against Nim-Vala.

While the assistant general voiced his agreement, Coura rolled her eyes.

If the situation wasn't time sensitive, I'd let him know exactly how capable I am by throwing my experience in his face. He'd probably just poke holes in every instance though.

With the matter settled, she exited the tent, leaving the two to discuss whatever business followed their conversation. Her instinct urged her to depart in search of her father as soon as possible; however, she forced herself to focus on her current condition in order to be prepared for the upcoming assignment. Not only did her muscles and limbs ache, but her stomach also tightened enough to grow painful.

It's going to be a long journey if I don't eat right away and sleep for a few hours, she decided as she wandered in search of the bonfire serving the troops' meals. *That brings up another problem...*

Coura looked down at her left hand, which rested on the hilt of the ancestral weapon even though she didn't remember placing it there. Over the days since she acquired the sword, she noticed how she became attached to the bond the item forged, which reduced the amount of energy she spent on a spell by amplifying her own power. That, coupled with the sense of security it projected, made imagining giving it up difficult.

Evern is going to be able to wield this much more efficiently than I can now, but I hate to think about what I'll be like when I don't have its ability to rely on. Basically, my body will be useless, and my energy should return to what little amount I can recover. That makes it all the more imperative I find Father soon.

Trouble on the Border

Four days passed since Byron departed from the main site, yet nothing appeared out of the ordinary except for the camps. His strategy involved avoiding the Asteom troops if possible in order to approach the search at a methodical pace. Although he chose to resort to solitude instead of racing through the woods, he found himself trying not to consider his decision to also refrain from bringing a mount.

Horses create noise and need additional attention. Besides, my leisurely hike would probably bore the animal into misbehaving.

With Evern monitoring the border from above, Byron figured he could try a different approach by scouting along the edge of Asteom's territory, or what he remembered belonged to the country. The uneven terrain often left him traversing less ground; however, he soon found he preferred to wander instead of rush ahead.

A careless rabbit sprints headlong into a waiting fox, but the hare who uses its ears will know when a predator is near. Our eyes from the sky will cover much more space anyway. I just need to act as reconnaissance.

To Byron's relief, the time didn't slow to a crawl or go by in a flash, allowing him to assess the environment while savoring what freedom he found. The lack of direction aside from his goal invigorated him, so he made sure to find a suitable location where he could clear his mind and meditate. When the sunlight faded, he moved on to a new spot next to the rocky cliffside where he built a suitable fire and rested with solid stone at his back.

It's been too long since I evaluated my mental health and center of energy, he reflected after propping himself up and closing his eyes. The tendrils of dark power within his soul space jittered in response to his attention, prompting a smile. *I'll enjoy when I can choose to go off on my own, whether in a forest or a section of East*

Hoover, rather than follow an assignment. Perhaps my recent issues stemmed from my unacknowledged desire to decide for myself.

He drifted to sleep before he could thoroughly consider the idea and stirred just as dawn approached. By the time he prepared to move on, sunlight filled the area enough to hint at a warmer day; however, the afternoon was less uneventful.

The sound of footsteps alerted him of trouble when he paused for a break, leading him to seize his bag and dive under the cover of the nearest pine tree's lower branches. A minute later, a group of six men dressed in the Nim-Valans' uniforms emerged from the brush just behind where he had been. The charcoal-colored clothing looked worse for wear, as showcased by tears in the fabric, the dull, leather padding, and loose spots where the material stretched too far. Each possessed different face shapes, along with a beard, and carried packs wrapped around their shoulders by multiple straps.

Despite the enemy's intrusion, Byron didn't act right away.

Why only half a dozen? he wondered after a minute ticked by and no more appeared. *I suppose this could be a scouting party, but they don't look like the type.*

The enemy remained close together, as if they feared splitting apart or getting lost, making it difficult to figure out who led them. Their level of noise also remained the same, which quieted the otherwise active woods.

As he studied the six, Byron contemplated whether it would benefit him to strike first, reveal himself and assess their reaction, or simply stay put until they wandered away. Eventually, he settled on the third option.

If they continue heading east, they should be in range of the nearest camp. Otherwise, the Asteom soldiers lined up farther south will stop them. I doubt we speak the same language, so an interrogation is out of the question, and a fight could attract additional opponents if they aren't alone. My assignment doesn't hinge on dealing with this group.

His eyes lingered on the Nim-Valans until they disappeared thought the foliage. Then, he trusted his hearing to let him know when they moved out of range. Only when he felt sure he wouldn't be discovered did he emerge from the branches and brush off what needles and sap clung to his outer layer of clothing.

"What could have brought them in this direction?" Byron mused aloud as the sounds of the forest began returning. When he couldn't come up with an accurate answer, he crossed his arms and glanced up at the sky. "From what I heard and experienced, the enemy doesn't usually break away from their camps and into fractions. Could this be a new tactic? Perhaps I shouldn't have let them go."

Byron shifted his gaze in the direction the six went in, scratched his head, and decided to trail behind, just in case.

The best outcome is they lead me to the dark mage. I suppose that might end up being worse if I'm caught, but at least I can be certain of their fate should they attempt to enter farther into Asteom.

*

After two days of stalking the group of Nim-Valans, Byron began to reconsider his chosen route. The weather remained consistent, which he appreciated, yet he learned little he could report on. This forced him to contemplate his next steps that afternoon when he paused and leaned against the trunk of a nearby birch tree.

All I know is one holds some sort of map and guides the others. They hardly talk, I haven't seen them draw their swords, and we're heading due east now. At this rate, we'll meet the scouts from the nearest camp by tomorrow morning. What a waste of time.

He released a frustrated sigh before readjusting his bag over his shoulder in preparation for another hike. As soon as he took the first step, the earth beneath his feet shook for a couple seconds, as if struck by an unseen force. The unexpected movement sent a jolt of panic through his body and had him searching for the source. The landscape didn't change except for a lack of noise, which signaled danger.

A second tremor followed, though this didn't bother Byron as much since he prepared for additional disruptions. His eyes darted in every direction until he noticed movement above. When he looked up through a break in the canopy, a pair of white wings soared by in an instant.

Is that the commander? he wondered while he started jogging after the Yeluthian. *It could be another angel, and the shaking ground would make sense if they're using elemental spells. Is there an attack happening nearby? I'd prefer to find out than spy on these Nim-Valans.*

The earth didn't tremble again as he hurried after the being above the woods. He stopped several times to monitor the sky and relocate his target; however, a blast of lightning shot upward during one of his pauses, sending a shiver along his spine.

The enemy's leader is the lone magic wielder among their ranks, as far as we know. That also makes sense since I don't sense any light or dark energy to signal their presence. The commander must have found the advisor and is probably pursuing.

Byron took pride in keeping his composure during stressful situations, yet his heartbeat increased with each step as he chased after his ally yet toward a potentially powerful opponent. His deep breaths created puffs in the freezing air until he slowed when no more spells appeared and the angel seemingly disappeared.

"Great," he growled through his teeth before halting to scan his new location, which appeared similar to everywhere else he'd visited. "I lost them."

After muttering a curse at his luck, he contemplated waiting and selecting a new direction if the excitement truly ended; however, the quiet surrounding him allowed distant voices to come across, though the words were undiscernible.

It could be Nim-Valan troops, their leader, or both. I'd better be cautious if I'm going to risk my life without support.

Byron inhaled a deep breath to reinvigorate his lungs before heading east. The brush met him like an old friend, clinging to his clothing and swiping at his face when he wasn't careful, yet searching for an easier path would waste time. He valued what cover it provided when the strangers' continued speaking, and his hunch had been correct when male voices spoke in the Nim-Valan language.

Still, he crept closer. Not a branch stirred when he shifted to crawl on his hands and knees under the branches until footsteps began right in front of him, leading him to freeze. The enemy's black boots shuffled just beyond his hiding spot, so he committed to remaining in place once he tilted his head into a position where he could look through the ferns.

Dozens of Nim-Valans packed and hauled bags in various directions while a hooded figure stood alone in the middle of the area. Their dark cloak prevented Byron from memorizing any noteworthy features, yet he sensed a wrongness coming from that individual. Before he could put his finger on why the feeling seemed familiar, a flash of light blinded him while the rumble of thunder followed at a deafening volume.

The entirety of the troops scattered then, as if they expected the interruption. Byron's control slipped at the sound when he instinctively covered his ears; however, nobody noticed the movement.

That has to be Evern, he realized and glanced out beyond the foliage again. *Has he been pursuing this group, or did their leader rejoin their troops when I started following them?*

All that remained after a minute was the lone figure, who merely glanced at the sky. Byron noticed then how the earth around the stranger hadn't been charred or disturbed in the slightest by the lightning spell.

Did they create a shield before the commander attacked? I didn't see this Nim-Valan lift a finger.

The flapping of wings returned his attention to the scene. His assumption had been correct, for Evern descended to drop onto the ground across from the hooded figure. Instead of dismissing the manifestation spell, the Yeluthian kept his extra, cloud-like limbs present and even extended them slightly as a method of intimidation.

"Enough games," the commander shouted while drawing his sword. "You are the leader of the Nim-Valans, correct?"

The figure didn't respond.

"If you are a human mage, I suggest you cooperate. Your life may be spared if-"

"What if I am not a human mage?" came a new voice.

Byron's body involuntarily shuddered at the question.

Even the commander paused, as if startled by the reply. "If you are anything less, then I will eliminate you."

The figure still didn't move, which looked more unnerving than if they physically reacted to the Yeluthian. When the answer prompted chuckling, Byron's heart dropped, and his worst fears became realized.

This must really be a...

"I assure you, I am above the feeble-minded humans. Only you vile, light-blooded beings are below them."

Byron considered revealing himself until Evern acted by charging at the stranger. A second later, the commander slid to a halt when a violet wall of energy appeared in front of the being without any sort of gesture.

A shielding spell cast without an exit point on the body, he noted. *It's possible yet risky unless a person's control is absolutely precise. There's no doubt the figure before us isn't human.*

"I'm afraid I must return to my business," the stranger commented before taking a couple steps back to signal a retreat. "I hope we meet again under less friendly circumstances."

As Evern yelled for the Nim-Valans' leader to stop, Byron leapt into action in order to take advantage of the opportunity. He rose from his position, outstretched his hands, and channeled his energy into a blast of fire that would cover the distance between his location and the figure's. At the same time, he walked toward his ally, alerting the Yeluthian of his support. In no way did he believe his spell would damage such a skilled mage, yet the distraction allowed him to enter the area undisturbed.

"Commander," he said by way of greeting after ending his spell without removing his eyes from their opponent. Once the flames and smoke cleared, he wasn't surprised to find the shield protecting its wielder, though he did frown when the eerily calm voice addressed him by name.

"Master Byron Rinod, what a pleasure." After the response, the violet wall shattered in a half-hearted dismissal, revealing the hooded figure.

At least he didn't flee when he had the chance.

"I'm not lying," the stranger continued. "I intended to eliminate you, though not so soon."

Byron prepared a retort but stayed his tongue when the Nim-Valan leader raised both arms, gripped the hood of their cloak, and threw it back in a dramatic fashion. What lied underneath proved without a doubt that the being before them was a demon.

Dark, beady eyes with a violet tint looked between the two before settling on Byron again. They seemed scrunched into the center, along with a slightly pointed nose and an unnaturally wide mouth, and no hair covered any part of its head. As expected of their kind, its pale skin stood out against the color of the cloak and what trees loomed behind.

"Now that the introductions are out of the way, I will give you an opportunity to return to Asteom's general with your tails between your legs," the creature continued in a matter-of-fact manner.

"Why would we leave when things are just getting started?" Byron responded while mustering a brave smile despite his caution. "You would rather flee than face your enemy? I suppose a demon has no loyalties."

His words prompted the being to laugh, which sounded frighteningly too natural.

"Believe me, human. I would enjoy putting an end to your lives, but I can't get ahead of myself."

Before they could question what the demon meant, it spun around, threw up its hood again, and sprinted in the opposite direction. Evern lunged forward, presumably to give chase, but Byron held out an arm and yelled for the Yeluthian to wait. His reaction halted the commander, yet the sapphire eyes bore into him when the interruption resulted in a glare.

"What is it?" Evern snapped impatiently.

"This is most likely a trap," Byron replied without backing down. "Besides, do you know where Asteom ends and Nim-Vala begins? We could be trespassing."

"Apprehending a purely evil being under any circumstances does not need the permission of the law."

"Maybe according to Yeluthia, but Nim-Vala might not see the situation that way. I'm not even sure if King Aaron and his council would permit that. The creature is an advisor to their ruler after all."

As Byron processed what he just said in a hasty manner to calm the commander, a curtain seemed to be lifted on some, unacknowledged fact. *The demon is using Nim-Vala as a front to prevent us from apprehending it. Their people don't realize what it truly is, only that it's pretending to act as an ally while manipulating their king. Still, they wouldn't believe anybody from Asteom if we tried to help, which makes sense.*

"What do you suggest we do?" the commander asked after resigning to wait for direction and crossing his arms. His impulsiveness, reluctance to accept support, and eventual acceptance to trust someone else reminded Byron of his daughter.

Evern controls his emotions much better than Coura, yet their mannerisms are so similar. Aren't I fortunate to have had experience working with her in preparation for moments like these.

"First, we need to figure out where we are," he decided after focusing on the issue at hand and gazing at the darkening sky. "The creature retreated north, so I'm guessing it plans to hide now that we confirmed its identity. I would also assume it won't return to this location as long as we're here."

"We should follow until we reach the border," the commander concluded with a nod and began heading in that direction. "When the being crosses again, we will be ready."

Byron shook his head and sidestepped to interrupt the Yeluthian's pursuit a second time. "What would that do except keep us in one spot? I'm assuming its plan would be to lure us closer and order the Nim-Valans to attack while it sneaks toward a different location."

"I refuse to abandon an opportunity to end the creature's manipulation."

"I agree, but if we're caught in a situation we're underprepared for, more than just our lives are at stake."

During the resulting pause, Evern's expression returned to the Yeluthian's normal, unbothered look, as if he seemed to calm down.

Then, he gazed at the spot the demon disappeared through. "I tracked the being and what Nim-Valan soldiers followed for hours already, so I will continue to do so if you intend to return to General Casner and report this encounter."

"It would take days to return on foot," Byron replied and rubbed his eyes. "Why don't you inform the general while I remain in this area."

"My position allows me to view the entire scope of the land that lays before us. Besides, you believe the enemy will retreat beyond the border anyway."

"It's their best approach unless they want us to go after them."

"I argue we should at least give chase until the demon reaches their territory."

"What if they prepared a trap for us or the creature challenges us like the one in Dala did? I disagree with acting when too many questions don't have answers."

"We will never know until we investigate."

Byron released a frustrated sigh before muttering, "I see where Coura gets her stubbornness from."

The Yeluthian didn't respond except to narrow his eyes.

I've been on assignments like this before, but I need to understand he is an experienced soldier as well. I suppose if there is actually danger ahead, he can flee to the sky after observing the situation.

"I'll return to the main camp to update General Casner," he decided, albeit with no shortage of reluctance. "Once he has the information, I can wait for his next order before returning; however, I advise against lingering along the border for more than a week, just to be safe."

Evern dipped his head a bit. "Perhaps I should heed your suggestion to practice caution. We would work better together anyway."

The comment startled Byron given the commander's behavior thus far, and he prepared to discuss what they would do when they returned to the camp until the Yeluthian continued.

"The Nim-Valans I trailed should not pose much of a threat, so we may be able to separate this demon or lure it back into Asteom."

"Now you want me to go along?"

"Master Byron, I respect your integrity and trust in your skills," Evern admitted in a serious manner. "We may just be enough to capture this threat or temporarily disable it. At the very least, consider what information we will get just by being present."

The idea didn't sound too treacherous when he recalled how the demon shared details about itself without much prompting. Still, he refused to disregard the consequences of entering Nim-Vala without permission.

"If their border patrol catches us, it would cause trouble for everybody," Byron stated instead of elaborating on the potential results and punishments.

The commander nodded before beginning to walk north. "We must not let them apprehend us then."

Byron remained in place while weighing his options; then, he struggled to dismiss his apprehension as he followed behind. Evern glanced over and shot him a grateful smile to show his appreciation for the support.

"I didn't expect Coura's impulsiveness to come from you either," he added, causing the Yeluthian to chuckle.

"My daughter once told me about how observant you are. I thought her remark stemmed from her admiration of you, but I see now she was just trying to warn me."

Byron savored his resulting laugh in case it would be his last.

*

The line distinguishing Asteom and Nim-Vala became clear once the pair noticed dozens of enemy troops lounging at the top of the rocky terrain's incline. Evern had guessed they would need to trek for three days in order to reach the northern country, yet it took them a day and a half since they didn't seem to need as much rest.

I'm blaming my anxiousness for the lack of sleep, Byron thought as he covered a yawn from where he crouched beside the commander in front of a cluster of bushes. *This is what I imagined we would find, but I never came up with a solution to dealing with the Nim-Valans.*

As if to shove that notion back into his face, the Yeluthian leaned over to ask what they should do in a whisper.

"I don't know," he replied honestly and at the same, hushed volume. "The demon doesn't look to be among them, so it's probably hiding farther behind."

He avoided the urge to remind the commander how he mentioned that before they set out; however, he accepted it was his decision to join with what knowledge they possessed.

Fortunately, Evern didn't appear dismayed. "We should focus on drawing it out while keeping the Nim-Valans from moving to attack. If we reveal ourselves, the creature should appear."

Byron shared his agreement before the pair stood, circled around the brush, and emerged into the open at the bottom of the slope.

Once they showed themselves, shouting steadily rose from the Nim-Valans at the front who noticed before several arrows flew through the air. Byron assumed their enemy would react first instead of questioning the pair, so he prepared his energy into a shielding spell, which he manifested after spotting the projectiles. Each struck and bounced off to land on the ground at his and Evern's feet until a single voice echoed across the distance and halted the arrows.

"I didn't think you two would be foolish enough to chase a demon," the being addressed them after.

Byron and Evern glanced up to find the Nim-Valans shuffling to the side so a lone figure could move to the front. Their target wore the dark cloak and kept its hood up to hide its true identity, yet a sense of amusement came across clearly. Byron dismissed his shield in order to address the enemy's leader.

"Asteom was already suspicious of your intentions, so we're prepared for another demon," he began while mustering his authority. "Nim-Vala will know soon enough. Surrender yourself to us."

The being placed its hands together in front of itself and tapped the tips of its fingers together while contemplating a response. "Perhaps you aren't aware, but few of their people speak Asteom's tongue. In fact, I doubt they even realize what's going on right now. I wonder if they would trust foreigners to steer them in another direction, especially if it means returning to their pitiful lives."

"You manipulate these men by abusing their nation's class system and lying," Evern retorted with more force than Byron expected. "You have no right to act as their leader!"

"Of course the light-blooded scum wants to intervene. Will you push your disgusting race's views on the humans to the north as well? As for your second point, I never lie. Just ask the master mage. Surely Soirée taught you about how we intelligent demons behave."

It took a moment for Byron to recall the first creature who possessed Coura, reminding him of his stomach injury during the fight outside the palace years ago. The memory shook him to his core, mainly because of how similar the two beings sounded.

"If it's a challenge you're looking for, then you're more than welcome to enter Nim-Vala and try to stop me," the figure continued.

"You underestimate our loyalty to Asteom," Evern replied before Byron could. "Just admit you intend to continue hiding beyond the border in order to lure us into invading these humans' country."

The creature's haunting laughter reached them from across the distance. "That is correct, but I'm not one who cares about such trivial ideals. In fact, let's play a game of sorts. I would like to test your self-proclaimed loyalty."

When the being raised an arm straight up, the troops surrounding it immediately drew their weapons and shuffled closer. The unexpected movement startled Byron into preparing another shielding spell, and even Evern rested a hand on the hilt of his sword.

"Shall you protect Asteom by halting an invasion, or will you continue to fight against me?" the demon asked before speaking in the Nim-Valan language.

It's sending the troops across the border, Byron realized when the area fell silent.

Then, the figure's arm dropped, signaling a charge.

Hundreds of footsteps caused the earth to tremble as the bodies came closer. Out of sheer instinct, Byron released his spell and created a wall against the mass of Nim-Valans before they reached the bottom of the slope. Meanwhile, Evern unsheathed his blade and assumed a fighting stance; however, there seemed to be a mutual understanding that the number of troops was simply too high for them to handle.

"We can't let them enter around us," Byron shouted to his companion.

When the commander didn't reply, he glanced over and caught the sapphire eyes lingering on the hooded demon. *He isn't planning on abandoning me, right?*

The lack of a confident answer to that question made him nervous, though the Yeluthian didn't rush forward or manifest the white wings yet. To Byron's dismay, the violet wall of energy only succeeded in deterring the enemy troops from attacking head on. Most of the Nim-Valans struck the shield with their dull or blunt weapons while the rest parted from the others and hurried around the outside of the spell's perimeter.

"Can you extend your shield?" Evern yelled without looking away from the opposite side of the area.

"Even if I could, they're focused on entering Asteom. They'll continue to go around unless we push them back."

"What about the demon?"

Byron muttered a curse before resigning to face the task at hand. "Leave it for now."

The commander began to argue until the Nim-Valans sprinted into the trees beyond without even attempting to confront either of them. Byron's heart sank when he realized what the decision meant and how their leader addressed the troops beforehand.

"Their orders aren't to fight us," he shared with Evern while formulating a strategy. "They only mean to enter Asteom while we're distracted."

"An unwise plan," came the Yeluthian's response. "There are soldiers farther south-"

"That doesn't matter," Byron interrupted and shook his head. "They won't stop unless we force them back, so I'm going to dismiss my shield and switch to elemental spells."

"Keep your spell up to act as a minor barricade. This way, we can turn our attention to the edges instead."

Without waiting for another word, the commander began sprinting toward the western side, leaving Byron to manage what enemy troops scrambled east. He dove into his center to utilize what energy awaited his command and shaped the tendrils into flames, which he released at the nearby Nim-Valans a second later. While he warded them off with fire, he sidestepped at a cautious pace until he reached the end of his shield. What men managed to get by escaped into the trees while the rest backed away and spat phrases at him, which he guessed were curses and insults.

As long as they remain bunched together, I can take down any who become brave enough to approach. We just need to use pressure to have them turning tail.

To Byron's relief, his magic continued acting as his best method of intimidation. The wide-eyed Nim-Valans avoided his flames, which shifted into ice shards after a minute, and didn't bother heading farther east when he sent bolts of lightning after any who strayed in that direction. This allowed him to use a showy display of spells that appeared more powerful than they actually were and utilized less energy.

If I can keep them in one spot, then perhaps targeting a few will cause them to retreat.

Before he could consider where to aim his next bolt of lightning, a flash to his left blinded him momentarily. His connection to the shield disappeared as his sight returned to normal, and the entire area fell silent for a split second when the wall's fragments dissipated.

Somebody destroyed my spell, Byron thought in a dazed state of mind. *Only one with more power could do so...*

His eyes shifted to the demon lingering at the top of the hill across the border. The creature's extended arm remained outstretched toward their location, and he swore he noticed the malicious grin from underneath the hood.

Without the shield blocking their path, the enemy troops started scattering again. Byron reacted by crafting another wall of energy in the same spot only for it to be struck by the demon's lightning spell again.

It's interfering to get the Nim-Valans past us. Either that, or it's still trying to taunt us into pursuing it. Unfortunately, both options are working.

Shield after shield rose and fell in less than a minute as he battled the magic of the creature. Although he struggled to keep up, the spells startled the enemy into hesitating; however, their leader's following shouts had them starting to move east again. The only words in Byron's mind became a stream of curses as he fought to avoid the urge to chase after the men instead of keeping the stragglers' distracted.

Removing the Disguise

The grueling pace at which Finn pushed Will and Clara left the pair practically alone as their leader remained just within sight for them to know what direction to go in. At night, the trio only stopped to rest when Clara demanded it since the Nim-Valan continued no matter the hour and Will trudged on to avoid causing issues.

As the days passed, nothing changed about the landscape to signal their entry into Asteom, yet Finn halted up ahead.

"What's the matter?" the light mage asked when she and Will caught up.

Their leader didn't move and seemed to be listening to the sounds of the wildlife around them.

"Is it the enemy troops?" Will pressed at a lower volume while preparing to draw his sword. "If they're already marching…"

Finn shook his head. "I'm not sure. It's too late in the year for storms, but I hear thunder farther to the west."

"Thunder? What could-"

"Will," Clara startled him by interrupting. "It could be a spell from a dark mage!"

"What? Are you sure-"

"It could be Advisor Lupin," the Nim-Valan interjected while facing them. "We should still be too far north to assume Asteom's troops marched right up to the border."

Although Will longed to ask what would prompt the advisor to appear and wield lightning, he figured one of his companions would cut him off again with an answer.

"I don't sense dark energy, so they must be masking their presence," the light mage added. Her face scrunched into a thoughtful expression. "That means it's either the advisor or somebody from General Casner's forces. We should investigate."

The Nim-Valan frowned. "At this point and at the distance we can travel in a single day, we should reach the main camp by tomorrow evening if we continue heading southwest. Going off that course will lose us time."

"What if it *is* the enemy's leader?" Clara countered. "We've been traveling to find his location anyway, so this might be what information the general needs."

"And if it isn't our target?"

"What's the risk?" Will decided to ask. "Asteom's troops should already be acting as the first line of defense. We would just be warning them about what they were already expecting."

Finn released a sigh through his nostrils to show his impatience. "Timing is crucial in a battle. We can't risk allowing our allies to be ambushed by a surprise attack because of a hunch."

A pause followed the comment when Will glanced at Clara. In that moment, he believed they shared the same idea.

"We'll go find out who's farther west," he began and faced the Nim-Valan again. "You can get to General Casner sooner without us slowing you down. Then once we discover the answer to who is using dark magic, we'll return to the main camp."

"We shouldn't split up," Finn startled him by replying in an oddly uncharacteristic manner. "If it is Advisor Lupin wielding magic, your lives will be at stake."

"As touching as your sentiment is, we're trained to handle ourselves," Clara responded matter-of-factly and crossed her arms, though not without an appreciative smile.

Will nodded to show his agreement. "She's right. Besides, I don't plan on charging in for a fight. We'll act as scouts and report back. That shouldn't be too dangerous."

The Nim-Valan still appeared to want to argue; however, he abandoned the effort, presumably after realizing how much time they wasted by standing around. "Fine. I will let you know when to head south in order to intersect the general's location."

Will and Clara expressed their gratitude for the information before their leader resumed the trek through the woods. A few minutes later, the thunder began to come across clearly, silencing the previously active wildlife.

This inconsistent rhythm isn't normal, he realized and hurried his pace. *This is definitely a mage's work. I would venture to guess more than one is involved based on sound alone.*

The three continued until movement within the trees ahead caught Will's eye and had him unsheathing his weapon. Silhouettes of at least half a dozen men stumbled south, as if in a hurry, yet none noticed the trio.

"Nim-Valan troops!" Finn warned before charging ahead and drawing his sword.

Their enemy reacted to his voice and their footsteps by sliding to a stop, scanning the area until one pointed at them, then yelling with various weapons raised to engage in combat. Will recalled his last encounter with the northerners when they invaded the camp while he and Clara snuck away. Back then, he had been lucky enough to avoid the initial, surprise attack, unlike his fellow guards, and his life changed drastically ever since.

I'm not a soldier, he reminded himself before focusing on a pair of Nim-Valans holding chipped swords. *Neither are the citizens the advisor rallied together, but they chose to kill innocent people.*

His first swing connected with a blade to produce a clang, then he twisted, pulled back, and sliced in the reverse direction at the man's knees, cutting through his opponent's upper leg. The wound was enough to send his enemy to the ground with a cry. Will poised his sword to block a stab from the second Nim-Valan, who slipped to the right, knocking the metal away before returning with a lunge of his own. Subconsciously, he didn't aim to kill and slid his blade through the man's shoulder. This caused the stranger to drop his weapon with a pained wail, place his other hand over the cut, and retreat into the trees to the west.

Will didn't pursue. Instead, he looked for his companions and found them standing nearby after Finn pulled his short sword out of an opponent on the ground. Two other bodies lied face down in the dry grass. However many enemies escaped, he didn't know, yet part of him pitied the men after remembering their vile leader.

I don't hate the northern country, he admitted to himself after reflecting on why he felt that way. *In fact, Finn, Geneva, and Yukin became some of my closest friends. I learned so much I wish to one day show the people in Asteom. We could all share our knowledge…*

Clara approached at a jog and wore a concerned expression. "Are you hurt?"

Will shook his head.

"We should keep moving then," Finn urged and glanced toward the continuing echoes of thunder. "There are bound to be more troops. The problem is whether or not they are our allies."

"You're coming with us?" Will asked without hiding his surprise.

"Let's just say I don't have faith that the enemy hasn't already crossed the border. Those who escaped us will most likely alert Asteom's forces before we reach the general. At this rate, our best option is to hope the advisor is the cause of the spells so we can return with valuable information at the very least and his head at best."

*

The closer the trio got to the noise, the slower they moved in order to avoid rushing into a fight already in progress. Several Nim-Valans hurried by farther ahead, yet Finn continued on their chosen path, seemingly to remain undetected; however, a pair engaged with them upon emerging from the trees to their right, forcing Will to support his friend.

I never considered the combat skills of a spy, he thought before they moved on after defeating the men. *He probably trained in Asteom and only knows enough to get by. I can tell he's used to acting swiftly and ending a fight sooner rather than dragging one out.*

Will became so engrossed in the idea that Finn's arm caught him in the gut when the Nim-Valan stopped suddenly and held out a hand to signal a halt.

"Get down," he ordered after shooting Will an unimpressed look for not paying attention.

Will sheepishly muttered an apology before obeying, then the three knelt behind the cover of a thick bunch of ferns. Farther ahead beyond a break in the foliage, a clearing revealed where the magic took place, as showcased by flashes of unnaturally tinted lightning. A group of bodies huddled together on the end of what appeared to be a violet wall Will recognized as a shielding spell manifested by dark mages.

"What's going on?" Clara asked without attempting to lower her voice given the consistent noise. "I can't tell."

Instead of answering, Finn glanced at Will, leading her to do the same.

He probably doesn't know what magic looks like during combat, Will realized before focusing on the activity again.

"I'm guessing two or three mages are trading lightning spells since somebody summoned a shield," he explained as he peered ahead. "There's a group on the edge closest to us, but they don't appear to be moving."

"That must be where the stragglers are coming from," the Nim-Valan added. "I see people on the opposite side as well."

"The enemy troops have to be fighting Asteom mages," Clara concluded.

"I agree, but I want to confirm whether or not our target is among them. Stay close to me."

With that, Finn rose into a crouch in order to stalk forward, leaving Will to follow behind his friends. The three continued until they reached the final mass of branches between them and the chaos taking place. From that position, they could make out the silhouette of a man on their side of the violet wall while the rest appeared blurry. What bolts they witnessed and heard came from a mage on the opposite end, who tore through the shield with every strike or two.

They both must be incredibly powerful to still be going, Will realized as a new wall of energy rose within seconds. *The person defending Asteom should be an ally while their opponent must be the advisor. Our mage is also using spells to prevent the Nim-Valans from crossing, though we faced those who escaped.*

In his mind, he knew the individual wouldn't stand a chance for much longer based on how the pattern of attacks didn't provide an opportunity to focus on a single spot at a time. Clara fortunately understood this as well.

"We need to help," she announced and stood straight.

Finn immediately seized her arm to prevent her from going forward. "It's too dangerous. We're only supposed to observe and relay our observations."

Clara's gaze shifted from the Nim-Valan to Will, prompting him to rise and voice his support.

"You're the spy here, right?" he joked despite the severity of the situation. "We'll manage. Besides, you have proof of the advisor's location. No other mage could be attacking Asteom."

Although Finn appeared to want to argue, he released his hold on Clara and remained under the foliage while the pair burst through their cover and out into the open. As soon as they sprinted for the safety of the shield, Will was glad he decided to help since the ally they hurried to join proved to be a familiar face underneath a heavy layer of sweat.

"Byron!" he shouted more out of surprise than to alert the master mage of their presence.

The figure either didn't hear them or ignored the sound, for he continued his pattern of casting a shield then sending blasts of fire at the enemy troops who began sneaking closer to the woods. In response, Clara slid to a stop, outstretched her arms toward the current shield, and crafted her own, which appeared with a faintly gold color. Will only halted when he reached Byron's side.

"What can we do?" he asked without glancing at the master mage. Part of him grew inexplicably anxious about interacting with his older friend and comrade after disappearing from Asteom for two years, so he hated the idea of unintentionally becoming a distraction.

Despite the lack of a proper reintroduction, the mage answered without pause. "If that shield can block the lightning, we need to push what's left of the enemy troops back into Nim-Vala."

Will glanced over his shoulder to repeat the order to Clara; however, she managed to catch the unspoken order.

"Go!" she yelled just as the first of the two shields shattered before the thunder erupted. "I'll protect you!"

Byron didn't question her. Instead, he sprinted to their right where the group of men started breaking apart and charging into Asteom's territory. With a single bolt of his own, he startled those who weren't struck into backing up. Then, their weapons rose at the challenge he presented.

Meanwhile, Will remained a step behind to avoid getting in the way. He slowed and selected his next targets before the swinging and stabbing began again. After the first two fell to his blade when he used all his strength to knock their swords away and lunge for their chests, he evaluated the remaining dozen or so.

None have proven to possess enough training to be a major threat. Their reaction to Byron's magic also shows their lack of experience around elemental spells. We might actually maintain an advantage at this rate.

Although he hoped his assumption was correct, the group shouted at one another to spread out, forcing him and Byron to divide their attention. The master mage unleashed another blast of lightning at an individual since the men would not get closer together, allowing the rest to charge.

"Watch my back," Will heard his partner order before more flashes filled the air, dropping two of their enemies.

He nodded instinctively and faced the next Nim-Valan who approached. The stranger bared crooked teeth and swung a short sword at him, though the lack of speed allowed him to connect his own blade with the duller of the two and push it away. Then, he attempted a horizontal slice for their legs, just as he did to a previous opponent in the woods; however, the Nim-Valan read his intent and stumbled backward to avoid being cut. Without considering his position, Will followed by lunging and pierced the man in the chest. He prepared to retract his weapon after, but the stranger startled him by reaching out and seizing the collar of Will's coat.

"You will die, servant of the mage!" the Nim-Valan growled as he poised his blade in preparation for a stabbing motion.

Will attempted to free himself from the grip to no avail. "We're trying to help Nim-Vala!" he begged when a sense of panic arose. "Please, just listen-"

When the man released a primal cry to dismiss the plea, Will abandoned his rationality, balled his hand into a fist, and swung upward, catching his opponent square in the jaw. The force of the blow threw the Nim-Valan's head back, though it also sent a minor stab of pain through his fingers, but the decision saved him from a potentially fatal strike when the hold on him released. Both stumbled away from the other, the man while cradling his chin and Will his hand, before the former swayed and dropped to the ground.

In the midst of his panting, Will muttered a curse when the remaining enemies eyed him up after realizing he abandoned his weapon. He rushed forward to seize the hilt of his blade before yanking it free from the man's torso just as the rest of the group charged at once. Warmth met the right side of his body then when Byron released a burst of fire to scorch the three there, allowing him to spin in the opposite direction and meet the sword of a new opponent. Unfortunately, the proximity of the men prevented additional support from the master mage, which Will noted when five backed up the one he faced.

A clink of metal and grunting sounded beneath the noise Will and his current opponent created before he managed to slice the Nim-Valan on the wrist during a parry, disarming his opponent. The man proceeded to retreat and sprang straight toward Byron. Will turned away before a flash of light sealed the stranger's fate, and he engaged with two enemies at once when they charged at the same time. Although the pair didn't seem to work well together, each proved to be formidable enough to have him backtracking.

I need to lure them toward Byron, Will decided before the opponent on his left slammed a bulky mace against his sword, throwing him off balance.

While he staggered, the second man began to pursue. His heart dropped once he realized he wouldn't be able to react fast enough to avoid the expected strike; however, a silhouette appeared behind the Nim-Valan before the tip of a sword burst through their chest from a stab in the back. The enemy took a couple steps forward before falling to the ground, and hiding behind the man's frame was Finn.

Will recovered his position in time to spot the second opponent shift to face his friend and ignored the rush of relief that followed his rescue. *He really didn't leave us...*

With two against one, the pair easily cut down their remaining enemy before glancing around for more. To their dismay, the lack of opponents meant the rest escaped into Asteom or retreated, though likely the former.

"I know you won't accept my gratitude, but I owe you," Will said to address the spy with a relieved smile.

As he expected, Finn merely nodded without meeting his eyes.

Meanwhile, Byron hurried over to join them. "We handled what we could here, but their leader got away. I didn't see if the creature retreated or not..."

"It didn't," came a familiar voice off to their left.

The three looked to where Clara jogged to meet them with somebody Will vaguely recognized. Neither appeared pleased, but it took their arrival to make him realize the blasts of lightning ended, the shielding spells had been dismissed, and the resulting aftermath of the chaos left the environment practically unrecognizable. What grass once occupied the clearing had been charred to nothing while the air remained heavy with thick smoke.

All this from less than an hour of fighting, Will reflected before he recalled the master mage's words.

"What did you say about the dark mage?" he pressed before anyone else could speak. "You called him a creature. Does that mean...?"

Byron stared at Will for a moment to seemingly assess his appearance and nodded. "The leader of their group is a demon."

"It revealed itself to us farther into Asteom's territory," the blond man added before pointing northwest. "We can discuss that later. Right now, we need to give chase."

"Do you have the authority?" Finn countered and sheathed his sword. "Forgive my bluntness, but General Casner's orders were to monitor the border, not invade Nim-Vala."

The question and comment startled Will, yet he figured the spy intended to remain professional given his connection to the northern country. *The advisor may be a demon, but his people don't know that. Besides, if it retreated, it shouldn't be Asteom's problem.*

Byron and the blond man shared a look, as if they recognized that information too.

"We do not," the latter replied after a moment. Then, he paused to eye up Finn, Will, and Clara. "I assume you three are allies from the general's camp?"

"We are," the Nim-Valan answered.

When he didn't continue, the master mage released an annoyed sigh. "I suppose you're right about how much we can do in our current position. Our next course of action should be to track down the enemy troops who entered Asteom and inform General Casner about the demon's identity and whereabouts."

Byron's partner voiced his agreement while maintaining a neutral expression, though Will sensed they planned to pursue the demon.

How flexible can Asteom be? he wondered while glancing at Clara, who seemed to be repressing the urge to argue with Finn's sense of responsibility. *On the other hand, how flexible can Nim-Vala be? I'm acting on behalf of the general, but Finn allowed Clara and I to assist him with Advisor Lupin. What if we extend the offer?*

"This is Finn," Will shared before he realized what he intended to accomplish. "He recruited us to go after the person leading the enemy troops named Lupin Olim. I can explain the rest later, but would you be able to go after him with us if Finn gives you permission on behalf of a Nim-Valan queen?"

He avoided the urge to look at either of his friends, mainly because he anticipated Finn's desire to strangle him and Clara's utter bafflement, yet Byron and the blond man seemed to be considering the offer once they recovered from their momentary confusion.

"It's not a matter of if we're able to go," the master mage mumbled while considering the question. "It's whether or not that will be a valid excuse for us to hunt down the demon."

"In any case, we are wasting time by discussing this," his partner added before addressing Finn. "On behalf of Yeluthia, I request to join you in apprehending the demon you are chasing. We share the same target, so I will accept whatever punishment may befall me by entering Nim-Vala as an ally of Asteom."

Will noticed Byron's surprised expression before chancing a glance at the spy, who didn't respond right away. *That means this man is an angel!*

"Perhaps we can work within our boundaries," his friend finally responded. "Let us track the advisor across the border while you two watch from a distance. If we can push him into Asteom again, you won't need to worry about trespassing."

The Yeluthian dipped his chin. "I can agree to that."

"Me too," Byron added with a slight smile. "Don't get too close to the creature though."

With that, the pair turned away before the angel manifested his pillowy wings and took to the sky while the master mage stayed close under the cover of the trees.

"That's that," Clara announced once the trio stood alone. "We'd better get going if we..."

Her voice faded into silence when Finn spun to confront Will. He already expected the Nim-Valan to berate him for his suggestion to use Elena's position for their plan, how he revealed the spy's identity, or both, so he met the glare with a brave face.

"You have no right to offer our services, let alone bring up business in Nim-Vala to outsiders," his friend began in a voice tight with vexation yet barely restrained. "You intend to use me and my master for yourself without considering the risks it brings to us!"

"For what it's worth, I'm sorry I dragged Elena into this," Will responded yet held his ground. "I trust them as much as I trust you and Clara, and we all need to stick together if we hope to catch Lupin."

"The politics you skim over could cost people their lives, including us!"

"I understand, but we have the same target."

"A target who manipulated the system in Nim-Vala in order to secure a place where he has control in the royal house. If we go about this wrong, he'll become a greater risk."

"If we stand here bickering about the potential results, the advisor is going to escape," Clara cut in to cease their arguing. "We agreed to support Byron and the Yeluthian, so let's go." With that, she moved south to climb over the rough terrain to where the enemy's camp lied empty.

Will looked after her for a moment and released a sigh of relief for her levelheadedness during the rising tension. Then, he glanced at Finn, drawing the Nim-Valan's attention. "After you."

Although the spy still appeared frustrated with the situation, he nodded and took off after Clara, leaving Will to follow.

*

As the afternoon wore on, the trio encountered the handiwork of the creature they pursued. They decided to let Finn take the lead again since the man's skills allowed him to track with ease, so Will and Clara remained a few paces behind and avoided distracting their friend from his work. Soon, bodies of Nim-Valans turned up with the results of various elemental spells.

"Could Lupin really be behind these deaths?" the light mage leaned over to ask Will when the pair spotted another, limp northerner with several icicles protruding from his torso. "Why would he sacrifice his own troops?"

The sight made Will shutter before he continued after their guide. "I wouldn't put it past a demon to use humans as a means to take out its pent-up aggression."

"But to waste the people who support its cause…"

What cause does a demon have that's for the betterment of those people anyway? he longed to counter when he remembered the previous being he faced in Verona. *They only serve their own interests, especially without considering how humans feel about it.*

The charred scent of a scorched body hung in the air while they crossed a short clearing, then they noticed Finn waving them forward. Will's insides twisted at the thought of fighting a second demon, especially considering how helpless he had been then, yet he repressed his rising worry as he crouched next to where the Nim-Valan knelt and pointed at the area beyond the foliage.

On the opposite side, a man lied face down in a patch of taller grass while their target circled him, like a predator cornering its prey. The advisor's lips moved, yet they heard none of the words being spoken. It raised a hand to blast a wave of flames at the corpse after.

While this took place, Finn glanced at Clara. "Can you protect us?"

"Yes, but what do you plan on doing?"

The Nim-Valan looked ahead again. "If Lupin is truly a demon, why bother with a war at all? What is he aiming to accomplish by provoking Asteom into attacking the inner circle? I wouldn't imagine their kind values gold, possessions, or titles."

Will considered the subject, though he assumed the obvious guess was probably the correct answer. "It's interested in power. What you just listed are things humans value, but demons aim to control the world through their own means."

"My thoughts exactly. Based on the advisor's behavior over these past few months, I doubt he would abandon his work with the outer circle by accepting casualties without reason."

"He wants to blame Asteom's mages for these people's deaths," Clara concluded without hiding her disgust. "The rest of Nim-Vala wouldn't know any better and have another reason to distrust us."

Finn grunted in confirmation. They remained silent for another minute before Lupin spun away from the burned body to stalk into the trees. Will prepared to rise when the spy held out a hand.

"I have a new idea," their leader began and addressed Clara. "I wish to test the advisor's commitment to his position by using my authority and pressuring him into escaping across the border. We shall see how he reacts when I bring up the inner circle. You will remain far enough away to avoid detection while Will and I confront him. If he decides to lash out…"

"I'll be there to shield you two and heal any injures," she finished with a nod.

He thanked her before motioning for Will to follow him through the brush. The pair purposefully created noise as they moved in order to alert their target of their presence, which succeeded when they caught Lupin pause and glance over one shoulder.

"Advisor Lupin Olim, we are here to bring you to the capital," Finn shouted.

Will jumped at the sound since he had never heard his friend's voice at such a loud volume. Meanwhile, the demon didn't flinch, though its stillness reflected how it debated its next course of action.

The spy slowed to a halt with enough distance between them to allow him and Will to avoid a magical projectile. "King Syrus requested we deliver you to him at once. If you are not the advisor, then state your name and business. The inner circle's guards will begin fortifying the border."

What is he saying? Will wondered when he couldn't put together a coherent message from his companion's statements. *Is he hoping to pressure Lupin into running in order to avoid any communication with the king?*

No matter what the reason, Finn's words evidently sparked a reaction from their target. The creature raised a hand in response, which prompted the pair to ready their weapons and prepare to jump or roll away; however, a glittering wall of violet energy manifested into a shield reaching the treetops and cutting across the woods. Then, Lupin fled in the opposite direction without a word.

"He's heading south," the Nim-Valan noted as he scanned the surface of the barrier. "We should continue to follow and keep track of his whereabouts."

Will nodded and prepared to go east only for his companion to jog west. Meanwhile, Clara emerged from her hiding spot and gestured for him to join them, which he did after rolling his eyes.

Death on the Horizon

With the canopy constantly blocking Byron's sight of the Yeluthian commander, he decided to rely on his other senses as he slowed to a walk in order to save his remaining energy. The spells he used earlier drained a portion of his reserves, yet he felt confident he would be able to keep up magically; however, his physical condition needed to as well.

The last time I fought a demon, it took advantage of my lack of a weapon. They're manipulative beings for sure, so I can't underestimate this one. Besides, Evern's intent on catching it alive or dead, though he may prefer the latter.

As he considered possible methods for subduing the creature, he heard crashing through the trees ahead, prompting him to halt and gaze up at the sky. The commander didn't appear, so he figured the Yeluthian already pounced on their target. Part of him also worried how well his comrade would behave given the angel's previous impatience and willingness to easily dismiss the politics behind their actions.

He shoved the doubts aside and hurried onward before the sound of thunder reached him, rumbling the earth below his feet. Just like he did days ago, Byron crept through the brush to use it as cover until he could safely join Evern. The opportunity presented itself once he parted a group of pine branches to reveal the commander facing the opposite direction where the demon stood. In its hands crackled sparks of bolts it prepared to send their way.

"I should have known you wouldn't abandon my scent," the creature teased from behind the hood of its cloak. "You're like a delusional mutt!"

In response, Evern raised his sword and charged, causing both their opponent to release the lightning and Byron to rush forward and cast a shielding spell in order to protect the Yeluthian. As soon as the wall of energy formed, flashes of light filled the area while thunder rumbled again from the opposite side. He approached the commander after and began illustrating some semblance of a strategy in his head until the Yeluthian turned to shout at him.

"Remove your spell!"

"Why?" he countered as the onslaught continued. "We need to plan how we can keep it here."

"The demon will escape again if given the opportunity," Evern practically snapped. "This is a diversion!"

Byron frowned. "It's a diversion that puts us in danger if we don't stop it."

The other's look of annoyance seemed to match what he felt, yet neither spoke as the bolts abruptly ended.

"Dismiss the shield," the commander ordered at a lower volume.

Although he hated how little visibility came from the other side given the resulting, gray smoke, Byron obliged. His energy shattered into fragments that floated to the ground like snow, and an eerie silence lingered.

Maybe the creature did run...

Suddenly, a shadow appeared amid the tainted air before the demon's cloak flew at them. Evern leapt forward to slash at the cloth in response before Byron could mention the possibility of another distraction. Then, the Yeluthian swung his head from side to side in search of their target.

It wouldn't remove its cover if it didn't intend to stay, Byron figured, leading him to draw his sword. *The smoke became enough of a hinderance for it to flee, so why throw the cloak from the front?*

Just when he put the pieces together, a silhouette moved out of the corner of his eye to the right, forcing him to turn and raise his weapon. An ebony blade connected with his regular one a heartbeat later when the demon appeared to ambush him from a new direction. Without the cloak, he could witness the creature's true form without the air of mystery.

Its body reminded him of a rat since its limbs looked thin and frail, though every muscle stuck out against the tightness of its pale skin. Like the other demon Byron remembered, their opponent possessed black fur, though this being's only covered the lower half of its body down to its ankles. The facial features were familiar since he committed them to memory after their first encounter, yet seeing the primal grin up close sent a shiver along his spine.

Despite appearing weak, the creature pushed him back with ease by pressing against the sword with its other hand. Byron stumbled at the unexpected show of strength before assuming his position in preparation for a follow-up attack; however, Evern jumped in from his left to begin swinging. The black blade met each of the Yeluthian's attempts, showing how well it kept up with physical combat, and it held its ground when the commander started circling it.

Byron hoped to insert himself into the fight, yet he didn't trust his comrade's ability to continue with support. *They're moving too fast, and I might throw off his rhythm. Perhaps I can use a spell when the moment's right.*

A sinister laugh from the demon caused him to freeze before Evern retreated a safe distance away. The pair still kept their opponent in the middle; however, for some reason, Byron sensed they didn't hold an advantage.

"Does this remind you of somebody?" the creature asked while raising its weapon. "Would you like to hear a secret?"

The violet eyes remained locked on Byron, though he refused to respond in case the questions were meant to lure him into a false sense of security.

"Not many humans are able to keep up with me, but you're not like the others. You've experienced the ferocity of a demon before, haven't you?"

Byron didn't answer, which amused their opponent.

"Decades ago, I climbed to the surface with a companion who shared my desire to test the limits of our kind's power. She taught me how to share our energy while I taught her how to manifest a blade like the one you see before you. Unfortunately, she also drove me north when she learned how humans manipulate both light and dark energy, which she became interested in studying. It didn't matter though. Mages like you only serve to distract from the purity of an ordinary vessel."

"What are you doing to the Nim-Valans?" Evern demanded before Byron could.

Their opponent's twisted smile flipped into a frown as it sent the Yeluthian a look reflecting its disgust. "Why should a despicable light-blooded care about the fate of those humans? Your kind seemed content to leave them alone so I could work."

"That's your goal," Byron interjected to pry as much information out of the creature as he could. "You want to possess the people here so they serve you."

The unnatural eyes lingered on him while the demon seemed to be contemplating a response. Then, the grin returned.

"Not in the slightest. Those who follow me do so purely because they believe in their pathetic cause. I am simply interested in witnessing which mass of humans will be fit for me to study next. Now that Soirée is gone, I would also like to test whether or not those who fought against her are actually formidable or just lucky."

Byron gripped his sword tighter upon hearing the name of the first demon and recalling how it manipulated Coura and terrorized the kingdom. He also wondered whether or not Evern recognized the connection and what the angel felt considering Yeluthia's involvement in ending the conflict. To his dismay, the creature chuckled at his reaction.

"What bothers you, master mage?" it teased. "Perhaps you're remembering the lives of those the Nim-Valans and I slayed to initiate this entertaining series of events. Or could it be your former pupil's attachment to the problem?"

"How do you know about her?" he growled against a sense of dread brought about by the creature's knowledge.

"I followed Soirée's previous endeavors in Asteom in order to fit into a role of power to the north, and thanks to a mutual acquaintance farther south, I'm aware of her pawn's connection to demonic energy. My eyes and ears have been alert for many years, master mage."

Byron tried not to let the creature's words get to him enough to hinder his focus, yet he couldn't avoid muttering a curse. *We ignored Nim-Vala because we didn't perceive them as a threat, but this demon has been steadily worming its way into a position where it could observe Asteom and build a following. Now we're facing the results of that ignorance.*

In order to push for an attack, he shifted his gaze to his comrade and hoped to convey that indirect instruction; however, Evern continued shooting daggers at their opponent, who didn't look away from Byron. A pause stretched between the three until he decided to act by charging at the creature.

He began with a lunge that the black blade deflected before sidestepping to avoid its retaliation in the form of a stab for his stomach. Then, he continued by mirroring a previous swipe meant to distract the demon. The tip of his weapon passed in front of the pointed nose when the creature didn't bother to dodge, yet Byron removed a hand from the hilt before swinging again and raising his empty palm to send a blast of fire in the creature's direction.

What he didn't expect was for the commander to be preparing a series of offensive strikes once he drove their opponent back. Instead of catching the demon with his flames, Byron abruptly ended the spell, yanked his arm away, and winced at the resulting burns from repressing the fire, which passed over the leather padding covering Evern's left shoulder.

Meanwhile, his comrade didn't seem to notice the error. The Yeluthian pursued their target as the creature danced away without engaging beyond blocking the attempts with the ebony blade, reminding Byron of how the first demon he faced enjoyed toying with him and his companions.

I can't hope to keep up with Evern if he continues using an aggressive pattern, he admitted as he watched the two beings move in a swift series of steps and motions. *That leaves magic, but again, I'm putting him in danger if he doesn't give me an opportunity to act. Does he actually believe he can defeat a demon all by himself?*

The question stemmed from the bitterness he felt about being left on the sidelines, yet part of him expected that to be the reason for the commander's decision to fight alone.

His moment to join came when their opponent took the offensive by using magic. The commander managed to poise his blade in a position to pierce straight through the demon's chest after twisting the edge of the metal underneath the other's sword, knocking it upward momentarily. As the weapon flew nearer to the creature, it leapt backward before manifesting a shielding spell in a staggering amount of time. Evern's attack connected with the wall of energy to produce a dull thud, which in turn ruined his fluid set of motions. In response, the Yeluthian retreated with a frustrated expression as sweat dripped from his brow.

Fortunately, Byron remained on the creature's side of the shield. Once he saw the spell, he readied a bolt of lightning and sent it forward before their opponent spun around. The resulting flashes hid the demon, but he knew better than to stop. Instead, a wave of ice shards followed while the smoke cleared, then he readied a wave of fire since he expected some sort of retaliation.

I need to monitor how much energy I expend, especially since it most likely won't be the way we end this fight. If my magic can keep its attention while Evern remains close, we'll attack from various distances. Then again, if the commander doesn't understand what I'm trying to do, he'll initiate another bout and leave me behind. We need to work together if we plan to succeed.

***

As Coura soared above the forests along the mysterious, northern border, she began to wonder if her father gave up on scouting from the sky. She stopped several times to rest after departing from Casner's camp two days ago due to her dwindling energy, which she needed to recover a bit before continuing. The issue with her lack of power bothered her immensely when she noticed conflicts taking place where she assumed Asteom's troops set up their stations.

If I could, I would jump in to help, especially since the ancestral weapon allows me to use my light magic without paying the usual cost. Witnessing a mage's spell could also deter the enemy from attempting another attack.

She forced herself to stop considering the possibilities after recognizing how distracted she became. Instead, she wished her allies the best before moving on.

Nothing else caught her attention until she faintly heard the sound of thunder in the distance. At first, she scanned the clouds ahead for signs of a storm; then, she wondered if she finally lost her mind when they didn't prove to be heavy with rain or snow. Still, the noise continued.

Perhaps I should land before I put myself in danger, Coura thought as she realized the potential risk of a dark mage inadvertently sending a bolt of lightning upward. *I didn't notice any elemental spells in use except for those wielding it against the Nim-Valans outside the camps. Even then, the thunder never sounded this loud.*

Curiosity pushed her forward before dim flashes beneath the canopy caught her eye. She paused to reevaluate her position, and once she confirmed she remained above Asteom, her wings pumped to send her nearer to the unnatural sight.

As she began accepting the likelihood of another conflict she wouldn't be able to join, her nerves rose at the threat she failed to dismiss, though the idea merely loomed in the back of her mind.

This is farther north than most of the other locations, so I can't ignore the dark mage wielding demonic energy. I hoped to sense their power ever since I left Dala in order to assist the soldiers on the ground. My rotten luck just isn't doing me any favors.

Coura slowed before hovering above where she noticed the thunder; however, the sound was replaced by voices and the clanging of metal, which became muffled thanks to the layers of leaves. With no leads pointing her toward her father, she steadily lowered herself to the ground in order to investigate the most suspicious activity she'd seen along the border. The canopy proved thick enough to force her to create plenty of noise just to break through the upper layer, but once she did, she easily climbed down until her feet touched the ground. Then, she dismissed her wings and crept in the direction of the fight.

I'm sure this is nothing different than what I already observed several times, but I should check it out, she thought to rationalize her decision. For some reason, her muscles grew tense, as if she expected an ambush, which prompted the comment.

When Coura discovered the source of the activity minutes later, her instinct had been correct, leading her to appreciate her cautious approach.

The safety of the brush allowed her to keep moving until she froze at the sight of familiar faces. Byron appeared first since he faced her direction from the center of a chaotic scene between two individuals who engaged in a flurry of sword strikes. That was when she recognized Evern attempting to subdue his opponent. Her eyes lingered on the stranger's black blade while the ghost of a hand tickled her throat.

It can't be…

Coura didn't want to believe a second demon caused such trouble and allied with Nim-Vala, yet she became surer once she could fully observe the creature's appearance. His features supported her hunch, especially the wicked grin and crazed, violet eyes. The longer she stared, the greater her body's discomfort felt as a weight fell onto her shoulders.

Terran nearly killed me, disabled Marcus, and controlled a legion of creatures to target Dala and the southern towns. I can't possibly pose a challenge, especially since this one seems to have the same skill and fierce desire to kill. That just leaves the ancestral weapon.

In response to her acknowledgement, the golden sword seemingly called to her, prompting her to place a hand on its hilt and savor what support the metal offered. Her heart also ached at the thought of giving up such a precious item, even to aid their cause.

With this, Father might stand a chance, she reminded herself. *Delivering it to him is my main priority; my life comes second to ending the enemy's tyranny.*

Coura focused on timing her participation after to prevent herself from abandoning the effort.

To her dismay, both Evern and Byron didn't look to be cooperating with each other. Her father obviously aimed to eliminate the threat himself by using close combat, likely to make certain the demon didn't escape or get a break and muster a spell in retaliation. Meanwhile, her former mentor inserted spells when their opponent lashed out, separating the creature from Evern, who then pursued. They attempted to utilize their strengths without much consideration for their comrade, though she figured they hadn't been given enough time to properly strategize.

They're stubborn too, she internally grumbled while continuing to watch for an opening.

An opportunity presented itself when the demon changed the pace of the fight. Until that moment, he didn't wield dark magic against her father due to the lack of time between swings and blocks. One hand parted from the black weapon's hilt momentarily in the midst of the bout before a sea of flames manifested and caught Evern along his right side, forcing him to retreat. Coura knew his armor would defend against a majority of the fire spell, yet the way he winced and ducked his head after worried her.

The master mage stepped in with a shielding spell to cover half the area when their opponent adjusted by launching dagger-like shards of ice at them both, pausing the combat again. Each icicle shattered once it connected with the slightly transparent wall of energy with a sound reminiscent of broken glass. As soon as she realized Byron would keep his spell up for more than a few seconds, she sprang into action and leapt out from the bushes.

Coura expected the creature to notice her at some point, whether she aimed to sneak around or not, so she continued sprinting toward the two men as fast as her feet would take her. To her relief, the enemy didn't bother to aim his icy blast toward her, allowing her to slip behind the cover of the shield. Neither Evern nor Byron addressed her at first, though the former studied her after he noticed the additional support. From that angle, Coura could see the skin around his right cheek growing scarlet to display minor burns from the demon's surprise attack.

She bent forward against the start of a cramp in her side and struggled to catch her breath. *I'm in worse shape than I thought*, she admitted before attempting to stand straighter.

By then, her former mentor eyed her with a hint of concern. "I'm assuming you're not just here to cheer us on."

"If I had the strength to join you, I would," she clarified and unsheathed the ancestral weapon. At the sight, both sets of eyes lit up, but she continued before they could comment. "It's a long story, but this is for you, Father."

Evern reached a hand toward the sword, let his hand rest against the golden blade, then accepted the gift. His shocked expression revealed how he didn't expect the item to make an appearance and likely provide the same sense of euphoria she experienced.

As soon as their secret weapon left her possession, Coura anticipated how terrible she would feel. Not much changed aside from her spirit, yet she avoided considering using magic or joining the fight.

"This didn't fall into your lap, did it?" Byron commented while shooting her a knowing look.

She shook her head and prepared to answer when a rumble of laughter filled the space and drew their attention.

"Now, isn't this a surprise," the demon began and offered a dramatic bow. His lips stretched farther into an unnaturally wide grin as his eye went wide with excitement. "It's a pleasure, Coura Galdwin. I had little faith in Terran, yet I figured he would have enough sense to finish squeezing the life out of you once he stole Soirée's energy. Alas, this is why I prefer to take care of business myself."

Coura tried her best to avoid letting his words bother her. Still, whatever warmth she generated during her sprint left her when he said her name. "Who are you?"

"Where are my manners? I am Lupin Olim, advisor to the king of Nim-Vala."

So this is who's been stirring up trouble to the north and controlling the so-called barbarian troops, she noted while Byron responded to the creature's introduction.

"Why are you pretending to be human? The demon we encountered never abandoned its pride, yet you seem to be focused on holding onto that fake name."

"Who says I'm abandoning my pride as a demon?" Lupin countered. "I believe you're projecting your own experiences on the humans to the north. You see, their ruler is aware of my true identity."

"What?" Coura exclaimed in amazement before her father joined the conversation.

"No living being would willingly ally with your kind. What sort of spell do you have on the man?"

"Or, what did you offer him?" Byron added.

Their questions fueled their enemy's amusement, spurring another laugh. "The people of Asteom always hold themselves in such high regard, like they wouldn't turn on their family or friends for power. Unlike what you became used to though, I am a god to these humans. They pray for a means to succeed, so I offer my services. The king desires to rule without issue and enjoy his wealth. I eliminated the competition and even brought gifts to keep his attention. Meanwhile, the citizens of the outer circle wish for the opportunity to fight for better lives; I gave them that chance."

"Why?" Evern demanded in a forceful manner. "Do you seek to rule Nim-Vala from the shadows? Are you building an army to overtake Asteom and manipulate the humans?"

Lupin's eyes narrowed slightly to show his impatience with the Yeluthian. "Why don't you ask your daughter? Surely she figured out the reason."

Although her father and the master mage glanced her way with a mild sense of alarm, Coura already processed the situation and why he called her out.

Demons enjoy nothing more than causing chaos and testing their power; it's that simple. Terran acted similarly, though through different means, and I grew up with Soirée's mentality planted in my mind. Only somebody with that connection would understand what it means to their kind.

"I suppose you want to take what energy I hold too," she said instead of trying to explain the answer. "You obviously worked with Soirée in the past."

For the first time since she arrived, Lupin's smile faltered. "You're correct."

When he didn't elaborate, Coura decided to push for more. "Did she drive you out of Asteom? Is that why you targeted Nim-Vala?"

"So many questions," the creature growled and allowed his expression to shift into annoyance. After a brief pause, he continued. "Soirée and I agreed to work together in order to share our knowledge. While she remained in the south, I moved north. Unfortunately, she kept her secrets once she grew bored of what we started."

"You weren't powerful enough to stand up to her."

"Watch your tongue," he snapped in response to her prodding. "My focus remained on what this country has to offer and didn't shift until Terran managed to enter from across the eastern mountains. Instead of challenging him, I inquired about his history, and we formed a pact of sorts. Without Soirée, he would raise an army in Asteom while I prepared mine in Nim-Vala."

"A war between humans for your own amusement," Byron summarized. "You treat us like pawns in a twisted game."

"I was looking forward to finding out which side would reign supreme," Lupin replied while flashing another grin. "It seems I won't get the pleasure, so I can settle for watching the northerners attempt to cause a rift in Asteom before they eventually turn to me again. In the meantime, I'll take out my frustrations and eliminate three threats to their success at once."

The creature raised his hands and sent dozens of bolts at Byron's shield, producing a deafening crash of thunder before smoke clouded the opposite end of the area. Although the earth beneath their feet trembled, the magical wall held.

"You should retreat," the master mage suggested without removing his eyes from his spell.

Coura knew he spoke to her and began backing up while her father positioned himself in front of her with the golden blade poised to defend against an attack. They managed a few steps before more lightning slammed against the shield, though the bolts reached above the limit of its height.

While the three glanced up at the unexpected direction of the demon's spell, movement out of the corner of her eye had her twisting to the left. Her father did the same a second later just as Lupin emerged from where he came around the farthest edge of the shield. Evern wasted no time lunging to meet the black blade as it swung for his head. The two initiated combat similar to what she witnessed earlier, drawing her father away. Byron dismissed his spell in order to hurry to her side where they studied the creature for a moment.

"If you can, return to General Casner," he instructed with a glance that projected his uncertainty. "We're close to the border, so he should be able to send backup or at least fortify the area. I'll cover you."

Coura ground her teeth yet knew her lack of energy, both physically and magically, prevented her from supporting the pair. *They need to figure out a new strategy. This demon fights as well as Soirée and Terran, and I needed to manipulate their pride in order to take the upper hand.*

Before she could offer the piece of advice, her father landed a scratch on the creature's thigh, sending Lupin stumbling away. Evern attempted to pursue only to be stopped by a shielding spell their opponent manifested that cut across the entire area. A jolt of panic shot through her when she realized she and Byron stood on the same side, which the demon acknowledged by sending a smirk their way.

"Go, now!" the master mage shouted as their enemy darted toward them.

Without allowing herself to observe the demon's progress, Coura spun around and began sprinting for the nearest cover as she sensed her former mentor craft another shield; however, the ground shook with a violent surge of thunder and blinding flashes before a wave of heat and crimson light washed over her body.

Don't stop, she told her legs despite the urge to see the remains of the magical bout. *I'm no match for an attack. I'm only distracting Byron and Evern.*

The bushes ahead would provide minimal protection, yet she didn't believe their enemy would pursue her with her father present. Unfortunately, her assumption proved incorrect.

Someone called her name to warn of a strike from behind just as she prepared to leap into the safety of the woods, prompting her to change tactics. A half-glance over her shoulder revealed the shadowy creature on her tail, so she followed her instinct and slowed enough to sidestep Lupin's next move. The black blade sliced downward right where she stood a second ago before stabbing for her torso. Coura expected the second attempt and repeated her move, then she retreated a few steps and prayed for a break when her breaths shortened.

To her relief, the creature didn't continue its assault. Any trace of amusement vanished from the unnatural face while the two stared each other down. Hurried footsteps sounded then, reminding her of Byron before a series of fireballs flew toward their opponent.

What she hadn't been expecting since the nearby shield continued to split the area in half was for the demon to be able to cast multiple spells. Lupin released his weapon, raised an arm, and created a second wall of energy at his side, blocking the flames as they soared through the air. At the same time, he aimed his other hand at Coura, grinned, and unleashed an icy blast.

Three spells at once, she noted and dove into what light energy remained in her center to manifest a shield. *He may not be as skilled a combatant, but there's no doubt he possesses more experience and power when it comes to magic.*

She learned from training with her father how a frail barrier wouldn't hold against strikes timed to land over a duration, so she anticipated needing to dodge what projectiles she could spot. The first, sharp icicle cracked her wall, the second shattered it into fragments the size of her hands, then the rest broke through. Although she lost count of the amount as she ducked and weaved, three found their mark to dig into her left shoulder, midsection, and right thigh. Meanwhile, a few grazed various parts of her body, drawing blood.

When icy spell abruptly ended, Coura locked her feet into place to avoid falling over as she stood panting. The pain from her fresh wounds grew numb because of the chill, yet the worst sensation came from the ache in her center from using what precious energy she could conjure. Still, her eyes remained glued to the ongoing fight.

Lupin's shield had disappeared, and Byron engaged in swordplay with the creature, presumably when their enemy became focused on her and didn't anticipate a physical retaliation. He managed to hold his ground until the black blade slipped past his weapon and pierced his side. With a grunt, the master mage shoved his opponent's sword far enough away so he could backtrack, leading the demon in the opposite direction.

Before Coura had time to consider what she could do to help, her father raced in from where Byron had been earlier to insert himself between the two, like a bolt of lightning. His sudden arrival created a rift in the combat, though he continued hammering the other's blade. She held her breath in anticipation until her head grew dizzy.

Father has the upper hand in close combat, and the ancestral weapon will boost his energy. Unless Lupin uses magic to keep him at a distance, I think Evern can manage a killing blow...

As if to echo her thoughts, the demon used his empty hand to scorch the grass and the Yeluthian's feet, separating the pair. He followed by casting another shielding spell, sending a final sneer at her father, then spinning around to disappear into the trees behind.

Coura muttered a curse in response to the creature's cowardice, though she recognized how fleeing meant their enemy most likely did so for protection. *He mentioned abandoning his efforts here, so he'll probably retreat into Nim-Vala or go into hiding until he can strike again.*

Although she fully expected Evern and Byron to chase after Lupin, she prepared to urge them to pursue anyway; however, neither figure moved. Instead, the pair gazed after the demon before turning toward her with a mixture of worry and reluctance.

"Go," she yelled against the lingering soreness in her throat. "I'll be fine. You can't let him get away!"

Her father nodded first and hurried to jog around the demon's shield, which remained firmly planted at the edge of the trees. After a moment, Byron did the same, though with a wince as he pressed a hand on the bloody spot where the creature managed to stab him.

Part of her wondered if they realized how weak she'd grown or if they sensed how she possessed no energy.

At the thought, the muscles in Coura's legs felt like they would stop working at any second, motivating her into finding a safer spot where she could recover. The closest tree seemed adequate, so she stumbled the few steps and threw herself at the wooden support. As soon as she propped herself against the trunk, what strength she mustered faded. Slowly, she lowered her body to the ground where she sat with her back against the tree keeping her upright, allowing her to view the entire area in front of her.

She remained in that position for a while before she felt prepared to evaluate her condition. The icicles froze to what clothing they touched, yet fresh blood oozed out of the wounds they created. Each area already grew numb to dilute the pain and remind her of the dropping temperatures later in the day. In addition, her limbs involuntarily shivered, which added to her concerns.

Do I have enough power for a healing spell? Coura's trembling hand hovered above the knife-like projectile in her stomach. *If I don't, I'll bleed out sooner when I remove them.*

Her hand dropped to her side after while she considered other options; however, her weariness extended to her mind, making her thoughts foggy. Both eyes drooped until she closed them and focused on steadying her breathing. For what felt like an eternity, she fought the desire to give into the temptation to fully relax, which would no doubt lead to her losing consciousness.

I need to…stay awake…and…wait for…

Lupin, the Nim-Valans, and her father and former mentor's safety became inconsequential until the sound of hurried footsteps reached her. Coura forced her heavy eyelids open when the noise grew louder off to her left. To her dismay, a stranger emerged from the brush instead of a familiar ally.

The man appeared as ordinary as anybody with brown hair, chestnut eyes, and an average height, yet his clothing sent a jolt of panic through her. Unlike the Asteom soldiers, he wore the dark, leather of the enemy troops. His eyes gazed over the charred and upturned earth before landing on her.

Before she could figure out what to do, a second stranger burst through the foliage and slowed to a stop behind the other. The woman looked quite the opposite and reminded Coura of a light mage, yet she donned the same type of clothing and armor. The pair spoke quietly with one another once the second's eyes found Coura until a third joined them at a less urgent pace. An additional man had her considering if the fight took place near an enemy's campsite or trek south. Part of her assumed they would decide to finish her off, yet the three huddled together and argued for a bit.

Despite the situation, what emotions they stirred lit a fire in her. *Even if they kill me, I refuse to go down without a fight.*

Their discussion ended when the woman broke away to approach her, leaving the two men to follow. All wore concerned expressions, which startled Coura, yet she reached across her chest with her right hand and tore out the icicle in her left shoulder before holding it out to defend herself, as she would a weapon. The trio halted in alarm at that and her resulting attempt at an intimidating glare.

Nobody moved for a few seconds while she panted in an effort to dismiss the mild pain and wave of dizziness that followed. Then, the third stranger raised his hands in a gesture of innocence and stepped forward. At a closer distance, she realized how familiar his face appeared, though she refused to acknowledge the person he reminded her of until he spoke.

"Coura, let her heal you."

It can't be, she told herself, yet her arm lowered without her realizing it. *Will died...and Marcus had been...*

As soon as her hand hit the ground and released the icicle from her grasp, the woman hurried to kneel and place both hands on her open injury. The first stranger took off at the same time to disappear in the direction Lupin, Evern, and Byron went, leaving the third to return his arms to his side, ball his hands into fists, and look after his companion. Then, he followed, and the woman and Coura were alone.

That's it then.

The toll of pushing herself exacted a heavy price after when every part of her body stopped responding. Even her head dropped so her chin touched her chest.

I'm actually dying… Will… His spirit came to…see me off…

Despite her acceptance of the situation, a jab of pain dragged her out of her slump. She craned her head back and whimpered before the woman's hands pressed against her midsection where the icicle had been.

"Don't give up now," the stranger chided as a warmth radiated from her glowing hands. "You wouldn't want to die without seeing Will again, right?"

"Who…are you?" Coura choked.

"It's a long story, but I'm a friend."

Coura felt too weak to argue, so she attempted to watch the woman work before her eyes closed again. The final, painful jolt of the last icicle's removal returned her focus to the healer until her skin mended.

"I took care of the worst wounds, but we won't make it back to the main camp if I continue," the stranger explained while wiping her hands on her pants. "Will and our friend Finn left to support Master Byron and the Yeluthian, so we'll just need to leave the demon to them."

The words spun around Coura's head, preventing her from processing what the woman shared. After a minute of silence, the other's sapphire eyes found her again.

"I'm Clara, by the way. Will told me about you, but I don't think we've ever been properly introduced."

While Coura faltered for a reply, the woman rose to stand and offered a hand.

"We should cover some ground tonight. It'll be a tough hike in your condition, and I mean that for both of us."

Coura tentatively accepted the support before Clara hauled her to her feet and slipped under one of her arms to prevent her from falling forward. Without another word, she let her new ally lead her away.

Faith in a Human

yron's heartbeat hammered in his chest for several minutes while he chased after the Yeluthian commander, who hunted their target like a predator chasing its prey. The wound in his side didn't bleed enough to concern him at the moment, though it hurt as much as he expected, and he felt better knowing Coura stayed behind to remove herself from the conflict.

If she says we should continue our mission without her, then I have to trust she'll manage on her own, he told himself before following her father into the woods. *She's experienced enough to know not to act tough in such a serious situation. I can't get distracted.*

Although he objectively focused on the task at hand, he couldn't vouch for the soldier he trailed behind. Byron knew from his time with Evern that the commander's sense of authority, as well as the Yeluthians' natural loathing of demons, likely clouded the angel's judgement. Coura's unexpected involvement also seemed to push her father into acting.

I can understand his dedication, but we won't succeed if he continues using the same strategy by attacking head on. Even if I act as a decoy, I'm not sure if that is the correct tactic. Luring it into a trap would be best. Unfortunately, demons are intelligent beings who can see through such tricks.

A surge of heat from farther ahead pulled his mind away before a growing, torch-like light alerted him of trouble. He slowed his steps and halted in order to process the situation as the eerie glow spread across the woods. Based on how their enemy behaved earlier, he figured the creature used a fire spell to hinder their pursuit, which spread in a matter of minutes given the dryness of the season.

After muttering a curse, Byron continued forward, albeit at a slower pace to both avoid a needless burn and use a sliver of his remaining energy to put out what flames got in his way. Part of him longed to eliminate the wildfire before it became too much for one mage to handle, yet that would take precious time. The sacrifice helped him catch up to where Evern began engaging with the demon again.

Unlike the previous area, their target didn't restrain itself when wielding elemental spells and eradicated much of the flora. The flames charred all the grass and leaves while several icicles found their way into the older tree trunks. He also noted the uneven terrain, which could prove detrimental to their success if they weren't careful.

I need to get closer to the commander, Byron decided once he recognized how repetitive the combat became. *Based on its behavior so far, the demon shouldn't flee as long as we don't hold the upper hand.*

Because of the familiar movements and pauses between the two, sword-wielding beings, he waited for a break before slipping into the open. The opportunity arose sooner than he expected given the ferocity of his comrade. Evern swung and lunged without giving the creature a chance to do more than block each strike, yet the violet eyes seemed to read each attempt clearly. Suddenly, a flash of lightning erupted from between the pair, causing the Yeluthian to stumble backward.

Byron kept his attention on their enemy through the blast since he expected a retaliation at some point. When the creature prepared to launch another bolt at the commander, he leapt forward, raised an arm, and cast the shielding spell he prepared. His magical wall stretched to protect his comrade just as their enemy released what lightning it conjured, resulting in a rumble of thunder that continued until the sparks faded.

"It's nice of you to finally catch up, master mage," came the demon's voice afterward when Byron slipped behind the safety of his spell to stand beside Evern. "I did commend you humans for your persistence, though I wonder if you'll ever realized just how outmatched you are."

Its cackling filled the clearing before another blast struck the shield. Despite the taunting, Byron didn't feel deterred and addressed the commander above the noise.

"We need a new strategy," he stated while glancing away from his spell to meet the other's eyes. "If we can keep it entertained, we might get a chance to surprise it with an unpredictable maneuver."

"What do you suggest?" the Yeluthian practically snapped. Despite Evern's exhausted appearance, he sounded full of energy and ready to argue. "Your magic interrupts my attempt to exhaust him and does not create a moment for me to deal the killing blow."

"What do *you* suggest?" Byron retorted while letting a hint of his temper show. "I can't keep up with you and that creature, I don't get a break to act until it uses magic, and you refuse to work as a team."

His honesty earned him a confused look from the commander, as if the angel hadn't realized he had been trying to assist. He released a sigh to calm his annoyance before another burst of lightning slammed against his spell. In the resulting silence, he remembered what he believed drove Evern to fight and seized that to support his point.

"We need to work together if we want to succeed. Our kingdoms are relying on us, and General Casner trusts our judgement. I also don't like how close this fight still is to Coura's location."

The Yeluthian's resulting, unreadable stare let Byron know the commander processed his words. Their eyes darted toward the demon when it began heckling them again; however, Evern replied to his plea at a lower volume.

"The enemy will keep an eye on me because of the ancestral weapon, which means you should be the distraction. I cannot come up with a way for you to do so, but I am willing to try whatever you settle on."

Byron scanned the surrounding area for a moment. "I don't see how I can keep its attention when there's nothing left to hide you besides the smoke. Despite that, I possess enough energy to trap it with shielding spells. You don't need to worry about me; just look for an opening."

Their plotting ended there when the creature stalked forward while wearing an amused grin.

"You've had a fair amount of time to plot your next move. Please, meet my expectations!"

In a tactic reminiscent of its earlier maneuver, their opponent extended both arms, launched a wave of flames to cover the opposite side of the magical wall, then sprinted toward the edge of the shield. Byron fixed his eyes on the shadow in order to follow the demon's position and initiate his next step. Meanwhile, he heard the commander's footsteps as the Yeluthian took off in another direction.

I assume he'll make a grand appearance from what's left of the woods, the smoke, or behind one of the spells. My center possesses enough dark energy for at least a few minutes. That's about all I can contribute without falling over.

Their enemy slowed a bit as it approached, as if hesitant to engage with Byron alone; however, he didn't give it a chance to search for his companion. He lifted both hands and kept the palms glued to his opponent while manifesting a shield between the two.

"Why not show me some real magic instead of these paper-thin walls?" it teased and halted to reach out and knock on Byron's solidified spell.

As it did so, he formed a new shield to the creature's right. The two sides met with his previous, wider barrier, nearly boxing the enemy in. It recognized his strategy before he could finish enclosing the space and sent an unamused glare in his direction.

"Let's test how powerful a master mage really is."

The demon placed both hands directly in front of the shield facing Byron before summoning a barrage of icicles similar to knives. They shattered when they connected, but because he quit managing the spell in order to cast more, the magical wall cracked under the pressure. After a moment, that side broke into fragments and floated to the ground where they disappeared with the remaining, icy blast.

By the time his previous shield fell, Byron constructed another at his opponent's back. This managed to catch the creature's eye, allowing him to form and maintain another to replace what had been destroyed.

I'll keep this a battle of endurance, he concluded once the enemy extended both arms to aim lightning bolts at the shields on either side. *It should continue the game until it gets bored or I outsmart it. Evern has plenty of time.*

His connection to the farthest spell ended when the demon broke through each side a few seconds later, so he started again with the right one. As he imagined, it didn't seem to be trying to get to him in a hurry, or else he would already be facing it in close combat. This allowed him to continue the game by replacing what walls fell when the creature selected an elemental spell in retaliation. Only when the being became visibly less entertained did Byron wonder about his comrade.

If the commander doesn't act soon, I might need to retreat, he realized against a tickle as beads of sweat slid down his temples. *The demon doesn't appear to be searching for him, at least as far as I can tell.*

After his observation, movement from the trees to his left caught his attention. He somehow understood what the Yeluthian waited for and dismissed the shield closest to that direction. The demon looked so focused on the barrier in front that it didn't notice Evern creeping toward it from behind.

Byron held his breath when the commander came within range of a strike. *Do it now!*

The golden weapon shot forward as the commander lunged for a stab from their enemy's blind spot; however, the metal only cut through the air as the lithe being pivoted to dodge the tip. Its lowered hand released another blast of fire after, hitting the Yeluthian directly in his upper torso.

Did it know Evern was stalking it the entire time? Byron wondered when he didn't remember the demon preparing a counter-spell.

As if in answer to his question, their opponent turned away from the commander, who retreated to a safe distance, and shattered his remaining shields using a surge of lightning. The eruption of thunder faded into the creature's haunting laughter.

"I must commend you for such a unique approach," it began while clapping its hands and grinning. "Fencing me in to control my position and lowering the rear wall. Well done, master mage! I assumed you would be the distraction though, which meant I just needed to be patient until the light-blooded appeared. Creative, but predictable."

The being shrugged, yet its violet eyes continued to pierce through Byron.

What should we do now?

He paused to assess what magic he possessed and avoided wincing at the remaining amount, which reflected the effort he spent ever since he engaged with the creature below the Nim-Valan's camp. With such a limited portion left, he didn't believe the pair would be victorious by depending on magic alone.

In the midst of his dilemma, the Yeluthian stepped forward to challenge their enemy again, drawing its eyes.

"I suppose you're aching to continue fighting," the demon grumbled with none of the pleasantry it showed Byron. "You must be desperate and ready to die if you believe-"

"Advisor Lupin!" a new voice shouted to interrupt its words. "Surrender yourself!"

From the remains of the woods behind Evern sprinted an unrecognizable figure who dismissed the commander entirely in order to raise his sword and swing at the demon. The black blade appeared and blocked the attempt, yet the creature backtracked when the Yeluthian joined the stranger's pursuit.

Before Byron could process the additional combatant, the sound of rustling from behind had him spinning around.

"It's just me," another voice added once he spotted a silhouette farther into the trees.

"Will?"

Saying the young man's name arose what mixed emotions stirred earlier during their previous encounter. He had dismissed what he felt in order to concentrate, but his current state of weariness reminded him of the pain and confusion. Still, the same, familiar face appeared as the herbalist hurried to stand beside Byron and observe the ongoing struggle.

"Finn thinks he can use the advisor's position and information from Nim-Vala as a distraction," he shared without looking away. "Let us keep its attention so the angel has a better chance, and you can support us from a distance."

Byron nodded in response, prompting the newcomer to rush into the fight.

At this point, I'm ready to try anything.

***

Evern's natural distain for the being in front of him only increased after it manifested flames to scorch his neck and likely burn what flesh lied beneath his breastplate. It took all his self-control to not engage with the creature again, especially since he longed to continue striking and locate its weakness.

What is wrong with me? a tiny voice demanded as his enemy addressed Master Byron. Despite their unfavorable position, the human mage never seemed to show more anger than mild irritation. *Yeluthians and demons possess opposite types of energy, so my hatred is fueled by instinct. I remember what I felt in the past too.*

Still, the uncertain part doubted his response.

I am an experienced soldier and leader. I should be able to hold myself in check better than this!

He stepped forward again to take on the demon until another human with the same idea barreled into the conflict. The human looked to be keeping their opponent occupied on close combat, so he jumped in when an opportunity presented itself. The flurry of swords grew even more hectic when a third ally appeared, though the two knew when to stay out of his way. As he expected, the pair moved slower and without his same intensity; however, the first's words seemed to distract the creature enough for Evern to nick its forearm. Their enemy released a pained growl, conjured sparks in its empty hand, and send bolts flying at him before aiming at the others.

He ducked his head behind the ancestral weapon in an attempt to block most of the blow despite the damage it would cause, but Master Byron reacted sooner. The man's signature shielding spell stretched in front of Evern and his new comrades just as the lightning shot for them. What flashes and thunder followed became a sensation he was growing accustomed to that day.

How can I get closer without it spotting me?

He clenched his jaw to repress the urge to growl in frustration until a sense of calmness emanated from the golden sword in his hand. That same essence captivated him when he first touched the precious metal and settled his emotions whenever he acknowledged it.

The master mage's shield cracked under the repeated pressure of the demon's spells to return his attention to their goal. Already, the pair of humans retreated far enough away yet on opposite sides of the area, making Evern consider if he should sneak up when their opponent focused on them.

It is the best option I can imagine right now, he admitted when the transparent wall of energy crumbled, allowing the newcomers to move again.

Evern steadily walked backward while the process repeated itself: After a brief skirmish, the swordsmen would trigger spells from the demon, resulting in their magic-wielding companion's intervention. By the time he reached the perimeter where he could dive into the woods, the shield's structure began to fracture.

Master Byron must be maintaining the spell in order to keep it up longer, he noted while surveying the layout of the space. *The two who joined us are already exhausted enough to need the support...*

His assumption fell flat a few seconds later when the barrier shattered. The slightly smaller human possessing spectacles charged at the creature with a cry before visibly giving every ounce of effort with each swing. Evern's eyes remained so glued to the combat that he didn't notice where the other one went until the demon whirled around with a snarl. Standing behind it and with an ink-like substance covering the top half of his blade stood the second man.

He managed to stab it?

Evern's surprise morphed into disbelief when their target stepped away, placed a hand on its left side, then stared at the bloody palm for a moment. The humans predicted its rage and backed away before the creature erupted into a series of spells. Unlike before though, Master Byron had not been expecting the reaction, resulting in a stray icicle striking one of the young men before his shielding spell manifested.

Witnessing the injury shook Evern from his daze when he remembered he was the only person in their group to wield light energy. He pushed through what aches his body reminded him of in order to hurry across the field where the newcomers knelt just beyond the dark wall protecting them from the typhoon of flame, lightning, and ice, which seemed to continue in a mindless manner.

"Let me see the wound," he said to announce his presence before throwing himself to his knees in front of them.

Immediately, the man with the spectacles rose to stand and place his back to his comrade, as if guarding them in case the demon acted sooner.

"It's not life-threatening," the other added while removing his hand from where the projectile landed.

Evern took a second to assess the injury before placing one hand on the human's torso and another on the icicle. "Ready?"

When his patient nodded, he yanked the shard of ice out, tossed it aside, and laid that hand over the hole. The wound didn't prove to be beyond his capability to heal, not by a long shot; however, his focus wavered as the man's successful attack came to mind.

How could this human damage our enemy so easily? I am naturally swifter, yet the being knew my location ever since we pursued.

"Who are you?" he asked as he finished his work.

The young man pressed on his freshly mended skin for a moment without showing a sense of amazement or doubt. "Call me Finn. I'm an ally from Asteom who works in Nim-Vala-"

"He's a spy," the second human clarified from over his shoulder, visibly irritating his comrade.

The volume of their voices sounded louder, and Evern realized the demon's spells diminished significantly as it only struck the shield in their direction. *I would guess Master Byron will not be able to maintain such a powerful barrier for much longer.*

The internal comment had him balling his hands into fists, though he reluctantly proposed a new idea to the spy named Finn. "You stabbed our opponent, correct?"

"I did."

"Do you believe you can do so again?"

The man didn't reply right away, yet he raised an eyebrow to show a bit of interest in the direction of their plotting.

To get to the point, Evern held out the ancestral weapon. "This blade will seal a demon's power within its body. I have not been able to do more than scratch its limbs, but you are skilled enough to sneak past its defenses."

This is not my area of expertise, he admitted to himself after the spy accepted the sword. Although what sense of security the item provided left him, he let his newly developed trust in the humans affirm his resolve. *I wish to end the creature myself, but it just is not possible given the circumstances. Plenty of people proved me wrong about their kind being weak, least of all Master Byron.*

He stood and offered a hand to Finn, who accepted and allowed him to pull the man up. Meanwhile, the glimmering, violet wall showcased dozens of cracks that caused whisps of fire to escape.

"We don't have much time," the other human announced as he backed away from the shield. "What's the plan?"

"I'll need you two to continue distracting it," Finn instructed and handed Evern his ordinary sword. "Don't look for me."

"Got it," his comrade called.

Evern voiced his agreement before the spy turned on a heel to jog toward the edge of the woods. Then, he addressed the remaining human. "Stay by my side. I am not certain if it will notice I wield a different weapon, but I would prefer to act as though I still possess the ancestral blade."

"What about Byron?" the man asked as the shield fractured and shattered into glittering pieces.

"I am sure he will understand and join at the appropriate time."

With that, Evern charged forward to throw himself through the magical remains and swing for the demon's head. Its eyes followed his every motion, prompting it to block the swing with the manifested, black weapon.

"Enough games," it snarled before the two began another bout, just like earlier.

This time, Evern maintained a hold on his temper in order to create pauses where his allies could act. The newcomer was by no means an accomplished swordsman, yet he managed not to earn cuts or bruises more detrimental than he could handle. The master mage didn't intervene during the fight, so Evern figured he intended to recover what energy he could for another shield in case the creature shifted to using elemental spells again.

Where is the spy? he absentmindedly wondered before catching himself letting his eyes wander behind his opponent, who twisted and arched its sword upward, forcing Evern to step to the side. The tip of the black blade slid against his breastplate and hissed as it created a shallow scratch in the armor. This amused the creature enough to laugh maniacally.

"The humans have lost their spirit, but I suppose your pride as a light-blooded won't let you lose to a demon," it began and swung to the right. "You might die a warrior, but it will be by my hand!"

The comment released some of Evern's inner rage, pushing him into retaliating. His blade connected with his opponent's when he threw all his weight into knocking the metal away. This succeeded in producing an opening, but the demon sidestepped and brought its sword up immediately after for another strike. Instead of parrying, he decided to block, and the being held its weapon against his. He glared at the demon while matching its strength. The scraping of the weapons as they fought to prove their physical dominance grated on his nerves to further irritate him, yet their enemy continued grinning like a mad dog.

For that moment, he forgot about the plan until the violet eyes lingered on his sword, and the wicked smile faded. Evern cursed his carelessness before movement from the right signaled the spy's intent.

I cannot allow our efforts to go to waste!

Instead of letting his gaze wander toward the human, he got the idea to look left, as if the approach came from that side instead, so his eyes darted in the opposite direction as his ally. The creature noticed, threw itself forward to shove him away with its shoulder and separate the two, then spun to Evern's left; however, it inadvertently turned its back on Finn. He held his breath as the spy adapted to the movement by keeping in their enemy's blind spot before lunging to plunge the golden blade straight through the demon's stomach.

***

As Will witnessed his friend's successful maneuvering pay off, a cry of joy sat like a lump in his throat. The entire area fell into a heavy silence once Finn pierced Lupin, so he didn't want to be the one to interrupt the moment in case the threat still lingered; however, Byron's voice seemed to move time forward again.

"Don't remove the sword!" the master mage shouted, catching their attention.

The sound made Will jump, which caused every scratch, bruise, and aching muscle to hurt, and he winced while growing tense.

I may not have contributed much, yet that lack of participation kept me alive, he realized once the situation caught up to him. *There's no way I could insert myself in a fight between a Yeluthian and a demon. I'm reckless, not stupid.*

The thought reminded him of the creature, who remained on its feet with its head craned around to glare at Finn. He considered rushing over and assisting the Nim-Valan until their enemy's body wavered. Then, the spy rose to wrap a free arm around the advisor's waist before steadily lowering the being to the ground, presumably to avoid risking the ancestral weapon sliding out.

Did we do it? he wondered a minute later when his friend stood again.

Byron crossed the area at a walk while holding his side, and the Yeluthian commander closed the distance between the three. Their movement prompted Will to go over too. Every sweat-covered face showcased their exhaustion, though their flushed cheeks were likely a result of the dropping temperature, and their chests rose and fell. Despite their physical appearances, everyone projected a sense of relief.

"The demonic energy has been sealed within the creature," Byron began to initiate their next steps. "As long as that blade remains in place, it can't act freely."

Before Will could process what that meant, Finn turned to begin walking away.

"Where are you going?" he asked the Nim-Valan without hiding his concern.

"We must inform the general about this," came the man's curt reply. "If the weapon can't be removed, someone needs to guard the body."

"You're correct, but we should stay together," Byron interjected, halting Finn's steps. "The enemy troops are still around. We can't predict their movements, so separating could become dangerous. Besides, we left a wounded companion nearby."

The master mage and his comrade shared a look, reminding Will of where he left Clara.

"Are you referring to Coura?" he added. When the question earned him nods from the two, he continued. "We found her on our way here, and our friend Clara stayed behind to heal her injuries. I'd guess they'll either catch up to us or return to the main camp."

A sigh of relief from the Yeluthian drew their attention before he offered a weary smile. "I owe your friend a debt. Since that is the case, I will return to update General Casner. Master Byron is correct about keeping guards here, and my wings allow me to traverse the distance more efficiently."

"Do you have the strength?" Byron countered while raising an eyebrow.

"Your concern is appreciated, but I will be able to reach the camp and plan to send Lavine north to lead Asteom's troops to your location."

No one argued with the angel's decision, especially when the sun dipped below the trees to shade the entire area. The angel bid them farewell after.

For a while, Will stared up at the sky as the weight from his journey began lifting from his shoulders and the implications of their victory dawned on him. Finn seemed to be doing the same sort of reflection, though he doubted the spy would ever reveal such feelings.

Byron seemed to be the only person ready to make progress for the evening. The mage took his time collecting sticks from the perimeter of the space after patching a shallow wound in his side, then he managed to start and build a decent fire as darkness covered the land. Only then did Will allow his body to relax by dropping to sit next to the older man.

"It's been days since we enjoyed the warmth of a fire," he commented absentmindedly, rubbed his hands together, then held his palms closer to the flames. "We abandoned our bags so they wouldn't slow us down. If I had time to consider how much rations we still had, I'd have argued against it."

His stomach tightened in response, as if to nag him. *We were so focused on finding Lupin that we threw caution to the wind. Then again, what would've happened if we didn't hurry here?*

When Byron didn't offer a comment, Will tentatively glanced over only to find the mage staring at him. The unexpected gaze startled him until he considered when the two last spoke.

"We don't need to catch up right now," Byron began with a slight smile before reaching out to clap him on the back. "Just tell me it's actually you, Will."

"It is. I mean… I am."

The comment spurred a laugh from Byron. "I can already tell your adventure is going to be an interesting tale."

*

Nothing unexpected interrupted the three during the night, which Will appreciated since they all ended up falling asleep. He knew Finn grew displeased with their relaxed mentality, as well as the spy's decision to remain near the advisor's body instead of being more useful, yet his friend dismissed the subject when he tried bringing it up. Meanwhile, Byron slept often to recover what energy he could in order to hunt that afternoon. In the evening, they enjoyed what few hares he caught before settling down again.

"It took me about four days to reach the border on foot," the master mage explained when Will wondered how long they would be at that location. "Commander Evern should reach the main camp in half the time, then we just wait for the Yeluthian's subordinate to return with the general's orders."

Will prepared to press for details on what those would be until the spy cut in.

"May I ask you about the ancestral weapon?"

Byron raised an eyebrow. "I suppose you've never heard of them before."

"Not at all," Finn admitted and let his eyes drift to where Lupin continued to lie undisturbed. "Can you share what you know?"

Although the master mage agreed, what he revealed proved to be what Will learned over the years as well, including their origin and ability to repress and repel demonic energy.

"The kingdom just recently recovered one, though it wasn't this sword," Byron concluded and scratched his head.

Will planned on asking what he meant; however, it didn't seem like he felt quite certain.

"I appreciate the summary," Finn picked up after. "Can you explain why we can't remove the blade?"

The master mage released a sigh, reminding Will about their past experience when dealing with a demon.

If I remember correctly, its energy escaped from Coura's body and found new hosts, which grew to become monstrous beasts. Not touching the ancestral weapon is our best chance at protecting ourselves from repeating that mistake.

Byron explained this to the Nim-Valan, who appeared slightly concerned.

"What's the matter?" Will pried when his friend remained silent.

The hazel eyes scanned the woods surrounding them for a moment before the answer came. "If what you said is the truth, how can we kill a demon without releasing its power?"

Neither Will nor Byron reacted, prompting a frown from Finn. "We can't leave such a useful item tied to the creature."

"The risk is too great," the master mage responded, though he looked to be considering the dilemma. "During our last attempt to control the creature's energy, we had a mage along who could take the stray energy into herself, but I doubt that would work again."

"Why not?" Will asked before the Nim-Valan could.

"Coura told me about her ability to manipulate what flows into her soul space," Byron answered while addressing him. "It doesn't remain with her anymore. Instead, what demonic power she collects enters and exits naturally, like a stream. I'd need to discuss our intentions beforehand."

The subject of magic and dark energy became less familiar to Will over the years, so he trusted the man's knowledge and didn't argue. They remained quiet for a few minutes, so he figured the conversation had ended until Finn startled him with a new suggestion.

"What if we behead the demon?"

An uncomfortable silence followed as Will grew tense. *Would that work, or would the result be the same?*

"It's an idea I'd prefer to bring up with General Casner," Byron startled him by replying. "At least he'll be aware of the situation and can organize precautions in case..."

"I understand," Finn added when the master mage paused to end their discussion.

As their second evening together approached, Will couldn't keep from rolling ideas around in his head. Whatever the solution to their problem was, it evaded him, so he tried to rest instead of struggle with the unknown.

***

The days following Evern's departure became arduous as their lack of resources took a toll with each passing morning. Byron found solace in being able to cast a minor spell and create their fire, but

414

that seemed to be the lone positive, aside from catching up with Will.

During their time together, he learned what befell the young herbalist and light mages, including how the group befriended the Asteom spy who pledged loyalty to a master in Nim-Vala. Finn didn't appear interested in much except what to do regarding the demon, but Byron expected such a skilled informant to always be listening and ready to act. Still, he thanked the man for rescuing Will and the others.

"It is my duty to Asteom," Finn responded nonchalantly. "I owe both countries my loyalty. Besides, Advisor Lupin proved to be a threat to humanity itself."

Byron soon picked up on how the demon assumed the role of a nobleman and why their people didn't question the lord's sudden appearance, as well as the being's influence over their king. At one point, he caught Will quietly urging the spy to return north and update a couple individuals on the situation. Although he didn't understand the purpose, he figured he would stay out of their business; however, Finn addressed him moments later to request his permission to depart.

"The advisor's death will no doubt impact the nobility in the capital," the man explained as his eyes drifted over the area. "I'm certain I'll receive enough questions to keep me occupied. They should also learn about the circumstances of our actions from a familiar face."

He means to say nobody will trust the rest of us because we're from Asteom, Byron concluded while wishing the spy a safe journey. *The situation favors their enemy, so of course they'll argue that we killed one of their leaders, presumably on their territory. I just hope Finn realizes how much weight is on his shoulders.*

With that, their ally from across the border returned to the north. Will fell silent for long enough to suggest a friendship had bloomed between the two, so he left the young man alone.

Evening approached to lull them to sleep once again, and they woke with stomachs knotted by hunger. Before Byron could volunteer to hunt, a commotion met them, signaling the promised arrival of their comrades. A handful of scouts emerged from beyond the wreckage to announce their presence, then the general led a group of about fifty troops into the open space a few minutes later.

Byron rose to greet Casner, yet the general extended a hand and spoke first.

"I'm glad to find you still in one piece."

He accepted the handshake with a relieved smile. "Another day and we might have starved."

The brown eyes slid left to note Will, who lingered near the fire, then the soldiers surrounding the demon's body. "I take it that's our target?"

"Yes, and it turned out to be what we feared."

"Commander Evern informed me of the situation," Casner picked up, saving Byron from having to explain the fight. "Now it's just a matter of what to do with the corpse."

"I assume the commander also mentioned the consequences of removing the ancestral weapon?"

"He did."

For a moment, the two contemplated their options until Byron recalled Finn's idea.

"We could try beheading the demon and seeing if that solves the issue of its energy getting loose. I personally wouldn't suggest doing so without thoroughly considering our options."

Casner crossed his arms and frowned. "We're also standing right on the border. If what Commander Evern said is true, we could be releasing a dangerous power if we mess with the item, which would cause more problems."

"Did the commander mention anything else?" Byron wondered aloud as he recalled their previous encounter with the creature in Verona.

"No. Why do you ask?"

"Commander Detrix used a Yeluthian spell called goddess fire to burn the demonic energy into nothing. I believe approaching either soldier, or even King Arval, would yield useful insight."

"That would mean leaving this being where it's at, assigning guards, and praying the enemy doesn't discover its location," Casner added and waved a hand at the figure.

"What's the alternative?" Byron countered with a tilt of his head. "The Nim-Valans will be aware of their advisor's fate thanks to our spy, but they may request the body for a proper burial."

The comment earned him a displeased huff.

"A proper burial for such a creature is to be tossed in a muddy river and left to float out to sea."

Byron shrugged. "It's your call, general."

Another pause followed while Casner looked in various directions before fixing his eyes on their target.

I don't envy his position. If a beheading still releases the demonic energy, then Asteom will need to remain on the boarder in order to contain the beasts it produces. Then there's the question of any that end up in Nim-Vala.

The man returned his attention to Byron after a moment. "The consequences are mine to bear, and mine alone," he warned at a lower volume. "I just want to let you know since you tend to offer your services for the betterment of Asteom. The way I view it, a demon is dangerous because of its power, and releasing that will guarantee destruction. It would be better to seek the advice of those with experience, knowledge, or ideas than take the matter into our own hands. Perhaps this will benefit our relationship with the northerners if we protect them, but they'll likely not trust us. That's part of the risk we're taking."

Byron dipped his chin. "I understand."

With that, the general turned to approach the being, drawing the troops' attention.

That's it then, he noted while the man issued orders for the soldiers to remain while he adjusted the defenses in their area. *There's no turning back if we miss our opportunity to end the creature once and for all. I suppose this allows us a break to recover, and Finn wouldn't reveal our location if he trusts us to handle the situation.*

He chose not to linger on the subject and closed the distance between himself and Casner when the general finished addressing the others.

"I'll return to the main camp with you and several guards," the man shared while pointing south. "Let's hope our friend across the border convinces the Nim-Valans that our actions are in the best interest of everyone. Otherwise, we can expect a retaliation sooner than we can handle."

Byron contemplated the new issue, what he could do to assist, and finally what he learned from the experience before the group moved out.

We should accept we can't kill a demon without unleashing its energy and act with that in mind, just to be safe. The notion stirred a sense of unease he masked behind his fatigue. *Our time is limited, and the second being near Dala needs to be dealt with as well. I should discuss this with Coura in addition to the Yeluthian leaders in case she has ideas. Hopefully none include her becoming directly involved this time.*

Unrest

Although Coura's physical state remained stable, her mentality steadily eroded during her journey to the main camp. The light mage named Clara talked her ear off about various topics, though she assumed it had to do with keeping her awake and thinking instead of nodding off. The pair trekked through the woods solely based on her companion's sense of direction since she could barely walk without tripping over herself. Every part of her body hurt, her insides ached from a lack of energy, and a dull pounding behind her temples added to the list of problems. Despite all that, they soon heard the familiar sounds of their allies before a scout called to them.

Coura stopped paying attention to how much time passed in favor of focusing on reaching their destination until they entered the camp. Many unfamiliar eyes landed on her, so she ducked her head to avoid their attention; however, the lack of distractions allowed her to pick out Byron's voice in the sea of noise. Her eyes snapped in the direction she believed him to be, and she dug her heels into the dirt to stop their procession.

"What's the matter?" Clara demanded. Her tone suggested she knew Coura halted their progress on purpose.

"We need to go this way."

The light mage refused to move when she attempted to lead them away. "What you need is to lie down. Have you forgotten how much energy you expended? I'm tired too, you know!"

"Then you should go rest," Coura retorted while removing her arm from around the other's shoulders in order to stumble ahead. She heard the beginning of an argument but continued anyway.

Byron needs to hear about the palace and Marcus. Evern too. The second ancestral weapon is still in Dala. What did they do with Lupin?

The question floated around in her head as she searched for the master mage. She caught her father's voice soon after before spotting the pair sitting around one of the bonfires with a dozen other people.

Evern noticed her approaching first. As he jumped to his feet to hurry over, the smile he wore disappeared. Byron did the same after realizing what caught her father's attention.

"Coura, you returned," her father began and reached out to place his hands on her shoulders.

As soon as the added pressure fell onto her body, she grimaced at the unexpectedly great amount of pain, prompting him to remove them.

"You should be resting," came Byron's voice as he stepped beside Evern and crossed his arms.

She recognized his disapproving expression from their years of working together yet dismissed the sentiment; however, as she opened her mouth to respond, Clara cut in from behind.

"That's what I said, but apparently the advice of a healer means nothing." The light mage slid next to Coura, took one arm, and returned it around her shoulders.

Still, Coura remained fixated on her update. "The Nim-Valans staged an attack in the palace by possessing several men with a single leader…"

"We heard," Byron interjected before she could elaborate further. "General Casner shared your report with us. We know about the status of those in Verona, as well as Dala and the southern base."

"What about the ancestral weapons?" she pressed after overcoming her initial surprise. "The dagger is-"

"Being used to restrain the second demon," Evern interrupted with a frown. "The sword sealed the creature we faced along the border."

Coura could only stare at the pair while her frantic thoughts vanished, leaving her mind quiet for the first time in days. The sight prompted an amused smile from her former mentor, which was a stark contrast from her concerned father.

"It's noble of you to consider informing us first, especially in your current condition," the master mage commented and projected his own sympathy. "We'll have time to talk later. Go build your strength. You've earned a break."

While she considered a reply, Clara forcibly turned them around by leading with her arm. The resulting jolt of pain from her overused muscles caused her to groan.

"Our superior is right. Now, let's get you to the medical station."

Those were the last words Coura remembered hearing that day. The world grew hazy again when she let her mind clear, and once they reached the place Clara mentioned, the other girl guided her to lie down as a wave of darkness swept her away.

*

Every instance Coura woke and asked the healer how much time had passed since her arrival, she received the same answer.

"It's been four days since you were admitted," each would reply with poorly concealed humor.

She thought nothing of the responses until her mind worked well enough to understand they were lying, which didn't seem to matter until she recognized it. Part of her hated the dishonesty while the other, more logical side figured there was a reason for their behavior. When she stirred enough to think properly, she decided to act on the hunch.

"Good morning," the blonde healer greeted her as she sat up to rub her eyes. "How are you feeling?"

Coura ignored the question to pose her own. "How long have I been here?"

The young woman raised an eyebrow, yet the corners of her lips curved upward. "It's been four days since you were admitted."

The two stared at each other for a few seconds before Coura shook her head.

"And how many days have you told me that?"

The comment earned her a grin from her healer, who proceeded to kneel beside her and begin a physical evaluation.

"I dragged you to the medical station a week and a half ago, then you slept for three days and only woke for long enough to drink a potion and ask how long you've been here. I didn't believe you actually knew what was going on, so I gave the same answer in order to gauge your condition."

Her lingering smirk showed she found the test entertaining as well, but Coura didn't dwell on the explanation. The young woman whose name escaped her performed a brief examination, instructing her to stretch, assess her current energy level, and attempt to stand, which she did without issue.

"You recovered far better than I gave you credit for," the healer concluded with both hands on her hips as her patient dropped onto the blankets again. "The next step is to eat something decent and start moving to build endurance. I'll fetch you lunch, then we'll go from there."

If she didn't need to recall the previous weeks' events and mentally prepare for what was ahead, Coura would have either argued against being left in the tent or exited when she found herself alone. The conflict in the palace, fight with Terran, and encounter with Lupin all seemed like memories from months ago instead of what happened recently, and once she accepted the demons were defeated, she wondered where she should go next. She started considering the ancestral weapons until the healer returned with two bowls full of a stew that smelled even more delicious due to her painful hunger. Her caretaker tentatively offered one before pulling it back when she eagerly reached forward.

"Don't make yourself sick by drinking this too fast," came the other girl's stern order.

Coura nodded while refraining from pouting as her mouth watered; however, as soon as she held the first portion, she consumed the warm contents in a couple minutes before gesturing for the second bowl. The healer released a disgruntled sigh yet obliged.

"I hoped your difficult behavior when we returned to camp stemmed from your weariness, but I guess I was being optimistic."

After another minute, Coura finished the rest of her meal and leaned back on her hands to savor the comfort a full stomach provided. Then, she addressed her caretaker in a less impersonal tone. "Thank you, both for the food and for saving my life in the woods."

"You're welcome," the light mage replied in a relaxed manner. She even offered a genuine smile after. "I don't know if you remember our introduction given the circumstances, but my name is Clara."

Coura opened her mouth to respond with her name only for the healer to raise a hand.

"I already met you," Clara chided, though in a friendly manner. "Besides, somebody told me about you before that."

When the other girl paused without masking a sense of uncertainty, Coura wondered if the healer expected a particular reaction, though she couldn't imagine what that would be. Evidently, it didn't matter. The light mage told her to rest after and exited the tent with the empty bowls, allowing her to lie down and drift into a nap.

*

Clara wasn't in the space when Coura woke for a second time that day. Judging by the same amount of light, she figured she only slept for an hour or two, which left plenty of time in the afternoon. She stood, stretched, and assessed her condition before opting to wait a bit in case her caretaker returned. When the light mage didn't make an appearance, she departed from the medical station.

If the weather in the main camp changed at all while she rested, she didn't notice. No snow covered the ground, yet the frigid air caused her breaths to release in puffs. Still, the sun's rays warmed her body enough to push her forward.

I wonder who I should look for first. Evern and Byron will probably be at or near Casner's tent in the center of the area, so I suppose I can start there.

With a yawn, Coura got her bearings amid the activity of the soldiers and mages. Her first stop involved cleaning up enough to appear presentable, then she went in search of a coat before she regretted the lack of clothing later. The attendants at the nearest supply station were able to assist with the request despite seeming to doubt her survival without the items already.

She scratched at her neck thanks to the itchiness of a gifted, woolen scarf as she wandered toward the general's tent while various scents bombarded her during the beginning of the evening meal. Her other senses dulled because of the distractions, but she still picked up a familiar voice in the mix of sounds at the center of the camp.

Byron is here somewhere, she noted with a relieved sigh and continued along the path. *Is he talking to Casner? I bet he's already planning our next steps.*

Soon, her former mentor's figure came into view as she circled around a cluster of tents. He faced her direction, though the individual he conversed with didn't, preventing her from identifying them. This led her to slow to a stop.

That's not the general, and it's not Evern...

She lingered awkwardly and waited awhile until Byron glanced around and noticed her. Then, she offered a timid wave. Instead of gesturing for her to join him, or even looking fazed by her appearance after a week and a half, he studied her before addressing the individual he had been speaking with. Together, they faced her and walked closer.

Coura didn't consider the second man until that moment. His curly brown hair, spectacles, and face reminded her of somebody, yet she could only think of one name: that of her deceased friend. The memories of Will she hadn't considered in months left her cold except for her clammy hands.

As they stopped in front of her, Byron remained silent and crossed his arms. The younger man averted his eyes in a bashful, frustratingly familiar manner while she continued staring. Silence stretched between the three for minutes, though her mind went blank and remained that way even when the third figure spoke.

"It's nice to see you again," he began, cleared his throat, and balled his hands into fists at his sides. His entire demeaner seemed like he was trying to form an apology. "I suppose I owe you and plenty of other people an explanation. After the ambush in the camp two years ago, I went north with a group of light mages..."

While he rambled, Coura stopped listening when the truth dawned on her.

This is Will… Not a stranger or his spirit… He's actually alive?

She held her breath until her chest ached against the thundering of her heart. Still, she remained in disbelief. "Will?"

The single word interrupted his long-winded story, and he stopped speaking to meet her eyes for the first time. With a blush, he nodded and dipped his chin.

That was all Coura needed to accept her once-lost friend's sudden appearance. One step followed another before she threw herself at him, wrapped both arms around his waist, and buried her face into his chest. An ecstatic huff escaped her when she accepted her giddiness, prompting her to tighten her hold.

Her friend returned the embrace and laughed at her reaction. Even Byron's amused chuckling joined theirs a moment later. Once she felt satisfied, Coura broke away and placed both hands on his shoulders.

"Where have you been this whole time?"

His smile faltered before he shook his head in a helpless manner. "Didn't you hear anything I just said?"

She grinned in response before wiping her eyes, which held tears she didn't acknowledge until that instant. Questions swirled around her head, yet her mind and mouth became disjointed, leaving her fumbling for a way to continue.

Byron took advantage of her shock to excuse himself from the discussion. "I'll let you two catch up," he threw out and backtracked toward Casner's tent.

Will nodded, thanked the master mage, then returned his attention to Coura. "I'm glad you're feeling better. Clara said you were practically on death's doorstep when we found you. I went to visit during your recovery, but you didn't seem attentive enough to recognize me."

She scratched at her neck again and wiped her nose as the severity of her previous injuries reminded her of how little rest she'd had over the last couple weeks.

"Anyway," Will picked up when she didn't respond. "Let's find a spot to sit and eat dinner so we can talk."

Coura's smile returned, and she took a few seconds to savor the sight of her friend. "I'd like that."

***

General Casner summoned Byron, Evern, and several other individuals every day after their return until the group felt somewhat confident with their upcoming route. A rotating selection of soldiers and mages would monitor the demon's body while the king's council decided on a fitting course of action after Byron shared the update. The Yeluthian commander admitted his lack of knowledge regarding the ancestral weapons, goddess fire spell, and his peoples' past decisions regarding the beings, leading him to volunteer to return to the capital as well.

Their second concern related to the northerns, both those who escaped into Asteom and those who fled from the border back to Nim-Vala. Because of his position, the general could only send messengers to the other camps with a warning regarding the invaders since his troops needed to continue maintaining the line. Evern eased part of the burden by offering to keep Lavine under the general's command temporarily, allowing the news to spread at a faster pace.

Because of the time-sensitive information, Casner requested the commander and master mage depart as soon as possible; however, Byron convinced Evern to wait until the following morning so he could discuss the journey with three individuals.

First, he figured Clearshot would want to return to Verona. His friend remained outside the general's business, which Byron thought was odd given the man's normal curiosity, but pressed for details once he extended the invitation. After promising to share the information that evening at dinner, the two parted on mutual terms.

Next, he found Will crossing through the camp. The young man seemed to possess a sense of independence and certainty ever since the demon had been dealt with. Byron needed a couple days to accept this new personality after what he became used to in the past.

Will always needed something or someone to motivate him into acting, but now he appears to have grown into an adult with the confidence to trust his abilities and instincts, he noted while the herbalist considered the idea of returning to the capital the following day. *Perhaps winding up in a situation where hesitation meant death forced him to confront his doubt. Given what he's been through, he could have turned out much worse for wear.*

He prepared for the young man's response when his eyes caught the familiar face of his former student lingering farther behind. The sight startled and relieved him in equal amounts due to their last interaction when she appeared bruised, worn, and drained and acted as if she couldn't think clearly. After he heard about the conflict in the palace and encounter in Dala, he understood she pushed herself too hard; however, he had a feeling she already knew that.

She offered a tentative wave to acknowledge her intent to speak with him, leading him to consider if she knew about her friend yet.

"Will, is Coura aware you're here?" he asked while returning his gaze to the herbalist. The chestnut eyes widened just enough for him to figure out the answer before the reply.

"I visited her a few times, but it didn't seem like she recognized me."

Will's quiet, somewhat deflated response pushed Byron into sharing her location, as well as mention his desire to request she join them and go to the capital. The young man nodded, so he closed the distance between them and Coura while studying her reaction.

She didn't look at Will until they came closer, and her casual expression hardened into an unreadable stare. Byron stepped aside so he wouldn't interrupt the natural pace of their reunion because he had no idea how either would react. Thankfully, his former student startled him in a pleasant manner by embracing her friend without restraining her positive emotions, which spurred a sheepish grin from Will and a chuckle from him.

Why did I expect hostility when they have been close for years? he reflected as he decided to remove himself before the inevitable recount of the herbalist's experience in Nim-Vala. *It must be the current circumstances. I'm not used to relaxing and enjoying the moment.*

He wandered around the camp sparking conversations with various soldiers until his stomach drove him to the area where he agreed to meet Clearshot. His friend arrived a few minutes later, then the duo made for the mess tent and received their portions.

"Should we head toward our fire?" the man asked while pointing in that direction.

Byron shook his head after recalling their departure the next morning. "I left Will with Coura and didn't get an opportunity to speak with her yet. I'd like to make that detour, if it's not too much trouble."

His friend gently elbowed him in the side without a vocal confirmation, so he led them to the medical station. His hunch proved correct when they entered and spotted the pair sitting cross-legged where she had been resting ever since her return. Several light mages wandered around the space, though nobody bothered the newcomers once they joined the younger occupants. Clearshot dove into a series of questions for Coura regarding her condition similar to his behavior when he reunited with Will, which she halfheartedly answered.

Although Byron grew curious about her thoughts on the situation, he focused on his goal and cleared his throat at the next opportunity. "Did Will tell you we're planning on heading back to Verona tomorrow?"

She tilted her head a bit. "He mentioned that's what you were discussing when I interrupted your conversation. I assume Evern is going too?"

He nodded before proceeding to summarize the general outline of their goals, including Casner's position along the border with the demon. All the while, he noted how she averted her eyes and appeared to be refraining from commenting.

That reserved behavior usually means something is on her mind, he realized once he finished the explanation. *Perhaps I should bring it up another time. I'd hate to sour the evening's mood by prying. Besides, she always reveals the reason when she's ready to talk.*

"Well?" Clearshot interjected when the group fell silent. "Have you had enough traveling yet?"

The question hadn't been directed at any one person, yet Coura and Will released a weary sigh at the same time, spurring a laugh from the archer.

"Don't worry, we'll get plenty of opportunities to rest and recover!"

"You're right, though I'd prefer the comfort of a featherbed, especially this far north," Will added while leaning back on his hands and staring up at the tent's ceiling.

The comment and resulting pause deflated Byron's spirits when he understood the message.

"You're not coming back to Verona?" Coura mumbled loudly enough for them to hear, though it sounded like more of a statement than a question.

Still, the herbalist nodded. "My friend Finn went across the border to share the news about Advisor Lupin. I would imagine he'll return and provide an update for General Casner, and I want to be here when he does."

"Are you sure?" Clearshot countered at a lower volume, catching the young man's attention. "This won't be a safe location if the northerners decide to retaliate. You and the surviving light mages saw what they can do, what lengths they're willing to go to for their idea of independence."

"I understand. Believe me, if I didn't have a personal stake in this conflict, I wouldn't hesitate to return to the palace. There are people in Nim-Vala I want to protect too. They deserve to live without hiding in fear from what havoc a demon wrecks."

The soldier crossed his arms. "It's up to you, but be careful."

Despite the severity of the subject, Will offered a reassuring smile. "I don't plan on charging headlong into danger..."

"That's how it always starts," Coura interrupted and glanced at her friend. "You never expect trouble to find you until it does. Then, you become invested in the outcome."

"Are you sharing from experience?" Byron couldn't refrain from asking in a joking manner.

She narrowed her eyes to show a hint of annoyance yet didn't deny the expected answer.

***

Although she preferred not to fly so soon after waking from the extended recovery, Coura rose and prepared for the trek ahead of her before meeting her father, Byron, and Clearshot as the sun began rising. Will seemed reluctant to join them for a farewell given the early hour, so they said their goodbyes the previous evening. She hated the idea of leaving him behind but kept her opinion to herself.

It's not my business if he wants to become involved with the conflict, she reminded herself once the group departed and she soared behind her father. *My worry is that he'll stay attached to Nim-Vala no matter the outcome, and I don't trust their people to accept Asteom citizens so easily. This may turn into a lengthy issue as well.*

The journey from the border to Asteom provided plenty of time to reflect on that concern, along with what took place over the past weeks. By the time Evern signaled for them to descend outside Verona days later, her thoughts seemed organized enough, though the demons still haunted her when she considered their current state. Byron and Clearshot arrived several minutes later, dismounted, and walked alongside the pair into the city.

"I plan on informing my king of the situation, and I would imagine you shall do the same for King Aaron," Evern commented while addressing the men, leading Byron to nod and Clearshot to shrug.

"I'll go wherever they let me," the latter commented before glancing at Coura. "You're in the same position."

She rolled her eyes yet didn't respond until she realized her father and former mentor seemed to be waiting for a reply. "I think I'll visit Grace if she is available. Otherwise, I could use a nap."

The comment was enough for the three to leave her out of their following discussion on when a council meeting would take place and who should be present.

I'd prefer to hear what Aaron and King Arval decide on when they have a chance to process the update. Based on Casner's orders for Byron and Evern, it doesn't sound like anybody is certain of what will happen to Terran and Lupin. I have a feeling the result is going to be disastrous either way.

*

Coura didn't see her father for three days following their return to the palace, unlike Byron who stopped by to inform her of the council's sessions every afternoon. At first, she appreciated being included given her involvement; however, nothing of note came from the meetings since more theories hung in the air than solid information. Grace had been called upon for her goddess gift in order to reach the Dalan base and Casner, which was why the meetings had been spread out: The younger Yeluthian could only use her spell for a brief period with the new master light mage's assistance.

In the meantime, Byron shared his own thoughts and asked for her opinion in a casual manner.

"The goddess fire Commander Detrix used on Hendal succeeded in eradicating the demonic energy, but no one is certain if the same would happen with a demon," he had explained after the first day. "There might not be an issue as long as the ancestral weapon is there. I wouldn't think so, yet we need to consider the risks."

"Is that the only suggestion the council came up with?" Coura asked to show she had been listening. In reality, she only wished for Asteom and Yeluthia's leaders to reach a decision and tried masking her impatience with curiosity.

The ancestral weapons aren't available; that's the main issue, in my opinion, she admitted while her former mentor elaborated on an idea to behead the creatures. *They can't stay where they are now, and the potential for them to somehow get removed increases every second they remain attached to Terran and Lupin. Perhaps I'm just being paranoid. I'm sure that's what Byron would say if I mention it.*

Part of her also wondered why he kept her involved at all. The likeliest reason she could come up with related to her connection to demonic energy, yet nothing hinted that she formed a particular bond with either creature compared to what Soirée forged. She also

431

knew the power would find hosts if released, leading her to hunt them down again.

As she lied in bed that evening to consider the reason, a realization dawned on her. *Soirée should be in the same position as Terran and Lupin since I cornered her with the ancestral sword. Only I know her location, though she should remain untouched in that space unless I go there or bring somebody along. I'd never considered returning because I didn't plan to need the weapon; however, would it benefit our current predicament if I retrieved it? This would be more of a solution if we knew how to stop a demon's power from being released.*

The thought kept her awake throughout the night until she rose to wander the halls instead of toss and turn on the mattress. Finally, weariness drove her toward her room for a restless sleep.

The following evening, Coura found herself in a similar situation where her concern regarding Soirée rose and her interest in the ancestral weapon piqued. More than anything, she longed to find a way to put the demons down for good, if only to get an answer, and the golden blades served Asteom best.

She remained attentive enough not to mention the subject to Byron, her father, or Grace when she saw them separately throughout the afternoon, yet the thought pursued her like a bloodthirsty insect until that night when she threw the sheets off her body to rise and pace the room.

I can't stand this, she admitted while dressing before heading to the training ground. *Soirée is the perfect test subject for me to learn whether or not demonic energy will return to me if the weapon is removed or a creature is beheaded. Besides, that location wouldn't put anyone in danger. I trust my skills enough not to become overconfident.*

With that sense of determination, Coura selected the sharpest blade she could find from those available in the stable while ignoring the stares of the soldiers on guard and nodded to them to acknowledge her intent to borrow the weapon. The men waved halfheartedly, presumably because they were familiar with her from her impromptu sessions every so often, then let her wander away from the palace.

No light reached the farthest edge of the perimeter where the stone barrier walled off the training ground from the forest beyond. When she stood alone and stared down at the sword in her hand, she paused to assess her mentality. Fortunately, it hadn't changed.

I'm the only person who can do this, and I'm not foolish enough to go without a plan. Once I spot her, I'll behead her and assess the situation from there. If the energy is released with the ancestral weapon still in place, then I can absorb what gets loose or it will wander in a place filled with demons anyway. I can also take the sword and return with answers for the council.

Despite her steady mind, her left hand trembled while she raised it and summoned her Yeluthian power. It leapt at her call, as it always did, before forming the outline of the portal in a shimmering, silver light. A few seconds later and the mirror-like image reflected a crimson glow from the realm. Coura stepped through before her doubts could catch up or remind her of her previous experience at that location.

Her body had been accustomed to the sensation of falling through the portal from her past travels when she used the goddess gift; however, distance played a key factor in how much the nausea and dizziness affected her afterward. That was why she halted as soon as she fully emerged instead of moving ahead. The expected reaction hit her a second later, and she doubled forward to catch her breath.

Last time, I used the ancestral weapon to assist me, she recalled once the toll pulled from her center, leaving her nearly drained. *I'll be able to use it for my return, but I'm sure I won't feel the best for a few days.*

No sounds or sights raised her guard any more than normal, which startled her a bit. Coura glanced around and found the space almost exactly as she remembered: a flat, circular rock possessing several boulders stretching above her head and molten earth far below. Smoke irritated her eyes and throat, though she remembered how dangerous the contaminated air was the longer she stayed, and the heat acted like a slap to the face. She squinted while scanning for any sign of the demon. Soon, her memories drove her toward the giant rocks.

I don't exactly know where I left her because I wasn't in an aware state.

After rubbing her eyes with the back of her free hand, she trudged onward before an unnatural, horrifying sight froze her in place. One of the boulders appeared to have been split in half down the middle with a single, jagged crack, and among its crumbled fragments lied an item reflecting what crimson light found its way to that spot. She recognized the shine came from something metal, but it wasn't until her lungs ached against the toxic air that she went to investigate.

Coura silently begged for the scene to defy her expectations, yet she couldn't mistake the shape of a blade as she stood above the rubble. *It's the ancestral weapon. How could Soirée have freed herself? Demons can't touch them, and she wouldn't be able to act with it in her chest.*

Too many questions flooded her head, though the most pressing rang the loudest.

Where is Soirée now?

She glanced from side to side yet found she remained the only living being on that section of earth. After, she assessed the scene again.

This split in the rock doesn't look like a strike from a weapon. It might have crumbled on its own, causing the blade to slip. I wonder...

A violent coughing fit interrupted her investigation, and she knew she needed to hurry when she tasted blood on her tongue. She cursed the limited time, Soirée's escape, and her rotten luck while avoiding the urge to cave into her concern. Instead, she reached for the hilt of the sword before procuring it and savoring its welcome warmth. The stability it projected mirrored the other ancestral weapons she recently utilized, projecting comfort to combat her despair.

There's nothing else I can do here, Coura reluctantly admitted to herself when another cough sat in her burning throat. *I need to leave with what I gathered. Soirée is gone, so I can warn the council, but we have this as a symbol of hope for the future.*

With those words echoing in her mind, she summoned her goddess gift once more, though this time directing it to her room for privacy; that, and she already felt her body protesting the effort and weakening as her energy worked. By the time she stepped into the silence of the enclosed space, her knees gave out, sending her to her hands and knees.

The blades clattered when they hit the stone floor, creating a chorus of clanging, which sounded louder given the hour. Coura listened in case a guard decided to investigate, though nobody interrupted her evening as she remained panting and coughing. It took at least an hour for the stinging to subside in her eyes. Her irritated throat continued itching, and her lungs ached from the unbalanced pressure she faced. Part of her believed she needed a healer's insight; however, visiting at that time would no doubt raise suspicion.

I should rest...

She dismissed the swords for the moment in order to pull herself into bed from a crawl. Then, her thoughts caught up to her, and she replayed the scene over in her head until sunlight from the window drew her attention.

What are we supposed to do now?

Glossary

CHARACTERS

Aimes Occaily – an older, former seaman from Clearwater who joins Coura during her venture to defeat the demonic creatures roaming Asteom

Aaron Vanstriann – heir to the kingdom of Asteom and son of King Hernan and Queen Freia

Assistant General Calin – leader of the Dalan base under General Tio

Barnelus Dagger-Diver – son of the Sie-Kie's *shimla* and their people's lead hunter

Bryn Leetle – a light mage who survives the ambush along the border

Byron Rinod – a master mage who wields dark magic and acts as Coura's mentor, an instructor at the Magical Arts Academy, and eventually the academy's representative in the palace

Califer Beackdal – former master light mage in Asteom's palace

Captain Harvey – leader of the Nim-Valan army who visited Asteom's capital

Cintra Amaldi – Byron's childhood friend who lives in Fester and works as a seer

Clara Waterton – a light mage who survives the ambush along the border and befriends Will

Commander Detrix – one of King Arval's trusted soldiers in Yeluthia

Commander Isan – one of King Arval's trusted soldiers in Yeluthia

Cornelius "Clearshot" Bayporter – a distinguished soldier who specializes in archery and Byron's close friend and comrade; he is married to Emilea and has two children: Mace and Lexie

Coura (core-ah) Galdwin – a dark mage and soldier with the ability to wield demonic energy and manifest black wings

Dianne Merker – an Asteom soldier assigned to act as Grace's guard

Drake Telkanar – a rouge Yeluthian working with the traitor in Verona

Elena Taymor – wife of King Syrus, one of Nim-Vala's six queens, and Finn's master

Emilea Bayporter – a master mage who wields light energy and acts as the palace's lead healer; she is married to Cornelius and has two children: Mace and Lexie

Evern Galdwin – commander of Yeluthia's army; he is married to Paulina and has three children: Coura, Odell, and Jackie

Finnley (Finn) – a Nim-Valan spy who assists Will and the light mages across the border

General Casner – commander stationed in Verona who is sent to the Nim-Valan border

General Garvish – new commander stationed in Verona

General Terrell – new commander stationed in Verona

General Tio – leader of the Dalan base

General Tont – commander stationed in Verona and Marcus' father

Geneva – a Nim-Valan woman who houses Will in Muld

Grace Zelnar – Yeluthia's ambassador sent to Asteom's capital; possesses a goddess gift that allows her to speak mind to mind with others

Harriette – a Mintelian woman who serves Sage Vidar and assists with Coura's training

Headmaster Symon – leader of the Magical Arts Academy and Byron's friend

Hector Lauple – a rouge Yeluthian working with the traitor in Verona

Hendal Duers – Asteom's former high priest

Jaspire Uskinor – leader of the rogue Yeluthian group assisting the traitor in the palace; possesses a goddess gift that allows him to heal from a distance

Jurek Younder – Asteom's new high priest

King Arval – leader of Yeluthia

Kline Galbourough – a rogue Yeluthian working with the traitor in Verona

Lady Katrina Neneme – wife of Lord Donovan Neneme and friend of Emilea

Lavine – Yeluthian soldier under Commander Evern who befriends Coura

Lissa Quentile – a light mage who survives the ambush along the border

Lupin Olim – King Syrus' mysterious advisor

Lydia Teller – a dark mage and Byron's second-in-command

Lyla Kroft – Wesley's apprentice and future priest of Kercher

Marcus Tont – an assistant general in Asteom's army and Prince Aaron's closest friend

Mary-Ann Weavu – a light mage who survives the ambush along the border

Marcy Kilguire – a woman from Dala who joins Coura during her venture to defeat the demonic creatures roaming Asteom

Nullan & Elenor Zelnar – Grace's parents and political leaders in Yeluthia

Paulina Galdwin – she is married to Evern and has three children: Coura, Odell, and Jackie

Rydar – a Mintelian man who serves Sage Vidar and assists with Coura's training

Sage Vidar – a Mintelian man who oversees a village and conducts soul cleansings

Soirée (sw-our-ae) – a demon who appears like an adult woman who forms a soul-bonding with Coura

Syrus Taymor – king of Nim-Vala and Elena's husband

Terran – a demon who appears to Coura during a scouting mission in search of Soirée

Thelma Boncarl – a rouge Yeluthian working with the traitor in Verona

Urvin Tsansa – a rouge Yeluthian working with the traitor in Verona

Verdic Ulshritz – former priest in Kercher and Hendal and Wesley's uncle

Wesley Ashre – priest in Kercher and Hendal's nephew

William "Will" Shairp – an herbalist from Clearwater who focuses on medicinal potions

Yukin Crowmald – a Nim-Valan lord and friend of Finn who Will treats and allies with

Zelma Vulan – a light mage who survives the ambush along the border

LOCATIONS

Clearwater – the southernmost city in Asteom primarily known for fishing

Dala – a city in southern Asteom housing a military base led by General Tio

East Hoover – northern town housing the Magical Arts Academy

Inner Circle – Nim-Vala's capital housing the royal family and nobility

Kercher – an eastern city known for housing messengers between Yeluthia and Asteom

Magical Arts Academy – often referred to as the MAA, this school houses primarily light and dark mage trainees and is located in East Hoover

Medina – a town located in the southwestern section of Asteom and the site of a demonic creature's massacre

Muld – a southern town in Nim-Vala where Finn brings Will, Clara, and the rest of their group

Neston – Coura's hometown located in the forest south of East Hoover

Nim-Vala – country north of Asteom

The Valley Beyond – open area between a series of tunnels connecting Dala, Clearwater, and Fester

Verona – Asteom's capital city

Western Woods – an extensive forest covering most of Asteom's western coast and home of the Sie-Kie people

Yeluthia – also referred to as the City of Angels, this kingdom consists of a people who are closely connected with light energy, allowing some to manifest wings and thus giving them the nickname angels

MISCELLANEOUS

Ancestral weapons – items gifted to Asteom's royal family consisting of two, golden swords, daggers, and bows; crafted with a sealing spell to protect against demonic energy

Chi-alve (key-al-ve) – term for soul space or center of power

Goddess gifts – special abilities used by certain Yeluthians involving telepathic communication, long-range healing, portal manifestation, and other spells

Mintelians – a secluded people who live in the Ghurun mountains and value artistic trades

Shalma – Sie-Kie's term for witch, or one who uses magic

Shimla – Sie-Kie's term for chief

Sie-Kie (sih-kai-e) – a tribe living in the Western Woods who value tradition over magic

Summa and Izina – god and goddess worshiped in Kercher

About the Author

Courtney Lillard was born and raised in Appleton, Wisconsin as the middle of five children. Growing up, she loved music and theater, and participating in both allowed her to develop a deeper interest in the arts. She graduated from Quincy University in 2015 with a B.A. degree in Broadcasting and Public Relations Communications and from Western Illinois University in 2018 with a M.A. degree in Communication Studies.

Aside from writing, Lillard is a fan of reading fantasy stories and the classics. Her other hobbies include cooking, playing video games, and doing puzzles, at least until her cats knock the pieces off the table.